COLONEL QUARITCH, V.C.

A TALE OF COUNTRY LIFE

H. RIDER HAGGARD

Colonel Quaritch, V.C.

H. Rider Haggard

PO Box 2211
Fairfield, IA 52556
www.1stworldlibrary.com
First Edition

LCCN: 2007901793

Softcover ISBN: 978-1-4218-4261-5
Hardcover ISBN: 978-1-4218-4163-2
eBook ISBN: 978-1-4218-4359-9

Purchase *"Colonel Quaritch, V.C."*
as a traditional bound book at:
www.1stWorldLibrary.com/purchase.asp?ISBN=978-1-4218-4261-5

1st World Library is a literary, educational organization dedicated to:

- Creating a free internet library of downloadable ebooks
- Hosting writing competitions and offering book publishing scholarships.

Interested in more 1st World Library books?
contact: literacy@1stworldlibrary.com
Check us out at: www.1stworldlibrary.com

1st World Library Literary Society

Giving Back to the World

"If you want to work on the core problem, it's early school literacy."

- James Barksdale, former CEO of Netscape

"No skill is more crucial to the future of a child, or to a democratic and prosperous society, than literacy."

- Los Angeles Times

Literacy... means far more than learning how to read and write... The aim is to transmit... knowledge and promote social participation."

- UNESCO

"Literacy is not a luxury, it is a right and a responsibility. If our world is to meet the challenges of the twenty-first century we must harness the energy and creativity of all our citizens."

- President Bill Clinton

"Parents should be encouraged to read to their children, and teachers should be equipped with all available techniques for teaching literacy, so the varying needs and capacities of individual kids can be taken into account."

- Hugh Mackay

I Dedicate

This Tale of Country Life

To

My Friend and Fellow-Sportsman,

CHARLES J. LONGMAN

CHAPTER I

HAROLD QUARITCH MEDITATES

There are things and there are faces which, when felt or seen for the first time, stamp themselves upon the mind like a sun image on a sensitized plate and there remain unalterably fixed. To take the instance of a face—we may never see it again, or it may become the companion of our life, but there the picture is just as we *first* knew it, the same smile or frown, the same look, unvarying and unvariable, reminding us in the midst of change of the indestructible nature of every experience, act, and aspect of our days. For that which has been, is, since the past knows no corruption, but lives eternally in its frozen and completed self.

These are somewhat large thoughts to be born of a small matter, but they rose up spontaneously in the mind of a soldierly-looking man who, on the particular evening when this history opens, was leaning over a gate in an Eastern county lane, staring vacantly at a field of ripe corn.

He was a peculiar and rather battered looking individual, apparently over forty years of age, and yet bearing upon him that unmistakable stamp of dignity and self-respect which, if it does not exclusively belong to, is still one of the distinguishing attributes of the English gentleman. In face he was ugly, no other word can express it. Here were not the long mustachios, the almond eyes, the aristocratic air of the Colonel of fiction—for our dreamer was a Colonel. These were—alas! that the truth should be so plain—represented by somewhat scrubby sandy-coloured whiskers, small but kindly blue eyes, a low broad forehead, with a deep line running across it from side to side, something like that to be seen upon the busts of Julius Caesar, and a long thin nose. One good feature, however, he did possess, a mouth of such sweetness and beauty that set, as it was, above a very square and manly-looking chin, it had the air of being ludicrously out of place. "Umph," said his old aunt, Mrs. Massey (who had just died and left him what she possessed), on the occasion of her first introduction to him five-and-thirty years before, "Umph! Nature meant to make a pretty girl of you, and changed her mind after she had finished the mouth. Well, never mind, better be a plain man than a pretty woman. There, go along, boy! I like your ugly face."

Nor was the old lady peculiar in this respect, for plain as the countenance of Colonel Harold Quaritch undoubtedly was, people found something very taking about it, when once they became accustomed to its rugged air and stern regulated expression. What that something was it would be hard to define, but perhaps the nearest approach to the truth would be to describe it as a light of purity which, notwithstanding the popular idea to the contrary, is quite as often to be found upon the faces of men as upon those of women. Any person of discernment looking on Colonel Quaritch must have felt that he was in the presence of a good man—not a prig or a milksop, but a man who had attained by virtue of thought and struggle that had left their marks upon him, a man whom it would not be well to tamper with, one to be respected by all, and feared of evildoers. Men felt this, and he was popular among those who knew him in his service, though not in any hail-fellow-well-met kind of way. But among women he was not popular. As a rule they both feared and disliked him. His presence jarred upon the frivolity of the lighter members of their sex, who dimly realised that his nature was antagonistic, and the more solid ones could not understand him. Perhaps this was the reason why Colonel Quaritch had never married, had never even had a love affair since he was five-and- twenty.

And yet it was of a woman that he was thinking as he leant over the gate, and looked at the field of yellowing corn, undulating like a golden sea beneath the pressure of the wind.

Colonel Quaritch had twice before been at Honham, once ten, and once four years ago. Now he was come to abide there for good. His old aunt, Mrs. Massey, had owned a place in the village—a very small place—called Honham Cottage, or Molehill, and on those two occasions he visited her. Mrs. Massey was dead and buried. She had left him the property, and with some reluctance, he had given up his profession, in which he saw no further prospects, and come to live upon it. This was his first evening in the place, for he had arrived by the last train on the previous night. All day he had been busy trying to get the house a little straight, and now, thoroughly tired, he was refreshing himself by leaning over a gate. It is, though a great many people will not believe it, one of the most delightful and certainly one of the cheapest refreshments in the world.

And then it was, as he leant over the gate, that the image of a woman's face rose before his mind as it had continually risen during the last five years. Five years had gone since he saw it, and those five years he spent in India and Egypt, that is with the exception of six months which he passed in hospital—the upshot of an Arab spear thrust in the thigh.

It had risen before him in all sorts of places and at all sorts of times; in his sleep, in his waking moments, at mess, out shooting, and even once in the hot rush of battle. He remembered it well—it was at El Teb. It happened that stern necessity forced him to shoot a man with his pistol. The bullet cut through his enemy, and with a few convulsions he died. He watched him die, he could not help doing so, there was some fascination in following the act of his own hand to its dreadful conclusion, and indeed conclusion and commencement were very near together. The terror of the sight, the terror of what in defence of his own life he was forced to do, revolted him even in the heat of the fight, and even then, over that ghastly and distorted face, another face spread itself like a mask, blotting it out from view— that woman's face. And now again it re-arose, inspiring him with the rather recondite reflections as to the immutability of things and impressions with which this domestic record opens.

Five years is a good stretch in a man's journey through the world. Many things happen to us in that time. If a thoughtful person were to set to work to record all the impressions which impinge upon his mind during that period, he would fill a library with volumes, the mere tale of its events would furnish a shelf. And yet how small they are to look back upon. It seemed but the other day that he was leaning over this very gate, and had turned to see a young girl dressed in black, who, with a spray of honeysuckle thrust in her girdle, and carrying a stick in her hand, was walking leisurely down the lane.

There was something about the girl's air that had struck him while she was yet a long way off—a dignity, a grace, and a set of the shoulders. Then as she came nearer he saw the soft dark eyes and the waving brown hair that contrasted so strangely and effectively with the pale and striking features. It was not a beautiful face, for the mouth was too large, and the nose was not as straight as it might have been, but there was a power about the broad brow, and a force and solid nobility stamped upon the features which had impressed him strangely. Just as she came opposite to where he was standing, a gust of wind, for there was a stiff breeze, blew the lady's hat off, taking it over the hedge, and he, as in duty bound, scrambled into the field and fetched it for her, and she had thanked him with a quick smile and a lighting up of the brown eyes, and then passed on with a bow.

Yes, with a little bow she had passed on, and he watched her walking down the long level drift, till her image melted into the stormy sunset light, and was gone. When he returned to the cottage he had described her to his old aunt, and asked who she might be, to learn that she was Ida de la Molle (which sounded like a name out of a novel), the only daughter of the old squire who lived at Honham Castle. Next day he had left for India, and saw Miss de la Molle no more.

And now he wondered what had become of her. Probably she was married; so striking a person would be almost sure to attract the notice of men. And after all what could it matter to him? He was not a marrying man, and women as a class had little attraction for him; indeed he disliked them. It has been said that he had never married, and never even had a love affair since he was five-and-twenty. But though he was not married, he once—before he was five-and-twenty—very nearly took that step. It was twenty years ago now, and nobody quite knew the history, for in twenty years many things are fortunately forgotten. But there was a history, and a scandal, and the marriage was broken off almost on the day it should have taken place. And after that it leaked out in the neighbourhood that the young lady, who by the way was a considerable heiress, had gone off her head, presumably with grief, and been confined in an asylum, where she was believed still to remain.

Perhaps it was the thought of this one woman's face, the woman he had once seen walking down the drift, her figure limned out against the stormy sky, that led him to think of the other face, the face hidden in the madhouse. At any rate, with a sigh, or rather a groan, he swung himself round from the gate and began to walk homeward at a brisk pace.

The drift that he was following is known as the mile drift, and had in ancient times formed the approach to the gates of Honham Castle, the seat of the ancient and honourable family of de la Molle (sometimes written "Delamol" in history and old writings). Honham Castle was now nothing but a ruin, with a manor house built out of the wreck on one side of its square, and the broad way that led to it from the high road which ran from Boisingham,[*] the local country town, was a drift or grass lane.

[*] Said to have been so named after the Boissey family, whose heiress a de la Molle married in the fourteenth

> century. As, however, the town of Boisingham is mentioned by one of the old chroniclers, this does not seem very probable. No doubt the family took their name from the town or hamlet, not the town from the family.

Colonel Quaritch followed this drift till he came to the high road, and then turned. A few minutes' walk brought him to a drive opening out of the main road on the left as he faced towards Boisingham. This drive, which was some three hundred yards long, led up a rather sharp slope to his own place, Honham Cottage, or Molehill, as the villagers called it, a title calculated to give a keen impression of a neat spick and span red brick villa with a slate roof. In fact, however, it was nothing of the sort, being a building of the fifteenth century, as a glance at its massive flint walls was sufficient to show. In ancient times there had been a large Abbey at Boisingham, two miles away, which, the records tell, suffered terribly from an outbreak of the plague in the fifteenth century. After this the monks obtained ten acres of land, known as Molehill, by grant from the de la Molle of the day, and so named either on account of their resemblance to a molehill (of which more presently) or after the family. On this elevated spot, which was supposed to be peculiarly healthy, they built the little house now called Honham Cottage, whereto to fly when next the plague should visit them.

And as they built it, so, with some slight additions, it had remained to this day, for in those ages men did not skimp their flint, and oak, and mortar. It was a beautiful little spot, situated upon the flat top of a swelling hill, which comprised the ten acres of grazing ground originally granted, and was, strange to say, still the most magnificently-timbered piece of ground in the country side. For on the ten acres of grass land there stood over fifty great oaks, some of them pollards of the most enormous antiquity, and others which had, no doubt, originally grown very close together, fine upstanding trees with a wonderful length and girth of bole. This place, Colonel Quaritch's aunt, old Mrs. Massey, had bought nearly thirty years before when she became a widow, and now, together with a modest income of two hundred a year, it had passed to him under her will.

Shaking himself clear of his sad thoughts, Harold Quaritch turned round at his own front door to contemplate the scene. The long, single-storied house stood, it has been said, at the top of the rising land, and to the south and west and east commanded as beautiful a view as is to be seen in the county. There, a mile or so away to the south, situated in the midst of grassy grazing grounds, and flanked on either side by still perfect towers, frowned the massive gateway of the old Norman castle. Then, to the west, almost at the foot of Molehill, the ground broke away in a deep bank clothed with timber, which led the eye down by slow descents into the beautiful valley of the Ell. Here the silver river wound its gentle way through lush and poplar-bordered marshes, where the cattle stand knee-deep in flowers; past quaint wooden mill-houses, through Boisingham Old Common, windy looking even now, and brightened here and there with a dash of golden gorse, till it was lost beneath the picturesque cluster of red-tiled roofs that marked the ancient town. Look which way he would, the view was lovely, and equal to any to be found in the Eastern counties, where the scenery is fine enough in its own way, whatever people may choose to say to the contrary, whose imaginations are so weak that they require a mountain and a torrent to excite them into activity.

Behind the house to the north there was no view, and for a good reason, for here in the very middle of the back garden rose a mound of large size and curious shape, which completely shut out the landscape. What this mound, which may perhaps have covered half an acre of ground, was, nobody had any idea. Some learned folk write it down a Saxon tumulus, a presumption to which its ancient name, "Dead Man's Mount," seemed to give colour. Other folk, however, yet more learned, declared it to be an ancient British dwelling, and pointed triumphantly to a hollow at the top, wherein the ancient Britishers were supposed to have moved, lived, and had their being—which must, urged the opposing party, have been a very damp one. Thereon the late Mrs. Massey, who was a British dwellingite, proceeded to show with much triumph *how* they had lived in the hole by building a huge mushroom-shaped roof over it, and thereby turning it into a summer-house, which, owing to unexpected difficulties in the construction of the roof, cost a great deal of money. But as the roof was slated, and as it was found necessary to pave the hollow with tiles and cut surface drains in it, the result did not clearly prove its use as a dwelling place before the Roman conquest. Nor did it make a very good summer house. Indeed it now served as a store place for the gardener's tools and for rubbish generally.

CHAPTER II

THE COLONEL MEETS THE SQUIRE

As Colonel Quaritch was contemplating these various views and reflecting that on the whole he had done well to come and live at Honham Cottage, he was suddenly startled by a loud voice saluting him from about twenty yards distance with such peculiar vigour that he fairly jumped.

"Colonel Quaritch, I believe," said, or rather shouted, the voice from somewhere down the drive.

"Yes," answered the Colonel mildly, "here I am."

"Ah, I thought it was you. Always tell a military man, you know. Excuse me, but I am resting for a minute, this last pull is an uncommonly stiff one. I always used to tell my dear old friend, Mrs. Massey, that she ought to have the hill cut away a bit just here. Well, here goes for it," and after a few heavy steps his visitor emerged from the shadow of the trees into the sunset light which was playing on the terrace before the house.

Colonel Quaritch glanced up curiously to see who the owner of the great voice might be, and his eyes lit upon as fine a specimen of humanity as he had seen for a long while. The man was old, as his white hair showed, seventy perhaps, but that was the only sign of decay about him. He was a splendid man, broad and thick and strong, with a keen, quick eye, and a face sharply chiselled, and clean shaved, of the stamp which in novels is generally known as aristocratic, a face, in fact, that showed both birth and breeding. Indeed, as clothed in loose tweed garments and a gigantic pair of top boots, his visitor stood leaning on his long stick and resting himself after facing the hill, Harold Quaritch thought that he had never seen a more perfect specimen of the typical English country gentleman—as the English country gentleman used to be.

"How do you do, sir, how do you do—my name is de la Molle. My man George, who knows everybody's business except his own, told me that you had arrived here, so I thought I would walk round and do myself the honour of making your acquaintance."

"That is very kind of you," said the Colonel.

"Not at all. If you only knew how uncommonly dull it is down in these parts you would not say that. The place isn't what it used to be when I was a boy. There are plenty of rich people about, but they are not the same stamp of people. It isn't what it used to be in more ways than one," and the old Squire gave something like a sigh, and thoughtfully removed his white hat, out of which a dinner napkin and two pocket-handkerchiefs fell to the ground, in a fashion that reminded Colonel Quaritch of the climax of a conjuring trick.

"You have dropped some—some linen," he said, stooping down to pick the mysterious articles up.

"Oh, yes, thank you," answered his visitor, "I find the sun a little hot at this time of the year. There is nothing like a few handkerchiefs or a towel to keep it off," and he rolled the mass of napery into a ball, and cramming it back into the crown, replaced the hat on his head in such a fashion that about eight inches of white napkin hung down behind. "You must have felt it in Egypt," he went on —"the sun I mean. It's a bad climate, that Egypt, as I have good reason to know," and he pointed again to his white hat, which Harold Quaritch now observed for the first time was encircled by a broad black band.

"Ah, I see," he said, "I suppose that you have had a loss."

"Yes, sir, a very heavy loss."

Now Colonel Quaritch had never heard that Mr. de la Molle had more than one child, Ida de la Molle, the young lady whose face remained so strongly fixed in his memory, although he had scarcely spoken to her on that one occasion five long years ago. Could it be possible that she had died in Egypt? The idea sent a tremor of fear through him, though of course there was no real reason why it should. Deaths are so common.

"Not—not Miss de la Molle?" he said nervously, adding, "I had the pleasure of seeing her once, a good many years ago, when I was stopping here for a few days with my aunt."

"Oh, no, not Ida, she is alive and well, thank God. Her brother James. He went all through that wretched war which we owe to Mr. Gladstone, as I say, though I don't know what your politics are, and then caught a fever, or as I think got touched by the sun, and died on his way home. Poor boy! He was a fine fellow, Colonel Quaritch, and my only son, but very reckless. Only a month or so before he died, I wrote to him to be careful always to put a towel in his helmet, and he answered, in that flippant sort of way he had, that he was not going to turn himself into a dirty clothes bag, and that he rather liked the heat than otherwise. Well, he's gone, poor fellow, in the service of his country, like many of his ancestors before him, and there's an end of him."

And again the old man sighed, heavily this time.

"And now, Colonel Quaritch," he went on, shaking off his oppression with a curious rapidity that was characteristic of him, "what do you say to coming up to the Castle for your dinner? You must be in a mess here, and I expect that old Mrs. Jobson, whom my man George tells me you have got to look after you, will be glad enough to be rid of you for to-night. What do you say?—take the place as you find it, you know. I believe that there is a leg of mutton for dinner if there is nothing else, because instead of minding his own business I saw George going off to Boisingham to fetch it this morning. At least, that is what he said he was going for; just an excuse to gossip and idle, I fancy."

"Well, really," said the Colonel, "you are very kind; but I don't think that my dress clothes are unpacked yet."

"Dress clothes! Oh, never mind your dress clothes. Ida will excuse you, I daresay. Besides, you have no time to dress. By Jove, it's nearly seven o'clock; we must be off if you are coming."

The Colonel hesitated. He had intended to dine at home, and being a methodical-minded man did not like altering his plans. Also, he was, like most military men, very punctilious about his dress and personal appearance, and objected to going out to dinner in a shooting coat. But all this notwithstanding, a feeling that he did not quite understand, and which it would have puzzled even an American novelist to analyse—something between restlessness and curiosity, with a dash of magnetic attraction thrown in—got the better of his scruples, and he accepted.

"Well, thank you," he said, "if you are sure that Miss de la Molle will not mind, I will come. Just allow me to tell Mrs. Jobson."

"That's right," halloaed the Squire after him, "I'll meet you at the back of the house. We had better go through the fields."

By the time that the Colonel, having informed his housekeeper that he should not want any dinner, and hastily brushed his not too luxuriant locks, had reached the garden which lay behind the house, the Squire was nowhere to be seen. Presently, however, a loud halloa from the top of the tumulus-like hill announced his whereabouts.

Wondering what the old gentleman could be doing there, Harold Quaritch walked up the steps that led to the summit of the mound, and found him standing at the entrance to the mushroom-shaped summer-house, contemplating the view.

"There, Colonel," he said, "there's a perfect view for you. Talk about Scotland and the Alps! Give me a view of the valley of Ell from the top of Dead Man's Mount on an autumn evening, and I never want to see anything finer. I have always loved it from a boy, and always shall so long as I live—look at those oaks, too. There are no such trees in the county that I know of. The old lady, your aunt, was wonderfully fond of them. I hope—" he went on in a tone of anxiety—"I hope that you don't mean to cut any of them down."

"Oh no," said the Colonel, "I should never think of such a thing."

"That's right. Never cut down a good tree if you can help it. I'm sorry to say, however," he added after a pause, "that I have been forced to cut down a good many myself. Queer place this, isn't it?" he continued, dropping the subject of the trees, which was evidently a painful one to him. "Dead Man's Mount is what the people about here call it, and that is what they called it at the time of the Conquest, as I can prove to you from ancient writings. I always believed that it was a tumulus, but of late years a lot of these clever people have been taking their oath that it is an ancient British dwelling, as though Ancient Britons, or any one else for that matter, could live in a kind of drainhole. But they got on the soft side of your old aunt—who, by the way, begging your pardon, was a wonderfully obstinate old lady when once she hammered an idea into her head—and so she set to work and built this slate mushroom over the place, and one way and another it cost her two hundred and fifty pounds. Dear me! I shall never forget her face when she saw the bill," and the old gentleman burst out into a Titanic laugh, such as Harold Quaritch had not heard for many a long day.

"Yes," he answered, "it is a queer spot. I think that I must have a dig at it one day."

"By Jove," said the Squire, "I never thought of that. It would be worth doing. Hulloa, it is twenty minutes past seven, and we dine at half past. I shall catch it from Ida. Come on, Colonel Quaritch; you don't know what it is to have a daughter—a daughter when one is late for dinner is a serious thing for any man," and he started off down the hill in a hurry.

Very soon, however, he seemed to forget the terrors in store, and strolled along, stopping now and again to admire some particular oak or view; chatting all the while in a discursive manner, which, though somewhat aimless, was by no means without its charm. He made a capital companion for a silent man like Harold Quaritch who liked to hear other people talk.

In this way they went down the slope, and crossing a couple of wheat fields came to a succession of broad meadows, somewhat sparsely timbered. Through these the footpath ran right up to the grim gateway of the ancient Castle, which now loomed before them, outlined in red lines of fire against the ruddy background of the sunset sky.

"Ay, it's a fine old place, Colonel, isn't it?" said the Squire, catching the exclamation of admiration that broke from his companion's lips, as a sudden turn brought them into line with the Norman ruin. "History—that's what it is; history in stone and mortar; this is historic ground, every inch of it. Those old de la Molles, my ancestors, and the Boisseys before them, were great folk in their day, and they kept up their position well. I will take you to see their tombs in the church yonder on Sunday. I always hoped to be buried beside them, but I can't manage it now, because of the Act. However, I mean to get as near to them as I can. I have a fancy for the companionship of those old Barons, though I expect that they were a roughish lot in their lifetimes. Look how squarely those towers stand out against the sky. They always remind me of the men who built them—sturdy, overbearing fellows, setting their shoulders against the sea of circumstance and caring neither for man nor devil till the priests got hold of them at the last. Well, God rest them, they helped to make England, whatever their faults. Queer place to choose for a castle, though, wasn't it? right out in an open plain."

"I suppose that they trusted to their moat and walls, and the hagger at the bottom of the dry ditch," said the Colonel. "You see there is no eminence from which they could be commanded, and their archers could sweep all the plain from the battlements."

"Ah, yes, of course they could. It is easy to see that you are a soldier. They were no fools, those old crusaders. My word, we must be getting on. They are hauling down the Union Jack on the west tower. I always have it hauled down at sunset," and he began walking briskly again.

In another three minutes they had crossed a narrow by-road, and were passing up the ancient drive that led to the Castle gates. It was not much of a drive, but there were still some half-dozen of old pollard oaks that had no doubt stood there before the Norman Boissey, from whose family, centuries ago, the de la Molles had obtained the property by marriage with the heiress, had got his charter and cut the first sod of his moat.

Right before them was the gateway of the Castle, flanked by two great towers, and these, with the exception of some ruins were, as a matter of fact, all that remained of the ancient building, which had been effectually demolished in the time of Cromwell. The space within, where the keep had once stood, was now laid out as a flower garden, while the house, which was of an unpretentious nature, and built in the Jacobean style, occupied the south side of the square, and was placed with its back to the moat.

"You see I have practically rebuilt those two towers," said the Squire, pausing underneath the Norman archway. "If I had not done it," he added apologetically, "they would have been in ruins by now, but it cost a pretty penny, I can tell you. Nobody knows what stuff that old flint masonry is to deal with, till he tries it. Well, they will stand now for many a long day. And here we are"—and he pushed open a porch door and then passed up some steps and through a passage into an oak-panelled vestibule, which was hung with tapestry originally taken, no doubt, from the old Castle, and decorated with coats of armour, spear heads, and ancient swords.

And here it was that Harold Quaritch once more beheld the face which had haunted his memory for so many months.

CHAPTER III

THE TALE OF SIR JAMES DE LA MOLLE

"Is that you, father?" said a voice, a very sweet voice, but one of which the tones betrayed the irritation natural to a healthy woman who has been kept waiting for her dinner. The voice came from the recesses of the dusky room in which the evening gloom had gathered deeply, and looking in its direction, Harold Quaritch could see the outline of a tall form sitting in an old oak chair with its hands crossed.

"Is that you, father? Really it is too bad to be so late for dinner—especially after you blew up that wretched Emma last night because she was five minutes after time. I have been waiting so long that I have almost been asleep."

"I am very sorry, my dear, very," said the old gentleman apologetically, "but—hullo! I've knocked my head—here, Mary, bring me a light!"

"Here is a light," said the voice, and at the same moment there was a sound of a match being struck.

In another moment the candle was burning, and the owner of the voice had turned, holding it in such a fashion that its rays surrounded her like an aureole—showing Harold Quaritch that face of which the memory had never left him. There were the same powerful broad brow, the same nobility of look, the same brown eyes and soft waving hair. But the girlhood had gone out of them, the face was now the face of a woman who knew what life meant, and had not found it too easy. It had lost some of its dreaminess, he thought, though it had gained in intellectual force. As for the figure, it was much more admirable than the face, which was strictly speaking not a beautiful one. The figure, however, was undoubtedly beautiful, indeed, it is doubtful if many women could show a finer. Ida de la Molle was a large, strong woman, and there was about her a swing and a lissom grace which is very rare, and as attractive as it is rare. She was now nearly six-and-twenty years of age, and not having begun to wither in accordance with the fate which overtakes all unmarried women after thirty, was at her very best. Harold Quaritch, glancing at her well-poised head, her perfect neck and arms (for she was in evening dress) and her gracious form, thought to himself that he had never seen a nobler-looking woman.

"Why, my dear father," she went on as she watched the candle burn up, "you made such a fuss this morning about the dinner being punctually at half-past seven, and now it is eight o'clock and you are not dressed. It is enough to ruin any cook," and she broke off for the first time, seeing that her father was not alone.

"Yes, my dear, yes," said the old gentleman, "I dare say I did. It is human to err, my dear, especially about dinner on a fine evening. Besides, I have made amends and brought you a visitor, our new neighbour, Colonel Quaritch. Colonel Quaritch, let me introduce you to my daughter, Miss de la Molle."

"I think that we have met before," said Harold, in a somewhat nervous fashion, as he stretched out his hand.

"Yes," answered Ida, taking it, "I remember. It was in the long drift, five years ago, on a windy afternoon, when my hat blew over the hedge and you went to fetch it."

"You have a good memory, Miss de la Molle," said he, feeling not a little pleased that she should have recollected the incident.

"Evidently not better than your own, Colonel Quaritch," was the ready answer. "Besides, one sees so few strangers here that one naturally remembers them. It is a place where nothing happens—time passes, that is all."

Meanwhile the old Squire, who had been making a prodigious fuss with his hat and stick, which he managed to send clattering down the flight of stone steps, departed to get ready, saying in a kind of roar as he went that Ida was to order in the dinner, as he would be down in a minute.

Accordingly she rang the bell, and told the maid to bring in the soup in five minutes and to lay another place. Then turning to Harold she began to apologise to him.

"I don't know what sort of dinner you will get, Colonel Quaritch," she said; "it is so provoking of my father; he never gives one the least warning when he is going to ask any one to dinner."

"Not at all—not at all," he answered hurriedly. "It is I who ought to apologise, coming down on you like—like—"

"A wolf on the fold," suggested Ida.

"Yes, exactly," he went on earnestly, looking at his coat, "but not in purple and gold."

"Well," she went on laughing, "you will get very little to eat for your pains, and I know that soldiers always like good dinners."

"How do you know that, Miss de la Molle?"

"Oh, because of poor James and his friends whom he used to bring here. By the way, Colonel Quaritch," she went on with a sudden softening of the voice, "you have been in Egypt, I know, because I have so often seen your name in the papers; did you ever meet my brother there?"

"I knew him slightly," he answered. "Only very slightly. I did not know that he was your brother, or indeed that you had a brother. He was a dashing officer."

What he did not say, however, was that he also knew him to have been one of the wildest and most extravagant young men in an extravagant regiment, and as such had to some extent shunned his society on the few occasions that he had been thrown in with him. Perhaps Ida, with a woman's quickness, divined from his tone that there was something behind his remark—at any rate she did not ask him for particulars of their slight acquaintance.

"He was my only brother," she continued; "there never were but we two, and of course his loss was a great blow to me. My father cannot get over it at all, although—" and she broke off suddenly, and rested her head upon her hand.

At this moment the Squire was heard advancing down the stairs, shouting to the servants as he came.

"A thousand pardons, my dear, a thousand pardons," he said as he entered the room, "but, well, if you will forgive particulars, I was quite unable to discover the whereabouts of a certain necessary portion of the male attire. Now, Colonel Quaritch, will you take my daughter? Stop, you don't know the way—perhaps I had better show you with the candle."

Accordingly he advanced out of the vestibule, and turning to the left, led the way down a long passage till he reached the dining-room. This apartment was like the vestibule, oak-panelled, but the walls were decorated with family and other portraits, including a very curious painting of the Castle itself, as it was before its destruction in the time of Cromwell. This painting was executed on a massive slab of oak, and conceived in a most quaint and formal style, being relieved in the foreground with stags at gaze and woodeny horses, that must, according to any rule of proportion, have been about half as large as the gateway towers. Evidently, also, it was of an older date than the present house, which is Jacobean, having probably been removed to its present position from the ruins of the Castle. Such as it was, however, it gave a very good idea of what the ancient seat of the Boisseys and de la Molles had been like before the Roundheads had made an end of its glory. The dining-room itself was commodious, though not large. It was lighted by three narrow windows which looked out upon the moat, and bore a considerable air of solid comfort. The table, made of black oak, of extraordinary solidity and weight, was matched by a sideboard of the same material and apparently of the same date, both pieces of furniture being, as Mr. de la Molle informed his guests, relics of the Castle.

On this sideboard were placed several pieces of old and massive plate, each of which was rudely engraved with three falcons *or*, the arms of the de la Molle family. One piece, indeed, a very ancient salver, bore those of the Boisseys—a ragged oak, in an escutcheon of pretence—showing thereby that it dated from that de la Molle who in the time of Henry the Seventh had obtained the property by marriage with the Boissey heiress.

Conversation having turned that way, as the dinner, which was a simple one, went on, the old Squire had this piece of plate brought to Harold Quaritch for him to examine.

"It is very curious," he said; "have you much of this, Mr. de la Molle?"

"No indeed," he said; "I wish I had. It all vanished in the time of Charles the First."

"Melted down, I suppose," said the Colonel.

"No, that is the odd part of it. I don't think it was. It was hidden somewhere—I don't know where, or perhaps it was turned into money and the money hidden. But I will tell you the story if you like as soon as we have done dinner."

Accordingly, when the servants had removed the cloth, and after the old fashion placed the wine upon the naked wood, the Squire began his tale, of which the following is the substance.

"In the time of James I. the de la Molle family was at the height of its prosperity, that is, so far as money goes. For several generations previous the representatives of the family had withdrawn themselves from any active participation in public affairs, and living here at small expense upon their lands, which were at that time very large, had amassed a quantity of wealth that, for the age, might fairly be called enormous. Thus, Sir Stephen de la Molle, the grandfather of the Sir James who lived in the time of James I., left to his son, also named Stephen, a sum of no less than twenty-three thousand pounds in gold. This Stephen was a great miser, and tradition says that he trebled the sum in his lifetime. Anyhow, he died rich as Croesus, and abominated alike by his tenants and by the country side, as might be expected when a gentleman of his race and fame degraded himself, as this Sir Stephen undoubtedly did, to the practice of usury.

"With the next heir, Sir James, however, the old spirit of the de la Molles seems to have revived, although it is sufficiently clear that he was by no means a spendthrift, but on the contrary, a careful man, though one who maintained his station and refused to soil his fingers with such base dealing as it had pleased his uncle to do. Going to court, he became, perhaps on account of his wealth, a considerable favourite with James I., to whom he was greatly attached and from whom he bought a baronetcy. Indeed, the best proof of his devotion is, that he on two occasions lent large sums of money to the King which were never repaid. On the accession of Charles I., however, Sir James left court under circumstances which were never quite cleared up. It is said that smarting under some slight which was put upon him, he made a somewhat brusque demand for the money that he had lent to James. Thereon the

King, with sarcastic wit, congratulated him on the fact that the spirit of his uncle, Sir Stephen de la Molle, whose name was still a byword in the land, evidently survived in the family. Sir James turned white with anger, bowed, and without a word left the court, nor did he ever return thither.

"Years passed, and the civil war was at its height. Sir James had as yet steadily refused to take any share in it. He had never forgiven the insult put upon him by the King, for like most of his race, of whom it was said that they never forgave an injury and never forgot a kindness, he was a pertinacious man. Therefore he would not lift a finger in the King's cause. But still less would he help the Roundheads, whom he hated with a singular hatred. So time went, till at last, when he was sore pressed, Charles, knowing his great wealth and influence, brought himself to write a letter to this Sir James, appealing to him for support, and especially for money.

"'I hear,' said the King in his letter, 'that Sir James de la Molle, who was aforetyme well affected to our person and more especially to the late King, our sainted father, doth stand idle, watching the growing of this bloody struggle and lifting no hand. Such was not the way of the race from which he sprang, which, unless history doth greatly lie, hath in the past been ever found at the side of their kings striking for the right. It is told to me also, that Sir James de la Molle doth thus place himself aside blowing neither hot nor cold, because of some sharp words which we spake in heedless jest many a year that's gone. We know not if this be true, doubting if a man's memory be so long, but if so it be, then hereby do we crave his pardon, and no more can we do. And now is our estate one of grievous peril, and sorely do we need the aid of God and man. Therefore, if the heart of our subject Sir James de la Molle be not rebellious against us, as we cannot readily credit it to be, we do implore his present aid in men and money, of which last it is said he hath large store, this letter being proof of our urgent need.'"

"These were, as nearly as I can remember, the very words of

the letter, which was written with the King's own hand, and show pretty clearly how hardly he was pressed. It is said that when he read it, Sir James, forgetting his grievance, was much affected, and, taking paper, wrote hastily as follows, which indeed he certainly did, for I have seen the letter in the Museum. 'My liege,—Of the past I will not speak. It is past. But since it hath graciously pleased your Majesty to ask mine aid against the rebels who would overthrow your throne, rest assured that all I have is at your Majesty's command, till such time as your enemies are discomfited. It hath pleased Providence to so prosper my fortunes that I have stored away in a safe place, till these times be past, a very great sum in gold, whereof I will at once place ten thousand pieces at the disposal of your Majesty, so soon as a safe means can be provided of conveying the same, seeing that I had sooner die than that these great moneys should fall into the hands of rebels to the furtherance of a wicked cause.'"

"Then the letter went on to say that the writer would at once buckle to and raise a troop of horse among his tenantry, and that if other satisfactory arrangements could not be made for the conveyance of the moneys, he would bring them in person to the King.

"And now comes the climax of the story. The messenger was captured and Sir James's incautious letter taken from his boot, as a result of which within ten days' time he found himself closely besieged by five hundred Roundheads under the command of one Colonel Playfair. The Castle was but ill-provisioned for a siege, and in the end Sir James was driven by sheer starvation to surrender. No sooner had he obtained an entry, then Colonel Playfair sent for his prisoner, and to his astonishment produced to Sir James's face his own letter to the King.

"'Now, Sir James,' he said, 'we have the hive, and I must ask you to lead us to the honey. Where be those great moneys whereof you talk herein? Fain would I be fingering these ten thousand pieces of gold, the which you have so snugly stored away.'"

"'Ay,' answered old Sir James, 'you have the hive, but the secret of the honey you have not, nor shall you have it. The ten thousand pieces in gold is where it is, and with it is much more. Find it if you may, Colonel, and take it if you can.'"

"'I shall find it by to-morrow's light, Sir James, or otherwise—or otherwise you die.'"

"'I must die—all men do, Colonel, but if I die, the secret dies with me.'"

"'This shall we see,' answered the Colonel grimly, and old Sir James was marched off to a cell, and there closely confined on bread and water. But he did not die the next day, nor the next, nor for a week, indeed."

"Every day he was brought up before the Colonel, and under the threat of immediate death questioned as to where the treasure was, not being suffered meanwhile to communicate by word or sign with any one, save the officers of the rebels. Every day he refused, till at last his inquisitor's patience gave out, and he was told frankly that if he did not communicate the secret he would be shot at the following dawn.

"Old Sir James laughed, and said that shoot him they might, but that he consigned his soul to the Devil if he would enrich them with his treasures, and then asked that his Bible might be brought to him that he might read therein and prepare himself for death."

"They gave him the Bible and left him. Next morning at the dawn, a file of Roundheads marched him into the courtyard of the Castle and here he found Colonel Playfair and his officers waiting."

"'Now, Sir James, for your last word,' said the Roundhead. 'Will you reveal where the treasure lies, or will you choose to die?'"

"'I will not reveal,' answered the old man. 'Murder me if ye will. The deed is worthy of Holy Presbyters. I have spoken and my mind is fixed.'"

"'Bethink you,' said the Colonel."

"'I have thought,' he answered, 'and I am ready. Slay me and seek the treasure. But one thing I ask. My young son is not here. In France hath he been these three years, and nought knows he of where I have hid this gold. Send to him this Bible when I am dead. Nay, search it from page to page. There is nought therein save what I have writ here upon this last sheet. It is all I have left to give.'"

"'The book shall be searched,' answered the Colonel, 'and if nought is found therein it shall be sent. And now, in the name of God, I adjure you, Sir James, let not the love of lucre stand between you and your life. Here I make you one last offer. Discover but to us the ten thousand pounds whereof you speak in this writing,' and he held up the letter to the King, 'and you shall go free—refuse and you die.'"

"'I refuse,' he answered."

"'Musqueteers, make ready,' shouted the Colonel, and the file of men stepped forward."

"But at that moment there came up so furious a squall of wind, and with it such dense and cutting rain, that for a while the execution was delayed. Presently it passed, the wild light of the November morning swept out from the sky, and revealed the doomed man kneeling in prayer upon the sodden turf, the water running from his white hair and beard.

"They called to him to stand up, but he would not, and continued praying. So they shot him on his knees."

"Well," said Colonel Quaritch, "at any rate he died like a gallant gentleman."

At that moment there was a knock at the door, and the servant came in.

"What is it?" asked the Squire.

"George is here, please, sir," said the girl, "and says that he would like to see you."

"Confound him," growled the old gentleman; "he is always here after something or other. I suppose it is about the Moat Farm. He was going to see Janter to-day. Will you excuse me, Quaritch? My daughter will tell you the end of the story if you care to hear any more. I will join you in the drawing-room."

CHAPTER IV

THE END OF THE TALE

As soon as her father had gone, Ida rose and suggested that if Colonel Quaritch had done his wine they should go into the drawing-room, which they accordingly did. This room was much more modern than either the vestibule or the dining-room, and had an air and flavour of nineteenth century young lady about it. There were the little tables, the draperies, the photograph frames, and all the hundred and one knick- knacks and odds and ends by means of which a lady of taste makes a chamber lovely in the eyes of brutal man. It was a very pleasant place to look upon, this drawing-room at Honham Castle, with its irregular recesses, its somewhat faded colours illuminated by the soft light of a shaded lamp, and its general air of feminine dominion. Harold Quaritch was a man who had seen much of the world, but who had not seen very much of drawing-rooms, or, indeed, of ladies at large. They had not come in his way, or if they did come in his way he had avoided them. Therefore, perhaps, he was the more susceptible to such influences when he was brought within their reach. Or perchance it was Ida's gracious presence which threw a charm upon the place that added to its natural attractiveness, as the china bowls of lavender and rose leaves added perfume to the air. Anyhow, it struck him that he had rarely before seen a room which conveyed to his mind such strong suggestions of refinement and gentle rest.

"What a charming room," he said, as he entered it.

"I am glad you think so," answered Ida; "because it is my own territory, and I arrange it."

"Yes," he said, "it is easy to see that."

"Well, would you like to hear the end of the story about Sir James and his treasure?"

"Certainly; it interests me very much."

"It positively *fascinates* me," said Ida with emphasis.

"Listen, and I will tell you. After they had shot old Sir James they took the Bible off him, but whether or no Colonel Playfair ever sent it to the son in France, is not clear.

"The story is all known historically, and it is certain that, as my father said, he asked that his Bible might be sent, but nothing more. This son, Sir Edward, never lived to return to England. After his father's murder, the estates were seized by the Parliamentary party, and the old Castle, with the exception of the gate towers, razed to the ground, partly for military purposes and partly in the long and determined attempt that was made to discover old Sir James's treasure, which might, it was thought, have been concealed in some secret chamber in the walls. But it was all of no use, and Colonel Playfair found that in letting his temper get the better of him and shooting Sir James, he had done away with the only chance of finding it that he was ever likely to have, for to all appearance the secret had died with its owner. There was a great deal of noise about it at the time, and the Colonel was degraded from his rank in reward for what he had done. It was presumed that old Sir James must have had accomplices in the hiding of so great a mass of gold, and every means was taken, by way of threats and promises of reward—which at last grew to half of the total amount that should be discovered—to induce these to come forward if they existed, but without result. And so the matter went on, till after a few years the quest died away and was forgotten.

"Meanwhile the son, Sir Edward, who was the second and last baronet, led a wandering life abroad, fearing or not caring to return to England now that all his property had been seized. When he was two- and-twenty years of age, however, he contracted an imprudent marriage with his cousin, a lady of the name of Ida Dofferleigh, a girl of good blood and great beauty, but without means. Indeed, she was the sister of Geoffrey Dofferleigh, who was a first cousin and companion in exile of Sir Edward's, and as you will presently see, my lineal ancestor. Well, within a year of this marriage, poor Ida, my namesake, died with her baby of fever, chiefly brought on, they say, by want and anxiety of mind, and the shock seems to have turned her husband's brain. At any rate, within three or four months of her death, he committed suicide. But before he did so, he formally executed a rather elaborate will, by which he left all his estates in England, 'now unjustly withheld from me contrary to the law and natural right by the rebel pretender Cromwell, together with the treasure hidden thereon or elsewhere by my late murdered father, Sir James de la Molle,' to John Geoffrey Dofferleigh, his cousin, and the brother of his late wife, and his heirs for ever, on condition only of his assuming the name and arms of the de la Molle family, the direct line of which became extinct with himself. Of course, this will, when it was executed, was to all appearance so much waste paper, but within three years from that date Charles II. was King of England.

"Thereon Geoffrey Dofferleigh produced the document, and on assuming the name and arms of de la Molle actually succeeded in obtaining the remains of the Castle and a considerable portion of the landed property, though the baronetcy became extinct. His son it was who built this present house, and he is our direct ancestor, for though my father talks of them as though they were—it is a little weakness of his—the old de la Molles are not our direct male ancestors."

"Well," said Harold, "and did Dofferleigh find the treasure?"

"No, ah, no, nor anybody else; the treasure has vanished. He hunted for it a great deal, and he did find those pieces of plate which you saw to-night, hidden away somewhere, I don't know where, but there was nothing else with them."

"Perhaps the whole thing was nonsense," said Harold reflectively.

"No," answered Ida shaking her head, "I am sure it was not, I am sure the treasure is hidden away somewhere to this day. Listen, Colonel Quaritch—you have not heard quite all the story yet—*I* found something."

"You, what?"

"Wait a minute and I will show you," and going to a cabinet in the corner, she unlocked it, and took out a despatch box, which she also unlocked.

"Here," she said, "I found this. It is the Bible that Sir James begged might be sent to his son, just before they shot him, you remember," and she handed him a small brown book. He took it and examined it carefully. It was bound in leather, and on the cover was written in large letters, "Sir James de la Molle. Honham Castle, 1611." Nor was this all. The first sheets of the Bible, which was one of the earliest copies of the authorised version, were torn out, and the top corner was also gone, having to all appearance been shot off by a bullet, a presumption that a dark stain of blood upon the cover and edges brought near to certainty.

"Poor gentleman," said Harold, "he must have had it in his pocket when he was shot. Where did you find it?"

"Yes, I suppose so," said Ida, "in fact I have no doubt of it. I found it when I was a child in an ancient oak chest in the basement of the western tower, quite hidden up in dusty rubbish and bits of old iron. But look at the end and you will see what he wrote in it to his son, Edward. Here, I will show you," and leaning over him she turned to the last page of the book. Between the bottom of the page and the conclusion of the final chapter of Revelations there had been a small blank space now densely covered with crabbed writing in faded ink, which she read aloud. It ran as follows:

"*Do not grieve for me, Edward, my son, that I am thus suddenly done to death by rebel murderers, for nought happeneth but according to God's will. And now farewell, Edward, till we shall meet in heaven. My monies have I hid and on account thereof I die unto this world, knowing that not one piece shall Cromwell touch. To whom God shall appoint, shall all my treasure be, for nought can I communicate.*"

"There," said Ida triumphantly, "what do you think of that, Colonel Quaritch? The Bible, I think, was never sent to his son, but here it is, and in that writing, as I solemnly believe," and she laid her white finger upon the faded characters, "lies the key to wherever it is that the money is hidden, only I fear I shall never make it out. For years I have puzzled over it, thinking that it might be some form of acrostic, but I can make nothing of it. I have tried it all ways. I have translated it into French, and had it translated into Latin, but still I can find out nothing—nothing. But some day somebody will hit upon it—at least I hope so."

Harold shook his head. "I am afraid," he said, "that what has remained undiscovered for so long will remain so till the end of the chapter. Perhaps old Sir James was hoaxing his enemies!"

"No," said Ida, "for if he was, what became of all the money? He was known to be one of the richest men of his day, and that he was rich we can see from his letter to the King. There was nothing found after his death, except his lands, of course. Oh, it will be found someday, twenty centuries hence, probably, much too late to be of any good to us," and she sighed deeply, while a pained and wearied expression spread itself over her handsome face.

"Well," said Harold in a doubtful voice, "there may be something in it. May I take a copy of that writing?"

"Certainly," said Ida laughing, "and if you find the treasure we will go shares. Stop, I will dictate it to you."

Just as this process was finished and Harold was shutting up his pocket-book, in which he put the fair copy he had executed on a half- sheet of note paper, the old Squire came into the room again. Looking at his face, his visitor saw that the interview with "George" had evidently been anything but satisfactory, for it bore an expression of exceedingly low spirits.

"Well, father, what is the matter?" asked his daughter.

"Oh, nothing, my dear, nothing," he answered in melancholy tones. "George has been here, that is all."

"Yes, and I wish he would keep away," she said with a little stamp of her foot, "for he always brings some bad news or other."

"It is the times, my dear, it is the times; it isn't George. I really don't know what has come to the country."

"What is it?" said Ida with a deepening expression of anxiety. "Something wrong with the Moat Farm?"

"Yes; Janter has thrown it up after all, and I am sure I don't know where I am to find another tenant."

"You see what the pleasures of landed property are, Colonel Quaritch," said Ida, turning towards him with a smile which did not convey a great sense of cheerfulness.

"Yes," he said, "I know. Thank goodness I have only the ten acres that my dear old aunt left to me. And now," he added, "I think that I must be saying good-night. It is half-past ten, and I expect that old Mrs. Jobson is sitting up for me."

Ida looked up in remonstrance, and opened her lips to speak, and then for some reason that did not appear changed her mind and held out her hand. "Good-night, Colonel Quaritch," she said; "I am so pleased that we are going to have you as a neighbour. By-the-way, I have a few people coming to play lawn tennis here to-morrow afternoon, will you come too?"

"What," broke in the Squire, in a voice of irritation, "more lawn tennis parties, Ida? I think that you might have spared me for once—with all this business on my hands, too."

"Nonsense, father," said his daughter, with some acerbity. "How can a few people playing lawn tennis hurt you? It is quite useless to shut oneself up and be miserable over things that one cannot help."

The old gentleman collapsed with an air of pious resignation, and meekly asked who was coming.

"Oh, nobody in particular. Mr. and Mrs. Jeffries—Mr. Jeffries is our clergyman, you know, Colonel Quaritch—and Dr. Bass and the two Miss Smiths, one of whom he is supposed to be in love with, and Mr. and Mrs. Quest, and Mr. Edward Cossey, and a few more."

"Mr. Edward Cossey," said the Squire, jumping off his chair; "really, Ida, you know I detest that young man, that I consider him an abominable young man; and I think you might have shown more consideration to me than to have asked him here."

"I could not help it, father," she answered coolly. "He was with Mrs. Quest when I asked her, so I had to ask him too. Besides, I rather like Mr. Cossey, he is always so polite, and I don't see why you should take such a violent prejudice against him. Anyhow, he is coming, and there is an end of it."

"Cossey, Cossey," said Harold, throwing himself into the

breach, "I used to know that name." It seemed to Ida that he winced a little as he said it. "Is he one of the great banking family?"

"Yes," said Ida, "he is one of the sons. They say he will have half a million of money or more when his father, who is very infirm, dies. He is looking after the branch banks of his house in this part of the world, at least nominally. I fancy that Mr. Quest really manages them; certainly he manages the Boisingham branch."

"Well, well," said the Squire, "if they are coming, I suppose they are coming. At any rate, I can go out. If you are going home, Quaritch, I will walk with you. I want a little air."

"Colonel Quaritch, you have not said if you will come to my party to-morrow, yet," said Ida, as he stretched out his hand to say good- bye.

"Oh, thank you, Miss de la Molle; yes, I think I can come, though I play tennis atrociously."

"Oh, we all do that. Well, good-night. I am so very pleased that you have come to live at Molehill; it will be so nice for my father to have a companion," she added as an afterthought.

"Yes," said the Colonel grimly, "we are almost of an age—good-night."

Ida watched the door close and then leant her arm on the mantelpiece, and reflected that she liked Colonel Quaritch very much, so much that even his not very beautiful physiognomy did not repel her, indeed rather attracted her than otherwise.

"Do you know," she said to herself, "I think that is the sort of man I should like to marry. Nonsense," she added, with an impatient shrug, "nonsense, you are nearly six-and-twenty, altogether too old for that sort of thing. And now there is this new trouble about the Moat Farm. My poor old father! Well, it is a hard world, and I think that sleep is about the best thing in it."

And with a sigh she lighted her candle to go to bed, then changed her mind and sat down to await her father's return.

CHAPTER V

THE SQUIRE EXPLAINS THE POSITION

"I don't know what is coming to this country, I really don't; and that's a fact," said the Squire to his companion, after they had walked some paces in silence. "Here is the farm, the Moat Farm. It fetched twenty-five shillings an acre when I was a young man, and eight years ago it used to fetch thirty-five. Now I have reduced it and reduced it to fifteen, just in order to keep the tenant. And what is the end of it? Janter—he's the tenant—gave notice last Michaelmas; but that stupid owl, George, said it was all nothing, and that he would continue at fifteen shillings when the time came. And now to-night he comes to me with a face as long as a yard-arm, and says that Janter won't keep it at any price, and that he does not know where he is to find another tenant, not he. It's quite heartbreaking, that's what it is. Three hundred acres of good, sound, food-producing land, and no tenant for it at fifteen shillings an acre. What am I to do?"

"Can't you take it in hand and farm it yourself?" asked Harold.

"How can I take it in hand? I have one farm of a hundred and fifty acres in hand as it is. Do you know what it would cost to take over that farm?" and he stopped in his walk and struck his stick into the ground. "Ten pounds an acre, every farthing of it—and say a thousand for the covenants—about four thousand pounds in all. Now where am I to get four thousand pounds to speculate with in that way, for it is a speculation, and one which I am too old to look after myself, even if I had the knowledge. Well, there you are, and now I'll say good-night, sir. It's getting chilly, and I have felt my chest for the last year or two. By-the-way, I suppose I shall see you to-morrow at this tennis party of Ida's. It's all very well for Ida to go in for her tennis parties, but how can I think of such things with all this worry on my hands? Well, good-night, Colonel Quaritch, good-night," and he turned and walked away through the moonlight.

Harold Quaritch watched him go and then stalked off home, reflecting, not without sadness, upon the drama which was opening up before him, that most common of dramas in these days of depression,—the break up of an ancient family through causes beyond control. It required far less acumen and knowledge of the world than he possessed to make it clear to him that the old race of de la Molle was doomed. This story of farms thrown up and money not forthcoming pointed its own moral, and a sad one it was. Even Ida's almost childish excitement about the legend of the buried treasure showed him how present to her mind must be the necessity of money; and he fell to thinking how pleasant it would be to be able to play the part of the Fairy Prince and step in with untold wealth between her and the ruin which threatened her family. How well that grand-looking open-minded Squire would become a great station, fitted as he was by nature, descent, and tradition, to play the solid part of an English country gentleman of the good old- fashioned kind. It was pitiful to think of a man of his stamp forced by the vile exigencies of a narrow purse to scheme and fight against the advancing tide of destitution. And Ida, too,—Ida, who was equipped with every attribute that can make wealth and power what they should be—a frame to show off her worth and state. Well, it was the way of the world, and he could not mend it; but it was with a bitter sense of the unfitness of things that with some little difficulty—for he was not yet fully accustomed to its twists and turns—he found his way past the swelling heap of Dead Man's Mount and round the house to his own front door.

He entered the house, and having told Mrs. Jobson that she could go to bed, sat down to smoke and think. Harold Quaritch, like many solitary men, was a great smoker, and never did he feel the need for the consolation of tobacco more than on this night. A few months ago, when he had retired from the army, he found himself in a great dilemma. There he was, a hale, active man of three-and-forty, of busy habits, and regular mind, suddenly thrown upon the world without occupation. What was he to do with himself? While he was asking this question and waiting blankly for an answer which did not come, his aunt, old Mrs. Massey, departed this life, leaving him heir to what she possessed, which might be three hundred a year in all. This, added to his pension and the little that he owned independently, put him beyond the necessity of seeking further employment. So he had made up his mind to come to reside at Molehill, and live the quiet, somewhat aimless, life of a small country gentleman. His reading, for he was a great reader, especially of scientific works, would, he thought, keep him employed. Moreover, he was a thorough sportsman, and an ardent, though owing to the smallness of his means, necessarily not a very extensive, collector of curiosities, and more particularly of coins.

At first, after he had come to his decision, a feeling of infinite rest and satisfaction had taken possession of him. The struggle of life was over for him. No longer would he be obliged to think, and contrive, and toil; henceforth his days would slope gently down towards the inevitable end. Trouble lay in the past, now rest and rest alone awaited him, rest that would gradually grow deeper and deeper as the swift years rolled by, till it was swallowed up in that almighty Peace to which, being a simple and religious man, he had looked forward from childhood as the end and object of his life.

Foolish man and vain imagining! Here, while we draw breath, there is no rest. We must go on continually, on from strength to strength, or weakness to weakness; we must always be troubled about this or that, and must ever have this desire or that to regret. It is an inevitable law within whose attraction all must fall; yes, even the purest souls, cradled in their hope of heaven; and the most swinish, wallowing in the mud of their gratified desires.

And so our hero had already begun to find out. Here, before he had been forty-eight hours in Honham, a fresh cause of troubles had arisen. He had seen Ida de la Molle again, and after an interval of between five and six years had found her face yet more charming than it was before. In short he had fallen in love with it, and being a sensible man he did not conceal this fact from himself. Indeed the truth was that he had been in love with her for all these years, though he had never looked at the matter in that light. At the least the pile had been gathered and laid, and did but require a touch of the match to burn up merrily enough. And now this was supplied, and at the first glance of Ida's eyes the magic flame began to hiss and crackle, and he knew that nothing short of a convulsion or a deluge would put it out.

Men of the stamp of Harold Quaritch generally pass through three stages with reference to the other sex. They begin in their youth by making a goddess of one of them, and finding out their mistake. Then for many years they look upon woman as the essence and incarnation of evil and a thing no more to be trusted than a jaguar. Ultimately, however, this folly wears itself out, probably in proportion as the old affection fades and dies away, and is replaced by contempt and regret that so much should have been wasted on that which was of so little worth. Then it is that the danger comes, for then a man puts forth his second venture, puts it forth with fear and trembling, and with no great hope of seeing a golden Argosy sailing into port. And if it sinks or is driven back by adverse winds and frowning skies, there is an end of his legitimate dealings with such frail merchandise.

And now he, Harold Quaritch, was about to put forth this second venture, not of his own desire or free will indeed, but because his reason and judgment were over-mastered. In short, he had fallen in love with Ida de la Molle when he first saw her five years ago, and was now in the process of discovering the fact. There he sat in his chair in the old half-furnished room, which he proposed to turn into his dining-room, and groaned in spirit over this portentous discovery. What had become of his fair prospect of quiet years sloping gently downwards, and warm with the sweet drowsy light of afternoon? How was it that he had not known those things that belonged to his peace? And probably it would end in nothing. Was it likely that such a splendid young woman as Ida would care for a super-annuated army officer, with nothing to recommend him beyond five or six hundred a year and a Victoria Cross, which he never wore. Probably if she married at all she would try to marry someone who would assist to retrieve the fallen fortunes of her family, which it was absolutely beyond his power to do. Altogether the outlook did not please him, as he sat there far into the watches of the night, and pulled at his empty pipe. So little did it please him, indeed, that when at last he rose to find his way to bed up the old oak staircase, the only imposing thing in Molehill, he had almost made up his mind to give up the idea of living at Honham at all. He would sell the place and emigrate to Vancouver's Island or New Zealand, and thus place an impassable barrier between himself and that sweet, strong face, which seemed to have acquired a touch of sternness since last he looked upon it five years ago.

Ah, wise resolutions of the quiet night, whither do you go in the garish light of day? To heaven, perhaps, with the mist wreaths and the dew drops.

When the Squire got back to the castle, he found his daughter still sitting in the drawing room.

"What, not gone to bed, Ida?" he said.

"No, father, I was going, and then I thought that I would wait to hear what all this is about Janter and the Moat Farm. It is best to get it over."

"Yes, yes, my dear—yes, but there is not much to tell you.

Janter has thrown up the farm after all, and George says that there is not another tenant to be had for love or money. He tried one man, who said that he would not have it at five shillings an acre, as prices are."

"That is bad enough in all conscience," said Ida, pushing at the fireirons with her foot. "What is to be done?"

"What is to be done?" answered her father irritably. "How can I tell you what is to be done? I suppose I must take the place in hand, that is all."

"Yes, but that costs money, does it not?"

"Of course it does, it costs about four thousand pounds."

"Well," said Ida, looking up, "and where is all that sum to come from? We have not got four thousand pounds in the world."

"Come from? Why I suppose that I must borrow it on the security of the land."

"Would it not be better to let the place go out of cultivation, rather than risk so much money?" she answered.

"Go out of cultivation! Nonsense, Ida, how can you talk like that? Why that strong land would be ruined for a generation to come."

"Perhaps it would, but surely it would be better that the land should be ruined than that we should be. Father, dear," she said appealingly, laying one hand upon his shoulder, "do be frank with me, and tell me what our position really is. I see you wearing yourself out about business from day to day, and I know that there is never any money for anything, scarcely enough to keep the house going; and yet you will not tell me what we really owe—and I think I have a right to know."

The Squire turned impatiently. "Girls have no head for these things," he said, "so what is the use of talking about it?"

"But I am not a girl; I am a woman of six-and-twenty; and putting other things aside, I am almost as much interested in your affairs as you are yourself," she said with determination. "I cannot bear this sort of thing any longer. I see that abominable man, Mr. Quest, continually hovering about here like a bird of ill-omen, and I cannot bear it; and I tell you what it is, father, if you don't tell me the whole truth at once I shall cry," and she looked as though she meant it.

Now the old Squire was no more impervious to a woman's tears than any other man, and of all Ida's moods, and they were many, he most greatly feared that rare one which took the form of tears. Besides, he loved his only daughter more dearly than anything in the world except one thing, Honham Castle, and could not bear to give her pain.

"Very well," he said, "of course if you wish to know about these things you have a right to. I have desired to spare you trouble, that is all; but as you are so very imperious, the best thing that I can do is to let you have your own way. Still, as it is rather late, if you have no objection I think that I had better put if off till to-morrow."

"No, no, father. By to-morrow you will have changed your mind. Let us have it now. I want to know how much we really owe, and what we have got to live on."

The old gentleman hummed and hawed a little, and after various indications of impatience at last began:

"Well, as you know, our family has for some generations depended upon the land. Your dear mother brought a small fortune with her, five or six thousand pounds, but that, with the sanction of her trustees, was expended upon improvements to the farms and in paying off a small mortgage. Well, for many years the land brought in about two thousand a year, but somehow we always found it difficult to keep within that income. For instance, it was necessary to repair the gateway, and you have no idea of the expense in which those repairs landed me. Then your poor brother James cost a lot of money, and always would have the shooting kept up in such an extravagant way. Then he went into the army, and heaven only knows what he spent there. Your brother was very extravagant, my dear, and well, perhaps I was foolish; I never could say him no. And that was not all of it, for when the poor boy died he left fifteen hundred pounds of debt behind him, and I had to find the money, if it was only for the honour of the family. Of course you know that we cut the entail when he came of age. Well, and then these dreadful times have come upon the top of it all, and upon my word, at the present moment I don't know which way to turn," and he paused and drummed his fingers uneasily upon a book.

"Yes, father, but you have not told me yet what it is that we owe."

"Well, it is difficult to answer that all in a minute. Perhaps twenty- five thousand on mortgage, and a few floating debts."

"And what is the place worth?"

"It used to be worth between fifty and sixty thousand pounds. It is impossible to say what it would fetch now. Land is practically a drug in the market. But things will come round, my dear. It is only a question of holding on.

"Then if you borrow a fresh sum in order to take up this farm, you will owe about thirty thousand pounds, and if you give five per cent., as I suppose you do, you will have to pay fifteen hundred a year in interest. Now, father, you said that in the good times the land brought in two thousand a year, so, of course, it can't bring in so much now. Therefore, by the time that you have paid the interest, there will be nothing, or less than nothing, left for us to live on."

Her father winced at this cruel and convincing logic.

"No, no," he said, "it is not so bad as that. You jump to conclusions, but really, if you do not mind, I am very tired, and should like to go to bed."

"Father, what is the use of trying to shirk the thing just because it is disagreeable?" she asked earnestly. "Do you suppose that it is more pleasant to me to talk about it than it is for you? I know that you are not to blame about it. I know that dear James was very thoughtless and extravagant, and that the times are crushing. But to go on like this is only to go to ruin. It would be better for us to live in a cottage on a couple of hundred a year than to try to keep our heads above water here, which we cannot do. Sooner or later these people, Quest, or whoever they are, will want their money back, and then, if they cannot have it, they will sell the place over our heads. I believe that man Quest wants to get it himself—that is what I believe —and set up as a country gentleman. Father, I know it is a dreadful thing to say, but we ought to leave Honham."

"Leave Honham!" said the old gentleman, jumping up in his agitation; "what nonsense you talk, Ida. How can I leave Honham? It would kill me at my age. How can I do it? And, besides, who is to look after the farms and all the business? No, no, we must hang on and trust to Providence. Things may come round, something may happen, one can never tell in this world."

"If we do not leave Honham, then Honham will leave us," answered his daughter, with conviction. "I do not believe in chances. Chances always go the wrong way—against those who are looking for them. We shall be absolutely ruined, that is all."

"Well, perhaps you are right, perhaps you are right, my dear," said the old Squire wearily. "I only hope that my time may come first. I have lived here all my life, seventy years and more, and I know that I could not live anywhere else. But God's will be done. And now, my dear, go to bed."

She leant down and kissed him, and as she did so saw that his eyes were filled with tears. Not trusting herself to speak, for she felt for him too deeply to do so, she turned away and went, leaving the old man sitting there with his grey head bowed upon his breast.

CHAPTER VI

LAWYER QUEST

The day following that of the conversation just described was one of those glorious autumn mornings which sometimes come as a faint compensation for the utter vileness and bitter disappointment of the season that in this country we dignify by the name of summer. Notwithstanding his vigils and melancholy of the night before, the Squire was up early, and Ida, who between one thing and another had not had the best of nights, heard his loud cheery voice shouting about the place for "George."

Looking out of her bedroom window, she soon perceived that functionary himself, a long, lean, powerful-looking man with a melancholy face and a twinkle in his little grey eyes, hanging about the front steps. Presently her father emerged in a brilliant but ancient dressing gown, his white locks waving on the breeze.

"Here, George, where are you, George?"

"Here I be, sir."

"Ah, yes; then why didn't you say so? I have been shouting myself hoarse for you."

"Yis, Squire," replied the imperturbable George, "I hev been a-standing here for the last ten minutes, and I heard you."

"You heard me, then why the dickens didn't you answer?"

"Because I didn't think as you wanted me, sir. I saw that you hadn't finished your letter."

"Well, then, you ought to. You know very well that my chest is weak, and yet I have to go hallooing all over the place after you. Now look here, have you got that fat pony of yours in the yard?"

"Yis, Squire, the pony is here, and if so be as it is fat it bean't for the want of movement."

"Very well, then, take this letter," and he handed him an epistle sealed with a tremendous seal, "take this letter to Mr. Quest at Boisingham, and wait for an answer. And look here, mind you are about the place at eleven o'clock, for I expect Mr. Quest to see me about the Moat Farm."

"Yis, Squire."

"I suppose that you have heard nothing more from Janter, have you?"

"No, Squire, nawthing. He means to git the place at his own price or chuck it."

"And what is his price?"

"Five shillings an acre. You see, sir, it's this way. That army gent, Major Boston, as is agent for all the College lands down the valley, he be a poor weak fule, and when all these tinants come to him and say that they must either hev the land at five shillings an acre or go, he gits scared, he du, and down goes the rent of some of the best meadow land in the country from thirty-five shillings to five. Of course it don't signify to him not a halfpenny, the College must pay him his salary all the same, and he don't know no more about farming, nor land, nor northing, than my old mare yinder. Well, and what comes of it? Of course every tinant on the place hears that those College lands be going for five shillings an acre, and they prick up their ears and say they must have their land at the same figger, and it's all owing to that Boston varmint, who ought to be kicked through every holl on the place and then drowned to dead in a dyke."

"Yes, you're right there, George, that silly man is a public enemy, and ought to be treated as such, but the times are very bad, with corn down to twenty-nine, very bad."

"I'm not a-saying that they ain't bad, Squire," said his retainer, his long face lighting up; "they are bad, cruel bad, bad for iverybody. And I'm not denying that they is bad for the tinants, but if they is bad for the tinants they is wus for the landlord. It all comes on his shoulders in the long run. If men find they can get land at five shillings an acre that's worth twenty, why it isn't in human natur to pay twenty, and if they find that the landlord must go as they drive him, of course they'll lay on the whip. Why, bless you, sir, when a tinant comes and says that he is very sorry but he finds he can't pay his rent, in nine cases out of ten, you'd find that the bank was paid, the tradesmen were paid, the doctor's paid, iverybody's paid before he thinks about his rent. Let the landlord suffer, because he can't help hisself; but Lord bless us, if a hundred pounds were overdue to the bank it would have the innards out of him in no time, and he knows it. Now as for that varmint, Janter, to tell me that he can't pay fifteen shillings an acre for the Moat Farm, is nonsense. I only wish I had the capital to take it at the price, that I du."

"Well, George," said the Squire, "I think that if it can be managed I shall borrow the money and take the farm on hand. I am not going to let Janter have it at five shillings an acre."

"Ah, sir, that's the best way. Bad as times be, it will go hard if I can't make the interest and the rent out of it too. Besides, Squire, if you give way about this here farm, all the others will come down on you. I'm not saying a word agin your tinants, but where there's money to be made you can't trust not no man."

"Well, well," said the Squire, "perhaps you are right and perhaps you ain't. Right or wrong, you always talk like Solomon in all his glory. Anyway, be off with that note and let me have the answer as soon as you get back. Mind you don't go loafing and jawing about down in Boisingham, because I want my answer."

"So he means to borrow the money if he can get it," said Ida to herself as she sat, an invisible auditor, doing her hair by the open window. "George can do more with him in five minutes than I can do in a week, and I know that he hates Janter. I believe Janter threw up the farm because of his quarrelling with George. Well, I suppose we must take our chance."

Meanwhile George had mounted his cart and departed upon the road to Boisingham, urging his fat pony along as though he meant to be there in twenty minutes. But so soon as he was well out of reach of the Squire's shouts and sight of the Castle gates, he deliberately turned up a bye lane and jogged along for a mile or more to a farm, where he had a long confabulation with a man about thatching some ricks. Thence he quietly made his way to his own little place, where he proceeded to comfortably get his breakfast, remarking to his wife that he was of opinion that there was no hurry about the Squire's letter, as the "lawyers" wasn't in the habit of coming to office at eight in the morning.

Breakfast over, the philosophic George got into his cart, the fat pony having been tied up outside, and leisurely drove into the picturesque old town which lay at the head of the valley. All along the main street he met many acquaintances, and with each he found it necessary to stop and have a talk, indeed with two he had a modest half-pint. At length, however, his labour o'er, he arrived at Mr. Quest's office, that, as all the Boisingham world knows, was just opposite the church, of which Mr. Quest was one of the churchwardens, and which but two years before was beautifully restored, mainly owing to his efforts and generous contributions. Driving up to the small and quiet-looking doorway of a very unpretentious building, George descended and knocked. Thereon a clerk opened the door, and in answer to his inquiries informed him that he believed Mr. Quest had just come over to the office.

In another minute he was shown into an inner room of the ordinary country lawyer's office stamp, and there at the table sat Mr. Quest himself.

Mr. Quest was a man of about forty years of age, rather under than over, with a pale ascetic cast of face, and a quiet and pleasant, though somewhat reserved, manner. His features were in no way remarkable, with the exception of his eyes, which seemed to have been set in his head owing to some curious error of nature. For whereas his general tone was dark, his hair in particular being jet black, these eyes were grey, and jarred extraordinarily upon their companion features. For the rest, he was a man of some presence, and with the manners of a gentleman.

"Well, George," he said, "what is it that brings you to Boisingham? A letter from the Squire. Thank you. Take a seat, will you, will I look through it? Umph, wants me to come and see him at eleven o'clock. I am very sorry, but I can't manage that anyway. Ah, I see, about the Moat Farm. Janter told me that he was going to throw it up, and I advised him to do nothing of the sort, but he is a dissatisfied sort of a fellow, Janter is, and Major Boston has upset the whole country side by his very ill-advised action about the College lands."

"Janter is a warmint and Major Boston, begging his pardon for the language, is an ass, sir. Anyway there it is, Janter has thrown up, and where I am to find a tinant between now and Michaelmas I don't know; in fact, with the College lands going at five shillings an acre there ain't no chance."

"Then what does the Squire propose to do—take the land

in hand?"

"Yes, sir, that's it; and that's what he wants to see you about."

"More money, I suppose," said Mr. Quest.

"Well, yis, sir. You see there will be covenants to meet, and then the farm is three hundred acres, and to stock it proper as it should be means nine pounds an acre quite, on this here heavy land."

"Yes, yes, I know, a matter of four thousand more or less, but where is it to come from, that's the question? Cossey's do not like land now, any more than other banks do. However, I'll see my principal about it. But, George, I can't possibly get up to the Castle at eleven. I have got a churchwardens' meeting at a quarter to, about that west pinnacle, you know. It is in a most dangerous condition, and by-the-way, before you go I should like to have your opinion, as a practical man, as to the best way to deal with it. To rebuild it would cost a hundred and twenty pounds, and that is more than we see our way to at present, though I can promise fifty if they can scape up the rest. But about the Squire. I think that the best thing I can do will be to come up to the Castle to lunch, and then I can talk over matters with him. Stay, I will just write him a note. By-the-way, you would like a glass of wine, wouldn't you, George? Nonsense man, here it is in the cupboard, a glass of wine is a good friend to have handy sometimes."

George, who like most men of his stamp could put away his share of liquor and feel thankful for it, drank his glass of wine while Mr. Quest was engaged in writing the note, wondering meanwhile what made the lawyer so civil to him. For George did not like Mr. Quest. Indeed, it would not be too much to say that he hated him. But this was a feeling which he never allowed to appear; he was too much afraid of the man for that, and in his queer way too much devoted to the old Squire's interests to run the risk of imperilling them by the exhibition of any aversion to Mr. Quest. He knew more of his master's affairs than anybody living, unless, perhaps, it was Mr. Quest himself, and was aware that the lawyer held the old gentleman in a bondage that could not be broken. Now, George was a man with faults. He was somewhat sly, and, perhaps within certain lines, at times capable of giving the word honesty a liberal interpretation. But amongst many others he had one conspicuous virtue: he loved the old Squire as a Highlandman loves his chief, and would almost, if not quite, have died to serve him. His billet was no easy one, for Mr. de la Molle's temper was none of the best at times, and when things went wrong, as they pretty frequently did, he was exceedingly apt to visit his wrath on the head of the devoted George, saying things to him which he should not have said. But his retainer took it all in the day's work, and never bore malice, continuing in his own cadging pigheaded sort of way to labour early and late to prop up his master's broken fortunes. "Lord, sir," as he once said to Harold Quaritch when the Colonel condoled with him after a violent and unjust onslaught made by the Squire in his presence, "Lord, sir, that ain't nawthing, that ain't. I don't pay no manner of heed to that. Folk du say how as I wor made for he, like a safety walve for a traction engine."

Indeed, had it not been for George's contrivings and procrastinations, Honham Castle and its owner would have parted company long before.

CHAPTER VII

EDWARD COSSEY, ESQUIRE

After George had drunk his glass of wine and given his opinion as to the best way to deal with the dangerous pinnacle on the Boisingham Church, he took the note, untied the fat pony, and ambled off to Honham, leaving the lawyer alone. As soon as he was gone, Mr. Quest threw himself back in his chair—an old oak one, by-the-way, for he had a very pretty taste in old oak and a positive mania for collecting it—and plunged into a brown study.

Presently he leant forward, unlocked the top drawer of his writing table, and extracted from it a letter addressed to himself which he had received that very morning. It was from the principals of the great banking firm of Cossey and Son, and dated from their head office in Mincing lane. This letter ran as follows:

"Private and confidential.

"Dear Sir,—

"We have considered your report as to the extensive mortgages which we hold upon the Honham Castle estates, and have allowed due weight to your arguments as to the advisability of allowing Mr. de la Molle time to give things a chance of righting. But we must tell you that we can see no prospect of any such solution of the matter, at any rate for some years to come. All the information that we are able to gather points to a further decrease in the value of the land rather than to a recovery. The interest on the mortgages in question is moreover a year in arrear, probably owing to the non-receipt of rents by Mr. de la Molle. Under these circumstances, much as it grieves us to take action against Mr. de la Molle, with whose family we have had dealings for five generations, we can see no alternative to foreclosure, and hereby instruct you to take the necessary preliminary steps to bring it about in the usual manner. We are, presuming that Mr. de la Molle is not in a position to pay off the mortgages, quite aware of the risks of a forced sale, and shall not be astonished if, in the present unprecedented condition of the land market, such a sale should result in a loss, although the sum recoverable does not amount to half the valuation of the estates, which was undertaken at our instance about twenty years ago on the occasion of the first advance. The only alternative, however, would be for us to enter into possession of the property or to buy it in. But this would be a course totally inconsistent with the usual practice of the bank, and what is more, our confidence in the stability of landed property is so utterly shattered by our recent experiences, that we cannot burden ourselves by such a course, preferring to run the risk of an immediate loss. This, however, we hope that the historical character of the property and its great natural advantages as a residential estate will avert, or at the least minimise.

"Be so good as to advise us by an early post of the steps you take in pursuance of these instructions.

"We are, dear sir,
"Your obedient servants,
"Cossey & Son.

"W. Quest, Esq.

"P.S.—We have thought it better to address you direct in this matter, but of course you will communicate the contents of this letter to Mr. Edward Cossey, and, subject to our instructions, which are final, act in consultation with him."

"Well," said Mr. Quest to himself, as he folded up the sheet of paper, "that is about as straight as it can be put. And this is the time that the old gentleman chooses to ask for another four thousand. He may ask, but the answer will be more than he bargains for."

He rose from the chair and began to walk up and down the room in evident perplexity. "If only," he said, "I had twenty-five thousand, I would take up the mortgages myself and foreclose at my leisure. It would be a good investment at that figure, even as things are, and besides, I should like to have that place. Twenty-five thousand, only twenty-five thousand, and now when I want it I have not got it. And I should have had it if it had not been for that tiger, that devil Edith. She has had more than that out of me in the last ten years, and still she is threatening and crying for more, more, more. Tiger; yes, that is the name for her, her own name, too. She would coin one's vitals into money if she could. All Belle's fortune she has had, or nearly all, and now she wants another five hundred, and she will have it too.

"Here we are," and he drew a letter from his pocket written in a bold, but somewhat uneducated, woman's hand.

"Dear Bill," it ran, "I've been unlucky again and dropped a pot. Shall want 500 pounds by the 1st October. No shuffling, mind; money down; but I think that you know me too well to play any more larx. When can you tear yourself away, and come and give your E—a look? Bring some tin when you come, and we will have times.—Thine, The Tiger."

"The Tiger, yes, the Tiger," he gasped, his face working with passion and his grey eyes glinting as he tore the epistle to fragments, threw them down and stamped on them. "Well, be careful that I don't one day cut your claws and paint your stripes. By heaven, if ever a man felt like murder, I do now. Five hundred more, and I haven't five thousand clear in the world. Truly we pay for the follies of our youth! It makes me mad to think of those fools Cossey and Son forcing that place into the market just now. There's a fortune in it at the price. In another year or two I might have recovered myself—that devil of a woman might be dead—and I have several irons in the fire, some of which are sure to turn up trumps. Surely there must be a way out of it somehow. There's a way out of everything except Death if only one thinks enough, but the thing is to find it," and he stopped in his walk opposite to the window that looked upon the street, and put his hand to his head.

As he did so he caught sight of the figure of a tall gentleman strolling idly towards the office door. For a moment he stared at him blankly, as a man does when he is trying to catch the vague clue to a new idea. Then, as the figure passed out of his view, he brought his fist down heavily upon the sill.

"Edward Cossey, by George!" he said aloud. "There's the way out of it, if only I can work him, and unless I have made a strange mistake, I think I know the road."

A couple of minutes afterwards a tall, shapely young man, of about twenty-four or five years of age, came strolling into the office where Mr. Quest was sitting, to all appearance hard at work at his correspondence. He was dark in complexion and decidedly distinguished-looking in feature, with large dark eyes, dark moustachios, and a pale, somewhat Spanish-looking skin. Young as the face was, it had, if observed closely, a somewhat worn and worried air, such as one would scarcely expect to see upon the countenance of a gentleman born to such brilliant fortunes, and so well fitted by nature to do them justice, as was Mr. Edward Cossey. For it is not every young man with dark eyes and a good figure who is destined to be the future head of one of the most wealthy private banks in England, and to inherit in due course a sum of money in hard cash variously estimated at from half a million to a million sterling. This, however, was the prospect in life that opened out before Mr. Edward Cossey, who was now supposed by his old and eminently business-like father to be in process of acquiring a sound knowledge of the provincial affairs of the house by attending to the working of their branch establishments in the Eastern counties.

"How do you do, Quest?" said Edward Cossey, nodding somewhat coldly to the lawyer and sitting down. "Any business?"

"Well, yes, Mr. Cossey," answered the lawyer, rising respectfully, "there is some business, some very serious business."

"Indeed," said Edward indifferently, "what is it?"

"Well, it is this, the house has ordered a foreclosure on the Honham Castle estates—at least it comes to that—"

On hearing this intelligence Edward Cossey's whole demeanour underwent the most startling transformation—his languor vanished, his eye brightened, and his form became instinct with active life and beauty.

"What the deuce," he said, and then paused. "I won't have it," he went on, jumping up, "I won't have it. I am not particularly fond of old de la Molle, perhaps because he is not particularly fond of me," he added rather drolly, "but it would be an infernal shame to break up that family and sell the house over them. Why they would be ruined! And then there's Ida—Miss de la Molle, I mean—what would become of her? And the old place too. After being in the family for all these centuries I suppose that it would be sold to some confounded counter-skipper or some retired thief of a lawyer. It must be prevented at any price—do you hear, Quest?"

The lawyer winced a little at his chief's contemptuous allusion, and then remarked with a smile, "I had no idea that you were so sentimental, Mr. Cossey, or that you took such a lively interest in Miss de la Molle," and he glanced up to observe the effect of his shot.

Edward Cossey coloured. "I did not mean that I took any particular interest in Miss de la Molle," he said, "I was referring to the family."

"Oh, quite so, though I'm sure I don't know why you shouldn't. Miss de la Molle is one of the most charming women that I ever met, I think the most charming except my own wife Belle," and he again looked up suddenly at Edward Cossey who, for his part, coloured for the second time.

"It seems to me," went on the lawyer, "that a man in your position has a most splendid opportunity of playing knight errant to the lovely damsel in distress. Here is the lady with her aged father about to be sold up and turned out of the estates which have belonged to her family for generations—why don't you do the generous and graceful thing, like the hero in a novel, and take up the mortgages?"

Edward Cossey did not reject this suggestion with the contempt that might have been expected; on the contrary he appeared to be turning the matter over in his mind, for he drummed a little tune with his knuckles and stared out of the window.

"What is the sum?" he said presently.

"Five-and-twenty thousand, and he wants four more, say thirty thousand."

"And where am I going to find thirty thousand pounds to take up a bundle of mortgages which will probably never pay a farthing of interest? Why, I have not got three thousand that I can come at. Besides," he added, recollecting himself, "why should I interfere?"

"I do not think," answered Mr. Quest, ignoring the latter part of the question, "that with your prospects you would find it difficult to get thirty thousand pounds. I know several who would consider it an honour to lend the money to a Cossey, if only for the sake of the introduction—that is, of course, provided the security was of a legal nature."

"Let me see the letter," said Edward.

Mr. Quest handed him the document conveying the commands of Cossey and Son, and he read it through twice.

"The old man means business," he said, as he returned it; "that letter was written by him, and when he has once made up his mind it is useless to try and stir him. Did you say that you were going to see the Squire to-day?"

"No, I did not say so, but as a matter of fact I am. His man, George—a shrewd fellow, by the way, for one of these bumpkins—came with a letter asking me to go up to the Castle, so I shall get round there to lunch. It is about this fresh loan that the old gentleman wishes to negotiate. Of course I shall be obliged to tell him that instead of giving a fresh loan we have orders to serve a notice on him."

"Don't do that just yet," said Edward with decision. "Write to the house and say that their instructions shall be attended to. There is no hurry about the notice, though I don't see how I am to help in the matter. Indeed there is no call upon me."

"Very well, Mr. Cossey. And now, by the way, are you going to the Castle this afternoon?"

"Yes, I believe so. Why?"

"Well, I want to get up there to luncheon, and I am in a fix. Mrs. Quest will want the trap to go there this afternoon. Can you lend me your dogcart to drive up in? and then perhaps you would not mind if she gave you a lift this afternoon."

"Very well," answered Edward, "that is if it suits Mrs. Quest.

Perhaps she may object to carting me about the country."

"I have not observed any such reluctance on her part," said the lawyer dryly, "but we can easily settle the question. I must go home and get some plans before I attend the vestry meeting about that pinnacle. Will you step across with me and we can ask her?"

"Oh yes," he answered. "I have nothing particular to do."

And accordingly, so soon as Mr. Quest had made some small arrangements and given particular directions to his clerks as to his whereabouts for the day, they set off together for the lawyer's private house.

CHAPTER VIII

MR. QUEST'S WIFE

Mr. Quest lived in one of those ugly but comfortably-built old red brick houses which abound in almost every country town, and which give us the clearest possible idea of the want of taste and love of material comfort that characterised the age in which they were built. This house looked out on to the market place, and had a charming old walled garden at the back, famous for its nectarines, which, together with the lawn tennis court, was, as Mrs. Quest would say, almost enough to console her for living in a town. The front door, however, was only separated by a little flight of steps from the pavement upon which the house abutted.

Entering a large, cool-looking hall, Mr. Quest paused and asked a servant who was passing there where her mistress was.

"In the drawing-room, sir," said the girl; and, followed by Edward Cossey, he walked down a long panelled passage till he reached a door on the left. This he opened quickly and passed through into a charming, modern-looking room, handsomely and even luxuriously furnished, and lighted by French windows opening on to the walled garden.

A little lady dressed in some black material was standing at one of these windows, her arms crossed behind her back, and absently gazing out of it. At the sound of the opening door she turned swiftly, her whole delicate and lovely face lighting up like a flower in a ray of sunshine, the lips slightly parted, and a deep and happy light shining in her violet eyes. Then, all in an instant, it was instructive to observe *how* instantaneously, her glance fell upon her husband (for the lady was Mrs. Quest) and her entire expression changed to one of cold aversion, the light fading out of her face as it does from a November sky, and leaving it cold and hard.

Mr. Quest, who was a man who saw everything, saw this also, and smiled bitterly.

"Don't be alarmed, Belle," he said in a low voice; "I have brought Mr. Cossey with me."

She flushed up to the eyes, a great wave of colour, and her breast heaved; but before she could answer, Edward Cossey, who had stopped behind to wipe some mud off his shoes, entered the room, and politely offered his hand to Mrs. Quest, who took it coldly enough.

"You are an early visitor, Mr. Cossey," she said.

"Yes," said her husband, "but the fault is mine. I have brought Mr. Cossey over to ask if you can give him a lift up to the Castle this afternoon. I have to go there to lunch, and have borrowed his dogcart."

"Oh yes, with pleasure. But why can't the dogcart come back for Mr. Cossey?"

"Well, you see," put in Edward, "there is a little difficulty; my groom is ill. But there is really no reason why you should be bothered. I have no doubt that a man can be found to bring it back."

"Oh no," she said, with a shrug, "it will be all right; only you had better lunch here, that's all, because I want to start early, and go to an old woman's at the other end of Honham about some fuchsia cuttings."

"I shall be very happy," said he.

"Very well then, that is settled," said Mr. Quest, "and now I must get my plans and be off to the vestry meeting. I'm late as it is. With your permission, Mr. Cossey, I will order the dogcart as I pass your rooms."

"Certainly," said Edward, and in another moment the lawyer was gone.

Mrs. Quest watched the door close and then sat down in a low armchair, and resting her head upon the back, looked up with a steady, enquiring gaze, full into Edward Cossey's face.

And he too looked at her and thought what a beautiful woman she was, in her own way. She was very small, rounded in her figure almost to stoutness, and possessed the tiniest and most beautiful hands and feet. But her greatest charm lay in the face, which was almost infantile in its shape, and delicate as a moss rose. She was exquisitely fair in colouring—indeed, the darkest things about her were her violet eyes, which in some lights looked almost black by contrast with her white forehead and waving auburn hair.

Presently she spoke.

"Has my husband gone?" she said.

"I suppose so. Why do you ask?"

"Because from what I know of his habits I should think it very likely that he is listening behind the door," and she laughed faintly.

"You seem to have a good opinion of him."

"I have exactly the opinion of him which he deserves," she said bitterly; "and my opinion of him is that he is one of the wickedest men in England."

"If he is behind the door he will enjoy that," said Edward Cossey. "Well, if he is all this, why did you marry him?"

"Why did I marry him?" she answered with passion, "because I was forced into it, bullied into it, starved into it. What would you do if you were a defenceless, motherless girl of eighteen, with a drunken father who beat you—yes, beat you with a stick—apologised in the most gentlemanlike way next morning and then went and got drunk again? And what would you do if that father were in the hands of a man like my husband, body and soul in his hands, and if between them pressure was brought to bear, and brought to bear, until at last—there, what is the good of going on it with—you can guess the rest."

"Well, and what did he marry you for—your pretty face?"

"I don't know; he said so; it may have had something to do with it. I think it was my ten thousand pounds, for once I had a whole ten thousand pounds of my own, my poor mother left it me, and it was tied up so that my father could not touch it. Well, of course, when I married, my husband would not have any settlements, and so he took it, every farthing."

"And what did he do with it?"

"Spent it upon some other woman in London—most of it. I found him out; he gave her thousands of pounds at once."

"Well, I should not have thought that he was so generous," he said with a laugh.

She paused a moment and covered her face with her hand, and then went on: "If you only knew, Edward, if you had the faintest idea what my life was till a year and a half ago, when I first saw you, you would pity me and understand why I am bad, and passionate, and jealous, and everything that I ought not to be. I never had any happiness as a girl —how could I in such a home as ours?—and then almost before I was a woman I was handed over to that man. Oh, how I hated him, and what I endured!"

"Yes, it can't have been very pleasant."

"Pleasant—but there, we have done with each other now—we don't even speak much except in public, that's my price for holding my tongue about the lady in London and one or two other little things—so what is the use of talking of it? It was a horrible nightmare, but it has gone. And then," she went on, fixing her beautiful eyes upon his face, "then I saw you, Edward, and for the first time in my life I learnt what love was, and I think that no woman ever loved like that before. Other women have had something to care for in their lives, I never had anything till I saw you. It may be wicked, but it's true."

He turned slightly away and said nothing.

"And yet, dear," she went on in a low voice, "I think it has been one of the hardest things of all—my love for you. For, Edward," and she rose and took his hand and looked into his face with her soft full eyes full of tears, "I should have liked to be a blessing to you, and not a curse, and—and—a cause of sin. Oh, Edward, I should have made you such a good wife, no man could have had a better, and I would have helped you too, for I am not such a fool as I seem, and now I shall do nothing but bring trouble upon you; I know I shall. And it was my fault too, at least most of it; don't ever think that I deceive myself, for I don't; I led you on, I know I did, I meant to—there! Think me as shameless as you like, I meant to from the first. And no good can come of it, I know that, although I would not have it undone. No good can ever come of what is wrong. I may be very wicked, but I know that—" and she began to cry outright.

This was too much for Edward Cossey, who, as any man must, had been much touched by this unexpected outburst. "Look here, Belle," he blurted out on the impulse of the moment, "I am sick and tired of all this sort of thing. For more than a year my life has been nothing but a living lie, and I can't stand it, and that's a fact. I tell you what it is: I think we had better just take the train to Paris and go off at once, or else give it all up. It is impossible to go on living in this atmosphere of continual falsehood."

She stopped crying. "Do you really care for me enough for that, Edward?" she said.

"Yes, yes," he said, somewhat impatiently, "you can see I do or I should not make the offer. Say the word and I'll do it."

She thought for a moment, and then looked up again. "No," she said, "no, Edward."

"Why?" he asked. "Are you afraid?"

"Afraid!" she answered with a gesture of contempt, "what have I to be afraid of? Do you suppose such women as I am have any care for consequences? We have got beyond that—that is, for ourselves. But we can still feel a little for others. It would ruin you to do such a thing, socially and in every other way. You know you have often said that your father would cut you out of his will if you compromised yourself and him like that."

"Oh, yes, he would. I am sure of it. He would never forgive the scandal; he has a hatred of that sort of thing. But I could get a few thousands ready money, and we could change our names and go off to a colony or something."

"It is very good of you to say so," she said humbly. "I don't deserve it, and I will not take advantage of you. You will be sorry that you made the offer by to-morrow. Ah, yes, I know it is only because I cried. No, we must go on as we are until the end comes, and then you can discard me; for all the blame will follow me, and I shall deserve it, too. I am older than you, you know, and a woman; and my husband will make some money out of you, and then it will all be forgotten, and I shall have had my day and go my own way to oblivion, like thousands of other unfortunate women before me, and it will be all the same a hundred years hence, don't you see? But, Edward, remember one thing. Don't play me any tricks, for I am not of the sort to bear it. Have patience and wait for the end; these things cannot last very long, and I shall never be a burden on you. Don't desert me or make me jealous, for I cannot bear it, I cannot, indeed, and I do not know what I might do—make a scandal or kill myself or you, I'm sure I can't say what. You nearly sent me wild the other day when you were carrying on with Miss de la Molle—ah, yes, I saw it all—I have suspected you for a long time, and sometimes I think that you are really in love with her. And now, sir, I tell you what it is, we have had enough of this melancholy talk to last me for a month. Why did you come here at all this morning, just when I wanted to get you out of my head for an hour or two and think about my garden? I suppose it was a trick of Mr. Quest's bringing you here. He has got some fresh scheme on, I am sure of it from his face. Well, it can't be helped, and, since you are here, Mr. Edward Cossey, tell me how you like my new dress," and she posed herself and courtesied before him. "Black, you see, to match my sins and show off my complexion. Doesn't it fit well?"

"Charmingly," he said, laughing in spite of himself, for he felt in no laughing mood, "and now I tell you what it is, Belle, I am not going to stop here all the morning, and lunch, and that sort of thing. It does not look well, to say the least of it. The probability is that half the old women in Boisingham have got their eyes fixed on the hall door to see how long I stay. I shall go down to the office and come back at half-past two."

"A very nice excuse to get rid of me," she said, "but I daresay you are right, and I want to see about the garden. There, good-bye, and mind you are not late, for I want to have a nice drive round to the Castle. Not that there is much need to warn you to be in time when you are going to see Miss de la Molle, is there? Good-bye, good-bye."

CHAPTER IX

THE SHADOW OF RUIN

Mr. Quest walked to his vestry meeting with a smile upon his thin, gentlemanly-looking face, and rage and bitterness in his heart.

"I caught her that time," he said to himself; "she can do a good deal in the way of deceit, but she can't keep the blood out of her cheeks when she hears that fellow's name. But she is a clever woman, Belle is—how well she managed that little business of the luncheon, and how well she fought her case when once she got me in a cleft stick about Edith and that money of hers, and made good terms too. Ah! that's the worst of it, she has the whip hand of me there; if I could ruin her she could ruin me, and it's no use cutting off one's nose to spite your face. Well! my fine lady," he went on with an ominous flash of his grey eyes, "I shall be even with you yet. Give you enough rope and you will hang yourself. You love this fellow, I know that, and it will go hard if I can't make him break your heart for you. Bah! you don't know the sort of stuff men are made of. If only I did not happen to be in love with you myself I should not care. If—Ah! here I am at the church."

The human animal is a very complicated machine, and can conduct the working of an extraordinary number of different interests and sets of ideas, almost, if not entirely, simultaneously. For instance, Mr. Quest—seated at the right hand of the rector in the vestry room of the beautiful old

Boisingham Church, and engaged in an animated and even warm discussion with the senior curate on the details of fourteenth century Church work, in which he clearly took a lively interest and understood far better than did the curate—would have been exceedingly difficult to identify with the scheming, vindictive creature whom we have just followed up the church path. But after all, that is the way of human nature, although it may not be the way of those who try to draw it and who love to paint the villain black as the Evil One and the virtuous heroine so radiant that we begin to fancy we can hear the whispering of her wings. Few people are altogether good or altogether bad; indeed it is probable that the vast majority are neither good nor bad—they have not the strength to be the one or the other. Here and there, however, we do meet a spirit with sufficient will and originality to press the scale down this way or that, though even then the opposing force, be it good or evil, is constantly striving to bring the balance equal. Even the most wicked men have their redeeming points and righteous instincts, nor are their thoughts continually fixed upon iniquity. Mr. Quest, for instance, one of the evil geniuses of this history, was, where his plots and passions were not immediately concerned, a man of eminently generous and refined tendencies. Many were the good turns, contradictory as it may seem, that he had done to his poorer neighbours; he had even been known to forego his bills of costs, which is about the highest and rarest exhibition of earthly virtue that can be expected from a lawyer. He was moreover eminently a cultured man, a reader of the classics, in translations if not in the originals, a man with a fine taste in fiction and poetry, and a really sound and ripe archaeological knowledge, especially where sacred buildings were concerned. All his instincts, also, were towards respectability. His most burning ambition was to secure a high position in the county in which he lived, and to be classed among the resident gentry. He hated his lawyer's work, and longed to accumulate sufficient means to be able to give it the good-bye and to indulge himself in an existence of luxurious and learned leisure. Such as he was he had made himself, for he was the son of a poor and inferior country dentist, and had begun life with a good education, it is true, which he chiefly owed to his own exertions, but with nothing else. Had his nature been a temperate nature with a balance of good to its credit to draw upon instead of a balance of evil, he was a man who might have gone very far indeed, for in addition to his natural ability he had a great power of work. But unfortunately this was not the case; his instincts on the whole were evil instincts, and his passions—whether of hate, or love, or greed, when they seized him did so with extraordinary violence, rendering him for the time being utterly callous to the rights or feelings of others, provided that he attained his end. In short, had he been born to a good position and a large fortune, it is quite possible, providing always that his strong passions had not at some period of his life led him irremediably astray, that he would have lived virtuous and respected, and died in good odour, leaving behind him a happy memory. But fate had placed him in antagonism with the world, and yet had endowed him with a gnawing desire to be of the world, as it appeared most desirable to him; and then, to complete his ruin circumstances had thrown him into temptations from which inexperience and the headlong strength of his passions gave him no opportunity to escape.

It may at first appear strange that a man so calculating and whose desires seemed to be fixed upon such a material end as the acquirement by artifice or even fraud of the wealth which he coveted, should also nourish in his heart so bitter a hatred and so keen a thirst for revenge upon a woman as Mr. Quest undoubtedly did towards his beautiful wife. It would have seemed more probable that he would have left heroics alone and attempted to turn his wife's folly into a means of wealth and self-advancement: and this would not doubt have been so had Mrs. Quest's estimate of his motives in marrying her been an entirely correct one. She had told Edward Cossey, it will be remembered, that her husband had married her for her money—the ten thousand pounds of which he stood so badly in need. Now this was the truth to a certain extent, and a certain extent only. He had wanted the ten thousand pounds, in fact at the moment money was necessary to him. But, and this his wife had never known or realised, he had been, and still was, also in love with her. Possibly the ten thousand pounds would have proved a sufficient inducement to him without the love, but the love was none the less there. Their relations, however, had never been happy ones. She had detested him from the fist, and had not spared to say so. No man with any refinement—and whatever he lacked Mr. Quest had refinement—could bear to be thus continually repulsed by a woman, and so it came to pass that their intercourse had always been of the most strained nature. Then when she at last had obtained the clue to the secret of his life, under threat of exposure she drove her bargain, of which the terms were complete separation in all but outward form, and virtual freedom of action for herself. This, considering the position, she was perhaps justified in doing, but her husband never forgave her for it. More than that, he determined, if by any means it were possible, to turn the passion which, although she did not know it, he was perfectly aware she bore towards his business superior, Edward Cossey, to a refined instrument of vengeance against her, with what success it will be one of the purposes of this history to show.

Such, put as briefly as possible, were the outlines of the character and aims of this remarkable and contradictory man.

Within an hour and a half of leaving his own house, "The Oaks," as it was called, although the trees from which it had been so named had long since vanished from the garden, Mr. Quest was bowling swiftly along behind Edward Cossey's powerful bay horse towards the towering gateway of Honham Castle. When he was within three hundred yards an idea struck him; he pulled the horse up sharply, for he was alone in the dogcart, and paused to admire the view.

"What a beautiful place!" he reflected to himself with enthusiasm, "and how grandly those old towers stand out against the sky. The Squire has restored them very well, too, there is no doubt about it; I could not have done it better myself. I wonder if that place will ever be mine. Things look black now, but they may come round, and I think I am beginning to see my way."

And then he started the horse on again, reflecting on the unpleasant nature of the business before him. Personally he both liked and respected the old Squire, and he certainly pitied him, though he would no more have dreamed of allowing his liking and pity to interfere with the prosecution of his schemes, than an ardent sportsman would dream of not shooting pheasants because he had happened to take a friendly interest in their nurture. He had also a certain gentlemanlike distaste to being the bearer of crushing bad news, for Mr. Quest disliked scenes, possibly because he had such an intimate personal acquaintance with them. Whilst he was still wondering how he might best deal with the matter, he passed over the moat and through the ancient gateway which he admired so fervently, and found himself in front of the hall door. Here he pulled up, looking about for somebody to take his horse, when suddenly the Squire himself emerged upon him with a rush.

"Hullo, Quest, is that you?" he shouted, as though his visitor had been fifty yards off instead of five. "I have been looking out for you. Here, William! William!" (crescendo), "William!" (fortissimo), "where on earth is the boy? I expect that idle fellow, George, has been sending him on some of his errands instead of attending to them himself. Whenever he is wanted to take a horse he is nowhere to be found, and then it is 'Please, sir, Mr. George,' that's what he calls him, 'Please, sir, Mr. George sent me up to the Moat Farm or somewhere to see how many eggs the hens laid last week,' or something of the sort. That's a very nice horse you have got there, by the way, very nice indeed."

"It is not my horse, Mr. de la Molle," said the lawyer, with a faint smile, "it is Mr. Edward Cossey's."

"Oh! it's Mr. Edward Cossey's, is it?" answered the old gentleman with a sudden change of voice. "Ah, Mr. Edward Cossey's? Well, it's a very good horse anyhow, and I suppose that Mr. Cossey can afford to buy good horses."

Just then a faint cry of "Coming, sir, coming," was heard, and a long hobble-de-hoy kind of youth, whose business it was to look after the not extensive Castle stables, emerged in a great heat from round the corner of the house.

"Now, where on earth have you been?" began the Squire, in a stentorian tone.

"If you please, sir, Mr. George—"

"There, what did I tell you?" broke in the Squire. "Have I not told you time after time that you are to mind your own business, and leave 'Mr. George' to mind his? Now take that horse round to the stables, and see that it is properly fed.

"Come, Quest, come in. We have a quarter of an hour before luncheon, and can get our business over," and he led the way through the passage into the tapestried and panelled vestibule, where he took his stand before the empty fireplace.

Mr. Quest followed him, stopping, ostensibly to admire a particularly fine suit of armour which hung upon the wall, but really to gain another moment for reflection.

"A beautiful suit of the early Stuart period, Mr. de la Molle," he said; "I never saw a better."

"Yes, yes, that belonged to old Sir James, the one whom the Roundheads shot."

"What! the Sir James who hid the treasure?"

"Yes. I was telling that story to our new neighbour, Colonel Quaritch, last night—a very nice fellow, by the way; you should go and call upon him."

"I wonder what he did with it," said Mr. Quest.

"Ah, so do I, and so will many another, I dare say. I wish that I could find it, I'm sure. It's wanted badly enough now-a-days. But that reminds me, Quest. You will have gathered my difficulty from my note and what George told you. You see this man Janter—thanks to that confounded fellow, Major Boston, and his action about those College Lands—has thrown up the Moat Farm, and George tells me that there is not another tenant to be had for love or money. In fact, you know what it is, one can't get tenants now-a-days, they simply are not to be had. Well, under these circumstances, there is, of course, only one thing to be done that I know of, and that is to take the farm in hand and farm it myself. It is quite impossible to let the place fall out of cultivation—and that is what would happen otherwise, for if I were to lay it down in grass it would cost a considerable sum, and be seven or eight years before I got any return."

The Squire paused and Mr. Quest said nothing.

"Well," he went on, "that being so, the next thing to do is to obtain the necessary cash to pay Janter his valuation and stock the place—about four thousand would do it, or perhaps," he added, with an access of generous confidence, "we had better say five. There are about fifty acres of those low-lying meadows which want to be thoroughly bush drained—bushes are quite as good as pipes for that stiff land, if they put in the right sort of stuff, and it don't cost half so much—but still it can't be done for nothing, and then there is a new wagon shed wanted, and some odds and ends; yes, we had better say five thousand."

Still Mr. Quest made no answer, so once more the Squire went on.

"Well, you see, under these circumstances—not being able to lay hands upon the necessary capital from my private resources, of course I have made up my mind to apply to Cossey and Son for the loan. Indeed, considering how long and intimate has been the connection between their house and the de la Molle family, I think it right and proper to do so;

indeed, I should consider it very wrong of me if I neglected to give them the opportunity of the investment"—here a faint smile flickered for an instant on Mr. Quest's face and then went out—"of course they will, as a matter of business, require security, and very properly so, but as this estate is unentailed, there will fortunately be very little difficulty about that. You can draw up the necessary deeds, and I think that under the circumstances the right thing to do would be to charge the Moat Farm specifically with the amount. Things are bad enough, no doubt, but I can hardly suppose it possible under any conceivable circumstances that the farm would not be good for five thousand pounds. However, they might perhaps prefer to have a general clause as well, and if it is so, although I consider it quite unnecessary, I shall raise no objection to that course."

Then at last Mr. Quest broke his somewhat ominous silence.

"I am very sorry to say, Mr. de la Molle," he said gently, "that I can hold out no prospect of Cossey and Son being induced, under any circumstances, to advance another pound upon the security of the Honham Castle estates. Their opinion of the value of landed property as security has received so severe a shock, that they are not at all comfortable as to the safety of the amount already invested."

Mr. de la Molle started when he heard this most unexpected bit of news, for which he was totally unprepared. He had always found it possible to borrow money, and it had never occurred to him that a time might perhaps come in this country, when the land, which he held in almost superstitious veneration, would be so valueless a form of property that lenders would refuse it as security.

"Why," he said, recovering himself, "the total encumbrances on the property do not amount to more than twenty-five thousand pounds, and when I succeeded to my father, forty years ago, it was valued at fifty, and the Castle and premises have been thoroughly repaired since then at a cost of five thousand, and most of the farm buildings too."

"Very possibly, de la Molle, but to be honest, I very much doubt if Honham Castle and the lands round it would now fetch twenty-five thousand pounds on a forced sale. Competition and Radical agitation have brought estates down more than people realise, and land in Australia and New Zealand is now worth almost as much per acre as cultivated lands in England. Perhaps as a residential property and on account of its historical interest it might fetch more, but I doubt it. In short, Mr. de la Molle, so anxious are Cossey and Son in the matter, that I regret to have to tell you that so far from being willing to make a further advance, the firm have formally instructed me to serve the usual six months' notice on you, calling in the money already advanced on mortgage, together with the interest, which I must remind you is nearly a year overdue, and this step I propose to take to-morrow."

The old gentleman staggered for a moment, and caught at the mantelpiece, for the blow was a heavy one, and as unexpected as it was heavy. But he recovered himself in an instant, for it was one of the peculiarities of his character that his spirits always seemed to rise to the occasion in the face of urgent adversity—in short, he possessed an extraordinary share of moral courage.

"Indeed," he said indignantly, "indeed, it is a pity that you did not tell me that at once, Mr. Quest; it would have saved me from putting myself in a false position by proposing a business arrangement which is not acceptable. As regards the interest, I admit that it is as you say, and I very much regret it. That stupid fellow George is always so dreadfully behindhand with his accounts that I can never get anything settled." (He did not state, and indeed did not know, that the reason that the unfortunate George was behindhand was that there were no accounts to make up, or rather that they were all on the wrong side of the ledger). "I will have that matter seen to at once. Of course, business people are quite right to consider their due, and I do not blame Messrs. Cossey in the matter, not in the least. Still, I must say that, considering the long and intimate relationship that has for nearly two centuries existed between their house and my family, they might—well—have shown a little more consideration."

"Yes," said Mr. Quest, "I daresay that the step strikes you as a harsh one. To be perfectly frank with you, Mr. de la Molle, it struck me as a very harsh one; but, of course, I am only a servant, and bound to carry out my instructions. I sympathise with you very much—very much indeed."

"Oh, don't do that," said the old gentleman. "Of course, other arrangements must be made; and, much as it will pain me to terminate my connection with Messrs. Cossey, they shall be made."

"But I think," went on the lawyer, without any notice of his interruption, "that you misunderstand the matter a little. Cossey and Son are only a trading corporation, whose object is to make money by lending it, or otherwise—at all hazards to make money. The kind of feeling that you allude to, and that might induce them, in consideration of long intimacy and close connection in the past, to forego the opportunity of so doing and even to run a risk of loss, is a thing which belongs to former generations. But the present is a strictly commercial age, and we are the most commercial of the trading nations. Cossey and Son move with the times, that is all, and they would rather sell up a dozen families who had dealt with them for two centuries than lose five hundred pounds, provided, of course, that they could do so without scandal and loss of public respect, which, where a banking house is concerned, also means a loss of custom. I am a great lover of the past myself, and believe that our ancestors' ways of doing business were, on the whole, better and more charitable than ours, but I have to make my living and take the world as I find it, Mr. de la Molle."

"Quite so, Quest; quite so," answered the Squire quietly. "I had no idea that you looked at these matters in such a light.

Certainly the world has changed a good deal since I was a young man, and I do not think it has changed much for the better. But you will want your luncheon; it is hungry work talking about foreclosures." Mr. Quest had not used this unpleasant word, but the Squire had seen his drift. "Come into the next room," and he led the way to the drawing-room, where Ida was sitting reading the *Times*.

"Ida," he said, with an affectation of heartiness which did not, however, deceive his daughter, who knew how to read every change of her dear father's face, "here is Mr. Quest. Take him in to luncheon, my love. I will come presently. I want to finish a note."

Then he returned to the vestibule and sat down in his favourite old oak chair.

"Ruined," he said to himself. "I can never get the money as things are, and there will be a foreclosure. Well, I am an old man and I hope that I shall not live to see it. But there is Ida. Poor Ida! I cannot bear to think of it, and the old place too, after all these generations—after all these generations!"

CHAPTER X

THE TENNIS PARTY

Ida shook hands coldly enough with the lawyer, for whom she cherished a dislike not unmixed with fear. Many women are by nature gifted with an extraordinary power of intuition which fully makes up for their deficiency in reasoning force. They do not conclude from the premisses of their observation, they *know* that this man is to be feared and that trusted. In fact, they share with the rest of breathing creation that self-protective instinct of instantaneous and almost automatic judgment, given to guard it from the dangers with which it is continually threatened at the hands of man's over-mastering strength and ordered intelligence. Ida was one of these. She knew nothing to Mr. Quest's disadvantage, indeed she always heard him spoken of with great respect, and curiously enough she liked his wife. But she could not bear the man, feeling in her heart that he was not only to be avoided on account of his own hidden qualities, but that he was moreover an active personal enemy.

They went into the dining-room, where the luncheon was set, and while Ida allowed Mr. Quest to cut her some cold boiled beef, an operation in which he did not seem to be very much at home, she came to a rapid conclusion in her own mind. She had seen clearly enough from her father's face that his interview with the lawyer had been of a most serious character, but she knew that the chances were that she would never be able to get its upshot out of him, for the old gentleman had a curious habit of keeping such unpleasant matters to himself until he was absolutely forced by circumstances to reveal them. She also knew that her father's affairs were in a most critical condition, for this she had extracted from him on the previous night, and that if any remedy was to be attempted it must be attempted at once, and on some heroic scale. Therefore, she made up her mind to ask her *bete noire*, Mr. Quest, what the truth might be.

"Mr. Quest," she said, with some trepidation, as he at last triumphantly handed her the beef, "I hope you will forgive me for asking you a plain question, and that, if you can, you will favour me with a plain answer. I know my father's affairs are very much involved, and that he is now anxious to borrow some more money; but I do not know quite how matters stand, and I want to learn the exact truth."

"I am very glad to hear you speak so, Miss de la Molle," answered the lawyer, "because I was trying to make up my mind to broach the subject, which is a painful one to me. Frankly, then—forgive me for saying it, your father is absolutely ruined. The interest on the mortgages is a year in arrear, his largest farm has just been thrown upon his hands, and, to complete the tale, the mortgagees are going to call in their money or foreclose."

At this statement, which was almost brutal in its brief comprehensiveness, Ida turned pale as death, as well she might, and dropped her fork with a clatter upon the plate.

"I did not realise that things were quite so bad," she murmured. "Then I suppose that the place will be taken from us, and we shall—shall have to go away."

"Yes, certainly, unless money can be found to take up the mortgages, of which I see no chance. The place will be sold for what it will fetch, and that now-a-days will be no great sum."

"When will that be?" she asked.

"In about six or nine months' time."

Ida's lips trembled, and the sight of the food upon her plate became nauseous to her. A vision arose before her mind's eye of herself and her old father departing hand in hand from the Castle gates, behind and about which gleamed the hard wild lights of a March sunset, to seek a place to hide themselves. The vivid horror of the phantasy almost overcame her.

"Is there no way of escape?" she asked hoarsely. "To lose this place would kill my father. He loves it better than anything in the world; his whole life is wrapped up in it."

"I can quite understand that, Miss de la Molle; it is a most charming old place, especially to anybody interested in the past. But unfortunately mortgagees are no respecters of feelings. To them land is so much property and nothing more."

"I know all that," she said impatiently, "you do not answer my question;" and she leaned towards him, resting her hand upon the table. "Is there no way out of it?"

Mr. Quest drank a little claret before he answered. "Yes," he said, "I think that there is, if only you will take it."

"What way?" she asked eagerly.

"Well, though as I said just now, the mortgagees of an estate as a body are merely a business corporation, and look at things from a business point of view only, you must remember that they are composed of individuals, and that individuals can be influenced if they can be got at. For instance, Cossey and Son are an abstraction and harshly disposed in their abstract capacity, but Mr. Edward Cossey is an individual, and I should say, so far as this particular matter is concerned, a benevolently disposed individual. Now Mr. Edward Cossey is not himself at the present moment actually one of the firm of Cossey and Son, but he is the hair of the head of the house, and of course has authority, and, what is better still, the command of money."

"I understand," said Ida. "You mean that my father should try to win over Mr. Edward Cossey. Unfortunately, to be frank, he dislikes him, and my father is not a man to keep his dislikes to himself."

"People generally do dislike those to whom they are crushingly indebted; your father dislikes Mr. Cossey because his name is Cossey, and for no other reason. But that is not quite what I meant—I do not think that the Squire is the right person to undertake a negotiation of the sort. He is a little too outspoken and incautious. No, Miss de la Molle, if it is to be done at all *you* must do it. You must put the whole case before him at once—this very afternoon, there is no time for delay; you need not enter into details, he knows all about them—only ask him to avert this catastrophe. He can do so if he likes, how he does it is his own affair."

"But, Mr. Quest," said Ida, "how can I ask such a favour of any man? I shall be putting myself in a dreadfully false position."

"I do not pretend, Miss de la Molle, that it is a pleasant task for any young lady to undertake. I quite understand your shrinking from it. But sometimes one has to do unpleasant things and make compromises with one's self-respect. It is a question whether or no your family shall be utterly ruined and destroyed. There is, as I honestly believe, no prospect whatever of your father being able to get the money to pay off Cossey and Son, and if he did, it would not help him, because he could not pay the interest on it. Under these circumstances you have to choose between putting yourself in an equivocal position and letting events take their course. It would be useless for anybody else to undertake the task, and of course I cannot guarantee that even you will succeed, but I will not mince matters—as you doubtless know, any man would find it hard to refuse a favour asked by such a suppliant. And now you must make up your own mind. I have shown you a path that may lead your family from a position of the most imminent peril. If you are the woman I take you for, you will not shrink from following it."

Ida made no reply, and in another moment the Squire came in to take a couple of glasses of sherry and a biscuit. But Mr. Quest, furtively watching her face, said to himself that she had taken the bait and that she would do it. Shortly after this a diversion occurred, for the clergyman, Mr. Jeffries, a pleasant little man, with a round and shining face and a most unclerical eyeglass, came up to consult the Squire upon some matter of parish business, and was shown into the dining-room. Ida took advantage of his appearance to effect a retreat to her own room, and there for the present we may leave her to her meditations.

No more business was discussed by the Squire that afternoon. Indeed it interested Mr. Quest, who was above all things a student of character, to observe how wonderfully the old gentleman threw off his trouble. To listen to him energetically arguing with the Rev. Mr. Jeffries as to whether or no it would be proper, as had hitherto been the custom, to devote the proceeds of the harvest festival collection (1 pound 18s. 3d. and a brass button) to the county hospital, or whether it should be applied to the repair of the woodwork in the vestry, was under the circumstances most instructive. The Rev. Mr. Jeffries, who suffered severely from the condition of the vestry, at last gained his point by triumphantly showing that no patient from Honham had been admitted to the hospital for fifteen months, and that therefore the hospital had no claim on this particular year, whereas the draught in the vestry was enough to cut any clergyman in two.

"Well, well," said the old gentleman, "I will consent for this year, and this year only. I have been churchwarden of this parish for between forty and fifty years, and we have always given the harvest festival collection to the hospital, and although under these exceptional circumstances it may possibly be desirable to diverge from that custom, I cannot and will not consent to such a thing in a permanent way. So I shall write to the secretary and explain the matter, and tell him that next year and in the future generally the collection will be devoted to its original purpose."

"Great heavens!" ejaculated Mr. Quest to himself. "And the man must know that in all human probability the place will be sold over his head before he is a year older. I wonder if he puts it on or if he deceives himself. I suppose he has lived here so long that he cannot realise a condition of things under which he will cease to live here and the place will belong to somebody else. Or perhaps he is only brazening it out." And then he strolled away to the back of the house and had a look at the condition of the outhouses, reflecting that some of them would be sadly expensive to repair for whoever came into possession here. After that he crossed the moat and walked through the somewhat extensive plantations at the back of the house, wondering if it would not be possible to get enough timber out of them, if one went to work judiciously, to pay for putting the place in order. Presently he came to a hedgerow where a row of very fine timber oaks had stood, of which the Squire had been notoriously fond, and of which he had himself taken particular and admiring notice in the course of the previous winter. The trees were gone. In the hedge where they had grown were a series of gaps like those in an old woman's jaw, and the ground was still littered with remains of bark and branches and of faggots that had been made up from the brushwood.

"Cut down this spring fell," was Mr. Quest's ejaculation. "Poor old gentleman, he must have been pinched before he consented to part with those oaks."

Then he turned and went back to the house, just in time to see Ida's guests arriving for the lawn tennis party. Ida herself was standing on the lawn behind the house, which, bordered as it was by the moat and at the further end by a row of ruined arches, was one of the most picturesque in the country and a very effective setting to any young lady. As the people came they were shown through the house on to the lawn, and here she was receiving them. She was dressed in a plain, tight-fitting gown of blue flannel, which showed off her perfect figure to great advantage, and a broad-brimmed hat, that shaded her fine and dignified face. Mr. Quest sat down on a bench beneath the shade of an arbutus, watching her closely, and indeed, if the study of a perfect English lady of the noblest sort has any charms, he was not without his reward. There are some women—most of us know one or two—who are born to hold a great position and to sail across the world like a swan through meaner fowl. It would be very hard to say to what their peculiar charm and dignity is owing. It is not to beauty only, for though they have presence, many of these women are not beautiful, while some are even plain. Nor does it spring from native grace and tact alone; though these things must be present. Rather perhaps it is the reflection of a cultivated intellect acting upon a naturally pure and elevated temperament, which makes these ladies conspicuous and fashions them in such kind that all men, putting aside the mere charm of beauty and the natural softening of judgment in the atmosphere of sex, must recognise in them an equal mind, and a presence more noble than their own.

Such a woman was Ida de la Molle, and if any one doubted it, it was sufficient to compare her in her simplicity to the various human items by whom she was surrounded. They were a typical county society gathering, such as needs no description, and would not greatly interest if described; neither very good nor very bad, very handsome nor very plain, but moving religiously within the lines of custom and on the ground of commonplace.

It is no wonder, then, that a woman like Ida de la Molle was *facile princeps* among such company, or that Harold Quaritch, who was somewhat poetically inclined for a man of his age, at any rate where the lady in question was concerned, should in his heart have compared her to a queen. Even Belle Quest, lovely as she undoubtedly was in her own way, paled and looked shopgirlish in face of that gentle dignity, a fact of which she was evidently aware, for although the two women were friendly, nothing would induce the latter to stand long near Ida in public. She would tell Edward Cossey that it made her look like a wax doll beside a live child.

While Mr. Quest was still watching Ida with complete satisfaction, for she appealed to the artistic side of his nature, Colonel Quaritch arrived upon the scene, looking, Mr. Quest thought, particularly plain with his solid form, his long thin nose, light whiskers, and square massive chin. Also he looked particularly imposing in contrast to the youths and maidens and domesticated clergymen. There was a gravity, almost a solemnity, about his bronzed countenance and deliberate ordered conversation, which did not, however, favourably impress the aforesaid youths and maidens, if a judgment might be formed from such samples of conversational criticism as Mr. Quest heard going on on the further side of his arbutus.

CHAPTER XI

IDA'S BARGAIN

When Ida saw the Colonel coming, she put on her sweetest smile and took his outstretched hand.

"How do you do, Colonel Quaritch?" she said. "It is very good of you to come, especially as you don't play tennis much—by the way, I hope you have been studying that cypher, for I am sure it is a cypher."

"I studied it for half-an-hour before I went to bed last night, Miss de la Molle, and for the life of me I could not make anything out of it, and what's more, I don't think that there is anything to make out."

"Ah," she answered with a sigh, "I wish there was."

"Well, I'll have another try at it. What will you give me if I find it out?" he said with a smile which lighted up his rugged face most pleasantly.

"Anything you like to ask and that I can give," she answered in a tone of earnestness which struck him as peculiar, for of course he did not know the news that she had just heard from Mr. Quest.

Then for the first time for many years, Harold Quaritch delivered himself of a speech that might have been capable of a tender and hidden meaning.

"I am afraid," he said, bowing, "that if I came to claim the reward, I should ask for more even that you would be inclined to give."

Ida blushed a little. "We can consider that when you do come, Colonel Quaritch—excuse me, but here are Mrs. Quest and Mr. Cossey, and I must go and say how do you do."

Harold Quaritch looked round, feeling unreasonably irritated at this interruption to his little advances, and for the first time saw Edward Cossey. He was coming along in the wake of Mrs. Quest, looking very handsome and rather languid, when their eyes met, and to speak the truth, the Colonel's first impression was not a complimentary one. Edward Cossey was in some ways not a bad fellow, but like a great many young men who are born with silver spoons in their mouths, he had many airs and graces, one of which was the affectation of treating older and better men with an assumption of off-handedness and even of superiority that was rather obnoxious. Thus while Ida was greeting Mr. Quest, he was engaged in taking in the Colonel in a way which irritated that gentleman considerably.

Presently Ida turned and introduced Colonel Quaritch, first to Mrs. Quest and then to Mr. Cossey. Harold bowed to each, and then strolled off to meet the Squire, whom he noted advancing with his usual array of protective towels hanging out of his hat, and for a while saw neither of them any more.

Meanwhile Mr. Quest had emerged from the shelter of his arbutus, and going from one person to another, said some pleasant and appropriate word to each, till at last he reached the spot where his wife and Edward Cossey were standing. Nodding affectionately at the former, he asked her if she was not going to play tennis, and then drew Cossey aside.

"Well, Quest," said the latter, "have you told the old man?"

"Yes, I told him."

"How did he take it?"

"Oh, talked it off and said that of course other arrangements must be made. I spoke to Miss de la Molle too."

"Indeed," said Edward, in a changed tone, "and how did she take it?"

"Well," answered the lawyer, putting on an air of deep concern (and as a matter of fact he really did feel sorry for her), "I think it was the most painful professional experience that I ever had. The poor woman was utterly crushed. She said that it would kill her father."

"Poor girl!" said Mr. Cossey, in a voice that showed his sympathy to be of a very active order, "and how pluckily she is carrying it off too—look at her," and he pointed to where Ida was standing, a lawn tennis bat in her hand and laughingly arranging a "set" of married *versus* single.

"Yes, she is a spirited girl," answered Mr. Quest, "and what a splendid woman she looks, doesn't she? I never saw anybody who was so perfect a lady—there is nobody to touch her round here, unless," he added meditatively, "perhaps it is Belle."

"There are different types of beauty," answered Edward Cossey, flinching.

"Yes, but equally striking in their separate ways. Well, it can't be helped, but I feel sorry for that poor woman, and the old gentleman too—ah, there he is."

As he was speaking the Squire, who was walking past with Colonel Quaritch, with the object of showing him the view from the end of the moat, suddenly came face to face with Edward Cossey. He at once stepped forward to greet him, but to his surprise was met by a cold and most stately bow from

Mr. de la Molle, who passed on without vouchsafing a single word.

"Old idiot!" ejaculated Mr. Quest to himself, "he will put Cossey's back up and spoil the game."

"Well," said Edward aloud and colouring almost to his eyes. "That old gentleman knows how to be insolent."

"You must not mind him, Mr. Cossey," answered Quest hastily. "The poor old boy has a very good idea of himself—he is dreadfully injured because Cossey and Son are calling in the mortgages after the family has dealt with them for so many generations; and he thinks that you have something to do with it."

"Well if he does he might as well be civil. It does not particularly incline a fellow to go aside to pull him out of the ditch, just to be cut in that fashion—I have half a mind to order my trap and go."

"No, no, don't do that—you must make allowances, you must indeed—look, here is Miss de la Molle coming to ask you to play tennis."

At this moment Ida arrived and took off Edward Cossey with her, not a little to the relief of Mr. Quest, who began to fear that the whole scheme was spoiled by the Squire's unfortunate magnificence of manner.

Edward played his game, having Ida herself as his partner. It cannot be said that the set was a pleasant one for the latter, who, poor woman, was doing her utmost to bring up her courage to the point necessary to the carrying out of the appeal *ad misericordiam*, which she had decided to make as soon as the game was over. However, chance put an opportunity in her way, for Edward Cossey, who had a curious weakness for flowers, asked her if she would show him her chrysanthemums, of which she was very proud. She consented readily enough.

They crossed the lawn, and passing through some shrubbery reached the greenhouse, which was placed at the end of the Castle itself. Here for some minutes they looked at the flowers, just now bursting into bloom. Ida, who felt exceedingly nervous, was all the while wondering how on earth she could broach so delicate a subject, when fortunately Mr. Cossey himself gave her the necessary opening.

"I can't imagine, Miss de la Molle," he said, "what I have done to offend your father—he almost cut me just now."

"Are you sure that he saw you, Mr. Cossey; he is very absent-minded sometimes?"

"Oh yes, he saw me, but when I offered to shake hands with him he only bowed in rather a crushing way and passed on."

Ida broke off a Scarlet Turk from its stem, and nervously began to pick the bloom to pieces.

"The fact is, Mr. Cossey—the fact is, my father, and indeed I also, are in great trouble just now, about money matters you know, and my father is very apt to be prejudiced,—in short, I rather believe that he thinks you may have something to do with his difficulties—but perhaps you know all about it."

"I know something, Miss de la Molle," said he gravely, "and I hope and trust you do not believe that I have anything to do with the action which Cossey and Son have thought fit to take."

"No, no," she said hastily. "I never thought anything of the sort—but I know that you have influence—and, well, to be plain, Mr. Cossey, I implore of you to use it. Perhaps you will understand that this is very humiliating for me to be obliged to ask this, though you can never guess *how* humiliating. Believe me, Mr. Cossey, I would never ask it for myself, but it is for my father—he loves this place better than his life; it would be much better he should die than that he should be obliged to leave it; and if this money is called in, that is what must happen, because the place will be sold over us. I believe he would go mad, I do indeed," and she stopped speaking and stood before him, the fragment of the flower in her hand, her breast heaving with emotion.

"What do you suggest should be done, Miss de la Molle?" said Edward Cossey gently.

"I suggest that—that—if you will be so kind, you should persuade Cossey and Son to forego their intention of calling in the money."

"It is quite impossible," he answered. "My father ordered the step himself, and he is a hard man. It is impossible to turn him if he thinks he will lose money by turning. You see he is a banker, and has been handling money all his life, till it has become a sort of god to him. Really I do believe that he would rather beggar every friend he has than lose five thousand pounds."

"Then there is no more to be said. The place must go, that's all," replied Ida, turning away her head and affecting to busy herself in removing some dried leaves from a chrysanthemum plant. Edward, watching her however, saw her shoulders shake and a big tear fall like a raindrop on the pavement, and the sight, strongly attracted as he was and had for some time been towards the young lady, was altogether too much for him. In an instant, moved by an overwhelming impulse, and something not unlike a gust of passion, he came to one of those determinations which so often change the whole course and tenour of men's lives.

"Miss de la Molle," he said rapidly, "there may be a way found out of it."

She looked up enquiringly, and there were the tear stains on her face.

"Somebody might take up the mortgages and pay off Cossey and Son."

"Can you find anyone who will?" she asked eagerly.

"No, not as an investment. I understand that thirty thousand pounds are required, and I tell you frankly that as times are I do not for one moment believe the place to be worth that amount. It is all very well for your father to talk about land recovering itself, but at present, at any rate, nobody can see the faintest chance of anything of the sort. The probabilities are, on the contrary, that as the American competition increases, land will gradually sink to something like a prairie value."

"Then how can money be got if nobody will advance it?"

"I did not say that nobody will advance it; I said that nobody would advance it as an investment—a friend might advance it."

"And where is such a friend to be found? He must be a very disinterested friend who would advance thirty thousand pounds."

"Nobody in this world is quite disinterested, Miss de la Molle; or at any rate very few are. What would you give to such a friend?"

"I would give anything and everything over which I have control in this world, to save my father from seeing Honham sold over his head," she answered simply.

Edward Cossey laughed a little. "That is a large order," he said. "Miss de la Molle, *I* am disposed to try and find the money to take up these mortgages. I have not got it, and I shall have to borrow it, and what is more, I shall have to keep the fact that I have borrowed it a secret from my father."

"It is very good of you," said Ida faintly, "I don't know what to say."

For a moment he made no reply, and looking at him, Ida saw that his hand was trembling.

"Miss de la Molle," he said, "there is another matter of which I wish to speak to you. Men are sometimes put into strange positions, partly through their own fault, partly by force of circumstances, and when in those positions, are forced down paths that they would not follow. Supposing, Miss de la Molle, that mine were some such position, and supposing that owing to that position I could not say to you words which I should wish to say—"

Ida began to understand now and once more turned aside.

"Supposing, however, that at some future time the difficulties of that position of which I have spoken were to fade away, and I were then to speak those words, can you, supposing all this—tell me how they would be received?"

Ida paused, and thought. She was a strong-natured and clear-headed woman, and she fully understood the position. On her answer would depend whether or no the thirty thousand pounds were forthcoming, and therefore, whether or no Honham Castle would pass from her father and her race.

"I said just now, Mr. Cossey," she answered coldly, "that I would give anything and everything over which I have control in the world, to save my father from seeing Honham sold over his head. I do not wish to retract those words, and I think that in them you will find an answer to your question."

He coloured. "You put the matter in a very business-like way," he said.

"It is best put so, Mr. Cossey," she answered with a faint shade of bitterness in her tone; "it preserves me from feeling under an obligation—will you see my father about these mortgages?"

"Yes, to-morrow. And now I will say good-bye to you," and he took her hand, and with some little hesitation kissed it. She made no resistance and showed no emotion.

"Yes," she answered, "we have been here some time; Mrs. Quest will wonder what has become of you."

It was a random arrow, but it went straight home, and for the third time that day Edward Cossey reddened to the roots of his hair. Without answering a word he bowed and went.

When Ida saw this, she was sorry she had made the remark, for she had no wish to appear to Mr. Cossey (the conquest of whom gave her neither pride nor pleasure) in the light of a spiteful, or worst still, of a jealous woman. She had indeed heard some talk about him and Mrs. Quest, but not being of a scandal-loving disposition it had not interested her, and she had almost forgotten it. Now however she learned that there was something in it.

"So that is the difficult position of which he talks," she said to herself; "he wants to marry me as soon as he can get Mrs. Quest off his hands. And I have consented to that, always provided that Mrs. Quest can be disposed of, in consideration of the receipt of a sum of thirty thousand pounds. And I do not like the man. It was not nice of him to make that bargain, though I brought it on myself. I wonder if my father will ever know what I have done for him, and if he will appreciate it when he does. Well, it is not a bad price—thirty thousand pounds—a good figure for any woman in the present state of the market." And with a hard and bitter laugh, and a prescience of sorrow to come lying at the heart, she threw down the remains of the Scarlet Turk and turned away.

CHAPTER XII

GEORGE PROPHESIES

Ida, for obvious reasons, said nothing to her father of her interview with Edward Cossey, and thus it came to pass that on the morning following the lawn tennis party, there was a very serious consultation between the faithful George and his master. It appeared to Ida, who was lying awake in her room, to commence somewhere about daybreak, and it certainly continued with short intervals for refreshment till eleven o'clock in the forenoon. First the Squire explained the whole question to George at great length, and with a most extraordinary multiplicity of detail, for he began at his first loan from the house of Cossey and Son, which he had contracted a great many years before. All this while George sat with a very long face, and tried to look as though he were following the thread of the argument, which was not possible, for his master had long ago lost it himself, and was mixing up the loan of 1863 with the loan of 1874, and the money raised in the severance of the entail with both, in a way which would have driven anybody except George, who was used to this sort of thing, perfectly mad. However he sat it through, and when at last the account was finished, remarked that things "sartainly did look queer."

Thereupon the Squire called him a stupid owl, and having by means of some test questions discovered that he knew very little of the details which had just been explained to him at such portentous length, in spite of the protest of the wretched

George, who urged that they "didn't seem to be gitting no forrader somehow," he began and went through every word of it again.

This brought them to breakfast time, and after breakfast, George's accounts were thoroughly gone into, with the result that confusion was soon worse confounded, for either George could not keep accounts or the Squire could not follow them. Ida, sitting in the drawing-room, could occasionally hear her father's ejaculatory outbursts after this kind:

"Why, you stupid donkey, you've added it up all wrong, it's nine hundred and fifty, not three hundred and fifty;" followed by a "No, no, Squire, you be a-looking on the wrong side—them there is the dibits," and so on till both parties were fairly played out, and the only thing that remained clear was that the balance was considerably on the wrong side.

"Well," said the Squire at last, "there you are, you see. It appears to me that I am absolutely ruined, and upon my word I believe that it is a great deal owing to your stupidity. You have muddled and muddled and muddled till at last you have muddled us out of house and home."

"No, no, Squire, don't say that—don't you say that. It ain't none of my doing, for I've been a good sarvant to you if I haven't had much book larning. It's that there dratted borrowing, that's what it is, and the interest and all the rest on it, and though I says it as didn't ought, poor Mr. James, God rest him and his free-handed ways. Don't you say it's me, Squire."

"Well, well," answered his master, "it doesn't much matter whose fault it is, the result is the same, George; I'm ruined, and I suppose that the place will be sold if anybody can be found to buy it. The de la Molles have been here between four and five centuries, and they got it by marriage with the Boisseys, who got it from the Norman kings, and now it will go to the hammer and be bought by a picture dealer, or a manufacturer of brandy, or someone of that sort. Well, everything has its end and God's will be done."

"No, no, Squire, don't you talk like that," answered George with emotion. "I can't bear to hear you talk like that. And what's more it ain't so."

"What do you mean by that?" asked the old gentleman sharply. "It *is* so, there's no getting over it unless you can find thirty thousand pounds or thereabouts, to take up these mortgages with. Nothing short of a miracle can save it. That's always your way. 'Oh, something will turn up, something will turn up.'"

"Thin there'll be a miricle," said George, bringing down a fist like a leg of mutton with a thud upon the table, "it ain't no use of your talking to me, Squire. I knaw it, I tell you I knaw it. There'll never be no other than a de la Molle up at the Castle while we're alive, no, nor while our childer is alive either. If the money's to be found, why drat it, it will be found. Don't you think that God Almighty is going to put none of them there counter jumpers into Honham Castle, where gentlefolk hev lived all these ginerations, because He ain't. There, and that's the truth, because I knaw it and so help me God—and if I'm wrong it's a master one."

The Squire, who was striding up and down the room in his irritation, stopped suddenly in his walk, and looked at his retainer with a sharp and searching gaze upon his noble features. Notwithstanding his prejudices, his simplicity, and his occasional absurdities, he was in his own way an able man, and an excellent judge of human nature. Even his prejudices were as a rule founded upon some solid ground, only it was as a general rule impossible to get at it. Also he had a share of that marvellous instinct which, when it exists, registers the mental altitude of the minds of others with the accuracy of an aneroid. He could tell when a man's words rang true and when they rang false, and what is more when the conviction of the true, and the falsity of the false, rested upon a substantial basis of fact or error. Of course the instinct was a vague, and from its nature an undefinable one, but it existed, and in the present instance arose in strength. He looked at the ugly melancholy countenance of the faithful George with that keen glance of his, and observed that for the moment it was almost beautiful—beautiful in the light of conviction which shone upon it. He looked, and it was borne in upon him that what George said was true, and that George knew it was true, although he did not know where the light of truth came from, and as he looked half the load fell from his heart.

"Hullo, George, are you turning prophet in addition to your other occupations?" he said cheerfully, and as he did so Edward Cossey's splendid bay horse pulled up at the door and the bell rang.

"Well," he added as soon as he saw who his visitor was, "unless I am much mistaken, we shall soon know how much truth there is in your prophecies, for here comes Mr. Cossey himself."

Before George could sufficiently recover from his recent agitation to make any reply, Edward Cossey, looking particularly handsome and rather overpowering, was shown into the room.

The Squire shook hands with him this time, though coldly enough, and George touched his forelock and said, "Sarvant, sir," in the approved fashion. Thereon his master told him that he might retire, though he was to be sure not to go out of hearing, as he should want him again presently.

"Very well, sir," answered George, "I'll just step up to the Poplars. I told a man to be round there to-day, as I want to see if I can come to an understanding with him about this year's fell in the big wood."

"There," said the Squire with an expression of infinite disgust, "there, that's just like your way, your horrid cadging way; the idea of telling a man to be 'round about the Poplars' sometime or other to-day, because you wanted to speak to him about a fell. Why didn't you write him a letter like an ordinary Christian and make an offer, instead of dodging him round a farm for half a day like a wild Indian? Besides, the Poplars is half a mile off, if it's a yard."

"Lord, sir," said George as he retired, "that ain't the way that folks in these parts like to do business, that ain't. Letter writing is all very well for Londoners and other furriners, but it don't do here. Besides, sir, I shall hear you well enough up there. Sarvant, sir!" this to Edward Cossey, and he was gone.

Edward burst out laughing, and the Squire looked after his retainer with a comical air.

"No wonder that the place has got into a mess with such a fellow as that to manage it," he said aloud. "The idea of hunting a man round the Poplars Farm like—like an Indian squaw! He's a regular cadger, that's what he is, and that's all he's fit for. However, it's his way of doing business and I shan't alter him. Well, Mr. Cossey," he went on, "this is a very sad state of affairs, at any rate so far as I am concerned. I presume of course that you know of the steps which have been taken by Cossey and Son to force a foreclosure, for that is what it amounts to, though I have not as yet received the formal notice; indeed, I suppose that those steps have been taken under your advice."

"Yes, Mr. de la Molle, I know all about it, and here is the notice calling in the loans," and he placed a folded paper on the table.

"Ah," said the Squire, "I see. As I remarked to your manager, Mr. Quest, yesterday, I think that considering the nature of the relationship which has existed for so many generations between our family and the business firm of which you are a member, considering too the peculiar circumstances in which the owners of land find themselves at this moment, and the ruinous loss—to put questions of sentiment aside—that must be inflicted by such sale upon the owner of property, more consideration might have been shown. However, it is useless to try to make a silk purse out of a sow's ear, or to get blood from a stone, so I suppose that I must make the best of a bad job—and," with a most polite bow—"I really do not know that I have anything more to say to you, Mr. Cossey. I will forward the notice to my lawyers; indeed I think that it might have been sent to them in the first instance."

Edward Cossey had all this while been sitting on an old oak chair, his eyes fixed upon the ground, and slowly swinging his hat between his legs. Suddenly he looked up and to the Squire's surprise said quietly:

"I quite agree with you. I don't think that you can say anything too bad about the behaviour of my people. A Shoreditch Jew could not have done worse. And look here, Mr. de la Molle, to come to the point and prevent misunderstanding, I may as well say at once that with your permission, I am anxious to take up these mortgages myself, for two reasons; I regard them as a desirable investment even in the present condition of land, and also I wish to save Cossey and Son from the discredit of the step which they meditate."

For the second time that morning the Squire looked up with the sharp and searching gaze he occasionally assumed, and for the second time his instinct, for he was too heady a man to reason overmuch, came into play and warned him that in making this offer Edward Cossey had other motives than those which he had brought forward. He paused to consider what they might be. Was he anxious to get the estate for himself? Was he put forward by somebody else? Quest, perhaps; or was it something to do with Ida? The first alternative seemed the most probable to him. But whatever the lender's object, the result to him was the same, it gave him a respite. For Mr. de la Molle well knew that he had no more chance of raising the money from an ordinary source, than he had of altering the condition of agriculture.

"Hum," he said, "this is an important matter, a most important matter. I presume, Mr. Cossey, that before making this definite offer you have consulted a legal adviser."

"Oh yes, I have done all that and am quite satisfied with the security —an advance of thirty thousand charged on all the Honham Castle estates at four per cent. The question now is if you are prepared to consent to the transfer. In that case all the old charges on the property will be paid off, and Mr. Quest, who will act for me in the matter, will prepare a single deed charging the estate for the round total."

"Ah yes, the plan seems a satisfactory one, but of course in so important a matter I should prefer to consult my legal adviser before giving a final answer, indeed I think that it would be better if the whole affair were carried out in a proper and formal way?"

"Surely, surely, Mr. de la Molle," said the younger man with some irritation, for the old gentleman's somewhat magnificent manner rather annoyed him, which under the circumstances was not unnatural. "Surely you do not want to consult a legal adviser to make up your mind as to whether or no you will allow a foreclosure. I offer you the money at four per cent. Cannot you let me have an answer now, yes or no?"

"I don't like being hurried. I can't bear to be hurried," said the Squire pettishly. "These important matters require consideration, a great deal of consideration. Still," he added, observing signs of increasing irritation upon Edward Cossey's face, and not having the slightest intention of throwing away the opportunity, though he would dearly have liked to prolong the negotiations for a week or two, if it was only to enjoy the illusory satisfaction of dabbling with such a large sum of money. "Still, as you are so pressing about it, I really, speaking off hand, can see no objection to your taking up the mortgages on the terms you mention."

"Very well, Mr. de la Molle. Now I have on my part one

condition and one only to attach to this offer of mine, which is that my name is not mentioned in connection with it. I do not wish Cossey and Son to know that I have taken up this investment on my own account. In fact, so necessary to me is it that my name should not be mentioned, that if it does transpire before the affair is completed I shall withdraw my offer, and if it transpires afterwards I shall call the money in. The loan will be advanced by a client of Mr. Quest's. Is that understood between us?"

"Hum," said the Squire, "I don't quite like this secrecy about these matters of business, but still if you make a point of it, why of course I cannot object."

"Very good. Then I presume that you will write officially to Cossey and Son stating that the money will be forthcoming to meet their various charges and the overdue interest. And now I think that we have had about enough of this business for once, so with your permission I will pay my respects to Miss de la Molle before I go."

"Dear me," said the Squire, pressing his hand to his head, "you do hurry me so dreadfully—I really don't know where I am. Miss de la Molle is out; I saw her go out sketching myself. Sit down and we will talk this business over a little more."

"No, thank you, Mr. de la Molle, I have to talk about money every day of my life and I soon have enough of the subject. Quest will arrange all the details. Good-bye, don't bother to ring, I will find my horse." And with a shake of the hand he was gone.

"Ah!" said the old gentleman to himself when his visitor had departed, "he asked for Ida, so I suppose that is what he is after. But it is a queer sort of way to begin courting, and if she finds it out I should think that it would go against him. Ida is not the sort of woman to be won by a money consideration. Well, she can very well look after herself, that's certain. Anyway it has been a good morning's work, but somehow I don't like that young man any the better for it. I have it—there's something wanting. He is not quite a gentleman. Well, I must find that fellow George," and he rushed to the front door and roared for "George," till the whole place echoed and the pheasants crowed in the woods.

After a while there came faint answering yells of "Coming, Squire, coming," and in due course George's long form became visible, striding swiftly up the garden.

"Well!" said his master, who was in high good humour, "did you find your man?"

"Well no, Squire—that is, I had a rare hunt after him, and I had just happened of him up a tree when you began to halloa so loud, that he went nigh to falling out of it, so I had to tell him to come back next week, or the week after."

"You happened of him up a tree. Why what the deuce was the man doing up a tree—measuring it?"

"No, Squire, I don't rightly know what he wor after, but he is a curious kind of a chap, and he said he had a fancy to wait there."

"Good heavens! no wonder the place is going to ruin, when you deal with men who have a fancy to transact their business up a tree. Well, never mind that, I have settled the matter about the mortgages. Of course somebody, a client of Mr. Quest's, has been found without the least difficulty to take them up at four per cent. and advance the other five thousand too, so that there be no more anxiety about that."

"Well that's a good job at any rate," answered George with a sigh of relief.

"A good job? Of course it's a good job, but it is no more than I expected. It wasn't likely that such an eligible investment, as they say in the advertisements, would be allowed to go begging for long. But that's just the way with you; the moment there's a hitch you come with your long face and your uneducated sort of way, and swear that we are all ruined and that the country is breaking up, and that there's nothing before us but the workhouse, and nobody knows what."

George reflected that the Squire had forgotten that not an hour before he himself had been vowing that they were ruined, while he, George, had stoutly sworn that something would turn up to help them. But his back was accustomed to those vicarious burdens, nor to tell the truth did they go nigh to the breaking of it.

"Well, it's a good job anyway, and I thank God Almighty for it," said he, "and more especial since there'll be the money to take over the Moat Farm and give that varmint Janter the boot."

"Give him *what?*"

"Why, kick him out, sir, for good and all, begging your pardon, sir."

"Oh, I see. I do wish that you would respect the Queen's English a little more, George, and the name of the Creator too. By the way the parson was speaking to me again yesterday about your continued absence from church. It really is disgraceful; you are a most confirmed Sabbath-breaker. And now you mustn't waste my time here any longer. Go and look after your affairs. Stop a minute, would you like a glass of port?"

"Well, thank you, sir," said George reflectively, "we hev had a lot of talk and I don't mind if I do, and as for that there parson, begging his pardon, I wish he would mind his own affairs and leave me to mind mine."

CHAPTER XIII

ABOUT ART

Edward Cossey drove from the Castle in a far from happy frame of mind. To begin with, the Squire and his condescending way of doing business irritated him very much, so much that once or twice in the course of the conversation he was within an ace of breaking the whole thing off, and only restrained himself with difficulty from doing so. As it was, notwithstanding all the sacrifices and money risks which he was undergoing to take up these mortgages, and they were very considerable even to a man of his great prospects, he felt that he had been placed in the position of a person who receives a favour rather than of a person who grants one. Moreover there was an assumption of superiority about the old man, a visible recognition of the gulf which used to be fixed between the gentleman of family and the man of business who has grown rich by trading in money and money's worth, which was the more galling because it was founded on actual fact, and Edward Cossey knew it. All his foibles and oddities notwithstanding, it would have been impossible for any person of discernment to entertain a comparison between the half-ruined Squire and the young banker, who would shortly be worth between half a million and a million sterling. The former was a representative, though a somewhat erratic one, of all that is best in the old type of Englishmen of gentle blood, which is now so rapidly vanishing, and of the class to which to a large extent this country owes her greatness. His very eccentricities were wandering lights that showed unsuspected heights and depths in his character—love of country and his country's honour, respect for the religion of his fathers, loyalty of mind and valour for the right. Had he lived in other times, like some of the old Boisseys and de la Molles, who were at Honham before him, he would probably have died in the Crusades or at Cressy, or perhaps more uselessly, for his King at Marston Moor, or like that last but one of the true de la Molles, kneeling in the courtyard of his Castle and defying his enemies to wring his secret from him. Now few such opportunities are left to men of his stamp, and they are, perhaps as a consequence, dying out of an age which is unsuited to them, and indeed to most strong growths of individual character. It would be much easier to deal with a gentleman like the Squire of this history if we could only reach down one of those suits of armour from the walls of his vestibule, and put it on his back, and take that long two-handled sword which last flashed on Flodden Field from its resting-place beneath the clock, and at the end see him die as a loyal knight should do in the forefront of his retainers, with the old war cry of "*a Delamol— a Delamol*" upon his lips. As it is, he is an aristocratic anachronism, an entity unfitted to deal with the elements of our advanced and in some ways emasculated age. His body should have been where his heart was—in the past. What chance have such as he against the Quests of this polite era of political economy and penny papers?

No wonder that Edward Cossey felt his inferiority to this symbol and type of the things that no more are, yes even in the shadow of his thirty thousand pounds. For here we have a different breed. Goldsmiths two centuries ago, then bankers from generation to generation, money bees seeking for wealth and counting it and hiving it from decade to decade, till at last gold became to them what honour is to the nobler stock—the pervading principle, and the clink of the guinea and the rustling of the bank note stirred their blood as the clank of armed men and the sound of the flapping banner with its three golden hawks flaming in the sun, was wont to set the hearts of the race of Boissey, of Dofferleigh and of de la Molle, beating to that tune to which England marched on to win the world.

It is a foolish and vain thing to scoff at business and those who do it in the market places, and to shout out the old war cries of our fathers, in the face of a generation which sings the song of capital, or groans in heavy labour beneath the banners of their copyrighted trade marks; and besides, who would buy our books (also copyrighted except in America) if we did? Let us rather rise up and clothe ourselves, and put a tall hat upon our heads and do homage to the new Democracy.

And yet in the depths of our hearts and the quiet of our chambers let us sometimes cry to the old days, and the old men, and the old ways of thought, let us cry "*Ave atque vale*,— Hail and farewell." Our fathers' armour hangs above the door, their portraits decorate the wall, and their fierce and half-tamed hearts moulder beneath the stones of yonder church. Hail and farewell to you, our fathers! Perchance a man might have had worse company than he met with at your boards, and even have found it not more hard to die beneath your sword-cuts than to be gently cozened to the grave by duly qualified practitioners at two guineas a visit.

And the upshot of all this is that the Squire was not altogether wrong when he declared in the silence of *his* chamber that Edward Cossey was not quite a gentleman. He showed it when he allowed himself to be guided by the arts of Mr. Quest into the adoption of the idea of obtaining a lien upon Ida, to be enforced if convenient. He showed it again, and what is more he committed a huge mistake, when tempted thereto by the opportunity of the moment, he made a conditional bargain with the said Ida, whereby she was placed in pledge for a sum of thirty thousand pounds, well knowing that her honour would be equal to the test, and that if convenient to him she would be ready to pay the debt. He made a huge mistake, for had he been quite a gentleman, he would have known that he could not have adopted a worse road to the affections of a lady. Had he been content to advance the money and then by-and-bye, though even that would not have been gentlemanlike, have gently let transpire what he had done at great personal expense and inconvenience, her imagination might have been touched and her gratitude would certainly have been excited. But the idea of bargaining, the idea of purchase, which after what had passed could never be put aside, would of necessity be fatal to any hope of tender feeling. Shylock might get his bond, but of his own act he had debarred himself from the possibility of ever getting more.

Now Edward Cossey was not lacking in that afterglow of refinement which is left by a course of public school and university education. No education can make a gentleman of a man who is not a gentleman at heart, for whether his station in life be that of a ploughboy or an Earl, the gentleman, like the poet, is born and not made. But it can and does if he be of an observant nature, give him a certain insight into the habits of thought and probable course of action of the members of that class to which he outwardly, and by repute, belongs. Such an insight Edward Cossey possessed, and at the present moment its possession was troubling him very much. His trading instincts, the desire bred in him to get something for his money, had led him to make the bargain, but now that it was done his better judgment rose up against it. For the truth may as well be told at once, although he would as yet scarcely acknowledge it to himself, Edward Cossey was already violently enamoured of Ida. He was by nature a passionate man, and as it chanced she had proved the magnet with power to draw his passion. But as the reader is aware, there existed another complication in his life for which he was not perhaps entirely responsible. When still quite a youth in mind, he had suddenly found himself the object of the love of a beautiful and enthralling woman, and had after a more or less severe struggle yielded to the temptation, as, out of a book, many young men would have done. Now to be the object of the violent affection of such a woman as Belle Quest is no doubt very flattering and even charming for a while. But if that affection is not returned in kind, if in short the gentleman does not love the lady quite as warmly as she loves him, then in course of time the charm is apt to vanish and even the flattery to cease to give pleasure. Also, when as in the present case the connection is wrong in itself and universally condemned by society, the affection which can still triumph and endure on both sides must be of a very strong and lasting order. Even an unprincipled man dislikes the acting of one long lie such as an intimacy of the sort necessarily involves, and if the man happens to be rather weak than unprincipled, the dislike is apt to turn to loathing, some portion of which will certainly be reflected on to the partner of his ill-doing.

These are general principles, but the case of Edward Cossey offered no exception to them, indeed it illustrated them well. He had never been in love with Mrs. Quest; to begin with she had shown herself too much in love with him to necessitate any display of emotion on his part. Her violent and unreasoning passion wearied and alarmed him, he never knew what she would do next and was kept in a continual condition of anxiety and irritation as to what the morrow might bring forth. Too sure of her unaltering attachment to have any pretext for jealousy, he found it exceedingly irksome to be obliged to avoid giving cause for it on his side, which, however, he dreaded doing lest he should thereby bring about some overwhelming catastrophe. Mrs. Quest was, as he well knew, not a woman who would pause to consider consequences if once her passionate jealousy were really aroused. It was even doubtful if the certainty of her own ruin would check her. Her love was everything to her, it was her life, the thing she lived for, and rather than tamely lose it, it seemed extremely probable to Edward Cossey that she would not hesitate to face shame, or even death. Indeed it was through this great passion of hers, and through it only, that he could hope to influence her. If he could persuade her to release him, by pointing out that a continuance of the intrigue must involve him in ruin of some sort, all might yet go well with him. If not his future was a dark one.

This was the state of affairs before he became attached to Ida de la Molle, after which the horizon grew blacker than ever. At first he tried to get out of the difficulty by avoiding Ida, but it did not answer. She exercised an irresistible attraction over him. Her calm and stately presence was to him what the sight of mountain snows is to one scorched by continual heat. He was weary of passionate outbursts, tears, agonies, alarms, presentiments, and all the paraphernalia of secret love. It appeared to him, looking up at the beautiful snow, that if once he could reach it life would be all sweetness and light, that there would be no more thirst, no more fear, and no more forced marches through those ill-odoured quagmires of deceit. The more he allowed his imagination to dwell upon the picture, the fiercer grew his longing to possess it. Also, he knew well enough that to marry a woman like Ida de la Molle would be the greatest blessing that could happen to him, for she would of necessity lift him up above himself. She had little money it was true, but that was a very minor matter to him, and she had birth and breeding and beauty, and a presence which commands homage. And so it came to pass that he fell deeply and yet more deeply in love with Ida, and that as he did so his connection with Mrs. Quest (although we have seen him but yesterday offering in a passing fit of tenderness and remorse to run away with her) became more and more irksome to him. And now, as he drove leisurely back to Boisingham, he felt that he had imperilled all his hopes by a rash indulgence in his trading instincts.

Presently the road took a turn and a sight was revealed that did not tend to improve his already irritable mood. Just here the roadway was bordered by a deep bank covered with trees which sloped down to the valley of the Ell, at this time of the year looking its loveliest in the soft autumn lights. And here, seated on a bank of turf beneath the shadow of a yellowing chestnut tree, in such position as to get a view of the green valley and flashing river where cattle red and white stood chewing the still luxuriant aftermath, was none other than Ida herself, and what was more, Ida accompanied by Colonel Quaritch. They were seated on campstools, and in front of each of them was an easel. Clearly they were painting together, for as Edward gazed, the Colonel rose, came up close behind his companion's stool made a ring of his thumb and first finger, gazed critically through it at the lady's performance, then sadly shook his head and made some remark. Thereupon

Ida turned round and began an animated discussion.

"Hang me," said Edward to himself, "if she has not taken up with that confounded old military frump. Painting together! Ah, I know what that means. Well, I should have thought that if there was one man more than another whom she would have disliked, it would have been that battered-looking Colonel."

He pulled up his horse and reflected for a moment, then handing the reins to his servant, jumped out, and climbing through a gap in the fence walked up to the tree. So engrossed were they in their argument, that they neither saw nor heard him.

"It's nonsense, Colonel Quaritch, perfect nonsense, if you will forgive me for telling you so," Ida was saying with warmth. "It is all very well for you to complain that my trees are a blur, and the castle nothing but a splotch, but I am looking at the water, and if I am looking at the water, it is quite impossible that I should see the trees and the cows otherwise than I have rendered them on the canvas. True art is to paint what the painter sees and as he sees it."

Colonel Quaritch shook his head and sighed.

"The cant of the impressionist school," he said sadly; "on the contrary, the business of the artist is to paint what he knows to be there," and he gazed complacently at his own canvas, which had the appearance of a spirited drawing of a fortified place, or of the contents of a child's Noah's ark, so stiff, so solid, so formidable were its outlines, trees and animals.

Ida shrugged her shoulders, laughed merrily, and turned round to find herself face to face with Edward Cossey. She started back, and her expression hardened—then she stretched out her hand and said, "How do you do?" in her very coldest tones.

"How do you do, Miss de la Molle?" he said, assuming as unconcerned an air as he could, and bowing stiffly to Harold

Quaritch, who returned the bow and went back to his canvas, which was placed a few paces off.

"I saw you painting," went on Edward Cossey in a low tone, "so I thought I would come and tell you that I have settled the matter with Mr. de la Molle."

"Oh, indeed," answered Ida, hitting viciously at a wasp with her paint brush. "Well, I hope that you will find the investment a satisfactory one. And now, if you please, do not let us talk any more about money, because I am quite tired of the subject." Then raising her voice she went on, "Come here, Colonel Quaritch, and Mr. Cossey shall judge between us," and she pointed to her picture.

Edward glanced at the Colonel with no amiable air. "I know nothing about art," he said, "and I am afraid that I must be getting on. Good- morning," and taking off his hat to Ida, he turned and went.

"Umph," said the Colonel, looking after him with a quizzical expression, "that gentleman seems rather short in his temper. Wants knocking about the world a bit, I should say. But I beg your pardon, I suppose that he is a friend of yours, Miss de la Molle?"

"He is an acquaintance of mine," answered Ida with emphasis.

CHAPTER XIV

THE TIGER SHOWS HER CLAWS

After this very chilling reception at the hands of the object of his affection, Edward Cossey continued his drive in an even worse temper than before. He reached his rooms, had some luncheon, and then in pursuance of a previous engagement went over to the Oaks to see Mrs. Quest.

He found her waiting for him in the drawing-room. She was standing at the window with her hands behind her, a favourite attitude of hers. As soon as the door was shut, she turned, came up to him, and grasped his hand affectionately between her own.

"It is an age since I have seen you, Edward," she said, "one whole day. Really, when I do not see you, I do not live, I only exist."

He freed himself from her clasp with a quick movement. "Really, Belle," he said impatiently, "you might be a little more careful than to go through that performance in front of an open window—especially as the gardener must have seen the whole thing."

"I don't much care if he did," she said defiantly. "What does it matter? My husband is certainly not in a position to make a fuss about other people."

"What does it matter?" he said, stamping his foot. "What does it *not* matter? If you have no care for your good name, do you suppose that I am indifferent to mine?"

Mrs. Quest opened her large violet eyes to the fullest extent, and a curious light was reflected from them.

"You have grown wonderfully cautious all of a sudden, Edward," she said meaningly.

"What is the use of my being cautious when you are so reckless? I tell you what it is, Belle. We are talked of all over this gossiping town, and I don't like it, and what is more, once and for all, I won't have it. If you will not be more careful, I will break with you altogether, and that is the long and short of it."

"Where have you been this morning?" she asked in the same ominously calm voice.

"I have been to Honham Castle on a matter of business."

"Oh, and yesterday you were there on a matter of pleasure. Now did you happen to see Ida in the course of your business?"

"Yes," he answered, looking her full in the face, "I did see her, what about it?"

"By appointment, I suppose."

"No, not by appointment. Have you done your catechism?"

"Yes—and now I am going to preach a homily on it. I see through you perfectly, Edward. You are getting tired of me, and you want to be rid of me. I tell you plainly that you are not going the right way to work about it. No woman, especially if she be in my—unfortunate position, can tamely bear to see herself discarded for another. Certainly I cannot—

and I caution you—I caution you to be careful, because when I think of such a thing I am not quite myself," and suddenly, without the slightest warning (for her face had been hard and cold as stone), she burst into a flood of tears.

Now Edward Cossey was naturally somewhat moved at this sight. Of course he did his best to console her, though with no great results, for she was still sobbing bitterly when suddenly there came a knock at the door. Mrs. Quest turned her face towards the wall and pretended to be reading a letter, and he tried to look as unconcerned as possible.

"A telegram for you, sir," said the girl with a sharp glance at her mistress. "The telegraph boy brought it on here, when he heard that you were not at home, because he said he would be sure to find you here—and please, sir, he hopes that you will give him sixpence for bringing it round, as he thought it might be important."

Edward felt in his pocket and gave the girl a shilling, telling her to say that there was no answer. As soon as she had gone, he opened the telegram. It was from his sister in London, and ran as follows:

> "Come up to town at once. Father has had a stroke of paralysis. Shall expect you by the seven o'clock train."

"What is it?" said Mrs. Quest, noting the alarm on his face.

"Why, my father is very ill. He has had a stroke of paralysis, and I must go to town by the next train."

"Shall you be long away?"

"I do not know. How can I tell? Good-bye, Belle. I am sorry that we should have had this scene just as I am going, but I can't help it."

"Oh, Edward," she said, catching him by the arm and turning

her tear- stained face up towards his own, "you are not angry with me, are you? Do not let us part in anger. How can I help being jealous when I love you so? Tell me that you do not hate me—or I shall be wretched all the time that you are away."

"No, no, of course not—but I must say, I wish that you would not make such shocking scenes—good-bye."

"Good-bye," she answered as she gave him her shaking hand. "Good-bye, my dear. If only you knew what I feel here," she pointed to her breast, "you would make excuses for me." Almost before she had finished her sentence he was gone. She stood near the door, listening to his retreating footsteps till they had quite died away, and then flung herself in the chair and rested her head upon her hands. "I shall lose him," she said to herself in the bitterness of her heart. "I know I shall. What chance have I against her? He already cares for Ida a great deal more than he does for me, in the end he will break from me and marry her. Oh, I had rather see him dead—and myself too."

Half-an-hour later, Mr. Quest came in.

"Where is Cossey?" he asked.

"Mr. Cossey's father has had a stroke of paralysis and he has gone up to London to look after him."

"Oh," said Mr. Quest. "Well, if the old gentleman dies, your friend will be one of the wealthiest men in England."

"Well, so much the better for him. I am sure money is a great blessing. It protects one from so much."

"Yes," said Mr. Quest with emphasis, "so much the better for him, and all connected with him. Why have you been crying? Because Cossey has gone away—or have you quarrelled with him?"

"How do you know that I have been crying? If I have, it's my affair. At any rate my tears are my own."

"Certainly, they are—I do not wish to interfere with your crying—cry when you like. It will be lucky for Cossey if that old father of his dies just now, because he wants money."

"What does he want money for?"

"Because he has undertaken to pay off the mortgages on the Castle estates."

"Why has he done that, as an investment?"

"No, it is a rotten investment. I believe that he has done it because he is in love with Miss de la Molle, and is naturally anxious to ingratiate himself with her. Don't you know that? I thought perhaps that was what you had been crying about?"

"It is not true," she answered, her lips quivering with pain.

Mr. Quest laughed gently. "I think you must have lost your power of observation, which used to be sufficiently keen. However, of course it does not matter to you. It will in many ways be a most suitable marriage, and I am sure they will make a very handsome couple."

She made no answer, and turned her back to hide the workings of her face. For a few moments her husband stood looking at her, a gentle smile playing on his refined features. Then remarking that he must go round to the office, but would be back in time for tea, he went, reflecting with satisfaction that he had given his wife something to think about which would scarcely be to her taste.

As for Belle Quest, she waited till the door had closed, and then turned round towards it and spoke aloud, as though she were addressing her vanished husband.

"I hate you," she said, with bitter emphasis. "I hate you. You have ruined my life, and now you torment me as though I were a lost soul. Oh, I wish I were dead! I wish I were dead!"

On reaching his office, Mr. Quest found two letters for him, one of which had just arrived by the afternoon post. The first was addressed in the Squire's handwriting and signed with his big seal, and the other bore a superscription, the sight of which made him turn momentarily faint. Taking up this last with a visible effort, he opened it.

It was from the "Tiger," alias Edith, and its coarse contents need not be written here. Put shortly they came to this. She was being summoned for debt. She wanted more money and would have it. If five hundred pounds were not forthcoming and that shortly—within a week, indeed—she threatened with no uncertain voice to journey down to Boisingham and put him to an open shame.

"Great heavens!" he said, "this woman will destroy me. What a devil! And she'd be as good as her word unless I found her the money. I must go up to town at once. I wonder how she got that idea into her head. It makes me shudder to think of her in Boisingham," and he dropped his face upon his hands and groaned in the bitterness of his heart.

"It is hard," he thought to himself; "here have I for years and years been striving and toiling, labouring to become a respectable and respected member of society, but always this old folly haunts my steps and drags me down, and by heaven I believe that it will destroy me after all." With a sigh he lifted his head, and taking a sheet of paper wrote on it, "I have received your letter, and will come and see you to-morrow or the next day." This note he placed in an envelope, which he directed to the high-sounding name of Mrs. d'Aubigne, Rupert St., Pimlico—and put it in his pocket.

Then with another sigh he took up the Squire's letter, and glanced through it. Its length was considerable, but in substance it announced his acceptance of the arrangement proposed by Mr. Edward Cossey, and requested that he would prepare the necessary deeds to be submitted to his lawyers. Mr. Quest read the letter absently enough, and threw it down with a little laugh.

"What a queer world it is," he said to himself, "and what a ludicrous side there is to it all. Here is Cossey advancing money to get a hold over Ida de la Molle, whom he means to marry if he can, and who is probably playing her own hand. Here is Belle madly in love with Cossey, who will break her heart. Here am I loving Belle, who hates me, and playing everybody's game in order to advance my own, and become a respected member of a society I am superior to. Here is the Squire blundering about like a walrus in a horse-pond, and fancying everything is being conducted for his sole advantage, and that all the world revolves round Honham Castle. And there at the end of the chain is this female harpy, Edith Jones, otherwise d'Aubigne, alias the Tiger, gnawing at my vitals and holding my fortunes in her hand.

"Bah! it's a queer world and full of combinations, but the worst of it is that plot as we will the solution of them does not rest with us, no —not with us."

CHAPTER XV

THE HAPPY DAYS

This is a troublesome world enough, but thanks to that mitigating fate which now and again interferes to our advantage, there do come to most of us times and periods of existence which, if they do not quite fulfil all the conditions of ideal happiness, yet go near enough to that end to permit in after days of our imagining that they did so. I say to most of us, but in doing so I allude chiefly to those classes commonly known as the "upper," by which is understood those who have enough bread to put into their mouths and clothes to warm them; those, too, who are not the present subjects of remorseless and hideous ailments, who are not daily agonised by the sight of their famished offspring; who are not doomed to beat out their lives against the madhouse bars, or to see their hearts' beloved and their most cherished hope wither towards that cold space from whence no message comes. For such unfortunates, and for their million-numbered kin upon the globe—the victims of war, famine, slave trade, oppression, usury, over-population, and the curse of competition, the rays of light must be few indeed; few and far between, only just enough to save them from utter hopelessness. And even to the favoured ones, the well warmed and well fed, who are to a great extent lifted by fortune or by their native strength and wit above the degradations of the world, this light of happiness is but as the gleam of stars, uncertain, fitful, and continually lost in clouds. Only the utterly selfish or the utterly ignorant can be happy with the happiness of savages or children, however prosperous their own affairs, for to the rest, to those who think and have hearts to feel, and imagination to realise, and a redeeming human sympathy to be touched, the mere weight of the world's misery pressing round them like an atmosphere, the mere echoes of the groans of the dying and the cries of the children are sufficient, and more than sufficient, to dull, aye, to destroy the promise of their joys. But, even to this finer sort there do come rare periods of almost complete happiness—little summers in the tempestuous climate of our years, green-fringed wells of water in our desert, pure northern lights breaking in upon our gloom. And strange as it may seem, these breadths of happy days, when the old questions cease to torment, and a man can trust in Providence and without one qualifying thought bless the day that he was born, are very frequently connected with the passion which is known as love; that mysterious symbol of our double nature, that strange tree of life which, with its roots sucking their strength from the dust-heap of humanity, yet springs aloft above our level and bears its blooms in the face of heaven.

Why it is and what it means we shall perhaps never know for certain. But it does suggest itself, that as the greatest terror of our being lies in the utter loneliness, the unspeakable identity, and unchanging self-completeness of every living creature, so the greatest hope and the intensest natural yearning of our hearts go out towards that passion which in its fire heats has the strength, if only for a little while, to melt down the barriers of our individuality and give to the soul something of the power for which it yearns of losing its sense of solitude in converse with its kind. For alone we are from infancy to death!—we, for the most part, grow not more near together but rather wider apart with the widening years. Where go the sympathies between the parent and the child, and where is the close old love of brother for his brother?

The invisible fates are continually wrapping us round and round with the winding sheets of our solitude, and none may know all our heart save He who made it. We are set upon the world as the stars are set upon the sky, and though in following our fated orbits we pass and repass, and each shine out on each, yet are we the same lonely lights, rolling obedient to laws we cannot understand, through spaces of which none may mark the measure.

Only, as says the poet in words of truth and beauty:

"Only but this is rare—
When a beloved hand is laid in ours,
When jaded with the rush and glare
Of the interminable hours,
Our eyes can in another's eyes read clear;
When our world-deafened ear
Is by the tones of a loved voice caressed
A bolt is shot back somewhere in our breast
And a lost pulse of feeling stirs again—
And what we mean we say and what we would we know.

* * * * *

And then he thinks he knows
The hills where his life rose
And the sea whereunto it goes."

Some such Indian summer of delight and forgetfulness of trouble, and the tragic condition of our days, was now opening to Harold Quaritch and Ida de la Molle. Every day, or almost every day, they met and went upon their painting expeditions and argued the point of the validity or otherwise of the impressionist doctrines of art. Not that of all this painting came anything very wonderful, although in the evening the Colonel would take out his canvases and contemplate their rigid proportions with singular pride and satisfaction. It was a little weakness of his to think that he could paint, and one of which he was somewhat tenacious. Like many another man he could do a number of things exceedingly well and one thing very badly, and yet had more faith in that bad thing than in all the good.

But, strange to say, although he affected to believe so firmly in his own style of art and hold Ida's in such cheap regard, it was a little painting of the latter's that he valued most, and which was oftenest put upon his easel for purposes of solitary admiration. It was one of those very impressionist productions that faded away in the distance, and full of soft grey tints, such as his soul loathed. There was a tree with a blot of brown colour on it, and altogether (though as a matter of fact a clever thing enough) from his point of view of art it was utterly "anathema." This little picture in oils faintly shadowed out himself sitting at his easel, working in the soft grey of the autumn evening, and Ida had painted it and given it to him, and that was why he admired it so much. For to speak the truth, our friend the Colonel was going, going fast—sinking out of sight of his former self into the depths of the love that possessed his soul.

He was a very simple and pure-minded man. Strange as it may appear, since that first unhappy business of his youth, of which he had never been heard to speak, no living woman had been anything to him. Therefore, instead of becoming further vulgarised and hardened by association with all the odds and ends of womankind that a man travelling about the globe comes into contact with, generally not greatly to his improvement, his faith had found time to grow up stronger even than at first. Once more he looked upon woman as a young man looks before he has had bitter experience of the world—as a being to be venerated and almost worshipped, as something better, brighter, purer than himself, hardly to be won, and when won to be worn like a jewel prized at once for value and for beauty.

Now this is a dangerous state of mind for a man of three or four and forty to fall into, because it is a soft state, and this is a world in which the softest are apt to get the worst of it. At four and forty a man, of course, should be hard enough to get the better of other people, as indeed he generally is.

When Harold Quaritch, after that long interval, set his eyes again upon Ida's face, he felt a curious change come over him. All the vague ideas and more or less poetical aspirations which for five long years had gathered themselves about that memory, took shape and form, and in his heart he knew he loved her. Then as the days went on and he came to know her better, he grew to love her more and more, till at last his whole heart went out towards his late found treasure, and she became more than life to him, more than aught else had been or could be. Serene and happy were those days which they spent in painting and talking as they wandered about the Honham Castle grounds. By degrees Ida's slight but perceptible hardness of manner wore away, and she stood out what she was, one of the sweetest and most natural women in England, and with it all, a woman having brains and force of character.

Soon Harold discovered that her life had been anything but an easy one. The constant anxiety about money and her father's affairs had worn her down and hardened her till, as she said, she began to feel as though she had no heart left. Then too he heard all her trouble about her dead and only brother James, how dearly she had loved him, and what a sore trouble he had been with his extravagant ways and his continual demands for money, which had to be met somehow or other. At last came the crushing blow of his death, and with it the certainty of the extinction of the male line of the de la Molles, and she said that for a while she had believed her father would never hold up his head again. But his vitality was equal to the shock, and after a time the debts began to come in, which although he was not legally bound to do so, her father would insist upon meeting to the last farthing for the honour of the family and out of respect for his son's memory. This increased their money troubles, which had gone on and on, always getting worse as the agricultural depression deepened, till things had reached their present position.

All this she told him bit by bit, only keeping back from him the last development of the drama with the part that Edward Cossey had played in it, and sad enough it made him to think of that ancient house of de la Molle vanishing into the night of ruin.

Also she told him something of her own life, how companionless it had been since her brother went into the army, for she had no real friends about Honham, and not even an acquaintance of her own tastes, which, without being gushingly so, were decidedly artistic and intellectual. "I should have wished," she said, "to try to do something in the world. I daresay I should have failed, for I know that very few women meet with a success which is worth having. But still I should have liked to try, for I am not afraid of work. But the current of my life is against it; the only thing that is open to me is to strive and make both ends meet upon an income which is always growing smaller, and to save my father, poor dear, from as much worry as I can.

"Don't think that I am complaining," she went on hurriedly, "or that I want to rush into pleasure-seeking, because I do not—a little of that goes a long way with me. Besides, I know that I have many things to be thankful for. Few women have such a kind father as mine, though we do quarrel at times. Of course we cannot have everything our own way in this world, and I daresay that I do not make the best of things. Still, at times it does seem a little hard that I should be forced to lead such a narrow life, just when I feel that I could work in a wide one."

Harold looked up at her face and saw that a tear was gathering in her dark eyes and in his heart he registered a vow that if by any means it ever lay within his power to improve her lot he would give everything he had to do it. But all he said was:

"Don't be downhearted, Miss de la Molle. Things change in a wonderful way, and often they mend when they look worst. You know," he went on a little nervously, "I am an old-fashioned sort of individual, and I believe in Providence and all that sort of thing, you see, and that matters generally come pretty well straight in the long run if people deserve it."

Ida shook her head a little doubtfully and sighed.

"Perhaps," she said, "but I suppose that we do not deserve it. Anyhow, our good fortune is a long while coming," and the conversation dropped.

Still her friend's strong belief in the efficacy of Providence, and generally his masculine sturdiness, did cheer her up considerably. Even the strongest women, if they have any element that can be called feminine left in them, want somebody of the other sex to lean on, and she was no exception to the rule. Besides, if Ida's society had charms for Colonel Quaritch, his society had almost if not quite as much charm for her. It may be remembered that on the night when they first met she had spoken to herself of him as the kind of man whom she would like to marry. The thought was a passing one, and it may be safely said that she had not since entertained any serious idea of marriage in connection with Colonel Quaritch. The only person whom there seemed to be the slightest probability of her marrying was Edward Cossey, and the mere thought of this was enough to make the whole idea of matrimony repugnant to her.

But this notwithstanding, day by day she found Harold Quaritch's society more congenial. Herself by nature, and also to a certain degree by education, a cultured woman, she rejoiced to find in him an entirely kindred spirit. For beneath his somewhat rugged and unpromising exterior, Harold Quaritch hid a vein of considerable richness. Few of those who associated with him would have believed that the man had a side to his nature which was almost poetic, or that he was a ripe and finished scholar, and, what is more, not devoid of a certain dry humour. Then he had travelled far and seen much of men and manners, gathering up all sorts of quaint odds and ends of information. But perhaps rather than these accomplishments it was the man's transparent honesty and simplemindedness, his love for what is true and noble, and his contempt of what is mean and base, which, unwittingly peeping out through his conversation, attracted her more than all the rest. Ida was no more a young girl, to be caught by a handsome face or dazzled by a superficial show of mind. She was a thoughtful, ripened woman, quick to perceive, and with the rare talent of judgment wherewith to weigh the proceeds of her perception. In plain, middle-aged Colonel Quaritch she found a very perfect gentleman, and valued him accordingly.

And so day grew into day through that lovely autumn-tide. Edward Cossey was away in London, Quest had ceased from troubling, and journeying together through the sweet shadows of companionship, by slow but sure degrees they drew near to the sunlit plain of love. For it is not common, indeed, it is so uncommon as to be almost impossible, that a man and woman between whom there stands no natural impediment can halt for very long in those shadowed ways. There is throughout all nature an impulse that pushes ever onwards towards completion, and from completion to fruition. Liking leads to sympathy, sympathy points the path to love, and then love demands its own. This is the order of affairs, and down its well-trodden road these two were quickly travelling.

George the wily saw it, and winked his eye with solemn meaning. The Squire also saw something of it, not being wanting in knowledge of the world, and after much cogitation and many solitary walks elected to leave matters alone for the present. He liked Colonel Quaritch, and thought that it would be a good thing for Ida to get married, though the idea of parting from her troubled his heart sorely. Whether or no it would be desirable from his point of view that she should marry the Colonel was a matter on which he had not as yet fully made up his mind. Sometimes he thought it would, and sometimes he thought the reverse. Then at times vague ideas suggested by Edward Cossey's behaviour about the loan would come to puzzle him. But at present he was so much in the dark that he could come to no absolute decision, so with unaccustomed wisdom for so headstrong and precipitate a man, he determined to refrain from interference, and for a while at any rate allow events to take their natural course.

CHAPTER XVI

THE HOUSE WITH THE RED PILLARS

Two days after his receipt of the second letter from the "Tiger," Mr. Quest announced to his wife that he was going to London on business connected with the bank, and expected to be away for a couple of nights.

She laughed straight out. "Really, William," she said, "you are a most consummate actor. I wonder that you think it worth while to keep up the farce with me. Well, I hope that Edith is not going to be very expensive this time, because we don't seem to be too rich just now, and you see there is no more of my money for her to have."

Mr. Quest winced visibly beneath this bitter satire, which his wife uttered with a smile of infantile innocence playing upon her face, but he made no reply. She knew too much. Only in his heart he wondered what fate she would mete out to him if ever she got possession of the whole truth, and the thought made him tremble. It seemed to him that the owner of that baby face could be terribly merciless in her vengeance, and that those soft white hands would close round the throat of a man she hated and utterly destroy him. Now, if never before, he realised that between him and this woman there must be enmity and a struggle to the death; and yet strangely enough he still loved her!

Mr. Quest reached London about three o'clock, and his first

act was to drive to Cossey and Son's, where he was informed that old Mr. Cossey was much better, and having heard that he was coming to town had sent to say that he particularly wished to see him, especially about the Honham Castle estates. Accordingly Mr. Quest drove on to the old gentleman's mansion in Grosvenor Street, where he asked for Mr. Edward Cossey. The footman said that Mr. Edward was upstairs, and showed him to a study while he went to tell him of the arrival of his visitor. Mr. Quest glanced round the luxuriously-furnished room, which he saw was occupied by Edward himself, for some letters directed in his handwriting lay upon the desk, and a velveteen lounging coat that Mr. Quest recognised as belonging to him was hanging over the back of a chair. Mr. Quest's eye wandering over this coat, was presently caught by the corner of a torn flap of an envelope which projected from one of the pockets. It was of a peculiar bluish tinge, in fact of a hue much affected by his wife. Listening for a moment to hear if anybody was coming, he stepped to the coat and extracted the letter. It *was* in his wife's handwriting, so he took the liberty of hastily transferring it to his own pocket.

In another minute Edward Cossey entered, and the two men shook hands.

"How do you do, Quest?" said Edward. "I think that the old man is going to pull through this bout. He is helpless but keen as a knife, and has all the important matters from the bank referred to him. I believe that he will last a year yet, but he will scarcely allow me out of his sight. He preaches away about business the whole day long and says that he wants to communicate the fruits of his experience to me before it is too late. He wishes to see you, so if you will you had better come up."

Accordingly they went upstairs to a large and luxurious bedroom on the first floor, where the stricken man lay upon a patent couch.

When Mr. Quest and Edward Cossey entered, a lady, old Mr. Cossey's eldest daughter, put down a paper out of which she had been reading the money article aloud, and, rising, informed her father that Mr. Quest had come.

"Mr. Quest?" said the old man in a high thin voice. "Ah, yes, I want to see Mr. Quest very much. Go away now, Anna, you can come back by-and-by, business before pleasure—most instructive, though, that sudden fall in American railways. But I thought it would come and I got Cossey's clear of them," and he sniffed with satisfaction and looked as though he would have rubbed his hands if he had not been physically incapacitated from so doing.

Mr. Quest came forward to where the invalid lay. He was a gaunt old man with white hair and a pallid face, which looked almost ghastly in contrast to his black velvet skull cap. So far as Mr. Quest could see, he appeared to be almost totally paralysed, with the exception of his head, neck, and left arm, which he could still move a little. His black eyes, however, were full of life and intelligence, and roamed about the room without ceasing.

"How do you do, Mr. Quest?" he said; "sorry that I can't shake hands with you but you see I have been stricken down, though my brain is clear enough, clearer than ever it was, I think. And I ain't going to die yet—don't think that I am, because I ain't. I may live two years more—the doctor says I am sure to live one at least. A lot of money can be made in a year if you keep your eyes open. Once I made a hundred and twenty thousand for Cossey's in one year; and I may do it again before I die. I may make a lot of money yet, ah, a lot of money!" and his voice went off into a thin scream that was not pleasant to listen to.

"I am sure I hope you will, sir," said Mr. Quest politely.

"Thank you; take that for good luck, you know. Well, well, Mr. Quest, things haven't done so bad down in your part of the world; not at all bad considering the times. I thought we should have had to sell that old de la Molle up, but I hear that he is going to pay us off. Can't imagine who has been fool enough to lend him the money. A client of yours, eh? Well, he'll lost it I expect, and serve him right for his pains. But I am not sorry, for it is unpleasant for a house like ours to have to sell an old client up. Not that his account is worth much, nothing at all—more trouble than profit—or we should not have done it. He's no better than a bankrupt and the insolvency court is the best place for him. The world is to the rich and the fulness thereof. There's an insolvency court especially provided for de la Molle and his like—empty old windbags with long sounding names; let him go there and make room for the men who have made money—hee! hee! hee!" And once more his voice went off into a sort of scream.

Here Mr. Quest, who had enjoyed about enough of this kind of thing, changed the conversation by beginning to comment on various business transactions which he had been conducting on behalf of the house. The old man listened with the greatest interest, his keen black eyes attentively fixed upon the speaker's face, till at last Mr. Quest happened to mention that amongst others a certain Colonel Quaritch had opened an account with their branch of the bank.

"Quaritch?" said the old man eagerly, "I know that name. Was he ever in the 105th Foot?"

"Yes," said Mr. Quest, who knew everything about everybody, "he was an ensign in that regiment during the Indian Mutiny, where he was badly wounded when still quite young, and got the Victoria Cross. I found it all out the other day."

"That's the man; that's the man," said old Mr. Cossey, jerking his head in an excited manner. "He's a blackguard; I tell you he's a blackguard; he jilted my wife's sister. She was twenty years younger than my wife—jilted her a week before her marriage, and would never give a reason, and she went mad and is in a madhouse how. I should like to have the ruining of him for it. I should like to drive him into the poor-house."

Mr. Quest and Edward looked at each other, and the old man let his head fall back exhausted.

"Now good-bye, Mr. Quest, they'll give you a bit of dinner downstairs," he said at length. "I'm getting tired, and I want to hear the rest of that money article. You've done very well for Cossey's and Cossey's will do well for you, for we always pay by results; that's the way to get good work and make a lot of money. Mind, Edward, if ever you get a chance don't forget to pay that blackguard Quaritch out pound for pound, and twice as much again for compound interest—hee! hee! hee!"

"The old gentleman keeps his head for business pretty well," said Mr. Quest to Edward Cossey as soon as they were well outside the door.

"Keeps his head?" answered Edward, "I should just think he did. He's a regular shark now, that's what he is. I really believe that if he knew I had found thirty thousand for old de la Molle he would cut me off with a shilling." Here Mr. Quest pricked up his ears. "And he's close, too," he went on, "so close that it is almost impossible to get anything out of him. I am not particular, but upon my word I think that it is rather disgusting to see an old man with one foot in the grave hanging on to his moneybags as though he expected to float to heaven on them."

"Yes," said Mr. Quest, "it is a curious thing to think of, but, you see, money *is* his heaven."

"By the way," said Edward, as they entered the study, "that's queer about that fellow Quaritch, isn't it? I never liked the look of him, with his pious air."

"Very queer, Mr. Cossey," said he, "but do you know, I almost think that there must be some mistake? I do not believe that Colonel Quaritch is the man to do things of that sort without a very good reason. However, nobody can tell, and it is a long while ago."

"A long while ago or not I mean to let him know my opinion of him when I get back to Boisingham," said Edward viciously. "By Jove! it's twenty minutes past six, and in this establishment we dine at the pleasant hour of half-past. Won't you come and wash your hands."

Mr. Quest had a very good dinner, and contrary to his custom drank the best part of a bottle of old port after it. He had an unpleasant business to face that evening, and felt as though his nerves required bracing. About ten o'clock he took his leave, and getting into a hansom bade the cabman drive to Rupert Street, Pimlico, where he arrived in due course. Having dismissed his cab, he walked slowly down the street till he reached a small house with red pillars to the doorway. Here he rang the bell. The door was opened by a middle-aged woman with a cunning face and a simper. Mr. Quest knew her well. Nominally the Tiger's servant, she was really her jackal.

"Is Mrs. d'Aubigne at home, Ellen?" he said.

"No, sir," she answered with a simper, "but she will be back from the music hall before long. She does not appear in the second part. But please come in, sir, you are quite a stranger here, and I am sure that Mrs. d'Aubigne will be very glad to see you, for she have been dreadfully pressed for money of late, poor dear; nobody knows the trouble that I have had with those sharks of tradesmen."

By this time they were upstairs in the drawing-room, and Ellen had turned the gas up. The room was well furnished in a certain gaudy style, which included a good deal of gilt and plate glass. Evidently, however, it had not been tidied since the Tiger had left it, for there on the table were cards thrown this way and that amidst an array of empty soda-water bottles, glasses with dregs of brandy in them, and other *debris*, such as the ends of cigars and cigarettes, and a little copper and silver money. On the sofa, too, lay a gorgeous tea gown resplendent with pink satin, also a pair of gold embroidered slippers, not over small, and an odd gant de Suede, with such an extraordinary number of buttons that it almost looked like the cast-off skin of a brown snake.

"I see that your mistress has been having company, Ellen," he said coldly.

"Yes, sir, just a few lady friends to cheer her up a bit," answered the woman, with her abominable simper; "poor dear, she do get that low with you away so much, and no wonder; and then all these money troubles, and she night by night working hard for her living at the music hall. Often and often have I seen her crying over it all—"

"Ah," said he, breaking in upon her eloquence, "I suppose that the lady friends smoke cigars. Well, clear away this mess and leave me—stop, give me a brandy-and-soda first. I will wait for your mistress."

The woman stopped talking and did as she was bid, for there was a look in Mr. Quest's eye which she did not quite like. So having placed the brandy-and-soda-water before him she left him to his own reflections.

Apparently they were not very pleasant ones. He walked round the room, which was reeking of patchouli or some such compound, well mixed with the odour of stale cigar smoke, looking absently at the gee-gar ornaments. On the mantelpiece were some photographs, and among them, to his disgust, he saw one of himself taken many years ago. With something as near an oath as he ever indulged in, he seized it, and setting fire to it over the gas, waited till the flames began to scorch his fingers, and then flung it, still burning, into the grate. Then he looked at himself in the glass in the mantelpiece—the room was full of mirrors—and laughed bitterly at the incongruity of his gentlemanlike, respectable, and even refined appearance, in that vulgar, gaudy, vicious-looking room.

Suddenly he bethought him of the letter in his wife's handwriting which he had stolen from the pocket of Edward

Cossey's coat. He drew it out, and throwing the tea gown and the interminable glove off the sofa, sat down and began to read it. It was, as he had expected, a love letter, a wildly passionate love letter, breathing language which in some places almost touched the beauty of poetry, vows of undying affection that were throughout redeemed from vulgarity and even from silliness by their utter earnestness and self-abandonment. Had the letter been one written under happier circumstances and innocent of offence against morality, it would have been a beautiful letter, for passion at its highest has always a wild beauty of its own.

He read it through and then carefully folded it and restored it to his pocket. "The woman has a heart," he said to himself, "no one can doubt it. And yet I could never touch it, though God knows however much I wronged her I loved her, yes, and love her now. Well, it is a good bit of evidence, if ever I dare to use it. It is a game of bluff between me and her, and I expect that in the end the boldest player will win."

He rose from the sofa—the atmosphere of the place stifled him, and going to the window threw it open and stepped out on to the balcony. It was a lovely moonlight night, though chilly, and for London the street was a quiet one.

Taking a chair he sat down there upon the balcony and began to think. His heart was softened by misery and his mind fell into a tender groove. He thought of his long-dead mother, whom he had dearly loved, and of how he used to say his prayers to her, and of how she sang hymns to him on Sunday evenings. Her death had seemed to choke all the beauty out of his being at the time, and yet now he thanked heaven that she was dead. And then he thought of the accursed woman who had been his ruin, and of how she had entered into his life and corrupted and destroyed him. Next there rose up before him a vision of Belle, Belle as he had first seen her, a maid of seventeen, the only child of that drunken old village doctor, now also long since dead, and of how the sight of her had for a while stayed the corruption of his heart because he grew to love her. And then he married Belle by foul means, and the woman rose up in his path again, and he learnt that his wife hated him with all the energy of her passionate heart. Then came degradation after degradation, and the abandonment of principle after principle, replaced only by a fierce craving for respectability and rest, a long, long struggle, which ever ended in new lapses from the right, till at length he saw himself a hardened schemer, remorselessly pursued by a fury from whom there was no escape. And yet he knew that under other circumstances he might have been a good and happy man—leading an honourable life. But now all hope had gone, that which he was he must be till the end. He leaned his head upon the stone railing in front of him and wept, wept in the anguish of his soul, praying to heaven for deliverance from the burden of his sins, well knowing that he had none to hope for.

For his chance was gone and his fate fixed.

CHAPTER XVII

THE TIGRESS IN HER DEN

Presently a hansom cab came rattling down the street and pulled up at the door.

"Now for it," said Mr. Quest to himself as he metaphorically shook himself together.

Next minute he heard a voice, which he knew only too well, a loud high voice say from the cab, "Well, open the door, stupid, can't you?"

"Certainly, my lady fair," replied another voice—a coarse, somewhat husky male voice—"adored Edithia, in one moment."

"Come stow that and let me out," replied the adored Edithia sharply; and in another moment a large man in evening clothes, a horrible vulgar, carnal-looking man with red cheeks and a hanging under-lip, emerged into the lamp-light and turned to hand the lady out. As he did so the woman Ellen advanced from the doorway, and going to the cab door whispered something to its occupant.

"Hullo, Johnnie," said the lady, as she descended from the cab, so loudly that Mr. Quest on the balcony could hear every word, "you must be off; Mr. d'Aubigne has turned up, and perhaps he won't think three good company, so you had just best take this cab back again, my son, and that will save me the trouble of paying it. Come, cut."

"D'Aubigne," growled the flashy man with an oath, "what do I care about d'Aubigne? Advance, d'Aubigne, and all's well! You needn't be jealous of me, I'm—"

"Now stop that noise and be off. He's a lawyer and he might not freeze on to you; don't you understand?"

"Well I'm a lawyer too and a pretty sharp one—*arcades ambo*," said Johnnie with a coarse laugh; "and I tell you what it is, Edith, it ain't good enough to cart a fellow down in this howling wilderness and then send him away without a drink; lend us another fiver at any rate. It ain't good enough, I say."

"Good enough or not you'll have to go and you don't get any fivers out of me to-night. Now pack sharp, or I'll know the reason why," and she pointed towards the cab in a fashion that seemed to cow her companion, for without another word he got into it.

In another moment the cab had turned, and he was gone, muttering curses as he went.

The woman, who was none other than Mrs. d'Aubigne, *alias* Edith Jones, *alias* the Tiger, turned and entered the house accompanied by her servant, Ellen, and presently Mr. Quest heard the rustle of her satin dress upon the stairs. He stepped back into the darkness of the balcony and waited. She opened the door, entered, and closed it behind her, and then, a little dazzled by the light, stood for some seconds looking about for her visitor. She was a thin, tall woman, who might have been any age between forty and fifty, with the wrecks of a very fine agile-looking figure. Her face, which was plentifully bedaubed with paint and powder, was sharp, fierce, and handsome, and crowned with a mane of false yellow hair. Her eyes were cold and blue, her lips thin and rather drawn, so as to show a double line of large and gleaming teeth. She was dressed in a rich and hideous tight-fitting gown of yellow satin, barred with black, and on her arms were long bright yellow gloves. She moved lightly and silently, and looked around her with a long-searching gaze, like that of a cat, and her general appearance conveyed an idea of hunger and wicked ferocity. Such was the outward appearance of the Tiger, and of a truth it justified her name. "Why, where the dickens has he got to?" she said aloud; "I wonder if he has given me the slip?"

"Here I am, Edith," said Mr. Quest quietly, as he stepped from the balcony into the room.

"Oh, there you are, are you?" she said, "hiding away in the dark—just like your nasty mean ways. Well, my long-lost one, so you have come home at last, and brought the tin with you. Well, give us a kiss," and she advanced on him with her long arms outspread.

Mr. Quest shivered visibly, and stretching out his hand, stopped her from coming near him.

"No, thank you," he said; "I don't like paint."

The taunt stopped her, and for a moment an evil light shone in her cold eyes.

"No wonder I have to paint," she said, "when I am so worn out with poverty and hard work—not like the lovely Mrs. Q., who has nothing to do all day except spend the money that I ought to have. I'll tell you what it is, my fine fellow: you had better be careful, or I'll have that pretty cuckoo out of her soft nest, and pluck her borrowed feathers off her, like the monkey did to the parrot."

"Perhaps you had better stop that talk, and come to business. I am in no mood for this sort of thing, Edith," and he turned round, shut the window, and drew the blind.

"Oh, all right; I'm agreeable, I'm sure. Stop a bit, though—I must have a brandy-and-soda first. I am as dry as a lime-kiln, and so would you be if you had to sing comic songs at a music hall for a living. There, that's better," and she put down the empty glass and threw herself on to the sofa. "Now then, tune up as much as you like. How much tin have you brought?"

Mr. Quest sat down by the table, and then, as though suddenly struck by a thought, rose again, and going to the door, opened it and looked out into the passage. There was nobody there, so he shut the door again, locked it, and then under cover of drawing the curtain which hung over it, slipped the key into his pocket.

"What are you at there?" said the woman suspiciously.

"I was just looking to see that Ellen was not at the key-hole, that's all. It would not be the first time that I have caught her there."

"Just like your nasty low ways again," she said. "You've got some game on. I'll be bound that you have got some game on."

Mr. Quest seated himself again, and without taking any notice of this last remark began the conversation.

"I have brought you two hundred and fifty pounds," he said.

"Two hundred and fifty pounds!" she said, jumping up with a savage laugh. "No, my boy, you don't get off for that if I know it. Why, I owe all that at this moment."

"You had better sit down and be quiet," he said, "or you will not get two hundred and fifty pence. In your own interest I recommend you to sit down."

There was something about the man's voice and manner that scared the female savage before him, fierce as she was, and she sat down.

"Listen," he went on, "you are continually complaining of

poverty; I come to your house—your house, mind you, not your rooms, and I find the *debris* of a card party lying about. I see champagne bottles freshly opened there in the corner. I see a dressing gown on the sofa that must have cost twenty or thirty pounds. I hear some brute associate of yours out in the street asking you to lend him another 'fiver.' You complain of poverty and you have had over four hundred pounds from me this year alone, and I know that you earn twelve pounds a week at the music hall, and not five as you say. No, do not trouble to lie to me, for I have made enquiries."

"Spying again," said the woman with a sneer.

"Yes, spying, if you like; but there it is. And now to the point—I am not going on supplying you with money at this rate. I cannot do it and I will not do it. I am going to give you two hundred and fifty pounds now, and as much every year, and not one farthing more."

Once more she sat up. "You must be mad," she said in a tone that sounded more like a snarl than a human voice. "Are you such a fool as to believe that I will be put off with two hundred and fifty pounds a year, I, *your legal wife?* I'll have you in the dock first, in the dock for bigamy."

"Yes," he answered, "I do believe it for a reason that I shall give you presently. But first I want to go though our joint history, very briefly, just to justify myself if you like. Five-and-twenty years ago, or was it six-and-twenty, I was a boy of eighteen and you were a woman of twenty, a housemaid in my mother's house, and you made love to me. Then my mother was called away to nurse my brother who died at school at Portsmouth, and I fell sick with scarlet fever and you nursed me through it—it would have been kinder if you had poisoned me, and in my weak state you got a great hold over my mind, and I became attached to you, for you were handsome in those days. Then you dared me to marry you, and partly out of bravado, partly from affection, I took out a licence, to do which I made a false declaration that I was over age, and gave false names of the parishes in which we resided. Next day, half tipsy and not knowing what I did, I went through the form of marriage with you, and a few days afterwards my mother returned, observed that we were intimate, and dismissed you. You went without a word as to our marriage, which we both looked on a farce, and for years I lost sight of you. Fifteen years afterwards, when I had almost forgotten this adventure of my youth, I became acquainted with a young lady with whom I fell in love, and whose fortune, though not large, was enough to help me considerably in my profession as a country lawyer, in which I was doing well. I thought that you were dead, or that if you lived, the fact of my having made the false declaration of age and locality would be enough to invalidate the marriage, as would certainly have been the case if I had also made a false declaration of names; and my impulses and interests prompting me to take the risk, I married that lady. Then it was that you hunted me down, and then for the first time I did what I ought to have done before, and took the best legal opinions as to the validity of the former marriage, which, to my horror, I found was undoubtedly a binding one. You also took opinions and came to the same conclusion. Since then the history has been a simple one. Out of my wife's fortune of ten thousand pounds, I paid you no less than seven thousand as hush money, on your undertaking to leave this country for America, and never return here again. I should have done better to face it out, but I feared to lose my position and practice. You left and wrote to me that you too had married in Chicago, but in eighteen months you returned, having squandered every farthing of the money, when I found that the story of your marriage was an impudent lie."

"Yes," she put in with a laugh, "and a rare time I had with that seven thousand too."

"You returned and demanded more blackmail, and I had no choice but to give, and give, and give. In eleven years you had something over twenty-three thousand pounds from me, and you continually demand more. I believe you will admit that this is a truthful statement of the case," and he paused.

"Oh, yes," she said, "I am not going to dispute that, but what then? I am your wife, and you have committed bigamy; and if you don't go on paying me I'll have you in gaol, and that's all about it, old boy. You can't get out of it any way, you nasty mean brute," she went on, raising her voice and drawing up her thin lips so as to show the white teeth beneath. "So you thought that you were going to play it down low on me in that fashion, did you? Well, you've just made a little mistake for once in your life, and I'll tell you what it is, you shall smart for it. I'll teach you what it is to leave your lawful wife to starve while you go and live with another woman in luxury. You can't help yourself; I can ruin you if I like. Supposing I go to a magistrate and ask for a warrant? What can you do to keep me quiet?"

Suddenly the virago stopped as though she were shot, and her fierce countenance froze into an appearance of terror, as well it might. Mr. Quest, who had been sitting listening to her with his hand over his eyes, had risen, and his face was as the face of a fiend, alight with an intense and quiet fury which seemed to be burning inwardly. On the mantelpiece lay a sharp-pointed Goorka knife, which one of Mrs. d'Aubigne's travelled admirers had presented to her. It was an awful looking weapon, and keen-edged as a razor. This he had taken up and held in his right hand, and with it he was advancing towards her as she lounged on the sofa.

"If you make a sound I will kill you at once," he said, speaking in a low and husky voice.

She had been paralysed with terror, for like most bullies, male and female, she was a great coward, but the sound of his voice roused her. The first note of a harsh screech had already issued from her lips, when he sprang upon her, and placing the sharp point of the knife against her throat, pricked her with it. "Be quiet," he said, "or you are a dead woman."

She stopped screaming and lay there, her face twitching, and her eyes bright with terror.

"Now listen," he said, in the same husky voice. "You incarnate fiend, you asked me just now how I could keep you quiet. I will tell you; I can keep you quiet by running this knife up to the hilt in your throat," and once more he pricked her with its point. "It would be murder," he went on, "but I do not care for that. You and others between you have not made my life so pleasant for me that I am especially anxious to preserve it. Now, listen. I will give you the two hundred and fifty pounds that I have brought, and you shall have the two hundred and fifty a year. But if you ever again attempt to extort more, or if you molest me either by spreading stories against my character or by means of legal prosecution, or in any other way, I swear by the Almighty that I will murder you. I may have to kill myself afterwards—I don't care if I do, provided I kill you first. Do you understand me? you tiger, as you call yourself. If I have to hunt you down, as they do tigers, I will come up with you at last and *kill* you. You have driven me to it, and, by heaven! I will! Come, speak up, and tell me that you understand, or I may change my mind and do it now," and once more he touched her with the knife.

She rolled off the sofa on to the floor and lay there, writhing in abject terror, looking in the shadow of the table, where her long lithe form was twisting about in its robe of yellow barred with black, more like one of the great cats from which she took her name than a human being. "Spare me," she gasped, "spare me, I don't want to die. I swear that I will never meddle with you again."

"I don't want your oaths, woman," answered the stern form bending over her with the knife. "A liar you have been from your youth up, and a liar you will be to the end. Do you understand what I have said?"

"Yes, yes, I understand. Ah! put away that knife, I can't bear it! It makes me sick."

"Very well then, get up."

She tried to rise, but her knees would not support her, so she sat upon the floor.

"Now," said Mr. Quest, replacing the knife upon the mantelpiece, "here is your money," and he flung a bag of notes and gold into her lap, at which she clutched eagerly and almost automatically. "The two hundred and fifty pounds will be paid on the 1st of January in each year, and not one farthing more will you get from me. Remember what I tell you, try to molest me by word or act, and you are a dead woman; I forbid you even to write to me. Now go to the devil in your own way," and without another word he took up his hat and umbrella, walked to the door, unlocked it and went, leaving the Tiger huddled together upon the floor.

For half-an-hour or more the woman remained thus, the bag of money in her hand. Then she struggled to her feet, her face livid and her body shaking.

"Ugh," she said, "I'm as weak as a cat. I thought he meant to do it that time, and he will too, for sixpence. He's got me there. I am afraid to die. I can't bear to die. It is better to lose the money than to die. Besides, if I blow on him he'll be put in chokey and I shan't be able to get anything out of him, and when he comes out he'll do for me." And then, losing her temper, she shook her fist in the air and broke out into a flood of language such as would neither be pretty to hear nor good to repeat.

Mr. Quest was a man of judgment. At last he had realised that in one way, and one only, can a wild beast be tamed, and that is by terror.

CHAPTER XVIII

"WHAT SOME HAVE FOUND SO SWEET"

Time went on. Mr. Quest had been back at Boisingham for ten days or more, and was more cheerful than Belle (we can no longer call her his wife) had seen him for many a day. Indeed he felt as though ten years had been lifted off his back. He had taken a great and terrible decision and had acted upon it, and it had been successful, for he knew that his evil genius was so thoroughly terrified that for a long while at least he would be free from her persecution. But with Belle his relations remained as strained as ever.

Now that the reader is in the secret of Mr. Quest's life, it will perhaps help him to understand the apparent strangeness of his conduct with reference to his wife and Edward Cossey. It is quite true that Belle did not know the full extent of her husband's guilt. She did not know that he was not her husband, but she did know that nearly all of her little fortune had been paid over to another woman, and that woman a common, vulgar woman, as one of Edith's letters which had fallen into her hands by chance very clearly showed her. Therefore, had he attempted to expose her proceedings or even to control her actions, she had in her hand an effective weapon of defence wherewith she could and would have given blow for blow. This state of affairs of necessity forced each party to preserve an armed neutrality towards the other, whilst they waited for a suitable opportunity to assert themselves. Not that their objects were quite the same. Belle merely wished to be free from her husband, whom she had always disliked, and whom she now positively hated with that curious hatred which women occasionally conceive toward those to whom they are legally bound, when they have been bad enough or unfortunate enough to fall in love with somebody else. He, on the contrary, had that desire for revenge upon her which even the gentler stamp of man is apt to conceive towards one who, herself the object of his strong affection, daily and hourly repels and repays it with scorn and infidelity. He did love her truly; she was the one living thing in all his bitter lonely life to whom his heart had gone out. True, he put pressure on her to marry him, or what comes to the same thing, allowed and encouraged her drunken old father to do so. But he had loved her and still loved her, and yet she mocked at him, and in the face of that fact about the money—her money, which he had paid away to the other woman, a fact which it was impossible for him to explain except by admission of guilt which would be his ruin, what was he to urge to convince her of this, even had she been open to conviction? But it was bitter to him, bitter beyond all conception, to have this, the one joy of his life, snatched from him. He threw himself with ardour into the pursuit after wealth and dignity of position, partly because he had a legitimate desire for these things, and partly to assuage the constant irritation of his mind, but to no purpose. These two spectres of his existence, his tiger wife and the fair woman who was his wife in name, constantly marched side by side before him, blotting out the beauty from every scene and souring the sweetness of every joy. But if in his pain he thirsted for revenge upon Belle, who would have none of him, how much more did he desire to be avenged upon Edward Cossey, who, as it were, had in sheer wantonness robbed him of the one good thing he had? It made him mad to think that this man, to whom he knew himself to be in every way superior, should have had the power thus to injure him, and he longed to pay him back measure for measure, and through *his* heart's affections to strike him as mortal a blow as he had himself received.

Mr. Quest was no doubt a bad man; his whole life was a fraud, he was selfish and unscrupulous in his schemes and relentless in their execution, but whatever may have been the measure of his iniquities, he was not doomed to wait for another world to have them meted out to him again. His life, indeed, was full of miseries, the more keenly felt because of the high pitch and capacity of his nature, and perhaps the sharpest of them all was the sickening knowledge that had it not been for that one fatal error of his boyhood, that one false step down the steep of Avernus, he might have been a good and even a great man.

Just now, however, his load was a little lightened, and he was able to devote himself to his money-making and to the weaving of the web that was to destroy his rival, Edward Cossey, with a mind a little less preoccupied with other cares.

Meanwhile, things at the Castle were going very pleasantly for everybody. The Squire was as happy in attending to the various details connected with the transfer of the mortgages as though he had been lending thirty thousand pounds instead of borrowing them. The great George was happy in the accustomed flow of cash, that enabled him to treat Janter with a lofty scorn not unmingled with pity, which was as balm to his harassed soul, and also to transact an enormous amount of business in his own peculiar way with men up trees and otherwise. For had he not to stock the Moat Farm, and was not Michaelmas at hand?

Ida, too, was happy, happier than she had been since her brother's death, for reasons that have already been hinted at. Besides, Mr. Edward Cossey was out of the way, and that to Ida was a very great thing, for his presence to her was what a policeman is to a ticket-of-leave man—a most unpleasant and suggestive sight. She fully realised the meaning and extent of the bargain into which she had entered to save her father and her house, and there lay upon her the deep shadow of evil that was to come. Every time she saw her father bustling about with his business matters and his parchments, every time the universal George arrived with an air of melancholy satisfaction and a long list of the farming stock and implements he had bought at some neighbouring Michaelmas sale, the shadow deepened, and she heard the clanking of her chains. Therefore she was the more thankful for her respite.

Harold Quaritch was happy too, though in a somewhat restless and peculiar way. Mrs. Jobson (the old lady who attended to his wants at Molehill, with the help of a gardener and a simple village maid, her niece, who smashed all the crockery and nearly drove the Colonel mad by banging the doors, shifting his papers and even dusting his trays of Roman coins) actually confided to some friends in the village that she thought the poor dear gentleman was going mad. When questioned on what she based this belief, she replied that he would walk up and down the oak-panelled dining-room by the hour together, and then, when he got tired of that exercise, whereby, said Mrs. Jobson, he had already worn a groove in the new Turkey carpet, he would take out a "rokey" (foggy) looking bit of a picture, set it upon a chair and stare at it through his fingers, shaking his head and muttering all the while. Then—further and conclusive proof of a yielding intellect—he would get a half-sheet of paper with some writing on it and put it on the mantelpiece and stare at that. Next he would turn it upside down and stare at it so, then sideways, then all ways, then he would hold it before a looking-glass and stare at the looking-glass, and so on. When asked how she knew all this, she confessed that her niece Jane had seen it through the key-hole, not once but often.

Of course, as the practised and discerning reader will clearly understand, this meant only that when walking and wearing out the carpet the Colonel was thinking of Ida. When contemplating the painting that she had given him, he was admiring her work and trying to reconcile the admiration with his conscience and his somewhat peculiar views of art. And when glaring at the paper, he was vainly endeavouring to make head or tale of the message written to his son on the night before his execution by Sir James de la Molle in the reign of Charles I., confidently believed by Ida to contain a key to the whereabouts of the treasure he was supposed to have secreted.

Of course the tale of this worthy soul, Mrs. Jobson, did not lose in the telling, and when it reached Ida's ears, which it did at last through the medium of George—for in addition to his numberless other functions, George was the sole authorised purveyor of village and county news—it read that Colonel Quaritch had gone raving mad.

Ten minutes afterwards this raving lunatic arrived at the Castle in dress clothes and his right mind, whereon Ida promptly repeated her thrilling history, somewhat to the subsequent discomfort of Mrs. Jobson and Jane.

No one, as somebody once said with equal truth and profundity, knows what a minute may bring forth, much less, therefore, does anybody know what an evening of say two hundred and forty minutes may produce. For instance, Harold Quaritch—though by this time he had gone so far as to freely admit to himself that he was utterly and hopelessly in love with Ida, in love with her with that settled and determined passion which sometimes strikes a man or woman in middle age—certainly did not know that before the evening was out he would have declared his devotion with results that shall be made clear in their decent order. When he put on his dress clothes to come up to dinner, he had no more intention of proposing to Ida than he had of not taking them off when he went to bed. His love was deep enough and steady enough, but perhaps it did not possess that wild impetuosity which carries people so far in their youth, sometimes indeed a great deal further than their reason approves. It was essentially a middle-aged devotion, and bore the same resemblance to the picturesque passion of five-and- twenty that a snow-fed torrent does to a navigable river. The one rushes and roars and sweeps away the bridges and devastates happy homes, while the other bears upon its placid breast the argosies of peace and plenty and is generally serviceable to the necessities of man. Still, there is something attractive about torrents. There is a grandeur in that first rush of passion which results from the sudden melting of the snows of the heart's purity and faith and high unstained devotion.

But both torrents and navigable rivers are liable to a common fate, they may fall over precipices, and when this comes to pass even the latter cease to be navigable for a space. Now this catastrophe was about to overtake our friend the Colonel.

Well, Harold Quaritch had dined, and had enjoyed a pleasant as well as a good dinner. The Squire, who of late had been cheerful as a cricket, was in his best form, and told long stories with an infinitesimal point. In anybody else's mouth these stories would have been wearisome to a degree, but there was a gusto, an originality, and a kind of Tudor period flavour about the old gentleman, which made his worst and longest story acceptable in any society. The Colonel himself had also come out in a most unusual way. He possessed a fund of dry humour which he rarely produced, but when he did produce it, it was of a most satisfactory order. On this particular night it was all on view, greatly to the satisfaction of Ida, who was a witty as well as a clever woman. And so it came to pass that the dinner was a very pleasant one.

Harold and the Squire were still sitting over their wine. The latter was for the fifth time giving his guest a full and particular account of how his deceased aunt, Mrs. Massey, had been persuaded by a learned antiquarian to convert or rather to restore Dead Man's Mount into its supposed primitive condition of an ancient British dwelling, and of the extraordinary expression of her face when the bill came in, when suddenly the servant announced that George was waiting to see him.

The old gentleman grumbled a great deal, but finally got up and went to enjoy himself for the next hour or so in talking about things in general with his retainer, leaving his guest to find his way to the drawing-room.

When the Colonel reached the room, he found Ida seated at the piano, singing. She heard him shut the door, looked round, nodded prettily, and then went on with her singing. He came and sat down on a low chair some two paces from her, placing himself in such a position that he could see her face, which indeed he always found a wonderfully pleasant object of contemplation. Ida was playing without music—the only light in the room was that of a low lamp with a red fringe to it. Therefore, he could not see very much, being with difficulty able to trace the outlines of her features, but if the shadow thus robbed him, it on the other hand lent her a beauty of its own, clothing her face with an atmosphere of wonderful softness which it did not always possess in the glare of day. The Colonel indeed (we must remember that he was in love and that it was after dinner) became quite poetical (internally of course) about it, and in his heart compared her first to St. Cecilia at her organ, and then to the Angel of the Twilight. He had never seen her look so lovely. At her worst she was a handsome and noble-looking woman, but now the shadow from without, and though he knew nothing of that, the shadow from her heart within also, aided maybe by the music's swell, had softened and purified her face till it did indeed look almost like an angel's. It is strong, powerful faces that are capable of the most tenderness, not the soft and pretty ones, and even in a plain person, when such a face is in this way seen, it gathers a peculiar beauty of its own. But Ida was not a plain person, so on the whole it is scarcely wonderful that a certain effect was produced upon Harold Quaritch. Ida went on singing almost without a break—to outward appearance, at any rate, all unconscious of what was passing in her admirer's mind. She had a good memory and a sweet voice, and really liked music for its own sake, so it was no great effort to her to do so.

Presently, she sang a song from Tennyson's "Maud," the tender and beautiful words whereof will be familiar to most readers of her story. It began:

> "O let the solid ground
> Not fail beneath my feet
> Before my life has found
> What some have found so sweet."

The song is a lovely one, nor did it suffer from her rendering, and the effect it produced upon Harold was of a most peculiar nature. All his past life seemed to heave and break beneath the magic of the music and the magic of the singer, as a northern field of ice breaks up beneath the outburst of the summer sun. It broke, sank, and vanished into the depths of his nature, those dread unmeasured depths that roll and murmur in the vastness of each human heart as the sea rolls beneath its cloak of ice; that roll and murmur here, and set towards a shore of which we have no chart or knowledge. The past was gone, the frozen years had melted, and once more the sweet strong air of youth blew across his heart, and once more there was clear sky above, wherein the angels sailed. Before the breath of that sweet song the barrier of self fell down, his being went out to meet her being, and all the sleeping possibilities of life rose from the buried time.

He sat and listened, trembling as he listened, till the gentle echoes of the music died upon the quiet air. They died, and were gathered into the emptiness which receives and records all things, leaving him broken.

She turned to him, smiling faintly, for the song had moved her also, and he felt that he must speak.

"That is a beautiful song," he said; "sing it again if you do not mind."

She made no answer, but once more she sang:

"O let the solid ground
Not fail beneath my feet
Before my life has found
What some have found so sweet;"

and then suddenly broke off.

"Why are you looking at me?" she said. "I can feel you looking at me and it makes me nervous."

He bent towards her and looked her in the eyes.

"I love you, Ida," he said, "I love you with all my heart," and he stopped suddenly.

She turned quite pale, even in that light he could see her pallor, and her hands fell heavily on the keys.

The echo of the crashing notes rolled round the room and slowly died away—but still she said nothing.

CHAPTER XIX

IN PAWN

At last she spoke, apparently with a great effort.

"It is stifling in here," she said, "let us go out." She rose, took up a shawl that lay beside her on a chair, and stepped through the French window into the garden. It was a lovely autumn night, and the air was still as death, with just a touch of frost in it.

Ida threw the shawl over her shoulders and followed by Harold walked on through the garden till she came to the edge of the moat, where there was a seat. Here she sat down and fixed her eyes upon the hoary battlements of the gateway, now clad in a solemn robe of moonlight.

Harold looked at her and felt that if he had anything to say the time had come for him to say it, and that she had brought him here in order that she might be able to listen undisturbed. So he began again, and told her that he loved her dearly.

"I am some seventeen years older than you," he went on, "and I suppose that the most active part of my life lies in the past; and I don't know if, putting other things aside, you could care to marry so old a man, especially as I am not rich. Indeed, I feel it presumptuous on my part, seeing what you are and what I am not, to ask you to do so. And yet, Ida, I believe if you could care for me that, with heaven's blessing, we should be very happy together. I have led a lonely life, and have had little to do with women—once, many years ago, I was engaged, and the matter ended painfully, and that is all. But ever since I first saw your face in the drift five years and more ago, it has haunted me and been with me. Then I came to live here and I have learnt to love you, heaven only knows how much, and I should be ashamed to try to put it into words, for they would sound foolish. All my life is wrapped up in you, and I feel as though, should you see me no more, I could never be a happy man again," and he paused and looked anxiously at her face, which was set and drawn as though with pain.

"I cannot say 'yes,' Colonel Quaritch," she answered at length, in a tone that puzzled him, it was so tender and so unfitted to the words.

"I suppose," he stammered, "I suppose that you do not care for me? Of course, I have no right to expect that you would."

"As I have said that I cannot say 'yes,' Colonel Quaritch, do you not think that I had better leave that question unanswered?" she replied in the same soft notes which seemed to draw the heart out of him.

"I do not understand," he went on. "Why?"

"Why?" she broke in with a bitter little laugh, "shall I tell you why? Because I am *in pawn!* Look," she went on, pointing to the stately towers and the broad lands beyond. "You see this place. *I* am security for it, I *myself* in my own person. Had it not been for me it would have been sold over our heads after having descended in our family for all these centuries, put upon the market and sold for what it would fetch, and my old father would have been turned out to die, for it would have killed him. So you see I did what unfortunate women have often been driven to do, I sold myself body and soul; and I got a good price too—thirty thousand pounds!" and suddenly she burst into a flood of tears, and began to sob as though her heart would break.

For a moment Harold Quaritch looked on bewildered, not in the least understanding what Ida meant, and then he followed the impulse common to mankind in similar circumstances and took her in his arms. She did not resent the movement, indeed she scarcely seemed to notice it, though to tell the truth, for a moment or two, which to the Colonel seemed the happiest of his life, her head rested on his shoulder.

Almost instantly, however, she raised it, freed herself from his embrace and ceased weeping.

"As I have told you so much," she said, "I suppose that I had better tell you everything. I know that whatever the temptation," and she laid great stress upon the words, "under any conceivable circumstances—indeed, even if you believed that you were serving me in so doing—I can rely upon you never to reveal to anybody, and above all to my father, what I now tell you," and she paused and looked up at him with eyes in which the tears still swam.

"Of course, you can rely on me," he said.

"Very well. I am sure that I shall never have to reproach you with the words. I will tell you. I have virtually promised to marry Mr. Edward Cossey, should he at any time be in a position to claim fulfilment of the promise, on condition of his taking up the mortgages on Honham, which he has done."

Harold Quaritch took a step back and looked at her in horrified astonishment.

"*What?*" he asked.

"Yes, yes," she answered hastily, putting up her hand as though to shield herself from a blow. "I know what you mean; but do not think too hardly of me if you can help it. It was not for myself. I would rather work for my living with my hands than take a price, for there is no other word for it. It was for my father, and my family too. I could not bear to think of the old place going to the hammer, and I did it all in a minute without consideration; but," and she set her face, "even as things are, I believe I should do it again, because I think that no one woman has a right to destroy her family in order to please herself. If one of the two must go, let it be the woman. But don't think hardly of me for it," she added almost pleadingly, "that is if you can help it."

"I am not thinking of you," he answered grimly; "by heaven I honour you for what you have done, for however much I may disagree with the act, it is a noble one. I am thinking of the man who could drive such a bargain with any woman. You say that you have promised to marry him should he ever be in a position to claim it. What do you mean by that? As you have told me so much you may as well tell me the rest."

He spoke clearly and with a voice full of authority, but his bearing did not seem to jar upon Ida.

"I meant," she answered humbly, "that I believe—of course I do not know if I am right—I believe that Mr. Cossey is in some way entangled with a lady, in short with Mrs. Quest, and that the question of whether or no he comes forward again depends upon her."

"Upon my word," said the Colonel, "upon my word the thing gets worse and worse. I never heard anything like it; and for money too! The thing is beyond me."

"At any rate," she answered, "there it is. And now, Colonel Quaritch, one word before I go in. It is difficult for me to speak without saying too much or too little, but I do want you to understand how honoured and how grateful I feel for what you have told me to-night—I am so little worthy of all you have given me, and to be honest, I cannot feel as pained about it as I ought to feel. It is feminine vanity, you know, nothing else. I am sure that you will not press me to say more."

"No," he answered, "no. I think that I understand the

position. But, Ida, there is one thing that I must ask—you will forgive me if I am wrong in doing so, but all this is very sad for me. If in the end circumstances should alter, as I pray heaven that they may, or if Mr. Cossey's previous entanglement should prove too much for him, will you marry me, Ida?"

She thought for a moment, and then rising from the seat, gave him her hand and said simply:

"Yes, I *will* marry you."

He made no answer, but lifting her hand touched it gently with his lips.

"Meanwhile," she went on, "I have your promise, and I am sure that you will not betray it, come what may."

"No," he said, "I will not betray it."

And they went in.

In the drawing-room they found the Squire puzzling over a sheet of paper, on which were scrawled some of George's accounts, in figures which at first sight bore about as much resemblance to Egyptian hieroglyphics as they did to those in use to-day.

"Hullo!" he said, "there you are. Where on earth have you been?"

"We have been looking at the Castle in the moonlight," answered Ida coolly. "It is beautiful."

"Um—ah," said the Squire, dryly, "I have no doubt that it is beautiful, but isn't the grass rather damp? Well, look here," and he held up the sheet of hieroglyphics, "perhaps you can add this up, Ida, for it is more than I can. George has bought stock and all sorts of things at the sale to-day and here is his account; three hundred and seventy-two pounds he makes it, but I make it four hundred and twenty, and hang me if I can find out which is right. It is most important that these accounts should be kept straight. Most important, and I cannot get this stupid fellow to do it."

Ida took the sheet of paper and added it up, with the result that she discovered both totals to be wrong. Harold, watching her, wondered at the nerve of a woman who, after going through such a scene as that which had just occurred, could deliberately add up long rows of badly-written figures.

And this money which her father was expending so cheerfully was part of the price for which she had bound herself.

With a sigh he rose, said good-night, and went home with feelings almost too mixed to admit of accurate description. He had taken a great step in his life, and to a certain extent that step had succeeded. He had not altogether built his hopes upon sand, for from what Ida had said, and still more from what she had tacitly admitted, it was necessarily clear to him that she did more or less regard him as a man would wish to be regarded by a woman whom he dearly loved. This was a great deal, more indeed than he had dared to believe, but then, as is usually the case in this imperfect world, where things but too often seem to be carefully arranged at sixes and sevens, came the other side of the shield. Of what use to him was it to have won this sweet woman's love, of what use to have put this pure water of happiness to his lips in the desert of his lonely life, only to see the cup that held it shattered at a blow? To him the story of the money loan—in consideration of which, as it were, Ida had put herself in pawn, as the Egyptians used to put the mummies of their fathers in pawn—was almost incredible. To a person of his simple and honourable nature, it seemed a preposterous and unheard of thing that any man calling himself a gentleman should find it possible to sink so low as to take such advantage of a woman's dire necessity and honourable desire to save her father from misery and her race from ruin, and to extract from her a promise of marriage in consideration of value received. Putting aside his overwhelming personal interest in the matter, it made his blood boil to think that such a thing could be. And yet it was, and what was more, he believed he knew Ida well enough to be convinced that she would not shirk the bargain. If Edward Cossey came forward to claim his bond it would be paid down to the last farthing. It was a question of thirty thousand pounds; the happiness of his life and of Ida's depended upon a sum of money. If the money were forthcoming, Cossey could not claim his flesh and blood. But where was it to come from? He himself was worth perhaps ten thousand pounds, or with the commutation value of his pension, possibly twelve, and he had not the means of raising a farthing more. He thought the position over till he was tired of thinking, and then with a heavy heart and yet with a strange glow of happiness shining through his grief, like sunlight through a grey sky, at last he went to sleep and dreamed that Ida had gone from him, and that he was once more utterly alone in the world.

But if he had cause for trouble, how much more was it so with Ida? Poor woman! under her somewhat cold and stately exterior lay a deep and at times a passionate nature. For some weeks she had been growing strangely attracted to Harold Quaritch, and now she knew that she loved him, so that there was no one thing that she desired more in this wide world than to become his wife. And yet she was bound, bound by a sense of honour and a sense too of money received, to stay at the beck and call of a man she detested, and if at any time it pleased him to throw down the handkerchief, to be there to pick it up and hold it to her breast. It was bad enough to have had this hanging over her head when she was herself more or less in a passive condition, and therefore to a certain extent reckless as to her future; but now that her heart was alight with the holy flame of a good woman's love, now that her whole nature rebelled and cried out aloud against the sacrilege involved, it was both revolting and terrible.

And yet so far as she could see there was no great probability of escape. A shrewd and observant woman, she could gauge Mr. Cossey's condition of mind towards herself with more or less accuracy. Also she did not think it in the least likely that having spent thirty thousand pounds to advance his object, he would be content to let his advantage drop. Such a course would be repellent to his trading instincts. She knew in her heart that the hour was not far off when he would claim his own, and that unless some accident occurred to prevent it, it was practically certain that she would be called upon to fulfil her pledge, and whilst loving another man to become the wife of Edward Cossey.

CHAPTER XX

"GOOD-BYE TO YOU, EDWARD"

It was on the day following the one upon which Harold proposed to Ida, that Edward Cossey returned to Boisingham. His father had so far recovered from his attack as to be at last prevailed upon to allow his departure, being chiefly moved thereto by the supposition that Cossey and Son's branch establishments were suffering from his son's absence.

"Well," he said, in his high, piercing voice, "business is business, and must be attended to, so perhaps you had better go. They talk about the fleeting character of things, but there is one thing that never changes, and that is money. Money is immortal; men may come and men may go, but money goes on for ever. Hee! hee! money is the honey-pot, and men are the flies; and some get their fill and some stick their wings, but the honey is always there, so never mind the flies. No, never mind me either; you go and look after the honey, Edward. Money—honey, honey—money, they rhyme, don't they? And look here, by the way, if you get a chance—and the world is full of chances to men who have plenty of money—mind you don't forget to pay out that half-pay Colonel—what's his name?—Quaritch. He played our family a dirty trick, and there's your poor Aunt Julia in a lunatic asylum to this moment and a constant source of expense to us."

And so Edward bade his estimable parent farewell and departed. Nor in truth did he require any admonition from

Mr. Cossey, Senior, to make him anxious to do Colonel Quaritch an ill-turn if the opportunity should serve. Mrs. Quest, in her numerous affectionate letters, had more than once, possibly for reasons of her own, given him a full and vivid *resume* of the local gossip about the Colonel and Ida, who were, she said, according to common report, engaged to be married. Now, absence had not by any means cooled Edward's devotion to Miss de la Molle, which was a sincere one enough in its own way. On the contrary, the longer he was away from her the more his passion grew, and with it a vigorous undergrowth of jealousy. He had, it is true, Ida's implied promise that she would marry him if he chose to ask her, but on this he put no great reliance. Hence his hurry to return to Boisingham.

Leaving London by an afternoon train, he reached Boisingham about half-past six, and in pursuance of an arrangement already made, went to dine with the Quests. When he reached the house he found Belle alone in the drawing-room, for her husband, having come in late, was still dressing, but somewhat to his relief he had no opportunity of private conversation with her, for a servant was in the room, attending to the fire, which would not burn. The dinner passed off quietly enough, though there was an ominous look about the lady's face which, being familiar with these signs of the feminine weather, he did not altogether like. After dinner, however, Mr. Quest excused himself, saying that he had promised to attend a local concert in aid of the funds for the restoration of the damaged pinnacle of the parish church, and he was left alone with the lady.

Then it was that all her pent-up passion broke out. She overwhelmed him with her affection, she told him that her life had been a blank while he was away, she reproached him with the scarcity and coldness of his letters, and generally went on in a way with which he was but too well accustomed, and, if the truth must be told, heartily tired. His mood was an irritable one, and to-night the whole thing wearied him beyond bearing.

"Come, Belle," he said at last, "for goodness' sake be a little more rational. You are getting too old for this sort of tom-foolery, you know."

She sprang up and faced him, her eyes flashing and her breast heaving with jealous anger. "What do you mean?" she said. "Are you tired of me?"

"I did not say that," he answered, "but as you have started the subject I must tell you that I think all this has gone far enough. Unless it is stopped I believe we shall both be ruined. I am sure that your husband is becoming suspicious, and as I have told you again and again, if once the business gets to my father's ears he will disinherit me."

Belle stood quite still till he had finished. She had assumed her favourite attitude and crossed her arms behind her back, and her sweet childish face was calm and very white.

"What is the good of making excuses and telling me what is not true, Edward?" she said. "One never hears a man who loves a woman talk like that; prudence comes with weariness, and men grow circumspect when there is nothing more to gain. You *are* tired of me. I have seen it a long time, but like a blind fool I have tried not to believe it. It is not a great reward to a woman who has given her whole life to a man, but perhaps it is as much as she can expect, for I do not want to be unjust to you. I am the most to blame, because we need never take a false step except of our own free will."

"Well, well," he said impatiently, "what of it?"

"Only this, Edward. I have still a little pride left, and as you are tired of me, why—*go*."

He tried hard to prevent it, but do what he would, a look of relief struggled into his face. She saw it, and it stung her almost to madness.

"You need not look so happy, Edward; it is scarcely decent; and, besides, you have not heard all that I have to say. I know what this arises from. You are in love with Ida de la Molle. Now *there* I draw the line. You may leave me if you like, but you shall not marry Ida while I am alive to prevent it. That is more than I can bear. Besides, like a wise woman, she wishes to marry Colonel Quaritch, who is worth two of you, Edward Cossey."

"I do not believe it," he answered; "and what right have you to say that I am in love with Miss de la Molle? And if I am in love with her, how can you prevent me from marrying her if I choose?"

"Try and you will see," she answered, with a little laugh. "And now, as the curtain has dropped, and it is all over between us, why the best thing that we can do is to put out the lights and go to bed," and she laughed again and courtesied with much assumed playfulness. "Good- night, Mr. Cossey; good-night, and good-bye."

He held out his hand. "Come, Belle," he said, "don't let us part like this."

She shook her head and once more put her arms behind her. "No," she answered, "I will not take your hand. Of my own free will I shall never touch it again, for to me it is like the hand of the dead. Good- bye, once more; good-bye to you, Edward, and to all the happiness that I ever had. I built up my life upon my love for you, and you have shattered it like glass. I do not reproach you; you have followed after your nature and I must follow after mine, and in time all things will come right—in the grave. I shall not trouble you any more, provided that you do not try to marry Ida, for that I will not bear. And now go, for I am very tired," and turning, she rang the bell for the servant to show him out.

In another minute he was gone. She listened till she heard the front door close behind him, and then gave way to her grief.

Flinging herself upon the sofa, she covered her face with her hands and moaned bitterly, weeping for the past, and weeping, too, for the long desolate years that were to come. Poor woman! whatever was the measure of her sin it had assuredly found her out, as our sins always do find us out in the end. She had loved this man with a love which has no parallel in the hearts of well-ordered and well-brought-up women. She never really lived till this fatal passion took possession of her, and now that its object had deserted her, her heart felt as though it was dead within her. In that short half-hour she suffered more than many women do in their whole lives. But the paroxysm passed, and she rose pale and trembling, with set teeth and blazing eyes.

"He had better be careful," she said to herself; "he may go, but if he tries to marry Ida I will keep my word—yes, for her sake as well as his."

When Edward Cossey came to consider the position, which he did seriously, on the following morning, he did not find it very satisfactory. To begin with, he was not altogether a heartless man, and such a scene as that which he had passed through on the previous evening was in itself quite enough to upset his nerves. At one time, at any rate, he had been much attached to Mrs. Quest; he had never borne her any violent affection; that had all been on her side, but still he had been fond of her, and if he could have done so, would probably have married her. Even now he was attached to her, and would have been glad to remain her friend if she would have allowed it. But then came the time when her heroics began to weary him, and he on his side began to fall in love with Ida de la Molle, and as he drew back so she came forward, till at length he was worn out, and things culminated as has been described. He was sorry for her too, knowing how deeply she was attached to him, though it is probable that he did not in the least realise the extent to which she suffered, for neither men nor women who have intentionally or otherwise been the cause of intense mental anguish to one of the opposite sex ever do quite realise this. They, not unnaturally, measure the trouble by the depth of their own, and are therefore very apt to come to erroneous conclusions. Of course this is said of cases where all the real passion is on one side, and indifference or comparative indifference on the other; for where it is mutual, the grief will in natures of equal depth be mutual also.

At any rate, Edward Cossey was quite sensitive enough to acutely feel parting with Mrs. Quest, and perhaps he felt the manner of it even more than the fact of the separation. Then came another consideration. He was, it is true, free from his entanglement, in itself an enormous relief, but the freedom was of a conditional nature. Belle had threatened trouble in the most decisive tones should he attempt to carry out his secret purpose of marrying Ida, which she had not been slow to divine. For some occult reason, at least to him it seemed occult, the idea of this alliance was peculiarly distasteful to her, though no doubt the true explanation was that she believed, and not inaccurately, that in order to bring it about he was bent upon deserting her. The question with him was, would she or would she not attempt to put her threat into execution? It certainly seemed to him difficult to imagine what steps she could take to that end, seeing that any such steps would necessarily involve her own exposure, and that too when there was nothing to gain, and when all hopes of thereby securing him for herself had passed away. Nor did he seriously believe that she would attempt anything of the sort. It is one thing for a woman to make such threats in the acute agony of her jealousy, and quite another for her to carry them out in cold blood. Looking at the matter from a man's point of view, it seemed to him extremely improbable that when the occasion came she would attempt such a move. He forgot how much more violently, when once it has taken possession of his being, the storm of passion sweeps through such a woman's heart than through a man's, and how utterly reckless to all consequence the former sometimes becomes. For there are women with whom all things melt in that white heat of anguished jealousy—honour, duty, conscience, and the restraint of religion—and of these Belle Quest was one.

But of this he was not aware, and though he recognised a risk, he saw in it no sufficient reason to make him stay his hand. For day by day the strong desire to make Ida his wife had grown upon him, till at last it possessed him body and soul. For a long while the intent had been smouldering in his breast, and the tale that he now heard, to the effect that Colonel Quaritch had been beforehand with him, had blown it into a flame. Ida was ever present in his thoughts; even at night he could not be rid of her, for when he slept her vision, dark-eyed and beautiful, came stealing down his dreams. She was his heaven, and if by any ladder known to man he might climb thereto, thither he would climb. And so he set his teeth and vowed that, Mrs. Quest or no Mrs. Quest, he would stake his fortune upon the hazard of the die, aye, and win, even if he loaded the dice.

While he was still thinking thus, standing at his window and gazing out on to the market place of the quiet little town, he suddenly saw Ida herself driving in her pony-carriage. It was a wet and windy day, the rain was on her cheek, and the wind tossed a little lock of her brown hair. The cob was pulling, and her proud face was set, as she concentrated her energies upon holding him. Never to Edward Cossey had she looked more beautiful. His heart beat fast at the sight of her, and whatever doubts might have lingered in his mind, vanished. Yes, he would claim her promise and marry her.

Presently the pony carriage pulled up at his door, and the boy who was sitting behind got down and rang the bell. He stepped back from the window, wondering what it could be.

"Will you please give that note to Mr. Cossey," said Ida, as the door opened, "and ask him to send an answer?" and she was gone.

The note was from the Squire, sealed with his big seal (the Squire always sealed his letters in the old-fashioned way), and contained an invitation to himself to shoot on the morrow. "George wants me to do a little partridge driving," it ended, "and to brush through one or two of the small coverts. There will only be Colonel Quaritch besides yourself and George, but I hope that you will have a fair rough day. If I don't hear from you I shall suppose that you are coming, so don't trouble to write."

"Oh yes, I will go," said Edward. "Confound that Quaritch. At any rate I can show him how to shoot, and what is more I will have it out with him about my aunt."

CHAPTER XXI

THE COLONEL GOES OUT SHOOTING

The next morning was fine and still, one of those lovely autumn days of which we get four or five in the course of a season. After breakfast Harold Quaritch strolled down his garden, stood himself against a gate to the right of Dead Man's Mount, and looked at the scene. All about him, their foliage yellowing to its fall, rose the giant oaks, which were the pride of the country side, and so quiet was the air that not a leaf upon them stirred. The only sounds that reached his ears were the tappings of the nut-hutches as they sought their food in the rough crannies of the bark, and the occasional falling of a rich ripe acorn from its lofty place on to the frosted grass beneath. The sunshine shone bright, but with a chastened heat, the squirrels scrambled up the oaks, and high in the blue air the rooks pursued their path. It was a beautiful morning, for summer is never more sweet than on its death-bed, and yet it filled him with solemn thoughts. How many autumns had those old trees seen, and how many would they still see, long after his eyes had lost their sight! And if they were old, how old was Dead Man's Mount there to his left! Old, indeed! for he had discovered it was mentioned in Doomday Book and by that name. And what was it—a boundary hill, a natural formation, or, as its name implied, a funeral barrow? He had half a mind to dig one day and find out, that is if he could get anybody to dig with him, for the people about Honham were so firmly convinced that Dead Man's Mount was haunted, a reputation which it had owned from time immemorial, that nothing would have persuaded them to touch it.

He contemplated the great mound carefully without coming to any conclusion, and then looked at his watch. It was a quarter to ten, time for him to start for the Castle for his day's shooting. So he got his gun and cartridges, and in due course arrived at the Castle, to find George and several myrmidons, in the shape of beaters and boys, already standing in the yard.

"Please, Colonel, the Squire hopes you'll go in and have a glass of summut before you start," said George; so accordingly he went, not to "have a glass of summut," but on the chance of seeing Ida. In the vestibule he found the old gentleman busily engaged in writing an enormous letter.

"Hullo, Colonel," he halloaed, without getting up, "glad to see you. Excuse me for a few moments, will you, I want to get this off my mind. Ida! Ida! Ida!" he shouted, "here's Colonel Quaritch."

"Good gracious, father," said that young lady, arriving in a hurry, "you are bringing the house down," and then she turned round and greeted Harold. It was the first time they had met since the eventful evening described a chapter or two back, so the occasion might be considered a little awkward; at any rate he felt it so.

"How do you do, Colonel Quaritch?" she said quite simply, giving him her hand. There was nothing in the words, and yet he felt that he was very welcome. For when a woman really loves a man there is about her an atmosphere of softness and tender meaning which can scarcely be mistaken. Sometimes it is only perceptible to the favoured individual himself, but more generally is to be discerned by any person of ordinary shrewdness. A very short course of observation in general society will convince the reader of the justice of this observation, and when once he gets to know the signs of the weather he will probably light upon more affairs of the heart than were ever meant for his investigation.

This softness, or atmospheric influence, or subdued glow of affection radiating from a light within, was clearly enough visible in Ida that morning, and certainly it made our friend the Colonel unspeakably happy to see it.

"Are you fond of shooting?" she asked presently.

"Yes, very, and have been all my life."

"Are you a good shot?" she asked again.

"I call that a rude question," he answered smiling.

"Yes, it is, but I want to know."

"Well," said Harold, "I suppose that I am pretty fair, that is at rough shooting; I never had much practice at driven birds and that kind of sport."

"I am glad of it."

"Why, it does not much matter. One goes out shooting for the sport of the thing."

"Yes, I know, but Mr. Edward Cossey," and she shrank visibly as she uttered the name, "is coming, and he is a *very* good shot and *very* conceited about it. I want you to beat him if you can—will you try?"

"Well," said Harold, "I don't at all like shooting against a man. It is not sportsmanlike, you know; and, besides, if Mr. Cossey is a crack shot, I daresay that I shall be nowhere; but I will shoot as well as I can."

"Do you know, it is very feminine, but I would give anything to see you beat him?" and she nodded and laughed, whereupon Harold Quaritch vowed in his heart that if it in him lay he would not disappoint her.

At that moment Edward Cossey's fast trotting horse drew up at the door with a prodigious crunching of gravel, and Edward himself entered, looking very handsome and rather pale. He was admirably dressed, that is to say, his shooting clothes were beautifully made and very new- looking, and so were his boots, and so was his hat, and so were his hammerless guns, of which he brought a pair. There exists a certain class of sportsmen who always appear to have just walked out of a sporting tailor's shop, and to this class Edward Cossey belonged. Everything about him was of the best and newest and most expensive kind possible; even his guns were just down from a famous maker, and the best that could be had for love or money, having cost exactly a hundred and forty guineas the pair. Indeed, he presented a curious contrast to his rival. The Colonel had certainly nothing new-looking about *him*; an old tweed coat, an old hat, with a piece of gut still twined round it, a sadly frayed bag full of brown cartridges, and, last of all, an old gun with the brown worn off the barrels, original cost, 17 pounds 10s. And yet there was no possibility of making any mistake as to which of the two looked more of a gentleman, or, indeed, more of a sportsman.

Edward Cossey shook hands with Ida, but when the Colonel was advancing to give him his hand, he turned and spoke to the Squire, who had at length finished his letter, so that no greeting was passed between them. At the time Harold did not know if this move was or was not accidental.

Presently they started, Edward Cossey attended by his man with the second gun.

"Hullo! Cossey," sang out the Squire after him, "it isn't any use bringing your two guns for this sort of work. I don't preserve much here, you know, at least not now. You will only get a dozen cock pheasants and a few brace of partridges."

"Oh, thank you," he answered, "I always like to have a second gun in case I should want it. It's no trouble, you know."

"All right," said the Squire. "Ida and I will come down with the luncheon to the grove. Good-bye."

After crossing the moat, Edward Cossey walked by himself, followed by his man and a very fine retriever, and the Colonel talked to George, who was informing him that Mr. Cossey was "a pretty shot, he wore, but rather snappy over it," till they came to a field of white turnips.

"Now, gentlemen, if you please," said George, "we will walk through these here turnips. I put two coveys of birds in here myself, and it's rare good 'lay' for them; so I think that we had better see if they will let us come nigh them."

Accordingly they started down the field, the Colonel on the right, George in the middle and Edward Cossey on the left.

Before they had gone ten yards, an old Frenchman got up in the front of one of the beaters and wheeled round past Edward, who cut him over in first-rate style.

From that one bird the Colonel could see that the man was a quick and clever shot. Presently, however, a leash of English birds rose rather awkwardly at about forty paces straight in front of Edward Cossey, and Harold noticed that he left them alone, never attempting to fire at them. In fact he was one of those shooters who never take a hard shot if they can avoid it, being always in terror lest they should miss it and so reduce their average.

Then George, who was a very fair shot of the "poking" order, fired both barrels and got a bird, and Edward Cossey got another. It was not till they were getting to the end of their last beat that Harold found a chance of letting off his gun. Suddenly, however, a brace of old birds sprang up out of the turnips in front of him at about thirty yards as swiftly as though they had been ejected from a mortar, and made off, one to the right and one to the left, both of them rising shots. He got the right-hand bird, and then turning killed the other also, when it was more than fifty yards away.

The Colonel felt satisfied, for the shots were very good. Mr. Cossey opened his eyes and wondered if it was a fluke, and George ejaculated, "Well, that's a master one."

After this they pursued their course, picking up another two brace of birds on the way to the outlying cover, a wood of about twenty acres through which they were to brush. It was a good holding wood for pheasants, but lay on the outside of the Honham estate, where they were liable to be poached by the farmers whose land marched, so George enjoined them particularly not to let anything go.

Into the details of the sport that followed we need not enter, beyond saying that the Colonel, to his huge delight, never shot better in his life. Indeed, with the exception of one rabbit and hen pheasant that flopped up right beneath his feet, he scarcely missed anything, though he took the shots as they came. Edward Cossey also shot well, and with one exception missed nothing, but then he never took a difficult shot if he could avoid it. The exception was a woodcock which rose in front of George, who was walking down an outside belt with the beaters. He loosed two barrels at it and missed, and on it came among the tree tops, past where Edward Cossey was standing, about half-way down the belt, giving him a difficult chance with the first barrel and a clear one with the second. Bang! bang! and on came the woodcock, now flying low, but at tremendous speed, straight at the Colonel's head, a most puzzling shot. However, he fired, and to his joy (and what joy is there like to the joy of a sportsman who has just killed a woodcock which everybody has been popping at?) down it came with a thump almost at his feet.

This was their last beat before lunch, which was now to be seen approaching down a lane in a donkey cart convoyed by Ida and the Squire. The latter was advancing in stages of about ten paces, and at every stage he stopped to utter a most fearful roar by way of warning all and sundry that they were not to shoot in his direction. Edward gave his gun to his bearer and at once walked off to join them, but the Colonel went with George to look after two running cocks which he had down, for he was an old-fashioned sportsman, and hated not picking up his game. After some difficulty they found one of the cocks in the hedgerow, but the other they could not find, so reluctantly they gave up the search. When they got to the lane they found the luncheon ready, while one of the beaters was laying out the game for the Squire to inspect. There were fourteen pheasants, four brace and a half of partridges, a hare, three rabbits, and a woodcock.

"Hullo," said the Squire, "who shot the woodcock?"

"Well, sir," said George, "we all had a pull at him, but the Colonel wiped our eyes."

"Oh, Mr. Cossey," said Ida, in affected surprise, "why, I thought you never missed *anything*."

"Everybody misses sometimes," answered that gentleman, looking uncommonly sulky. "I shall do better this afternoon when it comes to the driven partridges."

"I don't believe you will," went on Ida, laughing maliciously. "I bet you a pair of gloves that Colonel Quaritch will shoot more driven partridges than you do."

"Done," said Edward Cossey sharply.

"Now, do you hear that, Colonel Quaritch?" went on Ida. "I have bet Mr. Cossey a pair of gloves that you will kill more partridges this afternoon than he will, so I hope you won't make me lose them."

"Goodness gracious," said the Colonel, in much alarm. "Why, the last partridge-driving that I had was on the slopes of some mountains in Afghanistan. I daresay that I shan't hit anything. Besides," he said with some irritation, "I don't like being set up to shoot against people."

"Oh, of course," said Edward loftily, "if Colonel Quaritch does not like to take it up there's an end of it."

"Well," said the Colonel, "if you put it in that way I don't mind trying, but I have only one gun and you have two."

"Oh, that will be all right," said Ida to the Colonel. "You shall have George's gun; he never tries to shoot when they drive partridges, because he cannot hit them. He goes with the beaters. It is a very good gun."

The Colonel took up the gun and examined it. It was of about the same bend and length as his own, but of a better quality, having once been the property of James de la Molle.

"Yes," he said, "but then I haven't got a loader."

"Never mind. I'll do that, I know all about it. I often used to hold my brother's second gun when we drove partridges, because he said I was so much quicker than the men. Look," and she took the gun and rested one knee on the turf; "first position, second position, third position. We used to have regular drills at it," and she sighed.

The Colonel laughed heartily, for it was a curious thing to see this stately woman handling a gun with all the skill and quickness of a practised shot. Besides, as the loader idea involved a whole afternoon of Ida's society he certainly was not inclined to negative it. But Edward Cossey did not smile; on the contrary he positively scowled with jealousy, and was about to make some remark when Ida held up her finger.

"Hush," she said, "here comes my father" (the Squire had been counting the game); "he hates bets, so you mustn't say anything about our match."

Luncheon went off pretty well, though Edward Cossey did not

contribute much to the general conversation. When it was done the Squire announced that he was going to walk to the other end of the estate, whereon Ida said that she should stop and see something of the shooting, and the fun began.

CHAPTER XXII

THE END OF THE MATCH

They began the afternoon with several small drives, but on the whole the birds did very badly. They broke back, went off to one side or the other, and generally misbehaved themselves. In the first drive the Colonel and Edward Cossey got a bird each. In the second drive the latter got three birds, firing five shots, and his antagonist only got a hare and a pheasant that jumped out of a ditch, neither of which, of course, counted anything. Only one brace of birds came his way at all, but if the truth must be told, he was talking to Ida at the moment and did not see them till too late.

Then came a longer drive, when the birds were pretty plentiful. The Colonel got one, a low-flying Frenchman, which he killed as he topped the fence, and after that for the life of him he could not touch a feather. Every sportsman knows what a fatal thing it is to begin to miss and then get nervous, and that was what happened to the Colonel. Continually there came distant cries of "*Mark! mark over!*" followed by the apparition of half-a-dozen brown balls showing clearly against the grey autumn sky and sweeping down towards him like lightning. *Whizz* in front, overhead and behind; bang, bang; bang again with the second gun, and they were away—vanished, gone, leaving nothing but a memory behind them.

The Colonel swore beneath his breath, and Ida kneeling at his side, sighed audibly; but it was of no use, and presently the drive was done, and there he was with one wretched French partridge to show for it.

Ida said nothing, but she looked volumes, and if ever a man felt humiliated, Harold Quaritch was that man. She had set her heart upon his winning the match, and he was making an exhibition of himself that might have caused a schoolboy to blush.

Only Edward Cossey smiled grimly as he told his bearer to give the two and a half brace which he had shot to George.

"Last drive this next, gentlemen," said that universal functionary as he surveyed the Colonel's one Frenchman, and then glancing sadly at the tell-tale pile of empty cartridge cases, added, "You'll hev to shoot up, Colonel, this time, if you are a-going to win them there gloves for Miss Ida. Mr. Cossey hev knocked up four brace and a half, and you hev only got a brace. Look you here, sir," he went on in a portentous whisper, "keep forrard of them, well forrard, fire ahead, and down they'll come of themselves like. You're a better shot than he is a long way; you could give him 'birds,' sir, that you could, and beat him."

Harold said nothing. He was sorely tempted to make excuses, as any man would have been, and he might with truth have urged that he was not accustomed to partridge-driving, and that one of the guns was new to him. But he resisted manfully and said never a word.

George placed the two guns, and then went off to join the beaters. It was a capital spot for a drive, for on each side were young larch plantations, sloping down towards them like a V, the guns being at the narrow end and level with the points of the plantations, which were at this spot about a hundred and twenty yards apart. In front was a large stretch of open fields, lying in such a fashion that the birds were bound to fly straight over the guns and between the gap at the end of the

V-shaped covers.

They had to wait a long while, for the beat was of considerable extent, and this they did in silence, till presently a couple of single birds appeared coming down the wind like lightning, for a stiffish breeze had sprung up. One went to the left over Edward Cossey's head, and he shot it very neatly, but the other, catching sight of Harold's hat beneath the fence, which was not a high one, swerved and crossed, an almost impossible shot, nearer sixty than fifty yards from him.

"Now," said Ida, and he fired, and to his joy down came the bird with a thud, bounding full two feet into the air with the force of its impact, being indeed shot through the head.

"That's better," said Ida, as she handed him the second gun.

Another moment and a covey came over, high up. He fired both barrels and got a right and left, and snatching the second gun sent another barrel after them, hitting a third bird, which did not fall. And then a noble enthusiasm and certainty possessed him, and he knew that he should miss no more. Nor did he. With two almost impossible exceptions he dropped every bird that drive. But his crowning glory, a thing whereof he still often dreams, was yet to come.

He had killed four brace of partridge and fired eleven times, when at last the beaters made their appearance about two hundred yards away at the further end of rather dirty barley stubble.

"I think that is the lot," he said; "I'm afraid you have lost your gloves, Ida."

Scarcely were the words out of his mouth when there was a yell of "mark!" and a strong covey of birds appeared, swooping down the wind right on to him.

On they came, scattered and rather "stringy." Harold gripped his gun and drew a deep breath, while Ida, kneeling at his side, her lips apart, and her beautiful eyes wide open, watched their advent through a space in the hedge. Lovely enough she looked to charm the heart of any man, if a man out partridge-driving could descend to such frivolity, which we hold to be impossible.

Now is the moment. The leading brace are something over fifty yards away, and he knows full well that if there is to be a chance left for the second gun he must shoot before they are five yards nearer.

"Bang!" down comes the old cock bird; "bang!" and his mate follows him, falling with a smash into the fence.

Quick as light Ida takes the empty gun with one hand, and as he swings round passes him the cocked and loaded one with the other. "Bang!" Another bird topples head first out of the thinned covey. They are nearly sixty yards away now. "Bang!" again, and oh, joy and wonder! the last bird turns right over backwards, and falls dead as a stone some seventy paces from the muzzle of the gun.

He had killed four birds out of a single driven covey, which as shooters well know is a feat not often done even by the best driving shots.

"Bravo!" said Ida, "I was sure that you could shoot if you chose."

"Yes," he answered, "it was pretty good work;" and he commenced collecting the birds, for by this time the beaters were across the field. They were all dead, not a runner in the lot, and there were exactly six brace of them. Just as he picked up the last, George arrived, followed by Edward Cossey.

"Well I niver," said the former, while something resembling a smile stole over his melancholy countenance, "if that bean't the masterest bit of shooting that ever I did see. Lord Walsingham couldn't hardly beat that hisself—fifteen empty cases and twelve birds picked up. Why," and he turned to Edward, "bless me, sir, if I don't believe the Colonel has won them gloves for Miss Ida after all. Let's see, sir, you got two brace this last drive and one the first, and a leash the second, and two brace and a half the third, six and a half brace in all. And the Colonel, yes, he hev seven brace, one bird to the good."

"There, Mr. Cossey," said Ida, smiling sweetly, "I have won my gloves. Mind you don't forget to pay them."

"Oh, I will not forget, Miss de la Molle," said he, smiling also, but not too prettily. "I suppose," he said, addressing the Colonel, "that the last covey twisted up and you browned them."

"No," he answered quietly, "all four were clear shots."

Mr. Cossey smiled again, as he turned away to hide his vexation, an incredulous smile, which somehow sent Harold Quaritch's blood leaping through his veins more quickly than was good for him. Edward Cossey would rather have lost a thousand pounds than that his adversary should have got that extra bird, for not only was he a jealous shot, but he knew perfectly well that Ida was anxious that he should lose, and desired above all things to see him humiliated. And then he, the smartest shot within ten miles round, to be beaten by a middle-aged soldier shooting with a strange gun, and totally unaccustomed to driven birds! Why, the story would be told over the county; George would see to that. His anger was so great when he thought of it, that afraid of making himself ridiculous, he set off with his bearer towards the Castle without another word, leaving the others to follow.

Ida looked after him and smiled. "He is so conceited," she said; "he cannot bear to be beaten at anything."

"I think that you are rather hard on him," said the Colonel, for the joke had an unpleasant side which jarred upon his taste.

"At any rate," she answered, with a little stamp, "it is not for you to say so. If you disliked him as much as I do you would be hard on him, too. Besides, I daresay that his turn is coming."

The Colonel winced, as well he might, but looking at her handsome face, set just now like steel at the thought of what the future might bring forth, he reflected that if Edward Cossey's turn did come he was by no means sure that the ultimate triumph would rest with him. Ida de la Molle, to whatever extent her sense of honour and money indebtedness might carry her, was no butterfly to be broken on a wheel, but a woman whose dislike and anger, or worse still, whose cold, unvarying disdain, was a thing from which the boldest hearted man might shrink aghast.

Nothing more was said on the subject, and they began to talk, though somewhat constrainedly, about indifferent matters. They were both aware that it was a farce, and that they were playing a part, for beneath the external ice of formalities the river of their devotion ran strong—whither they knew not. All that had been made clear a few nights back. But what will you have? Necessity over-riding their desires, compelled them along the path of self-denial, and, like wise folk, they recognised the fact: for there is nothing more painful in the world than the outburst of hopeless affection.

And so they talked about painting and shooting and what not, till they reached the grey old Castle towers. Here Harold wanted to bid her good-bye, but she persuaded him to come in and have some tea, saying that her father would like to say good-night to him.

Accordingly he went into the vestibule, where there was a light, for it was getting dusk; and here he found the Squire and Mr. Cossey. As soon as he entered, Edward Cossey rose, said good-night to the Squire and Ida, and then passed towards the door, where the Colonel was standing, rubbing the mud off his shooting boots. As he came, Harold being slightly ashamed of the business of the shooting match, and very sorry to have humiliated a man who prided himself so much upon his skill in a particular branch of sport, held out his hand and said in a friendly tone:

"Good-night, Mr. Cossey. Next time that we are out shooting together I expect I shall be nowhere. It was an awful fluke of mine killing those four birds."

Edward Cossey took no notice of the friendly words or outstretched hand, but came straight on as though he intended to walk past him.

The Colonel was wondering what it was best to do, for he could not mistake the meaning of the oversight, when the Squire, who was sometimes very quick to notice things, spoke in a loud and decided tone.

"Mr. Cossey," he said, "Colonel Quaritch is offering you his hand."

"I observe that he is," he answered, setting his handsome face, "but I do not wish to take Colonel Quaritch's hand."

Then came a moment's silence, which the Squire again broke.

"When a gentleman in my house refuses to take the hand of another gentleman," he said very quietly, "I think that I have a right to ask the reason for his conduct, which, unless that reason is a very sufficient one, is almost as much a slight upon me as upon him."

"I think that Colonel Quaritch must know the reason, and will not press me to explain," said Edward Cossey.

"I know of no reason," replied the Colonel sternly, "unless indeed it is that I have been so unfortunate as to get the best of Mr. Cossey in a friendly shooting match."

"Colonel Quaritch must know well that this is not the reason to which I allude," said Edward. "If he consults his conscience he will probably discover a better one."

Ida and her father looked at each other in surprise, while the Colonel by a half involuntary movement stepped between his accuser and the door; and Ida noticed that his face was white with anger.

"You have made a very serious implication against me, Mr. Cossey," he said in a cold clear voice. "Before you leave this room you will be so good as to explain it in the presence of those before whom it has been made."

"Certainly, if you wish it," he answered, with something like a sneer. "The reason why I refused to take your hand, Colonel Quaritch, is that you have been guilty of conduct which proves to me that you are not a gentleman, and, therefore, not a person with whom I desire to be on friendly terms. Shall I go on?"

"Most certainly you will go on," answered the Colonel.

"Very well. The conduct to which I refer is that you were once engaged to my aunt, Julia Heston; that within three days of the time of the marriage you deserted and jilted her in a most cruel way, as a consequence of which she went mad, and is to this moment an inmate of an asylum."

Ida gave an exclamation of astonishment, and the Colonel started, while the Squire, looking at him curiously, waited to hear what he had to say.

"It is perfectly true, Mr. Cossey," he answered, "that I was engaged twenty years ago to be married to Miss Julia Heston, though I now for the first time learn that she was your aunt. It is also quite true that that engagement was broken off, under most painful circumstances, within three days of the time fixed for the marriage. What those circumstances were I am not at liberty to say, for the simple reason that I gave my word not to do so; but this I will say, that they were not to my discredit, though you may not be aware of that fact. But as you are one of the family, Mr. Cossey, my tongue is not tied, and I will do myself the honour of calling upon you to-morrow and explaining them to you. After that," he added significantly, "I shall require you to apologise to me as publicly as you have accused me."

"You may require, but whether I shall comply is another matter," said Edward Cossey, and he passed out.

"I am very sorry, Mr. de la Molle," said the Colonel, as soon as he had gone, "more sorry than I can say, that I should have been the cause of this most unpleasant scene. I also feel that I am placed in a very false position, and until I produce Mr. Cossey's written apology, that position must to some extent continue. If I fail to obtain that apology, I shall have to consider what course to take. In the meanwhile I can only ask you to suspend your judgment."

CHAPTER XXIII

THE BLOW FALLS

On the following morning, about ten o'clock, while Edward Cossey was still at breakfast, a dog-cart drew up at his door and out of it stepped Colonel Quaritch.

"Now for the row," said he to himself. "I hope that the governor was right in his tale, that's all. Perhaps it would have been wiser to say nothing till I had made sure," and he poured out some more tea a little nervously, for in the Colonel he had, he felt, an adversary not to be despised.

Presently the door opened, and "Colonel Quaritch" was announced. He rose and bowed a salutation, which the Colonel whose face bore a particularly grim expression, did not return.

"Will you take a chair?" he said, as soon as the servant had left, and without speaking Harold took one—and presently began the conversation.

"Last night, Mr. Cossey," he said, "you thought proper to publicly bring a charge against me, which if it were true would go a long way towards showing that I was not a fit person to associate with those before whom it was brought."

"Yes," said Edward coolly.

"Before making any remarks on your conduct in bringing such a charge, which I give you credit for believing to be true, I purpose to show to you that it is a false charge," went on the Colonel quietly. "The story is a very simple one, and so sad that nothing short of necessity would force me to tell it. I was, when quite young, engaged to your aunt, Miss Heston, to whom I was much attached, and who was then twenty years of age. Though I had little besides my profession, she had money, and we were going to be married. The circumstances under which the marriage was broken off were as follow:—Three days before the wedding was to take place I went unexpectedly to the house, and was told by the servant that Miss Heston was upstairs in her sitting- room. I went upstairs to the room, which I knew well, knocked and got no answer. Then I walked into the room, and this is what I saw. Your aunt was lying on the sofa in her wedding dress (that is, in half of it, for she had only the skirt on), as I first thought, asleep. I went up to her, and saw that by her side was a brandy bottle, half empty. In her hand also was a glass containing raw brandy. While I was wondering what it could mean, she woke up, got off the sofa, and I saw that she was intoxicated."

"It's a lie!" said Edward excitedly.

"Be careful what you say, sir," answered the Colonel, "and wait to say it till I have done."

"As soon as I realised what was the matter, I left the room again, and going down to your grandfather's study, where he was engaged in writing a sermon, I asked him to come upstairs, as I feared that his daughter was not well. He came and saw, and the sight threw him off his balance, for he broke out into a torrent of explanations and excuses, from which in time I extracted the following facts:—It appeared that ever since she was a child, Miss Heston had been addicted to drinking fits, and that it was on account of this constitutional weakness, which was of course concealed from me, that she had been allowed to engage herself to a penniless subaltern. It appeared, too, that the habit was hereditary, for her mother had died from the effects of drink, and one of her aunts had become mad from it.

"I went away and thought the matter over, and came to the conclusion that under these circumstances it would be impossible for me, much as I was attached to your aunt, to marry her, because even if I were willing to do so, I had no right to run the risk of bringing children into the world who might inherit the curse. Having come to this determination, which it cost me much to do, I wrote and communicated it to your grandfather, and the marriage was broken off."

"I do not believe it, I do not believe a word of it," said Edward, jumping up. "You jilted her and drove her mad, and now you are trying to shelter yourself behind a tissue of falsehood."

"Are you acquainted with your grandfather's handwriting?" asked the Colonel quietly.

"Yes."

"Is that it?" he went on, producing a yellow-looking letter and showing it to him.

"I believe so—at least it looks like it."

"Then read the letter."

Edward obeyed. It was one written in answer to that of Harold Quaritch to his betrothed's father, and admitted in the clearest terms the justice of the step that he had taken. Further, it begged him for the sake of Julia and the family at large, never to mention the cause of his defection to any one outside the family.

"Are you satisfied, Mr. Cossey? I have other letters, if you wish to see them."

Edward made no reply, and the Colonel went on:—"I gave the

promise your grandfather asked for, and in spite of the remarks that were freely made upon my behaviour, I kept it, as it was my duty to do. You, Mr. Cossey, are the first person to whom the story has been told. And now that you have thought fit to make accusations against me, which are without foundation, I must ask you to retract them as fully as you made them. I have prepared a letter which you will be so good as to sign," and he handed him a note addressed to the Squire. It ran:

> "Dear Mr. de la Molle,—
>
> "I beg in the fullest and most ample manner possible to retract the charges which I made yesterday evening against Colonel Quaritch, in the presence of yourself and Miss de la Molle. I find that those charges were unfounded, and I hereby apologise to Colonel Quaritch for having made them."

"And supposing that I refuse to sign," said Edward sulkily.

"I do not think," answered the Colonel, "that you will refuse."

Edward looked at Colonel Quaritch, and the Colonel looked at Edward.

"Well," said the Colonel, "please understand I mean that you should sign this letter, and, indeed, seeing how absolutely you are in the wrong, I do not think that you can hesitate to do so."

Then very slowly and unwillingly, Edward Cossey took up a pen, affixed his signature to the letter, blotted it, and pushed it from him.

The Colonel folded it up, placed it in an envelope which he had ready, and put it in his pocket.

"Now, Mr. Cossey," he said, "I will wish you good-morning. Another time I should recommend you to be more careful, both of your facts and the manner of your accusations," and with a slight bow he left the room.

"Curse the fellow," thought Edward to himself as the front door closed, "he had me there—I was forced to sign. Well, I will be even with him about Ida, at any rate. I will propose to her this very day, Belle or no Belle, and if she won't have me I will call the money in and smash the whole thing up"—and his handsome face bore a very evil look, as he thought of it.

That very afternoon he started in pursuance of this design, to pay a visit to the Castle. The Squire was out, but Miss de la Molle was at home. He was ushered into the drawing-room, where Ida was working, for it was a wet and windy afternoon.

She rose to greet him coldly enough, and he sat down, and then came a pause which she did not seem inclined to break.

At last he spoke. "Did the Squire get my letter, Miss de la Molle?" he asked.

"Yes," she answered, rather icily. "Colonel Quaritch sent it up."

"I am very sorry," he added confusedly, "that I should have put myself in such a false position. I hope that you will give me credit for having believed my accusation when I made it."

"Such accusations should not be lightly made, Mr. Cossey," was her answer, and, as though to turn the subject, she rose and rang the bell for tea.

It came, and the bustle connected with it prevented any further conversation for a while. At length, however, it subsided, and once more Edward found himself alone with Ida. He looked at her and felt afraid. The woman was of a different clay to himself, and he knew it— he loved her, but he did not understand her in the least. However, if the thing was to be done at all it must be done now, so, with a desperate effort, he brought himself to the point.

"Miss de la Molle," he said, and Ida, knowing full surely what was coming, felt her heart jump within her bosom and then stand still.

"Miss de la Molle," he repeated, "perhaps you will remember a conversation that passed between us some weeks ago in the conservatory?"

"Yes," she said, "I remember—about the money."

"About the money and other things," he said, gathering courage. "I hinted to you then that I hoped in certain contingencies to be allowed to make my addresses to you, and I think that you understood me."

"I understood you perfectly," answered Ida, her pale face set like ice, "and I gave you to understand that in the event of your lending my father the money, I should hold myself bound to—to listen to what you had to say."

"Oh, never mind the money," broke in Edward. "It is not a question of money with me, Ida, it is not, indeed. I love you with all my heart. I have loved you ever since I saw you. It was because I was jealous of him that I made a fool of myself last night with Colonel Quaritch. I should have asked you to marry me long ago only there were obstacles in the way. I love you, Ida; there never was a woman like you—never."

She listened with the same set face. Obviously he was in earnest, but his earnestness did not move her; it scarcely even flattered her pride. She disliked the man intensely, and nothing that he could say or do would lessen that dislike by one jot—probably, indeed, it would only intensify it.

Presently he stopped, his breast heaving and his face broken with emotion, and tried to take her hand.

She withdrew it sharply.

"I do not think that there is any need for all this," she said coldly. "I gave a conditional promise. You have fulfilled your share of the bargain, and I am prepared to fulfil mine in due course."

So far as her words went, Edward could find no fault with their meaning, and yet he felt more like a man who has been abruptly and finally refused than one declared chosen. He stood still and looked at her.

"I think it right to tell you, however," she went on in the same measured tones, "that if I marry you it will be from motives of duty, and not from motives of affection. I have no love to give you and I do not wish for yours. I do not know if you will be satisfied with this. If you are not, you had better give up the idea," and for the first time she looked up at him with more anxiety in her face than she would have cared to show.

But if she hoped that her coldness would repel him, she was destined to be disappointed. On the contrary, like water thrown on burning oil, it only inflamed him the more.

"The love will come, Ida," he said, and once more he tried to take her hand.

"No, Mr. Cossey," she said, in a voice that checked him. "I am sorry to have to speak so plainly, but till I marry I am my own mistress. Pray understand me."

"As you like," he said, drawing back from her sulkily. "I am so fond of you that I will marry you on any terms, and that is the truth. I have, however, one thing to ask of you, Ida, and it is that you will keep our engagement secret for the present, and get your father (I suppose I must speak to him) to do the same. I have reasons," he went on by way of explanation, "for not wishing it to become known."

"I do not see why I should keep it secret," she said; "but it does not matter to me."

"The fact is," he explained, "my father is a very curious man, and I doubt if he would like my engagement, because he thinks I ought to marry a great deal of money."

"Oh, indeed," answered Ida. She had believed, as was indeed the case, that there were other reasons not unconnected with Mrs. Quest, on account of which he was anxious to keep the engagement secret. "By the way," she went on, "I am sorry to have to talk of business, but this is a business matter, is it not? I suppose it is understood that, in the event of our marriage, the mortgage you hold over this place will not be enforced against my father."

"Of course not," he answered. "Look here, Ida, I will give you those mortgage bonds as a wedding present, and you can put them in the fire; and I will make a good settlement on you."

"Thank you," she said, "but I do not require any settlement on myself; I had rather none was made; but I consent to the engagement only on the express condition that the mortgages shall be cancelled before marriage, and as the property will ultimately come to me, this is not much to ask. And now one more thing, Mr. Cossey; I should like to know when you would wish this marriage to take place; not yet, I presume?"

"I could wish it to take place to-morrow," he said with an attempt at a laugh; "but I suppose that between one thing and another it can't come off at once. Shall we say this time six months, that will be in May?"

"Very good," said Ida; "this day six months I shall be prepared to become your wife, Mr. Cossey. I believe," she added with a flash of bitter sarcasm, "it is the time usually allowed for the redemption of a mortgage."

"You say very hard things," he answered, wincing.

"Do I? I daresay. I am hard by nature. I wonder that you can wish to marry me."

"I wish it beyond everything in the world," he answered earnestly. "You can never know how much. By the way, I know I was foolish about Colonel Quaritch; but, Ida, I cannot bear to see that man near you. I hope that you will now drop his acquaintance as much as possible."

Once more Ida's face set like a flint. "I am not your wife yet, Mr. Cossey," she said; "when I am you will have a right to dictate to me as to whom I shall associate with. At present you have no such right, and if it pleases me to associate with Colonel Quaritch, I shall do so. If you disapprove of my conduct, the remedy is simple—you can break off the engagement."

He rose absolutely crushed, for Ida was by far the stronger of the two, and besides, his passion gave her an unfair advantage over him. Without attempting a reply he held out his hand and said good-night, for he was afraid to venture on any demonstration of affection, adding that he would come to see her father in the morning.

She touched his outstretched hand with her fingers, and then fearing lest he should change his mind, promptly rang the bell.

In another minute the door had closed behind him and she was left alone.

CHAPTER XXIV

"GOOD-BYE, MY DEAR, GOOD-BYE!"

When Edward Cossey had gone, Ida rose and put her hands to her head. So the blow had fallen, the deed was done, and she was engaged to be married to Edward Cossey. And Harold Quaritch! Well, there must be an end to that. It was hard, too—only a woman could know how hard. Ida was not a person with a long record of love affairs. Once, when she was twenty, she had received a proposal which she had refused, and that was all. So it happened that when she became attached to Colonel Quaritch she had found her heart for the first time, and for a woman, somewhat late in life. Consequently her feelings were all the more profound, and so indeed was her grief at being forced not only to put them away, but to give herself to another man who was not agreeable to her. She was not a violent or ill-regulated woman like Mrs. Quest. She looked facts in the face, recognised their meaning and bowed before their inexorable logic. It seemed to her almost impossible that she could hope to avoid this marriage, and if that proved to be so, she might be relied upon to make the best of it. Scandal would, under any circumstances, never find a word to say against Ida, for she was not a person who could attempt to console herself for an unhappy marriage. But it was bitter, bitter as gall, to be thus forced to turn aside from her happiness—for she well knew that with Harold Quaritch her life would be very happy—and fit her shoulders to this heavy yoke. Well, she had saved the place to her father, and also to her descendants, if she had any, and that was all that could be said.

She thought and thought, wishing in the bitterness of her heart that she had never been born to come to such a heavy day, till at last she could think no more. The air of the room seemed to stifle her, though it was by no means overheated. She went to the window and looked out. It was a wild wet evening, and the wind drove the rain before it in sheets. In the west the lurid rays of the sinking sun stained the clouds blood red, and broke in arrows of ominous light upon the driving storm.

But bad as was the weather, it attracted Ida. When the heart is heavy and torn by conflicting passions, it seems to answer to the calling of the storm, and to long to lose its petty troubling in the turmoil of the rushing world. Nature has many moods of which our own are but the echo and reflection, and she can be companionable when all human sympathy must fail. For she is our mother from whom we come, to whom we go, and her arms are ever open to clasp the children who can hear her voices. Drawn thereto by an impulse which she could not have analysed, Ida went upstairs, put on a thick pair of boots, a macintosh and an old hat. Then she sallied out into the wind and wet. It was blowing big guns, and as the rain whirled down the drops struck upon her face like spray. She crossed the moat bridge, and went out into the parkland beyond. The air was full of dead leaves, and the grass rustled with them as though it were alive, for this was the first wind since the frost. The great boughs of the oaks rattled and groaned above her, and high overhead, among the sullen clouds, a flight of rooks were being blown this way and that.

Ida bent her tall form against the rain and gale, and fought her way through them. At first she had no clear idea as to where she was going, but presently, perhaps from custom, she took the path that ran across the fields to Honham Church. It was a beautiful old church, particularly as regards the tower, one of the finest in the county, which had been partially blown down and rebuilt about the time of Charles I. The church itself had originally been founded by the Boissey family, and considerably enlarged by the widow of a de la Molle, whose husband had fallen at Agincourt, "as a memorial for ever." There, upon the porch, were carved the "hawks" of the de la Molles, wreathed round with palms of victory; and there, too, within the chancel, hung the warrior's helmet and his dinted shield.

Nor was he alone, for all around lay the dust of his kindred, come after the toil and struggle of their stormy lives to rest within the walls of that old church. Some of them had monuments of alabaster, whereon they lay in effigy, their heads pillowed upon that of a conquered Saracen; some had monuments of oak and brass, and some had no monuments at all, for the Puritans had ruthlessly destroyed them. But they were nearly all there, nearly twenty generations of the bearers of an ancient name, for even those of them who perished on the scaffold had been borne here for burial. The place was eloquent of the dead and of the mournful lesson of mortality. From century to century the bearers of that name had walked in these fields, and lived in yonder Castle, and looked upon the familiar swell of yonder ground and the silver flash of yonder river, and now their ashes were gathered here and all the forgotten turmoil of their lives was lost in the silence of those narrow tombs.

Ida loved the spot, hallowed to her not only by the altar of her faith, but also by the human associations that clung around and clothed it as the ivy clothed its walls. Here she had been christened, and here among her ancestors she hoped to be buried also. Here as a girl, when the full moon was up, she had crept in awed silence with her brother James to look through the window at the white and solemn figures stretched within. Here, too, she had sat on Sunday after Sunday for more than twenty years, and stared at the quaint Latin inscriptions cut on marble slabs, recording the almost superhuman virtues of departed de la Molles of the eighteenth century, her own immediate ancestors. The place was familiar to her whole life; she had scarcely a recollection with which it was not in some way connected. It was not wonderful, therefore, that she loved it, and that in the trouble of her mind her feet shaped their course towards it.

Presently she was in the churchyard. Taking her stand under the shelter of a line of Scotch firs, through which the gale sobbed and sang, she leant against a side gate and looked. The scene was desolate enough. Rain dropped from the roof on to the sodden graves beneath, and ran in thin sheets down the flint facing of the tower; the dead leaves whirled and rattled about the empty porch, and over all shot one red and angry arrow from the sinking sun. She stood in the storm and rain, gazing at the old church that had seen the end of so many sorrows more bitter than her own, and the wreck of so many summers, till the darkness began to close round her like a pall, while the wind sung the requiem of her hopes. Ida was not of a desponding or pessimistic character, but in that bitter hour she found it in her heart, as most people have at one time or another in their lives, to wish the tragedy over and the curtain down, and that she lay beneath those dripping sods without sight or hearing, without hope or dread. It seemed to her that the Hereafter must indeed be terrible if it outweighs the sorrows of the Here.

And then, poor woman, she thought of the long years between her and rest, and leaning her head against the gate-post, began to cry bitterly in the gloom.

Presently she ceased crying and with a start looked up, feeling that she was no longer alone. Her instincts had not deceived her, for in the shadow of the fir trees, not more than two paces from her, was the figure of a man. Just then he took a step to the left, which brought his outline against the sky, and Ida's heart stood still, for now she knew him. It was Harold Quaritch, the man over whose loss she had been weeping.

"It's very odd," she heard him say, for she was to leeward of him, "but I could have sworn that I heard somebody sobbing; I suppose it was the wind."

Ida's first idea was flight, and she made a movement for that purpose, but in doing so tripped over a stick and nearly fell.

In a minute he was by her side. She was caught, and perhaps she was not altogether sorry, especially as she had tried to get away.

"Who is it? what's the matter?" said the Colonel, lighting a fusee under her eyes. It was one of those flaming fusees, and burnt with a blue light, showing Ida's tall figure and beautiful face, all stained with grief and tears, showing her wet macintosh, and the gate-post against which she had been leaning—showing everything.

"Why, Ida," he said in amaze, "what are you doing here, crying too?"

"I'm not crying," she said, with a sob; "it's the rain that has made my face wet."

Just then the light burnt out and he dropped it.

"What is it, dear, what is it?" he said in great distress, for the sight of her alone in the wet and dark, and in tears, moved him beyond himself. Indeed he would have been no man if it had not.

She tried to answer, but she could not, and in another minute, to tell the honest truth, she had exchanged the gate-post for Harold's broad shoulder, and was finishing her "cry" there.

Now to see a young and pretty woman weeping (more especially if she happens to be weeping on your shoulder) is a very trying thing. It is trying even if you do not happen to be in love with her at all. But if you are in love with her, however little, it is dreadful; whereas, if, as in the present case, you happen to worship her, more, perhaps, than it is good to worship any fallible human creature, then the sight is positively overpowering. And so, indeed, it proved in the present instance. The Colonel could not bear it, but lifting her head from his shoulder, he kissed her sweet face again and again.

"What is it, darling?" he said, "what is the matter?"

"Leave go of me and I will tell you," she answered.

He obeyed, though with some unwillingness.

She hunted for her handkerchief and wiped her eyes, and then at last she spoke:

"I am engaged to be married," she said in a low voice, "I am engaged to Mr. Cossey."

Then, for about the first time in his life, Harold Quaritch swore violently in the presence of a lady.

"Oh, damn it all!" he said.

She took no notice of the strength of the language, perhaps indeed she re-echoed it in some feminine equivalent.

"It is true," she said with a sigh. "I knew that it would come, those dreadful things always do—and it was not my fault—I am sure you will always remember that. I had to do it—he advanced the money on the express condition, and even if I could pay back the money, I suppose that I should be bound to carry out the bargain. It is not the money which he wants but his bond."

"Curse him for a Shylock," said Harold again, and groaned in his bitterness and jealousy.

"Is there nothing to be done?" he asked presently in a harsh voice, for he was very hard hit.

"Nothing," she answered sadly. "I do not see what can help us, unless the man died," she said; "and that is not likely. Harold," she went on, addressing him for the first time in her life by his Christian name, for she felt that after crying upon a man's shoulder it is ridiculous to scruple about calling him by his name; "Harold, there is no help for it. I did it myself, remember, because, as I told you, I do not think that any one woman has a right to place her individual happiness before the welfare of her family. And I am only sorry," she added, her voice breaking a little, "that what I have done should bring suffering upon you."

He groaned again, but said nothing.

"We must try to forget," she went on wildly. "Oh no! no! I feel it is not possible that we should forget. You won't forget me, Harold, will you? And though it must be all over between us, and we must never speak like this again—never—you will always know I have not forgotten you, will you not, but that I think of you always?"

"There is no fear of my forgetting," he said, "and I am selfish enough to hope that you will think of me at times, Ida."

"Yes, indeed I will. We all have our burdens to bear. It is a hard world, and we must bear them. And it will all be the same in the end, in just a few years. I daresay these dead people here have felt as we feel, and how quiet they are! And perhaps there may be something beyond, where things are not so. Who can say? You won't go away from this place, Harold, will you? Not until I am married at any rate; perhaps you had better go then. Say that you won't go till then, and you will let me see you sometimes; it is a comfort to see you."

"I should have gone, certainly," he said; "to New Zealand probably, but if you wish it I will stop for the present."

"Thank you; and now good-bye, my dear, good-bye! No, don't come with me, I can find my own way home. And—why do you wait? Good-bye, good - bye for ever in this way. Yes, kiss me once and swear that you will never forget me. Marry if you wish to; but don't forget me, Harold. Forgive me for speaking so plainly, but I speak as one about to die to you, and I wish things to be clear."

"I shall never marry and I shall never forget you," he answered. "Good-bye, my love, good-bye!"

In another minute she had vanished into the storm and rain, out of his sight and out of his life, but not out of his heart.

He, too, turned and went his way into the wild and lonely night.

An hour afterwards Ida came down into the drawing-room dressed for dinner, looking rather pale but otherwise quite herself. Presently the Squire arrived. He had been at a magistrate's meeting, and had only just got home.

"Why, Ida," he said, "I could not find you anywhere. I met George as I was driving from Boisingham, and he told me that he saw you walking through the park."

"Did he?" she answered indifferently. "Yes, I have been out. It was so stuffy indoors. Father," she went on, with a change of tone, "I have something to tell you. I am engaged to be married."

He looked at her curiously, and then said quietly—the Squire was always quiet in any matter of real emergency—"Indeed, my dear! That is a serious matter. However, speaking off-hand, I think that notwithstanding the disparity of age, Quaritch—"

"No, no," she said, wincing visibly, "I am not engaged to Colonel Quaritch, I am engaged to Mr. Cossey."

"Oh," he said, "oh, indeed! I thought from what I saw, that—that—"

At this moment the servant announced dinner.

"Well, never mind about it now, father," she said; "I am tired and want my dinner. Mr. Cossey is coming to see you to-morrow, and we can talk about it afterwards."

And though the Squire thought a good deal, he made no further allusion to the subject that night.

CHAPTER XXV

THE SQUIRE GIVES HIS CONSENT

Edward Cossey did not come away from the scene of his engagement in a very happy or triumphant tone of mind. Ida's bitter words stung like whips, and he understood, and she clearly meant he should understand, that it was only in consideration of the money advanced that she had consented to become his wife. Now, however satisfactory it is to be rich enough to purchase your heart's desire in this fashion, it is not altogether soothing to the pride of a nineteenth-century man to be continually haunted by the thought that he is a buyer in the market and nothing but a buyer. Of course, he saw clearly enough that there was an object in all this—he saw that Ida, by making obvious her dislike, wished to disgust him with his bargain, and escape from an alliance of which the prospect was hateful to her. But he had no intention of being so easily discouraged. In the first place his passion for the woman was as a devouring flame, eating ever at his heart. In that at any rate he was sincere; he did love her so far as his nature was capable of love, or at any rate he had the keenest desire to make her his wife. A delicate-minded man would probably have shrunken from forcing himself upon a woman under parallel circumstances; but Edward Cossey did not happen to fall into that category. As a matter of fact such men are not as common as they might be.

Another thing which he took into account was that Ida would probably get over her dislike. He was a close observer of women, in a cynical and half contemptuous way, and he remarked, or thought that he remarked, a curious tendency among them to submit with comparative complacency to the inevitable whenever it happened to coincide with their material advantage. Women, he argued, have not, as a class, outgrown the traditions of their primitive condition when their partners for life were chosen for them by lot or the chance of battle. They still recognise the claims of the wealthiest or strongest, and their love of luxury and ease is so keen that if the nest they lie in is only soft enough, they will not grieve long over the fact that it was not of their own choosing. Arguing from these untrustworthy premises, he came to the conclusion that Ida would soon get over her repugnance to marrying him, when she found how many comforts and good things marriage with so rich a man would place at her disposal, and would, if for no other reason, learn to look on him with affection and gratitude as the author of her gilded ease. And so indeed she might have done had she been of another and more common stamp. But, unfortunately for his reasoning, there exist members of her sex who are by nature of an order of mind superior to these considerations, and who realise that they have but one life to live, and that the highest form of happiness is *not* dependent upon money or money's worth, but rather upon the indulgence of mental aspirations and those affections which, when genuine, draw nearer to holiness than anything else about us. Such a woman, more especially if she is already possessed with an affection for another man, does not easily become reconciled to a distasteful lot, however quietly she may endure it, and such a woman was Ida de la Molle.

Edward Cossey, when he reached Boisingham on the evening of his engagement, at once wrote and posted a note to the Squire, saying that he would call on the following morning about a matter of business. Accordingly, at half-past ten o'clock, he arrived and was shown into the vestibule, where he found the old gentleman standing with his back to the fire and plunged in reflection.

"Well, Mr. de la Molle," said Edward, rather nervously, so

soon as he had shaken hands, "I do not know if Ida has spoken to you about what took place between us yesterday."

"Yes," he said, "yes, she told me something to the effect that she had accepted a proposal of marriage from you, subject to my consent, of course; but really the whole thing is so sudden that I have hardly had time to consider it."

"It is very simple," said Edward; "I am deeply attached to your daughter, and I have been so fortunate as to be accepted by her. Should you give your consent to the marriage, I may as well say at once that I wish to carry out the most liberal money arrangements in my power. I will make Ida a present of the mortgage that I hold over this property, and she may put it in the fire. Further, I will covenant on the death of my father, which cannot now be long delayed, to settle two hundred thousand pounds upon her absolutely. Also, I am prepared to agree that if we have a son, and he should wish to do so, he shall take the name of de la Molle."

"I am sure," said the Squire, turning round to hide his natural gratification at these proposals, "your offers on the subject of settlements are of a most liberal order, and of course so far as I am concerned, Ida will have this place, which may one day be again more valuable than it is now."

"I am glad that they meet with your approval," said Edward; "and now there is one more thing I want to ask you, Mr. de la Molle, and which I hope, if you give your consent to the marriage, you will not raise any objection to. It is, that our engagement should not be announced at present. The fact is," he went on hurriedly, "my father is a very peculiar man, and has a great idea of my marrying somebody with a large fortune. Also his state of health is so uncertain that there is no possibility of knowing how he will take anything. Indeed he is dying; the doctors told me that he might go off any day, and that he cannot last for another three months. If the engagement is announced to him now, at the best I shall have a great deal of trouble, and at the worst he might make me suffer in his will, should he happen to take a fancy against it."

"Umph," said the Squire, "I don't quite like the idea of a projected marriage with my daughter, Miss de la Molle of Honham Castle, being hushed up as though there were something discreditable about it, but still there may be peculiar circumstances in the case which would justify me in consenting to that course. You are both old enough to know your own minds, and the match would be as advantageous for you as it could be to us, for even now-a-days, family, and I may even say personal appearance, still go for something where matrimony is concerned. I have reason to know that your father is a peculiar man, very peculiar. Yes, on the whole, though I don't like hole and corner affairs, I shall have no objection to the engagement not being announced for the next month or two."

"Thank you for considering me so much," said Edward with a sigh of relief. "Then am I to understand that you give your consent to our engagement?"

The Squire reflected for a moment. Everything seemed quite straight, and yet he suspected crookedness. His latent distrust of the man, which had not been decreased by the scene of two nights before—for he never could bring himself to like Edward Cossey—arose in force and made him hesitate when there was no visible ground for hesitation. He possessed, as has been said, an instinctive insight into character that was almost feminine in its intensity, and it was lifting a warning finger before him now.

"I don't quite know what to say," he replied at length. "The whole affair is so sudden—and to tell you the truth, I thought that Ida had bestowed her affections in another direction."

Edward's face darkened. "I thought so too," he answered, "until yesterday, when I was so happy as to be undeceived. I ought to tell you, by the way," he went on, running away from the covert falsehood in his last words as quickly as he could, "how much I regret I was the cause of that scene with Colonel Quaritch, more especially as I find that there is an explanation of the story against him. The fact is, I was foolish enough to be vexed because he beat me out shooting, and also because, well I—I was jealous of him."

"Ah, yes," said the Squire, rather coldly, "a most unfortunate affair. Of course, I don't know what the particulars of the matter were, and it is no business of mine, but speaking generally, I should say never bring an accusation of that sort against a man at all unless you are driven to it, and if you do bring it be quite certain of your ground. However, that is neither here nor there. Well, about this engagement. Ida is old enough to judge for herself, and seems to have made up her mind, so as I know no reason to the contrary, and as the business arrangements proposed are all that I could wish, I cannot see that I have any ground for withholding my consent. So all I can say, sir, is that I hope you will make my daughter a good husband, and that you will both be happy. Ida is a high-spirited woman; but in my opinion she is greatly above the average of her sex, as I have known it, and provided you have her affection, and don't attempt to drive her, she will go through thick and thin for you. But I dare say you would like to see her. Oh, by the way, I forgot, she has got a headache this morning, and is stopping in bed. It isn't much in her line, but I daresay that she is a little upset. Perhaps you would like to come up to dinner to-night?"

This proposition Edward, knowing full well that Ida's headache was a device to rid herself of the necessity of seeing him, accepted with gratitude and went.

As soon as he had gone, Ida herself came down.

"Well, my dear," said the Squire cheerfully, "I have just had the pleasure of seeing Edward Cossey, and I have told him that, as you seemed to wish it—"

Here Ida made a movement of impatience, but remembered

herself and said nothing.

"That as you seemed to wish that things should be so, I had no ground of objection to your engagement. I may as well tell you that the proposals which he makes as regards settlements are of the most liberal nature."

"Are they?" answered Ida indifferently. "Is Mr. Cossey coming here to dinner?"

"Yes, I asked him. I thought that you would like to see him."

"Well, then, I wish you had not," she answered with animation, "because there is nothing to eat except some cold beef. Really, father, it is very thoughtless of you;" and she stamped her foot and went off in a huff, leaving the Squire full of reflection.

"I wonder what it all means," he said to himself. "She can't care about the man much or she would not make that fuss about his being asked to dinner. Ida isn't the sort of woman to be caught by the money, I should think. Well, I know nothing about it; it is no affair of mine, and I can only take things as I find them."

And then he fell to reflecting that this marriage would be an extraordinary stroke of luck for the family. Here they were at the last gasp, mortgaged up the eyes, when suddenly fortune, in the shape of an, on the whole, perfectly unobjectionable young man, appears, takes up the mortgages, proposes settlements to the tune of hundreds of thousands, and even offers to perpetuate the old family name in the person of his son, should he have one. Such a state of affairs could not but be gratifying to any man, however unworldly, and the Squire was not altogether unworldly. That is, he had a keen sense of the dignity of his social position and his family, and it had all his life been his chief and laudable desire to be sufficiently provided with the goods of this world to raise the de la Molles to the position which they had occupied in former centuries.

Hitherto, however, the tendency of events had been all the other way—the house was a sinking one, and but the other day its ancient roof had nearly fallen about their ears. But now the prospect changed as though by magic. On Ida's marriage all the mortgages, those heavy accumulations of years of growing expenditure and narrowing means, would roll off the back of the estate, and the de la Molles of Honham Castle would once more take the place in the county to which they were undoubtedly entitled.

It is not wonderful that the prospect proved a pleasing one to him, or that his head was filled with visions of splendours to come.

As it chanced, on that very morning it was necessary for Mr. Quest to pay the old gentleman a visit in order to obtain his signature to a lease of a bakery in Boisingham, which, together with two or three other houses, belonged to the estate.

He arrived just as the Squire was in the full flow of his meditations, and it would not have needed a man of Mr. Quest's penetration and powers of observation to discover that he had something on his mind which he was longing for an opportunity to talk about.

The Squire signed the lease without paying the slightest attention to Mr. Quest's explanations, and then suddenly asked him when the first interest on the recently-effected mortgages came due.

The lawyer mentioned a certain date.

"Ah," said the Squire, "then it will have to be met; but it does not matter, it will be for the last time."

Mr. Quest pricked up his ears and looked at him.

"The fact is, Quest," he went on by way of explanation, "that there are—well—family arrangements pending which will put an end to these embarrassments in a natural and a proper way."

"Indeed," said Mr. Quest, "I am very glad to hear it."

"Yes, yes," said the Squire, "unfortunately I am under some restraints in speaking about the matter at present, or I should like to ask your opinion, for which as you know I have a great respect. Really, though, I do not know why I should not consult my lawyer on a matter of business; I only consented not to trumpet the thing about."

"Lawyers are confidential agents," said Mr. Quest quietly.

"Of course they are. Of course, and it is their business to hold their tongues. I may rely upon your discretion, may I not?"

"Certainly," said Mr. Quest.

"Well, the matter is this: Mr. Edward Cossey is engaged to Miss de la Molle. He has just been here to obtain my consent, which, of course, I have not withheld, as I know nothing against the young man—nothing at all. The only stipulation that he made is, as I think, a reasonable one under the circumstances, namely, that the engagement is to be kept quiet for a little while on account of the condition of his father's health. He says that he is an unreasonable man, and that he might take a prejudice against it."

During this announcement Mr. Quest had remained perfectly quiet, his face showing no signs of excitement, only his eyes shone with a curious light.

"Indeed," he said, "this is very interesting news."

"Yes," said the Squire. "That is what I meant by saying that there would be no necessity to make any arrangements as to the future payment of interest, for Cossey has informed me that he proposes to put the mortgage bonds in the fire before his marriage."

"Indeed," said Mr. Quest; "well, he could hardly do less, could he? Altogether, I think you ought to be congratulated, Mr. de la Molle. It is not often that a man gets such a chance of clearing the encumbrances off a property. And now I am very sorry, but I must be getting home, as I promised my wife to be back for luncheon. As the thing is to be kept quiet, I suppose that it would be premature for me to offer my good wishes to Miss de la Molle."

"Yes, yes, don't say anything about it at present. Well, good-bye."

CHAPTER XXVI

BELLE PAYS A VISIT

Mr. Quest got into his dog-cart and drove homewards, full of feelings which it would be difficult to describe.

The hour of his revenge was come. He had played his cards and he had won the game, and fortune with it, for his enemy lay in the hollow of his hand. He looked behind him at the proud towers of the Castle, reflecting as he did so, that in all probability they would belong to him before another year was over his head. At one time he had earnestly longed to possess this place, but now this was not so much the object of his desire. What he wanted now was the money. With thirty thousand pounds in his hand he would, together with what he had, be a rich man, and he had already laid his plans for the future. Of Edith he had heard nothing lately. She was cowed, but he well knew that it was only for a while. By-and-by her rapacity would get the better of her fear and she would recommence her persecutions. This being so, he came to a determination—he would put the world between them. Once let him have this money in his hand and he would start his life afresh in some new country; he was not too old for it, and he would be a rich man, and then perhaps he might get rid of the cares which had rendered so much of his existence valueless. If Belle would go with him, well and good—if not, he could not help it. If she did go, there must be a reconciliation first, for he could not any longer tolerate the life they lived.

In due course he reached the Oaks and went in. Luncheon was on the table, at which Belle was sitting. She was, as usual, dressed in black, and beautiful to look on; but her round babyish face was pale and pinched, and there were black lines beneath her eyes.

"I did not know that you were coming back to luncheon," she said; "I am afraid there is not much to eat."

"Yes," he said, "I finished my business up at the Castle, so I thought I might as well come home. By-the-by, Belle, I have a bit of news for you."

"What is it?" she asked, looking up sharply, for something in his tone attracted her attention and awoke her fears.

"Your friend, Edward Cossey, is going to be married to Ida de la Molle."

She blanched till she looked like death itself, and put her hands to her heart as though she had been stabbed.

"The Squire told me so himself," he went on, keeping his eyes remorselessly fixed upon her face. She leaned forward and he thought that she was going to faint, but she did not. By a supreme effort she recovered herself and drank a glass of sherry which was standing by her side.

"I expected it," she said in a low voice.

"You mean that you dreaded it," answered Mr. Quest quietly. He rose and locked the door and then came and stood close to her and spoke.

"Listen, Belle. I know all about your affair with Edward Cossey. I have proofs of it, but I have forborne to use them, because I saw that in the end he would weary of you and desert you for some other woman, and that would be my best revenge upon you. You have all along been nothing but his toy, the light woman with whom he amused his leisure hours."

She put her hands back over her heart but said no word and he went on.

"Belle, I did wrong to marry you when you did not want to marry me, but, being married, you have done wrong to be unfaithful to your vows. I have been rewarded by your infidelity, and your infidelity has been rewarded by desertion. Now I have a proposal to make, and if you are wise you will accept it. Let us set the one wrong against the other; let both be forgotten. Forgive me, and I will forgive you, and let us make peace—if not now, then in a little while, when your heart is not so sore—and go right away from Edward Cossey and Ida de la Molle and Honham and Boisingham, into some new part of the world where we can begin life again and try to forget the past."

She looked up at him and shook her head mournfully, and twice she tried to speak and twice she failed. The third time her words came.

"You do not understand me," she said. "You are very kind and I am very grateful to you, but you do not understand me. I cannot get over things so easily as I know most women can; what I have done I never can undo. I do not blame him altogether, it was as much or more my fault than his, but having once loved him I cannot go back to you or any other man. If you like I will go on living with you as we live, and I will try to make you comfortable, but I can say no more."

"Think again, Belle," he said almost pleadingly; "I daresay that you have never given me credit for much tenderness of heart, and I know that you have as much against me as I have against you. But I have always loved you, and I love you now, really and truly love you, and I will make you a good husband if you will let me."

"You are very good," she said, "but it cannot be. Get rid of me if you like and marry somebody else. I am ready to take the penalty of what I have done."

"Once more, Belle, I beg you to consider. Do you know what kind of man this is for whom you are giving up your life? Not only has he deserted you, but do you know how he has got hold of Ida de la Molle? He has, as I know well, *bought* her. I tell you he has bought her as much as though he had gone into the open market and paid down a price for her. The other day Cossey and Son were going to foreclose upon the Honham estates, which would have ruined the old gentleman. Well, what did your young man do? He went to the girl—who hates him, by the way, and is in love with Colonel Quaritch—and said to her, 'If you will promise to marry me when I ask you, I will find the thirty thousand pounds and take up the mortgages.' And on those terms she agreed to marry him. And now he has got rid of you and he claims her promise. There is the history. I wonder that your pride will bear such a thing. By heaven, I would kill the man."

She looked up at him curiously. "Would you?" she said. "It is not a bad idea. I dare say it is all true. He is worthless. Why does one fall in love with worthless people? Well, there is an end of it; or a beginning of the end. As I have sown, so must I reap;" and she got up, and unlocking the door left the room.

"Yes," he said aloud when she had gone, "there is a beginning of the end. Upon my word, what between one thing and another, unlucky devil as I am, I had rather stand in my own shoes than in Edward Cossey's."

Belle went to her room and sat thinking, or rather brooding, sullenly. Then she put on her bonnet and cloak and started out, taking the road that ran past Honham Castle. She had not gone a hundred yards before she found herself face to face with Edward Cossey himself. He was coming out of a gunsmith's shop, where he had been ordering some cartridges.

"How do you do, Belle?" he said, colouring and lifting his hat.

"How do you do, Mr. Cossey?" she answered, coming to a stop and looking him straight in the face.

"Where are you going?" he asked, not knowing what to say.

"I am going to walk up to the Castle to call on Miss de la Molle."

"I don't think that you will find her. She is in bed with a headache."

"Oh! So you have been up there this morning?"

"Yes, I had to see the Squire about some business."

"Indeed." Then looking him in the eyes again, "Are you engaged to be married to Ida?"

He coloured once more, he could not prevent himself from doing so.

"No," he answered; "what makes you ask such a question?"

"I don't know," she said, laughing a little; "feminine curiosity I suppose. I thought that you might be. Good-bye," and she went on, leaving Edward Cossey to the enjoyment of a very peculiar set of sensations.

"What a coward!" said Belle to herself. "He does not even dare to tell me the truth."

Nearly an hour later she arrived at the Castle, and, asking for Ida, was shown into the drawing-room, where she found her sitting with a book in her hand.

Ida rose to greet her in friendly fashion, for the two women, although they were at the opposite poles of character, had a liking for each other. In a way they were both strong, and strength always recognises and respects strength.

"Have you walked up?" asked Ida.

"Yes, I came on the chance of finding you. I want to speak to you."

"Yes," said Ida, "what is it?"

"This. Forgive me, but are you engaged to be married to Edward Cossey?"

Ida looked at her in a slow, stately way, which seemed to ask by what right she came to question her. At least, so Belle read it.

"I know that I have no right to ask such a question," she said, with humility, "and, of course, you need not answer it, but I have a reason for asking."

"Well," said Ida, "I was requested by Mr. Cossey to keep the matter secret, but he appears to have divulged it. Yes, I am engaged to be married to him."

Belle's beautiful face turned a shade paler, if that was possible, and her eyes hardened.

"Do you wonder why I ask you this?" she said. "I will tell you, though probably when I have done so you will never speak to me again. I am Edward Cossey's discarded mistress," and she laughed bitterly enough.

Ida shrank a little and coloured, as a pure and high-minded woman naturally does when she is for the first time suddenly brought into actual contact with impurity and passion.

"I know," went on Belle, "that I must seem a shameful thing to you; but, Miss de la Molle, good and cold and stately as you are, pray God that you may never be thrown into temptation; pray God that you may never be married almost by force to a man whom you hate, and then suddenly learn what a thing it is to fall in love, and for the first time feel your life awake."

"Hush," said Ida gently, "what right have I to judge you?"

"I loved him," went on Belle, "I loved him passionately, and for a while it was as though heaven had opened its gates, for he used to care for me a little, and I think he would have taken me away and married me afterwards, but I would not hear of it, because I knew that it would ruin him. He offered to, once, and I refused, and within three hours of that I believe he was bargaining for you. Well, and then it was the old story, he fell more and more in love with you and of course I had no hold upon him."

"Yes," said Ida, moving impatiently, "but why do you tell me all this? It is very painful and I had rather not hear it."

"Why do I tell you? I tell you because I do not wish you to marry Edward Cossey. I tell you because I wish *him* to feel a little of what *I* have to feel, and because I have said that he should *not* marry you."

"I wish that you could prevent it," said Ida, with a sudden outburst. "I am sure you are quite welcome to Mr. Cossey so far as I am concerned, for I detest him, and I cannot imagine how any woman could ever have done otherwise."

"Thank you," said Belle; "but I have done with Mr. Cossey, and I think I hate him too. I know that I did hate him when I met him in the street just now and he told me that he was not engaged to you. You say that you detest him, why then do you marry him—you are a free woman?"

"Do you want to know?" said Ida, wheeling round and looking her visitor full in the face. "I am going to marry him for the same reason that you say caused you to marry—because I *must*. I am going to marry him because he lent us money on condition that I promised to marry him, and as I have taken the money, I must give him his price, even if it breaks my heart. You think that you are wretched; how do you know that I am not fifty times as wretched? Your lot is to lose your lover, mine is to have one forced upon me and endure him all my life. The worst of your pain is over, all mine is to come."

"Why? why?" broke in Belle. "What is such a promise as that? He cannot force you to marry him, and it is better for a woman to die than to marry a man she hates, especially," she added meaningly, "if she happens to care for somebody else. Be advised by me, I know what it is."

"Yes," said Ida, "perhaps it is better to die, but death is not so easy. As for the promise, you do not seem to understand that no gentleman or lady can break a promise in consideration of which money has been received. Whatever he has done, and whatever he is, I *must* marry Mr. Cossey, so I do not think that we need discuss the subject any more."

Belle sat silent for a minute or more, and then rising said that she must go. "I have warned you," she added, "although to warn you I am forced to put myself at your mercy. You can tell the story and destroy me if you like. I do not much care if you do. Women such as I grow reckless."

"You must understand me very little, Mrs. Quest" (it had always been Belle before, and she winced at the changed name), "if you think me capable of such conduct. You have nothing to fear from me."

She held out her hand, but in her humility and shame, Belle went without taking it, and through the angry sunset light walked slowly back to Boisingham. And as she walked there was a look upon her face that Edward Cossey would scarcely have cared to see.

CHAPTER XXVII

MR. QUEST HAS HIS INNINGS

All that afternoon and far into the evening Mr. Quest was employed in drafting, and with his own hand engrossing on parchment certain deeds, for the proper execution of which he seemed to find constant reference necessary to a tin box of papers labelled "Honham Castle Estates."

By eleven that night everything was finished, and having carefully collected and docketed his papers, he put the tin box away and went home to bed.

Next morning, about ten o'clock, Edward Cossey was sitting at breakfast in no happy frame of mind. He had gone up to the Castle to dinner on the previous evening, but it cannot be said that he had enjoyed himself. Ida was there, looking very handsome in her evening dress, but she was cold as a stone and unapproachable as a statue. She scarcely spoke to him, indeed, except in answer to some direct remark, reserving all her conversation for her father, who seemed to have caught the contagion of restraint, and was, for him, unusually silent and depressed.

But once or twice he found her looking at him, and then there was upon her face a mingled expression of contempt and irresistible aversion which chilled him to the marrow.

These qualities were indeed so much more plainly developed

towards himself than they had been before, that at last a conviction which he at first rejected as incredible forced itself into his mind. This conviction was, that Belle had disbelieved his denial of the engagement, and in her eagerness for revenge, must have told Ida the whole story. The thought made him feel faint. Well, there was but one thing to be done—face it out.

Once when the Squire's back was turned he had ventured to attempt some little verbal tenderness in which the word "dear" occurred, but Ida did not seem to hear it and looked straight over his head into space. This he felt was trying. So trying did he find the whole entertainment indeed that about half-past nine he rose and came away, saying that he had received some bank papers which must be attended to that night.

Now most men would in all human probability have been dismayed by this state of affairs into relinquishing an attempt at matrimony which it was evident could only be carried through in the face of the quiet but none the less vigorous dislike and contempt of the other contracting party. But this was not so with Edward Cossey. Ida's coldness excited upon his tenacious and obstinate mind much the same effect that may be supposed to be produced upon the benighted seeker for the North Pole by the sight of a frozen ocean of icebergs. Like the explorer he was convinced that if once he could get over those cold heights he would find a smiling sunny land beyond and perchance many other delights, and like the explorer again, he was, metaphorically, ready to die in the effort. For he loved her more every day, till now his passion dominated his physical being and his mental judgment, so that whatever loss was entailed, and whatever obstacles arose, he was determined to endure and overcome them if by so doing he might gain his end.

He was reflecting upon all this on the morning in question when Mr. Quest, looking very cool, composed and gentleman-like, was shown into his room, much as Colonel Quaritch had been shown in two mornings before.

"How do you do, Quest?" he said, in a from high to low tone, which he was in the habit of adopting towards his official subordinates. "Sit down. What is it?"

"It is some business, Mr. Cossey," the lawyer answered in his usual quiet tones.

"Honham Castle mortgages again, I suppose," he growled. "I only hope you don't want any more money on that account at present, that's all; because I can't raise another cent while my father lives. They don't entail cash and bank shares, you know, and though my credit's pretty good I am not far from the bottom of it."

"Well," said Mr. Quest, with a faint smile, "it has to do with the Honham Castle mortgages; but as I have a good deal to say, perhaps we had better wait till the things are cleared."

"All right. Just ring the bell, will you, and take a cigarette?"

Mr. Quest smiled again and rang the bell, but did not take the cigarette. When the breakfast things had been removed he took a chair, and placing it on the further side of the table in such a position that the light, which was to his back, struck full upon Edward Cossey's face, began to deliberately untie and sort his bundle of papers. Presently he came to the one he wanted—a letter. It was not an original letter, but a copy. "Will you kindly read this, Mr. Cossey?" he said quietly, as he pushed the letter towards him across the table.

Edward finished lighting his cigarette, then took the letter up and glanced at it carelessly. At sight of the first line his expression changed to one of absolute horror, his face blanched, the perspiration sprang out upon his forehead, and the cigarette dropped from his fingers to the carpet, where it lay smouldering. Nor was this wonderful, for the letter was a copy of one of Belle's most passionate epistles to himself. He had never been able to restrain her from writing these compromising letters. Indeed, this one was the very same that some little time before Mr. Quest had abstracted from the pocket of Mr. Cossey's lounging coat in the room in London.

He read on for a little way and then put the letter down upon the table. There was no need for him to go further, it was all in the same strain.

"You will observe, Mr. Cossey, that this is a copy," said Mr. Quest, "but if you like you can inspect the original document."

He made no answer.

"Now," went on Mr. Quest, handing him a second paper, "here is the copy of another letter, of which the original is in your handwriting."

Edward looked at it. It was an intercepted letter of his own, dated about a year before, and its contents, though not of so passionate a nature as the other, were of a sufficiently incriminating character.

He put it down upon the table by the side of the first and waited for Mr. Quest to go on.

"I have other evidence," said his visitor presently, "but you are probably sufficiently versed in such matters to know that these letters alone are almost enough for my purpose. That purpose is to commence a suit for divorce against my wife, in which you will, of course, in accordance with the provisions of the Act, be joined as co-respondent. Indeed, I have already drawn up a letter of instruction to my London agents directing them to take the preliminary steps," and he pushed a third paper towards him.

Edward Cossey turned his back to his tormentor and resting his head upon his hand tried to think.

"Mr. Quest," he said presently in a hoarse voice, "without admitting anything, there are reasons which would make it ruinous to me if such an action were commenced at present."

"Yes," he answered, "there are. In the first place there is no knowing in what light your father would look on the matter and how his view of it would affect your future interests. In the second your engagement to Miss de la Molle, upon which you are strongly set, would certainly be broken off."

"How do you know that I am engaged?" asked Edward in surprise.

"It does not matter how I know it," said the lawyer, "I do know it, so it will be useless for you to deny it. As you remark, this suit will probably be your ruin in every way, and therefore it is, as you will easily understand, a good moment for a man who wants his revenge to choose to bring it."

"Without admitting anything," answered Edward Cossey, "I wish to ask you a question. Is there no way out of this? Supposing that I have done you a wrong, wrong admits of compensation."

"Yes, it does, Mr. Cossey, and I have thought of that. Everybody has his price in this world and I have mine; but the compensation for such a wrong must be a heavy one."

"At what price will you agree to stay the action for ever?" he asked.

"The price that I will take to stay the action is the transfer into my name of the mortgages you hold over the Honham Castle Estates," answered Mr. Quest quietly.

"Great heavens!" said Edward, "why that is a matter of thirty thousand pounds."

"I know it is, and I know also that it is worth your while to pay thirty thousand pounds to save yourself from the scandal, the chance of disinheritance, and the certainty of the loss of the woman whom you want to marry. So well do I know it that I have prepared the necessary deeds for your signature, and here they are. Listen, sir," he went on sternly; "refuse to accept my terms and by to-night's post I shall send this letter of instructions. Also I shall send to Mr. Cossey, Senior, and to Mr. de la Molle copies of these two precious epistles," and he pointed to the incriminating documents, "together with a copy of the letter to my agents; and where will you be then? Consent, and I will bind myself not to proceed in any way or form. Now, make your choice."

"But I cannot; even if I will, I cannot," said he, almost wringing his hands in his perplexity. "It was on condition of my taking up those mortgages that Ida consented to become engaged to me, and I have promised that I will cancel them on our wedding. Will you not take money instead?"

"Yes," answered Mr. Quest, "I would take money. A little time ago I would not have taken it because I wanted that property; now I have changed my ideas. But as you yourself said, your credit is strained to the utmost, and while your father is alive you will not find it possible to raise another thirty thousand pounds. Besides, if this matter is to be settled at all it must be settled at once. I will not wait while you make attempts to raise the money."

"But about the mortgages? I promised to keep them. What shall I say to Ida?"

"Say? Say nothing. You can meet them if you choose after your father's death. Refuse if you like, but if you refuse you will be mad. Thirty thousand pounds will be nothing to you, but exposure will be ruin. Have you made up your mind? You must take my offer or leave it. Sign the documents and I will put the originals of those two letters into your hands; refuse and I will take my steps."

Edward Cossey thought for a moment and then said, "I will sign. Let me see the papers."

Mr. Quest turned aside to hide the expression of triumph which flitted across his face and then handed him the deeds. They were elaborately drawn, for he was a skilful legal draughtsman, quite as skilful as many a leading Chancery conveyancer, but the substance of them was that the mortgages were transferred to him by the said Edward Cossey in and for the consideration that he, the said William M. Quest, consented to abandon for ever a pending action for divorce against his wife, Belle Quest, whereto the said Edward Cossey was to be joined as co-respondent.

"You will observe," said Mr. Quest, "that if you attempt to contest the validity of this assignment, which you probably could not do with any prospect of success, the attempt must recoil upon your own head, because the whole scandal will then transpire. We shall require some witnesses, so with your permission I will ring the bell and ask the landlady and your servant to step up. They need know nothing of the contents of the papers," and he did so.

"Stop," said Edward presently. "Where are the original letters?"

"Here," answered Mr. Quest, producing them from an inner pocket, and showing them to him at a distance. "When the landlady comes up I will give them to her to hold in this envelope, directing her to hand them to you when the deeds are signed and witnessed. She will think that it is part of the ceremony."

Presently the man-servant and the landlady arrived, and Mr. Quest, in his most matter-of-fact way, explained to them that they were required to witness some documents. At the same time he handed the letters to the woman, saying that she was to give them to Mr. Cossey when they had all done signing.

Then Edward Cossey signed, and placing his thumb on the familiar wafer delivered the various documents as his act and deed. The witnesses with much preparation and effort affixed their awkward signatures in the places pointed out to them, and in a few minutes the thing was done, leaving Mr. Quest a richer man by thirty thousand pounds than when he had got up that morning.

"Now give Mr. Cossey the packet, Mrs. Jeffries," he said, as he blotted the signatures, "and you can go." She did so and went.

When the witnesses had gone Edward looked at the letters, and then with a savage oath flung them into the fire and watched them burn.

"Good-morning, Mr. Cossey," said Mr. Quest as he prepared to part with the deeds. "You have now bought your experience and had to pay dearly for it; but, upon my word, when I think of all you owe me, I wonder at myself for letting you off at so small a price."

As soon as he had gone, Edward Cossey gave way to his feelings in language forcible rather than polite. For now, in addition to all the money which he had lost, and the painful exposure to which he had been subjected, he was face to face with a new difficulty. Either he must make a clean breast of it to Ida about the mortgages being no longer in his hands or he must pretend that he still had them. In the first alternative, the consideration upon which she had agreed to marry him came to nothing. Moreover, Ida was thereby released from her promise, and he was well aware that under these circumstances she would probably break off the engagement. In the second, he would be acting a lie, and the lie would sooner or later be discovered, and what then? Well, if it was after marriage, what would it matter? To a woman of gentle birth there is only one thing more irretrievable than marriage, and that is death. Anyhow, he had suffered so much for the sake of this woman that he did not mean to give her up now. He must meet the mortgages after marriage, that was all.

Facilis est descensus Averni. When a man of the character of Edward Cossey, or indeed of any character, allows his passions to lead him into a course of deceit, he does not find it easy to check his wild career. From dishonour to dishonour shall he go till at length, in due season, he reaps as he has sown.

CHAPTER XXVIII

HOW GEORGE TREATED JOHNNIE

Some two or three days before the scene described in the last chapter the faithful George had suddenly announced his desire to visit London.

"What?" said the Squire in astonishment, for George had never been known to go out of his own county before. "Why, what on earth are you going to do in London?"

"Well, Squire," answered his retainer, looking marvellously knowing, "I don't rightly know, but there's a cheap train goes up to this here Exhibition on the Tuesday morning and comes back on the Thursday evening. Ten shillings both ways, that's the fare, and I see in the *Chronicle*, I du, that there's a wonnerful show of these new-fangled self-tying and delivering reapers, sich as they foreigners use over sea in America, and I'm rarely fell on seeing them and having a holiday look round Lunnon town. So as there ain't not nothing particler a-doing, if you hain't got anything to say agin it, I think I'll go, Squire."

"All right," said the Squire; "are you going to take your wife with you?"

"Why no, Squire; I said as I wanted to go for a holiday, and that ain't no holiday to take the old missus too," and George chuckled in a manner which evidently meant volumes.

And so it came to pass that on the afternoon of the day of the transfer of the mortgages from Edward Cossey to Mr. Quest the great George found himself wandering vaguely about the vast expanse of the Colinderies, and not enjoying himself in the least. He had been recommended by some travelled individual in Boisingham to a certain lodging near Liverpool Street Station, which he found with the help of a friendly porter. Thence he set out for the Exhibition, but, being of a prudent mind, thought that he would do well to save his money and walk the distance. So he walked and walked till he was tired, and then, after an earnest consultation with a policeman, he took a 'bus, which an hour later landed him—at the Royal Oak. His further adventures we need not pursue; suffice it to say that, having started from his lodging at three, it was past seven o'clock at night when he finally reached the Exhibition, more thoroughly wearied than though he had done a good day's harvesting.

Here he wandered for a while in continual dread of having his pocket picked, seeking reaping machines and discovering none, till at length he found himself in the gardens, where the electric light display was in full swing. Soon wearying of this, for it was a cold damp night, he made a difficult path to a buffet inside the building, where he sat down at a little table, and devoured some very unpleasant-looking cold beef. Here slumber overcame him, for his weariness was great, and he dozed.

Presently through the muffled roar and hum of voices which echoed in his sleep-dulled ears, he caught the sound of a familiar name, that woke him up "all of a heap," as he afterwards said. The name was "Quest." Without moving his body he opened his eyes. At the very next table to his own were seated two people, a man and a woman. He looked at the latter first. She was clad in yellow, and was very tall, thin and fierce-looking; so fierce-looking that George involuntarily jerked his head back, and brought it with painful force in contact with the wall. It was the Tiger herself, and her companion was the coarse, dreadful-looking man called Johnnie, whom she had sent away in the cab on the night of Mr. Quest's visit.

"Oh," Johnnie was saying, "so Quest is his name, is it, and he lives in a city called Boisingham, does he? Is he an off bird?" (rich)

"Rather," answered the Tiger, "if only one can make the dollars run, but he's a nasty mean boy, he is. Look here, not a cent, not a stiver have I got to bless myself with, and I daren't ask him for any more not till January. And how am I going to live till January? I got the sack from the music hall last week because I was a bit jolly. And now I can't get another billet any way, and there's a bill of sale over the furniture, and I've sold all my jewels down to my ticker, or at least most of them, and there's that brute," and her voice rose to a subdued scream, "living like a fighting-cock while his poor wife is left to starve."

"'Wife!' Oh, yes, we know all about that," said the gentleman called Johnnie.

A look of doubt and cunning passed across the woman's face. Evidently she feared that she had said too much. "Well, it's a good a name as another," she said. "Oh, don't I wish that I could get a grip of him; I'd wring him," and she twisted her long bony hands as washerwomen do when they squeeze a cloth.

"I'd back you to," said Johnnie. "And now, adored Edithia, I've had enough of this blooming show, and I'm off. Perhaps I shall look in down Rupert Street way this evening. Ta-ta."

"Well, you may as well stand a drink first," said the adored one. "I'm pretty dry, I can tell you."

"Certainly, with pleasure; I will order one. Waiter, a brandy-and-soda for this lady—*six* of brandy, if you please; she's very delicate and wants support."

The waiter grinned and brought the drink and the man

Johnnie turned round as though to pay him, but really he went without doing so.

George watched him go, and then looked again at the lady, whose appearance seemed to fascinate him.

"Well, if that ain't a master one," he said to himself, "and she called herself his wife, she did, and then drew up like a slug's horns. Hang me if I don't stick to her till I find out a bit more of the tale."

Thus ruminated George, who, be it observed, was no fool, and who had a hearty dislike and mistrust of Mr. Quest. While he was wondering how he was to go to work an unexpected opportunity occurred. The lady had finished her brandy-and-soda, and was preparing to leave, when the waiter swooped down upon her.

"Money please, miss," he said.

"Money!" she said, "why you're paid."

"Come, none of that," said the waiter. "I want a shilling for the brandy-and-soda."

"A shilling, do you? Then you'll have to want, you cheating white- faced rascal you; my friend paid you before he went away."

"Oh, we've had too much of that game," said the waiter, beckoning to a constable, to whom, in spite of the "fair Edithia's" very vigorous and pointed protestations, he went on to give her in charge, for it appeared that she had only twopence about her. This was George's opportunity, and he interfered.

"I think, marm," he said, "that the fat gent with you was a-playing of a little game. He only pretinded to pay the waiter."

"Playing a game, was he?" gasped the infuriated Tiger. "If I don't play a little game on him when I get a chance my name is not Edith d'Aubigne, the nasty mean beast—the—"

"Permit me, marm," said George, putting a shilling on the table, which the waiter took and went away. "I can't bear to see a real lady like you in difficulty."

"Well, you are a gentleman, you are," she said.

"Not at all, marm. That's my way. And now, marm, won't you have another?"

No objection was raised by the lady, who had another, with the result that she became if not exactly tipsy at any rate not far off it.

Shortly after this the building was cleared, and George found himself standing in Exhibition Road with the woman on his arm.

"You're going to give me a lift home, ain't you?" she said.

"Yes, marm, for sure I am," said George, sighing as he thought of the cab fare.

Accordingly they got into a hansom, and Mrs. d'Aubigne having given the address in Pimlico, of which George instantly made a mental note, they started.

"Come in and have a drink," she said when they arrived, and accordingly he paid the cab—half-a-crown it cost him—and was ushered by the woman with a simper into the gilded drawing-room.

Here the Tiger had another brandy-and-soda, after which George thought that she was about in a fit state for him to prosecute his inquiries.

"Wonderful place this Lunnon, marm; I niver was up here afore and had no idea that I should find folks so friendly. As I was a saying to my friend Laryer Quest down at Boisingham yesterday—"

"Hullo, what's that?" she said. "Do you know the old man?"

"If you means Laryer Quest, why in course I do, and Mrs. Quest too. Ah! she's a pretty one, she is."

Here the lady burst into a flood of incoherent abuse which tired her so much that she had a fourth brandy-and-soda; George mixed it for her and he mixed it strong.

"Is he rich?" she asked as she put down the glass.

"What! Laryer Quest? Well I should say that he is about the warmest man in our part of the county."

"And here am I starving," burst out the horrible woman with a flood of drunken tears. "Starving without a shilling to pay for a cab or a drink while my wedded husband lives in luxury with another woman. You tell him that I won't stand it; you tell him that if he don't find a 'thou.' pretty quick I'll let him know the reason why."

"I don't quite understand, marm," said George; "there's a lady down in Boisingham as is the real Mrs. Quest."

"It's a lie!" she shrieked, "it's a lie! He married me before he married her. I could have him in the dock to-morrow, and I would, too, if I wasn't afraid of him, and that's a fact."

"Come, marm, come," said George, "draw it mild from that tap."

"You won't believe me, won't you?" said the woman, on whom the liquor was now beginning to take its full effect; "then I'll show you," and she staggered to a desk, unlocked it and took from it a folded paper, which she opened.

It was a properly certified copy of a marriage certificate, or purported so to be; but George, who was not too quick at his reading, had only time to note the name Quest, and the church, St. Bartholomew's, Hackney, when she snatched it away from him and locked it up again.

"There," she said, "it isn't any business of yours. What right have you to come prying into the affairs of a poor lone woman?" And she sat down upon the sofa beside him, threw her long arm round him, rested her painted face upon his shoulder and began to weep the tears of intoxication.

"Well, blow me!" said George to himself, "if this ain't a master one! I wonder what my old missus would say if she saw me in this fix. I say, marm—"

But at that moment the door opened, and in came Johnnie, who had evidently also been employing the interval in refreshing himself, for he rolled like a ship in a sea.

"Well," he said, "and who the deuce are you? Come get out of this, you Methody parson-faced clodhopper, you. Fairest Edithia, what means this?"

By this time the fairest Edithia had realised who her visitor was, and the trick whereby he had left her to pay for the brandy-and-soda recurring to her mind she sprang up and began to express her opinion of Johnnie in violent and libellous language. He replied in appropriate terms, as according to the newspaper reports people whose healths are proposed always do, and fast and furious grew the fun. At length, however, it seemed to occur to Johnnie that he, George, was in some way responsible for this state of affairs, for without word or warning he hit him on the nose. This proved too much for George's Christian forbearance.

"You would, you lubber! would you?" he said, and sprang

at him.

Now Johnnie was big and fat, but Johnnie was rather drunk, and George was tough and exceedingly strong. In almost less time that it takes to write it he grasped the abominable Johnnie by the scruff of the neck and had with a mighty jerk hauled him over the sofa so that he lay face downwards thereon. By the door quite convenient to his hand stood George's ground ash stick, a peculiarly good and well-grown one which he had cut himself in Honham wood. He seized it. "Now, boar," he said, "I'll teach you how we do the trick where I come from," and he laid on without mercy. *Whack! whack! whack!* came the ground ash on Johnnie's tight clothes. He yelled, swore and struggled in the grip of the sturdy countryman, but it was of no use, the ash came down like fate; never was a Johnnie so bastinadoed before.

"Give it the brute, give it him," shrilled the fair Edithia, bethinking her of her wrongs, and he did till he was tired.

"Now, Johnnie boar," he panted at last, "I'm thinking I've pretty nigh whacked you to dead. Perhaps you'll larn to be more careful how you handles your betters by-and-by." Then seizing his hat he ran down the stairs without seeing anybody and slipping into the street crossed over and listened.

They were at it again. Seeing her enemy prostrate the Tiger had fallen on him, with the fire-irons to judge from the noise.

Just then a policeman hurried up.

"I say, master," said George, "the folk in that there house with the red pillars do fare to be a murdering of each other."

The policeman listened to the din and then made for the house. Profiting by his absence George retreated as fast as he could, his melancholy countenance shining with sober satisfaction.

On the following morning, before he returned to Honham, George paid a visit to St. Bartholomew's Church, Hackney. Here he made certain investigations in the registers, the results of which were not unsatisfactory to him.

CHAPTER XXIX

EDWARD COSSEY MEETS WITH AN ACCIDENT

At the best of times this is not a gay world, though no doubt we ought to pretend that humanity at large is as happy as it is represented to be in, let us say, the Christmas number of an illustrated paper. How well we can imagine the thoughtful inhabitant of this country Anno Domini 7500 or thereabouts disinterring from the crumbling remains of a fireproof safe a Christmas number of the *Illustrated London News* or the *Graphic*. The archaic letters would perhaps be unintelligible to him, but he would look at the pictures with much the same interest that we regard bushmen's drawings or the primitive clay figures of Peru, and though his whole artistic seventy-sixth century soul would be revolted at the crudeness of the colouring, surely he would moralise thus: "Oh, happy race of primitive men, how I, the child of light and civilisation, envy you your long-forgotten days! Here in these rude drawings, which in themselves reveal the extraordinary capacity for pleasure possessed by the early races, who could look upon them and gather gratification from the sight, may we trace your joyous career from the cradle to the grave. Here you figure as a babe, at whose appearance everybody seems delighted, even those of your race whose inheritance will be thereby diminished—and here a merry lad you revel in the school which the youth of our age finds so wearisome. There, grown more old, you stand at the altar of a beautiful lost faith, a faith that told of hope and peace beyond the grave, and by you stands your blushing bride. No hard fate, no considerations of means, no worldly-mindedness, come to snatch you from her arms as now they daily do. With her you spend your peaceful days, and here at last we see you old but surrounded by love and tender kindness, and almost looking forward to that grave which you believed would be but the gate of glory. Oh, happy race of simple-minded men, what a commentary upon our fevered, avaricious, pleasure-seeking age is this rude scroll of primitive and infantile art!"

So will some unborn *laudator temporis acti* speak in some dim century to be, when our sorrows have faded and are not.

And yet, though we do not put a record of them in our Christmas numbers, troubles are as troubles have been and will continually be, for however apparently happy the lot of individuals, it is not altogether a cheerful world in which we have been called to live. At any rate so thought Harold Quaritch on that night of the farewell scene with Ida in the churchyard, and so he continued to think for some time to come. A man's life is always more or less a struggle; he is a swimmer upon an adverse sea, and to live at all he must keep his limbs in motion. If he grows faint-hearted or weary and no longer strives, for a little while he floats, and then at last, morally or physically, he vanishes. We struggle for our livelihoods, and for all that makes life worth living in the material sense, and not the less are we called upon to struggle with an army of spiritual woes and fears, which now we vanquish and now are vanquished by. Every man of refinement, and many women, will be able to recall periods in his or her existence when life has seemed not only valueless but hateful, when our small successes, such as they are, dwindled away and vanished in the gulf of our many failures, when our hopes and aspirations faded like a little sunset cloud, and we were surrounded by black and lonely mental night, from which even the star of Faith had passed. Such a time had come to Harold Quaritch now. His days had not, on the whole, been happy days; but he was a good and earnest man, with that touching faith in Providence which is given to some among us, and which had brought with it the reward of an even thankful spirit. And then, out of the dusk of his contentment a hope of happiness had arisen like the Angel of the Dawn, and suddenly life was aflame with the light of love, and became beautiful in his eyes. And now the hope had passed: the woman whom he deeply loved, and who loved him back again, had gone from his reach and left him desolate—gone from his reach, not into the grave, but towards the arms of another man.

Our race is called upon to face many troubles; sickness, poverty, and death, but it is doubtful if Evil holds another arrow so sharp as that which pierced him now. He was no longer young, it is true, and therefore did not feel that intense agony of disappointed passion, that sickening sense of utter loss which in such circumstances sometimes settle on the young. But if in youth we feel more sharply and with a keener sympathy of the imagination, we have at least more strength to bear, and hope does not altogether die. For we know that we shall live it down, or if we do not know it then, we *do* live it down. Very likely, indeed, there comes a time when we look back upon our sorrow and he or she who caused it with wonder, yes even with scorn and bitter laughter. But it is not so when the blow falls in later life. It may not hurt so much at the time, it may seem to have been struck with the bludgeon of Fate rather than with her keen dividing sword, but the effect is more lasting, and for the rest of our days we are numb and cold, for Time has no salve to heal us.

These things Harold realised most clearly in the heavy days which followed that churchyard separation.

He took his punishment like a brave man indeed, and went about his daily occupations with a steadfast face, but his bold behaviour did not lessen its weight. He had promised not to go away till Ida was married and he would keep the promise, but in his heart he wondered how he should bear the sight of her. What would it be to see her, to touch her hand, to hear the rustle of her dress and the music of her beloved voice, and to realise again and yet again that all these things were not for him, that they had passed from him into the ownership of another man?

On the day following that upon which Edward Cossey had been terrified into transferring the Honham mortgages to Mr. Quest the Colonel went out shooting. He had lately become the possessor of a new hammerless gun by a well-known London maker, of which he stood in considerable need. Harold had treated himself to this gun when he came into his aunt's little fortune, but it was only just completed. The weapon was a beautiful one, and at any other time it would have filled his sportsman's heart with joy. Even as it was, when he put it together and balanced it and took imaginary shots at blackbirds in the garden, for a little while he forgot his sorrows, for the woe must indeed be heavy which a new hammerless gun by such a maker cannot do something towards lightening. So on the next morning he took this gun and went to the marshes by the river—where, he was credibly informed, several wisps of snipe had been seen—to attempt to shoot some of them and put the new weapon to the test.

It was on this same morning that Edward Cossey got a letter which disturbed him not a little. It was from Belle Quest, and ran thus:

> "Dear Mr. Cossey,—Will you come over and see me this afternoon about three o'clock? I shall *expect* you, so I am sure you will not disappoint me.—B.Q."

For a long while he hesitated what to do. Belle Quest was at the present juncture the very last person whom he wished to see. His nerves were shaken and he feared a scene, but on the other hand he did not know what danger might threaten him if he refused to go. Quest had got his price, and he knew that he had nothing more to fear from him; but a jealous woman has no price, and if he did not humour her it might, he felt, be at a risk which he could not estimate. Also he was nervously anxious to give no further cause for gossip. A sudden outward and visible cessation of his intimacy with the Quests might, he thought, give rise to surmises and suspicion in a little country town like Boisingham, where all his movements were known. So, albeit with a faint heart, he determined to go.

Accordingly, at three o'clock precisely, he was shown into the drawing-room at the Oaks. Mrs. Quest was not there; indeed he waited for ten minutes before she came in. She was pale, so pale that the blue veins on her forehead showed distinctly through her ivory skin, and there was a curious intensity about her manner which frightened him. She was very quiet also, unnaturally so, indeed; but her quiet was of the ominous nature of the silence before the storm, and when she spoke her words were keen, and quick, and vivid.

She did not shake hands with him, but sat down and looked at him, slowly fanning herself with a painted ivory fan which she took up from the table.

"You sent for me, Belle, and here I am," he said, breaking the silence.

Then she spoke. "You told me the other day," she said, "that you were not engaged to be married to Ida de la Molle. It is not true. You are engaged to be married to her."

"Who said so?" he asked defiantly. "Quest, I suppose?"

"I have it on a better authority," she answered. "I have it from Miss de la Molle herself. Now, listen, Edward Cossey. When I let you go, I made a condition, and that condition was that you should *not* marry Ida de la Molle. Do you still intend to marry her?"

"You had it from Ida," he said, disregarding her question; "then you must have spoken to Ida—you must have told her everything. I suspected as much from her manner the other night. You—"

"Then it is true," she broke in coldly. "It is true, and in addition to your other failings, Edward, you are a coward and—a liar."

"What is it to you what I am or what I am not?" he answered savagely. "What business is it of yours? You have no hold over me, and no claim upon me. As it is I have suffered enough at your hands and at those of your accursed husband. I have had to pay him thirty thousand pounds, do you know that? But of course you know it. No doubt the whole thing is a plant, and you will share the spoil."

"*Ah!*" she said, drawing a long breath.

"And now look here," he went on. "Once and for all, I will not be interfered with by you. I *am* engaged to marry Ida de la Molle, and whether you wish it or no I shall marry her. And one more thing. I will not allow you to associate with Ida. Do you understand me? I will not allow it."

She had been holding the fan before her face while he spoke. Now she lowered it and looked at him. Her face was paler than ever, paler than death, if that be possible, but in her eyes there shone a light like the light of a flame.

"Why not?" she said quietly.

"Why not?" he answered savagely. "I wonder that you think it necessary to ask such a question, but as you do I will tell you why. Because Ida is the lady whom I am going to marry, and I do not choose that she should associate with a woman who is what you are."

"*Ah!*" she said again, "I understand now."

At that moment a diversion occurred. The drawing-room looked on to the garden, and at the end of the garden was a door which opened into another street.

Through this door had come Colonel Quaritch accompanied by Mr. Quest, the former with his gun under his arm. They walked up the garden and were almost at the French window when Edward Cossey saw them. "Control yourself," he said in a low voice, "here is your husband."

Mr. Quest advanced and knocked at the window, which his wife opened. When he saw Edward Cossey he hesitated a little, then nodded to him, while the Colonel came forward, and placing his gun by the wall entered the room, shook hands with Mrs. Quest, and bowed coldly to Edward Cossey.

"I met the Colonel, Belle," said Mr. Quest, "coming here with the benevolent intention of giving you some snipe, so I brought him up by the short way."

"That is very kind of you, Colonel Quaritch," said she with a sweet smile (for she had the sweetest smile imaginable).

He looked at her. There was something about her face which attracted his attention, something unusual.

"What are you looking at?" she asked.

"You," he said bluntly, for they were out of hearing of the other two. "If I were poetically minded I should say that you looked like the Tragic Muse."

"Do I?" she answered, laughing. "Well, that is curious, because I feel like Comedy herself."

"There's something wrong with that woman," thought the Colonel to himself as he extracted two couple of snipe from his capacious coat tails. "I wonder what it is."

Just then Mr. Quest and Edward Cossey passed out into the garden talking.

"Here are the snipe, Mrs. Quest," he said. "I have had rather good luck. I killed four couple and missed two couple more; but then I had a new gun, and one can never shoot so well with a new gun."

"Oh, thank you," she said, "do pull out the 'painters' for me. I like to put them in my riding hat, and I can never find them myself."

"Very well," he answered, "but I must go into the garden to do it; there is not light enough here. It gets dark so soon now."

Accordingly he stepped out through the window, and began to hunt for the pretty little feathers which are to be found at the angle of a snipe's wing.

"Is that the new gun, Colonel Quaritch?" said Mrs. Quest presently; "what a beautiful one!"

"Be careful," he said, "I haven't taken the cartridges out."

If he had been looking at her, which at that moment he was not, Harold would have seen her stagger and catch at the wall for support. Then he would have seen an awful and malevolent light of sudden determination pass across her face.

"All right," she said, "I know about guns. My father used to shoot and I often cleaned his gun," and she took the weapon up and began to examine the engraving on the locks.

"What is this?" she said, pointing to a little slide above the locks on which the word "safe" was engraved in gold letters.

"Oh, that's the safety bolt," he said. "When you see the word 'safe,' the locks are barred and the gun won't go off. You have to push the bolt forward before you can fire."

"So?" she said carelessly, and suiting the action to the word.

"Yes, so, but please be careful, the gun is loaded."

"Yes, I'll be careful," she answered. "Well, it is a very pretty gun, and so light that I believe I could shoot with it myself."

Meanwhile Edward Cossey and Mr. Quest, who were walking up the garden, had separated, Mr. Quest going to the right across the lawn to pick up a glove which had dropped upon the grass, while Edward Cossey slowly sauntered towards them. When he was about nine paces off he too halted and, stooping a little, looked abstractedly at a white Japanese chrysanthemum which was still in bloom. Mrs. Quest turned, as the Colonel thought, to put the gun back against the wall. He would have offered to take it from her but at the moment both his hands were occupied in extracting one of the "painters" from a snipe. The next thing he was aware of was a loud explosion, followed by an exclamation or rather a cry from Mrs. Quest. He dropped the snipe and looked up, just in time to see the gun, which had leapt from her hands with the recoil, strike against the wall of the house and fall to the ground. Instantly, whether by instinct or by chance he never knew, he glanced towards the place where Edward Cossey stood, and saw that his face was streaming with blood and that his right arm hung helpless by his side. Even as he looked, he saw him put his uninjured hand to his head, and, without a word or a sound, sink down on the gravel path.

For a second there was silence, and the blue smoke from the gun hung heavily upon the damp autumn air. In the midst of it stood Belle Quest like one transfixed, her lips apart, her blue eyes opened wide, and the stamp of terror—or was it guilt?—upon her pallid face.

All this he saw in a flash, and then ran to the bleeding heap upon the gravel.

He reached it almost simultaneously with Mr. Quest, and together they turned the body over. But still Belle stood there enveloped in the heavy smoke.

Presently, however, her trance left her and she ran up, flung herself upon her knees, and looked at her former lover, whose face and head were now a mass of blood.

"He is dead," she wailed; "he is dead, and I have killed him! Oh, Edward! Edward!"

Mr. Quest turned on her savagely; so savagely that one might almost have thought he feared lest in her agony she should say something further.

"Stop that," he said, seizing her arm, "and go for the doctor, for if he is not dead he will soon bleed to death."

With an effort she rose, put her hand to her forehead, and then ran like the wind down the garden and through the little door.

CHAPTER XXX

HAROLD TAKES THE NEWS

Mr. Quest and Harold bore the bleeding man—whether he was senseless or dead they knew not—into the house and laid him on the sofa. Then, having despatched a servant to seek a second doctor in case the one already gone for was out, they set to work to cut the clothes from his neck and arm, and do what they could, and that was little enough, towards staunching the bleeding. It soon, however, became evident that Cossey had only got the outside portion of the charge of No. 7 that is to say, he had been struck by about a hundred pellets of the three or four hundred which would go to the ordinary ounce and an eighth. Had he received the whole charge he must, at that distance, have been instantly killed. As it was, the point of the shoulder was riddled, and so to a somewhat smaller extent was the back of his neck and the region of the right ear. One or two outside pellets had also struck the head higher up, and the skin and muscles along the back were torn by the passage of shot.

"By Jove!" said Mr. Quest, "I think he is done for."

The Colonel nodded. He had some experience of shot wounds, and the present was not of a nature to encourage hope of the patient's survival.

"How did it happen?" asked Mr. Quest presently, as he mopped up the streaming blood with a sponge.

"It was an accident," groaned the Colonel. "Your wife was looking at my new gun. I told her it was loaded, and that she must be careful, and I thought she had put it down. The next thing that I heard was the report. It is all my cursed fault for leaving the cartridges in."

"Ah," said Mr. Quest. "She always thought she understood guns. It is a shocking accident."

Just then one of the doctors, followed by Belle Quest, ran up the lawn carrying a box of instruments, and in another minute was at work. He was a quick and skilful surgeon, and having announced that the patient was not dead, at once began to tie one of the smaller arteries in the throat, which had been pierced, and through which Edward Cossey was rapidly bleeding to death. By the time that this was done the other doctor, an older man, put in an appearance, and together they made a rapid examination of the injuries.

Belle stood by holding a basin of water. She did not speak, and on her face was that same fixed look of horror which Harold had observed after the discharge of the gun.

When the examination was finished the two doctors whispered together for a few seconds.

"Will he live?" asked Mr. Quest.

"We cannot say," answered the older doctor. "We do not think it likely that he will. It depends upon the extent of his injuries, and whether or no they have extended to the spine. If he does live he will probably be paralysed to some extent, and must certainly lose the hearing of the right ear."

When she heard this Belle sank down upon a chair overwhelmed. Then the two doctors, assisted by Harold, set to work to carry Edward Cossey into another room which had been rapidly prepared, leaving Mr. Quest alone with his wife.

He came, stood in front of her, looked her in the face, and then laughed.

"Upon my word," he said, "we men are bad enough, but you women beat us in wickedness."

"What do you mean?" she said faintly.

"I mean that you are a murderess, Belle," he said solemnly. "And you are a bungler, too. You could not hold the gun straight."

"I deny it," she said, "the gun went off—"

"Yes," he said, "you are wise to make no admissions; they might be used in evidence against you. Let me counsel you to make no admissions. But now look here. I suppose the man will have to lie in this house until he recovers or dies, and that you will help to nurse him. Well, I will have none of your murderous work going on here. Do you hear me? You are not to complete at leisure what you have begun in haste."

"What do you take me for?" she asked, with some return of spirit; "do you think that I would injure a wounded man?"

"I do not know," he answered, with a shrug, "and as for what I take you for, I take you for a woman whose passion has made her mad," and he turned and left the room.

When they had carried Edward Cossey, dead or alive—and he looked more like death than life—up to the room prepared for him, seeing that he could be of no further use the Colonel left the house with a view of going to the Castle.

On his way out he looked into the drawing-room and there was Mrs. Quest, still sitting on the chair and gazing blankly before her. Pitying her he entered. "Come, cheer up, Mrs. Quest," he said kindly, "they hope that he will live."

She made no answer.

"It is an awful accident, but I am almost as culpable as you, for I left the cartridges in the gun. Anyhow, God's will be done."

"God's will!" she said, looking up, and then once more relapsed into silence.

He turned to go, when suddenly she rose and caught him by the arm.

"Will he die?" she said almost fiercely. "Tell me what you think—not what the doctors say; you have seen many wounded men and know better than they do. Tell me the truth."

"I cannot say," he answered, shaking his head.

Apparently she interpreted his answer in the affirmative. At any rate she covered her face with her hands.

"What would you do, Colonel Quaritch, if you had killed the only thing you loved in the whole world?" she asked dreamily. "Oh, what am I saying?—I am off my head. Leave me—go and tell Ida; it will be good news for Ida."

Accordingly he started for the Castle, having first picked up his gun on the spot where it had fallen from the hands of Mrs. Quest.

And then it was that for the first time the extraordinary importance of this dreadful accident in its bearing upon his own affairs flashed upon his mind. If Cossey died he could not marry Ida, that was clear. This was what Mrs. Quest must have meant when she said that it would be good news for Ida. But how did she know anything about Ida's engagement to Edward Cossey? And, by Jove! what did the woman mean when she asked what he would do if he had killed the only thing he loved in the world? Cossey must be the "only thing she loved," and now he thought of it, when she believed that he was dead she called him "Edward, Edward."

Harold Quaritch was as simple and unsuspicious a man as it would be easy to find, but he was no fool. He had moved about the world and on various occasions come in contact with cases of this sort, as most other men have done. He knew that when a woman, in a moment of distress, calls a man by his Christian name it is because she is in the habit of thinking of him and speaking to him by that name. Not that there was much in that by itself, but in public she called him "Mr. Cossey." "Edward" clearly then was the "only thing she loved," and Edward was secretly engaged to Ida, and Mrs. Quest knew it.

Now when a man who is not her husband has the fortune, or rather the misfortune, to be the only thing a married woman ever loved, and when that married woman is aware of the fact of his devotion and engagement to somebody else, it is obvious, he reflected, that in nine cases out of ten the knowledge will excite strong feelings in her breast, feelings indeed which in some natures would amount almost to madness.

When he had first seen Mrs. Quest that afternoon she and Cossey were alone together, and he had noticed something unusual about her, something unnatural and intense. Indeed, he remembered he had told her that she looked like the Tragic Muse. Could it be that the look was the look of a woman maddened by insult and jealousy, who was meditating some fearful crime? *How did that gun go off?* He did not see it, and he thanked heaven that he did not, for we are not always so anxious to bring our fellow creatures to justice as we might be, especially when they happen to be young and lovely women. How did it go off? She understood guns; he could see that from the way she handled it. Was it likely that it exploded of itself, or owing to an accidental touch of the trigger? It was possible, but not likely. Still, such things have been known to happen, and it would be very difficult to prove that it had not happened in this case. If it should be attempted murder it was very cleverly managed, because nobody could prove that it was not accidental. But could it be that this soft, beautiful, baby-faced woman had on the spur of the moment taken advantage of his loaded gun to wreak her jealousy and her wrongs upon her faithless lover? Well, the face is no mirror of the quality of the soul within, and it was possible. Further than that it did not seem to him to be his business to inquire.

By this time he had reached the Castle. The Squire had gone out but Ida was in, and he was shown into the drawing-room while the servant went to seek her. Presently he heard her dress rustle upon the stairs, and the sound of it sent the blood to his heart, for where is the music that is more sweet than the rustling of the dress of the woman whom we love?

"Why, what is the matter?" she said, noticing the disturbed expression on his face.

"Well," he said, "there has been an accident—a very bad accident."

"Who?" she said. "Not my father?"

"No, no; Mr. Cossey."

"Oh," she said, with a sigh of relief. "Why did you frighten me so?"

The Colonel smiled grimly at this unconscious exhibition of the relative state of her affections.

"What has happened to him?" asked Ida, this time with a suitable expression of concern.

"He has been accidentally shot."

"Who by?"

"Mrs. Quest."

"Then she did it on purpose—I mean—is he dead?"

"No, but I believe that he will die."

They looked at one another, and each read in the eyes of the other the thought which passed through their brains. If Edward Cossey died they would be free to marry. So clearly did they read it that Ida actually interpreted it in words.

"You must not think that," she said, "it is very wrong."

"It is wrong," answered the Colonel, apparently in no way surprised at her interpretation of his thoughts, "but unfortunately human nature is human nature."

Then he went on to tell her all about it. Ida made no comment, that is after those first words, "she did it on purpose," which burst from her in astonishment. She felt, and he felt too, that the question as to how that gun went off was one which was best left uninquired into by them. No doubt if the man died there would be an inquest, and the whole matter would be investigated. Meanwhile one thing was certain, Edward Cossey, whom she was engaged to, was shot and likely to die.

Presently, while they were still talking, the Squire came in from his walk. To him also the story was told, and to judge from the expression of his face he thought it grave enough. If Edward Cossey died the mortgages over the Honham property would, as he believed, pass to his heir, who, unless he had made a will, which was not probable, would be his father, old Mr. Cossey, the banker, from whom Mr. de la Molle well knew he had little mercy to expect. This was serious enough, and still more serious was it that all the bright prospects in which he had for some days been basking of the re-establishment of his family upon a securer basis than it had occupied for generations would vanish like a vision. He was not more worldly-minded than are other men, but he did fondly cherish a natural desire to see the family fortunes once more in the ascendant. The projected marriage between his daughter and Edward Cossey would have brought this about most fully, and however much he might in his secret heart distrust the man himself, and doubt whether the match was really acceptable to Ida, he could not view its collapse with indifference. While they were still talking the dressing-bell rang, and Harold rose to go.

"Stop and dine, won't you, Quaritch?" said the Squire.

Harold hesitated and looked at Ida. She made no movement, but her eyes said "stay," and he sighed and yielded. Dinner was rather a melancholy feast, for the Squire was preoccupied with his own thoughts, and Ida had not much to say. So far as the Colonel was concerned, the recollection of the tragedy he had witnessed that afternoon, and of all the dreadful details with which it was accompanied, was not conducive to appetite.

As soon as dinner was over the Squire announced that he should walk into Boisingham to inquire how the wounded man was getting on. Shortly afterwards he started, leaving his daughter and Harold alone.

They went into the drawing-room and talked about indifferent things. No word of love passed between them; no word, even, that could bear an affectionate significance, and yet every sentence which passed their lips carried a message with it, and was as heavy with unuttered tenderness as a laden bee with honey. For they loved each other dearly, and deep love is a thing that can hardly be concealed by lovers from each other.

It was happiness for him merely to sit beside her and hear her speak, to watch the changes of her face and the lamplight playing upon her hair, and it was happiness for her to know that he was sitting there and watching. For the most beautiful aspect of true affection is its accompanying sense of perfect companionship and rest. It is a sense which nothing else in this life can give, and, like a lifting cloud, reveals the white and distant peaks of that unbroken peace which we cannot hope to win in our stormy journey through the world.

And so the evening wore away till at last they heard the Squire's loud voice talking to somebody outside. Presently he came in.

"How is he?" asked Harold. "Will he live?"

"They cannot say," was the answer. "But two great doctors have been telegraphed for from London, and will be down to-morrow."

CHAPTER XXXI

IDA RECANTS

The two great doctors came, and the two great doctors pocketed their hundred guinea fees and went, but neither the one nor the other, nor eke the twain, would commit themselves to a fixed opinion as to Edward Cossey's chances of life or death. However, one of them picked out a number of shot from the wounded man, and a number more he left in because he could not pick them out. Then they both agreed that the treatment of their local brethren was all that could be desired, and so far as they were concerned there was an end of it.

A week had passed, and Edward Cossey, nursed night and day by Belle Quest, still hovered between life and death.

It was a Thursday, and Harold had walked up to the Castle to give the Squire the latest news of the wounded man. Whilst he was in the vestibule saying what he had to say to Mr. de la Molle and Ida, a man rung the bell, whom he recognised as one of Mr. Quest's clerks. He was shown in, and handed the Squire a fully-addressed brief envelope, which, he said, he had been told to deliver by Mr. Quest, and adding that there was no answer bowed himself out.

As soon as he had gone the envelope was opened by Mr. de la Molle, who took from it two legal-looking documents which he began to read. Suddenly the first dropped from his hand, and with an exclamation he snatched at the second.

"What is it, father?" asked Ida.

"What is it? Why it's just this. Edward Cossey has transferred the mortgages over this property to Quest, the lawyer, and Quest has served a notice on me calling in the money," and he began to walk up and down the room in a state of great agitation.

"I don't quite understand," said Ida, her breast heaving, and a curious light shining in her eyes.

"Don't you?" said her father, "then perhaps you will read that," and he pushed the papers to her. As he did so another letter which he had not observed fell out of them.

At this point Harold rose to go.

"Don't go, Quaritch, don't go," said the Squire. "I shall be glad of your advice, and I am sure that what you hear will not go any further."

At the same time Ida motioned him to stay, and though somewhat unwillingly he did so.

> "Dear Sir," began the Squire, reading the letter aloud,—
>
> "Inclosed you will find the usual formal notices calling in the sum of thirty thousand pounds recently advanced upon the mortgage of the Honham Castle Estates by Edward Cossey, Esq. These mortgages have passed into my possession for value received, and it is now my desire to realise them. I most deeply regret being forced to press an old client, but my circumstances are such that I am obliged to do so. If I can in any way facilitate your efforts to raise the sum I shall be very glad. But in the event of the money not being forthcoming at the end of six months' notice the ordinary steps will be taken to realise by foreclosure.
>
> "I am, dear sir, yours truly,

"W. Quest.

"James de la Molle, Esq., J.P., D.L."

"I see now," said Ida. "Mr. Cossey has no further hold on the mortgages or on the property."

"That's it," said the Squire; "he has transferred them to that rascally lawyer. And yet he told me—I can't understand it, I really can't."

At this point the Colonel insisted upon leaving, saying he would call in again that evening to see if he could be of any assistance. When he was gone Ida spoke in a cold, determined voice:

"Mr. Cossey told me that when we married he would put those mortgages in the fire. It now seems that the mortgages were not his to dispose of, or else that he has since transferred them to Mr. Quest without informing us."

"Yes, I suppose so," said the Squire.

"Very well," said Ida. "And now, father, I will tell you something. I engaged myself—or, to be more accurate, I promised to engage myself—to Edward Cossey on the condition that he would take up these mortgages when Cossey and Son were threatening to foreclose, or whatever it is called."

"Good heavens!" said her astonished father, "what an idea!"

"I did it," went on Ida, "and he took up the mortgages, and in due course he claimed my promise, and I became engaged to marry him, though that engagement was repugnant to me. You will see that having persuaded him to advance the money I could not refuse to carry out my share of the bargain."

"Well," said the Squire, "this is all new to me."

"Yes," she answered, "and I should never have told you of it had it not been for this sudden change in the position of affairs. What I did, I did to save our family from ruin. But now it seems that Mr. Cossey has played us false, and that we are to be ruined after all. Therefore, the condition upon which I promised to marry him has not been carried out, and my promise falls to the ground."

"You mean that supposing he lives, you will not marry Edward Cossey."

"Yes, I do mean it."

The Squire thought for a minute. "This is a very serious step, Ida," he said. "I don't mean that I think that the man has behaved well—but still he may have given up the mortgages to Quest under pressure of some sort and might be willing to find the money to meet them."

"I do not care if he finds the money ten times over," said Ida, "I will not marry him. He has not kept to the letter of his bond and I will not keep to mine."

"It is all very well, Ida," said the Squire, "and of course nobody can force you into a distasteful marriage, but I wish to point out one thing. You have your family to think of as well as yourself. I tell you frankly that I do not believe that as times are it will be possible to raise thirty thousand pounds to pay off the charges unless it is by the help of Edward Cossey. So if he lives—and as he has lasted so long I expect that he will live—and you refuse to go on with your engagement to him we shall be sold up, that is all; for this man Quest, confound him, will show us no mercy."

"I know it, father," answered Ida, "but I cannot and will not marry him, and I do not think you can expect me to do so. I became engaged, or rather promised to become engaged to him, because I thought that one woman had no right to put her own happiness before the welfare of an old family like ours, and I would have carried out that engagement at any cost. But since then, to tell you the truth," and she blushed deeply, "not only have I learned to dislike him a great deal more, but I have come to care for some one else who also cares for me, and who therefore has a right to be considered. Think, father, what it means to a woman to sell herself into bodily and mental bondage—when she cares for another man."

"Well, well," said her father with some irritation, "I am no authority upon matters of sentiment; they are not in my line and I know that women have their prejudices. Still you can't expect me to look at the matter in quite the same light as you do. And who is the gentleman? Colonel Quaritch?"

She nodded her head.

"Oh," said the Squire, "I have nothing to say against Quaritch, indeed I like the man, but I suppose that if he has 600 pounds a year, it is every sixpence he can count on."

"I had rather marry him upon six hundred a year than Edward Cossey upon sixty thousand."

"Ah, yes, I have heard young women talk like that before, though perhaps they think differently afterwards. Of course I have no right to obtrude myself, but when you are comfortably married, what is going to become of Honham I should like to know, and incidentally of me?"

"I don't know, father, dear," she answered, her eyes filling with tears; "we must trust to Providence, I suppose. I know you think me very selfish," she went on, catching him by the arm, "but, oh, father! there are things that are worse than death to women, or, at least, to some women. I almost think that I would rather die than marry Edward Cossey, though I should have gone through with it if he had kept his word."

"No, no," said her father. "I can't wonder at it, and certainly I do not ask you to marry a man whom you dislike. But still it is hard upon me to have all this trouble at my age, and the old place coming to the hammer too. It is enough to make a man wish that his worries were over altogether. However, we must take things as we find them, and we find them pretty rough. Quaritch said he was coming back this evening, didn't he? I suppose there will not be any public engagement at present, will there? And look here, Ida, I don't want him to come talking to me about it. I have got enough things of my own to think of without bothering my head with your love affairs. Pray let the matter be for the present. And now I am going out to see that fellow George, who hasn't been here since he came back from London, and a nice bit of news it will be that I shall have to tell him."

When her father had gone Ida did a thing she had not done for some time—she wept a little. All her fine intentions of self-denial had broken down, and she felt humiliated at the fact. She had intended to sacrifice herself upon the altar of her duty and to make herself the wedded wife of a man whom she disliked, and now on the first opportunity she had thrown up the contract on a quibble—a point of law as it were. Nature had been too strong for her, as it often is for people with deep feelings; she could not do it, no, not to save Honham from the hammer. When she had promised that she would engage herself to Edward Cossey she had not been in love with Colonel Quaritch; now she was, and the difference between the two states is considerable. Still the fall humiliated her pride, and what is more she felt that her father was disappointed in her. Of course she could not expect him at his age to enter into her private feelings, for when looked at through the mist of years sentiment appears more or less foolish. She knew very well that age often strips men of those finer sympathies and sensibilities which clothe them in youth, much as the winter frost and wind strip the delicate foliage from the trees. And to such the music of the world is dead. Love has vanished with the summer dews, and in its place are cutting blasts and snows and sere memories rustling like fallen leaves about the feet. As we grow old we are too apt to grow away from beauty and what is high and pure, our hearts harden by contact with the hard world. We examine love and find, or believe we find, that it is nought but a variety of passion; friendship, and think it self-interest; religion, and name it superstition. The facts of life alone remain clear and desirable. We know that money means power, and we turn our face to Mammon, and if he smiles upon us we are content to let our finer visions go where our youth has gone.

"Trailing clouds of glory do we come
From God, who is our home."

So says the poet, but alas! the clouds soon melt into the grey air of the world, and some of us, before our course is finished, forget that they ever were. And yet which is the shadow of the truth—those dreams, and hopes, and aspirations of our younger life, or the corruption with which the world cakes our souls?

Ida knew that she could not expect her father to sympathise with her; she knew that to his judgment, circumstances being the same, and both suitors being equally sound in wind and limb, the choice of one of them should, to a large extent, be a matter to be decided by the exterior considerations of wealth and general convenience.

However, she had made her choice, made it suddenly, but none the less had made it. It lay between her father's interest and the interest of the family at large and her own honour as a woman—for the mere empty ceremony of marriage which satisfies society cannot make dishonour an honourable thing. She had made her choice, and the readers of her history must judge if that choice was right or wrong.

After dinner Harold came again as he had promised. The Squire was not in the drawing-room when he was shown in.

Ida rose to greet him with a sweet and happy smile upon her face, for in the presence of her lover all her doubts and troubles vanished like a mist.

"I have a piece of news for you," said he, trying to look as though he was rejoiced to give it. "Edward Cossey has taken a wonderful turn for the better. They say that he will certainly recover."

"Oh," she answered, colouring a little, "and now I have a piece of news for you, Colonel Quaritch. My engagement with Mr. Edward Cossey is at an end. I shall not marry him."

"Are you sure?" said Harold with a gasp.

"Quite sure. I have made up my mind," and she held out her hand, as though to seal her words.

He took it and kissed it. "Thank heaven, Ida," he said.

"Yes," she answered, "thank heaven;" and at that moment the Squire came in, looking very miserable and depressed, and of course nothing more was said about the matter.

CHAPTER XXXII

GEORGE PROPHESIES AGAIN

Six weeks passed, and in that time several things happened. In the first place the miserly old banker, Edward Cossey's father, had died, his death being accelerated by the shock of his son's accident. On his will being opened, it was found that property and money to no less a value than 600,000 pounds passed under it to Edward absolutely, the only condition attached being that he should continue in the house of Cossey and Son and leave a certain share of his fortune in the business.

Edward Cossey also, thanks chiefly to Belle's tender nursing, had almost recovered, with one exception—he was, and would be for life, stone deaf in the right ear. The paralysis which the doctors feared had not shown itself. One of his first questions when he became convalescent was addressed to Belle Quest.

As in a dream, he had always seen her sweet face hanging over him, and dimly known that she was ministering to him.

"Have you nursed me ever since the accident, Belle?" he said.

"Yes," she answered.

"It is very good of you, considering all things," he murmured. "I wonder that you did not let me die."

But she turned her face to the wall and never said a word, nor did any further conversation on these matters pass between them.

Then as his strength came back so did his passion for Ida de la Molle revive. He was not allowed to write or even receive letters, and with this explanation of her silence he was fain to content himself. But the Squire, he was told, often called to inquire after him, and once or twice Ida came with him.

At length a time came—it was two days after he had been told of his father's death—when he was pronounced fit to be moved into his own rooms and to receive his correspondence as usual.

The move was effected without any difficulty, and here Belle bade him good-bye. Even as she did so George drove his fat pony up to the door, and getting down gave a letter to the landlady, with particular instructions that it was to be delivered into Mr. Cossey's own hands. As she passed Belle saw that it was addressed in the Squire's handwriting.

When it was delivered to him Edward Cossey opened it with eagerness. It contained an inclosure in Ida's writing, and this he read first. It ran as follows:

> "Dear Mr. Cossey,—
>
> "I am told that you are now able to read letters, so I hasten to write to you. First of all, let me say how thankful I am that you are in a fair way to complete recovery from your dreadful accident. And now I must tell you what I fear will be almost as painful to you to read as it is for me to write, namely, that the engagement between us is at an end. To put the matter frankly, you will remember that I rightly or wrongly became engaged to you on a certain condition. That condition has not been fulfilled, for Mr. Quest, to whom the mortgages on my father's property have been transferred by you, is pressing for their payment. Consequently the obligation on my part is at an end, and with it

the engagement must end also, for I grieve to tell you that it is not one which my personal inclination will induce me to carry out. Wishing you a speedy and complete recovery, and every happiness and prosperity in your future life, believe me, dear Mr. Cossey,

"Very truly yours,
"Ida de la Molle."

He put down this uncompromising and crushing epistle and nervously glanced at the Squire's, which was very short.

"My dear Cossey," it began,—

"Ida has shown me the inclosed letter. I think that you did unwisely when you entered into what must be called a money bargain for my daughter's hand. Whether under all the circumstances she does either well or wisely to repudiate the engagement after it has once been agreed upon, is not for me to judge. She is a free agent and has a natural right to dispose of her life as she thinks fit. This being so I have of course no option but to endorse her decision, so far as I have anything to do with the matter. It is a decision which I for some reasons regret, but which I am quite powerless to alter.

"Believe me, with kind regards,
"Truly yours,
"James de la Molle."

Edward Cossey turned his face to the wall and indulged in such meditations as the occasion gave rise to, and they were bitter enough. He was as bent upon this marriage as he had ever been, more so in fact, now that his father was out of the way. He knew that Ida disliked him, he had known that all along, but he had trusted to time and marriage to overcome the dislike. And now that accursed Quest had brought about the ruin of his hopes. Ida had seen her chance of escape, and, like a bold woman, had seized upon it. There was one ray of hope, and one only. He knew that the money would not be forthcoming to pay off the mortgages. He could see too from the tone of the Squire's letter that he did not altogether approve of his daughter's decision. And his father was dead. Like Caesar, he was the master of many legions, or rather of much money, which is as good as legions. Money can make most paths smooth to the feet of the traveller, and why not this? After much thought he came to a conclusion. He would not trust his chance to paper, he would plead his cause in person. So he wrote a short note to the Squire acknowledging Ida's and his letter, and saying that he hoped to come and see them as soon as ever the doctor would allow him out of doors.

Meanwhile George, having delivered his letter, had gone upon another errand. Pulling up the fat pony in front of Mr. Quest's office he alighted and entered. Mr. Quest was disengaged, and he was shown straight into the inner office, where the lawyer sat, looking more refined and gentlemanlike than ever.

"How do you do, George?" he said cheerily; "sit down; what is it?"

"Well, sir," answered that lugubrious worthy, as he awkwardly took a seat, "the question is what isn't it? These be rum times, they be, they fare to puzzle a man, they du."

"Yes," said Mr. Quest, balancing a quill pen on his finger, "the times are bad enough."

Then came a pause.

"Dash it all, sir," went on George presently, "I may as well get it out; I hev come to speak to you about the Squire's business."

"Yes," said Mr. Quest.

"Well, sir," went on George, "I'm told that these dratted mortgages hev passed into your hands, and that you hev called in the money."

"Yes, that is correct," said Mr. Quest again.

"Well, sir, the fact is that the Squire can't git the money. It can't be had nohow. Nobody won't take the land as security. It might be so much water for all folk to look at it."

"Quite so. Land is in very bad odour as security now."

"And that being so, sir, what is to be done?"

Mr. Quest shrugged his shoulders. "I do not know. If the money is not forthcoming, of course I shall, however unwillingly, be forced to take my legal remedy."

"Meaning, sir—"

"Meaning that I shall bring an action for foreclosure and do what I can with the lands."

George's face darkened.

"And that reads, sir, that the Squire and Miss Ida will be turned out of Honham, where they and theirs hev been for centuries, and that you will turn in?"

"Well, that is what it comes to, George. I am sincerely sorry to press the Squire, but it's a matter of thirty thousand pounds, and I am not in a position to throw away thirty thousand pounds."

"Sir," said George, rising in indignation, "I don't rightly know how you came by them there mortgages. There is some things as laryers know and honest men don't know, and that's one on them. But it seems that you've got 'em and are a-going to use 'em—and that being so, Mr. Quest, I have summut to say to you—and that is that no good won't come to you from this here move."

"What do you mean by that, George?" said the lawyer sharply.

"Niver you mind what I mean, sir. I means what I says. I means that sometimes people has things in their lives snugged away where nobody can't see 'em, things as quiet as though they was dead and buried, and that ain't dead nor buried neither, things so much alive that they fare as though they were fit to kick the lid off their coffin. That's what I means, sir, and I means that when folk set to work to do a hard and wicked thing those dead things sometimes gits up and walks where they is least wanting; and mayhap if you goes on for to turn the old Squire and Miss Ida out of the Castle, mayhap, sir, summut of that sort will happen to you, for mark my word, sir, there's justice in the world, sir, as mebbe you will find out. And now, sir, begging your pardon, I'll wish you good-morning, and leave you to think on what I've said," and he was gone.

"George!" called Mr. Quest after him, rising from his chair, "George!" but George was out of hearing.

"Now what did he mean by that—what the devil did he mean?" said Mr. Quest with a gasp as he sat down again. "Surely," he thought, "that man cannot have got hold of anything about Edith. Impossible, impossible; if he had he would have said more, he would not have confined himself to hinting, that would take a cleverer man, he would have shown his hand. He must have been speaking at random to frighten me, I suppose. By heaven! what a thing it would be if he *had* got hold of something. Ruin! absolute ruin! I'll settle up this business as soon as I can and leave the country; I can't stand the strain, it's like having a sword over one's head. I've half a mind to leave it in somebody else's hands and go at once. No, for that would look like running away. It must be all rubbish; how could he know anything about it?"

So shaken was he, however, that though he tried once and yet again, he found it impossible to settle himself down to work till he had taken a couple of glasses of sherry from the decanter in the cupboard. Even as he did so he wondered if the shadow of the sword disturbed him so much, how he would be affected if it ever was his lot to face the glimmer of its naked blade.

No further letter came to Edward Cossey from the Castle, but, impatient as he was to do so, another fortnight elapsed before he was able to see Ida and her father. At last one fine December morning for the first time since his accident he was allowed to take carriage exercise, and his first drive was to Honham Castle.

When the Squire, who was sitting in the vestibule writing letters, saw a poor pallid man, rolled up in fur, with a white face scarred with shot marks and black rings round his large dark eyes, being helped from a closed carriage, he did not know who it was, and called to Ida, who was passing along the passage, to tell him.

Of course she recognised her admirer instantly, and wished to leave the room, but her father prevented her.

"You got into this mess," he said, forgetting how and for whom she got into it, "and now you must get out of it in your own way."

When Edward, having been assisted into the room, saw Ida standing there, all the blood in his wasted body seemed to rush into his pallid face.

"How do you do, Mr. Cossey?" she said. "I am glad to see you out, and hope that you are better."

"I beg your pardon, I cannot hear you," he said, turning round; "I am stone deaf in my right ear."

A pang of pity shot through her heart. Edward Cossey, feeble, dejected, and limping from the jaws of Death, was a very different being to Edward Cossey in the full glow of his youth, health, and strength. Indeed, so much did his condition appeal to her sympathies that for the first time since her mental attitude towards him had been one of entire indifference, she looked on him without repugnance.

Meanwhile her father had shaken him by the hand, and led him to an armchair before the fire.

Then after a few questions and answers as to his accident and merciful recovery there came a pause.

At length he broke it. "I have come to see you both," he said with a faint nervous smile, "about the letters you wrote me. If my condition had allowed I should have come before, but it would not."

"Yes," said the Squire attentively, while Ida folded her hands in her lap and sat still with her eyes fixed upon the fire.

"It seems," he went on, "that the old proverb has applied to my case as to so many others—being absent I have suffered. I understand from these letters that my engagement to you, Miss de la Molle, is broken off."

She made a motion of assent.

"And that it is broken off on the ground that having been forced by a combination of circumstances which I cannot enter into to transfer the mortgages to Mr. Quest, consequently I broke my bargain with you?"

"Yes," said Ida.

"Very well then, I come to tell you both that I am ready to find the money to meet those mortgages and to pay them off in full."

"Ah!" said the Squire.

"Also that I am ready to do what I offered to do before, and which, as my father is now dead, I am perfectly in a position to do, namely, to settle two hundred thousand pounds absolutely upon Ida, and indeed generally to do anything else that she or you may wish," and he looked at the Squire.

"It is no use looking to me for an answer," said he with some irritation. "I have no voice in the matter."

He turned to Ida, who put her hand before her face and shook her head.

"Perhaps," said Edward, somewhat bitterly, "I should not be far wrong if I said that Colonel Quaritch has more to do with your change of mind than the fact of the transfer of these mortgages."

She dropped her hand and looked him full in the face.

"You are quite right, Mr. Cossey," she said boldly. "Colonel Quaritch and I are attached to each other, and we hope one day to be married."

"Confound that Quaritch," growled the Squire beneath his breath.

Edward winced visibly at this outspoken statement.

"Ida," he said, "I make one last appeal to you. I am devoted to you with all my heart; so devoted that though it may seem foolish to say so, especially before your father, I really think I would rather not have recovered from my accident than that I should have recovered for this. I will give you everything that a woman can want, and my money will make your family what it was centuries ago, the greatest in the country side. I don't pretend to have been a saint—perhaps you may have heard something against me in that way—or to be anything out of the common. I am only an ordinary every-day man, but I am devoted to you. Think, then, before you refuse me altogether."

"I have thought, Mr. Cossey," answered Ida almost passionately: "I have thought until I am tired of thinking, and I do not consider it fair that you should press me like this, especially before my father."

"Then," he said, rising with difficulty, "I have said all I have to say, and done all that I can do. I shall still hope that you may change your mind. I shall not yet abandon hope. Good-bye."

She touched his hand, and then the Squire offering him his arm, he went down the steps to his carriage.

"I hope, Mr. de la Molle," he said, "that bad as things look for me, if they should take a turn I shall have your support."

"My dear sir," answered the Squire, "I tell you frankly that I wish my daughter would marry you. As I said before, it would for obvious reasons be desirable. But Ida is not like ordinary women. When she sets her mind upon a thing she sets it like a flint. Times may change, however, and that is all I can say. Yes, if I were you, I should remember that this is a changeable world, and women are the most changeable things in it."

When the carriage was gone he re-entered the vestibule. Ida, who was going away much disturbed in mind, saw him come, and knew from the expression of his face that there would be trouble. With characteristic courage she turned, determined to brave it out.

CHAPTER XXXIII

THE SQUIRE SPEAKS HIS MIND

For a minute or more her father fidgeted about, moving his papers backwards and forwards but saying nothing.

At last he spoke. "You have taken a most serious and painful step, Ida," he said. "Of course you have a right to do as you please, you are of full age, and I cannot expect that you will consider me or your family in your matrimonial engagements, but at the same time I think it is my duty to point out to you what it is that you are doing. You are refusing one of the finest matches in England in order to marry a broken-down, middle-aged, half-pay colonel, a man who can hardly support you, whose part in life is played, or who is apparently too idle to seek another."

Here Ida's eyes flashed ominously, but she made no comment, being apparently afraid to trust herself to speak.

"You are doing this," went on her father, working himself up as he spoke, "in the face of my wishes, and with a knowledge that your action will bring your family, to say nothing of your father, to utter and irretrievable ruin."

"Surely, father, surely," broke in Ida, almost in a cry, "you would not have me marry one man when I love another. When I made the promise I had not become attached to Colonel Quaritch."

"Love! pshaw!" said her father. "Don't talk to me in that sentimental and school-girl way—you are too old for it. I am a plain man, and I believe in family affection and in *duty*, Ida. *Love*, as you call it, is only too often another word for self-will and selfishness and other things that we are better without."

"I can understand, father," answered Ida, struggling to keep her temper under this jobation, "that my refusal to marry Mr. Cossey is disagreeable to you for obvious reasons, though it is not so very long since you detested him yourself. But I do not see why an honest woman's affection for another man should be talked of as though there was something shameful about it. It is all very well to sneer at 'love,' but, after all a woman is flesh and blood; she is not a chattel or a slave girl, and marriage is not like anything else—it means many things to a woman. There is no magic about marriage to make that which is unrighteous righteous."

"There," said her father, "it is no good your lecturing to me on marriage, Ida. If you do not want to marry Cossey, I can't force you to. If you want to ruin me, your family and yourself, you must do so. But there is one thing. While it is over me, which I suppose will not be for much longer, my house is my own, and I will not have that Colonel of yours hanging about it, and I shall write to him to say so. You are your own mistress, and if you choose to walk over to church and marry him you can do so, but it will be done without my consent, which of course, however, is an unnecessary formality. Do you hear me, Ida?"

"If you have quite done, father," she answered coldly, "I should like to go before I say something which I might be sorry for. Of course you can write what you like to Colonel Quaritch, and I shall write to him, too."

Her father made no answer beyond sitting down at his table and grabbing viciously at a pen. So she left the room, indignant, indeed, but with as heavy a heart as any woman could carry in her breast.

"Dear Sir," wrote the not unnaturally indignant Squire, "I have been informed by my daughter Ida of her entanglement with you. It is one which, for reasons that I need not enter into, is distasteful to me, as well as, I am sorry to say, ruinous to Ida herself and to her family. Ida is of full age, and must, of course, do as she pleases with herself. But I cannot consent to become a party to what I disapprove of so strongly, and this being the case, I must beg you to cease your visits to my house.

"I am, sir, your obedient servant,
"James de la Molle.

"Colonel Quaritch, V.C."

Ida as soon as she had sufficiently recovered herself also wrote to the Colonel. She told him the whole story, keeping nothing back, and ended her letter thus:

"Never, dear Harold, was a woman in a greater difficulty and never have I more needed help and advice. You know and have good reason to know how hateful this marriage would be to me, loving you as I do entirely and alone, and having no higher desire than to become your wife. But of course I see the painfulness of the position. I am not so selfish as my father believes or says that he believes. I quite understand how great would be the material advantage to my father if I could bring myself to marry Mr. Cossey. You may remember I told you once that I thought no woman has a right to prefer her own happiness to the prosperity of her whole family. But, Harold, it is easy to speak thus, and very, very hard to act up to it. What am I to do? What am I to do? And yet how can I in common fairness ask you to answer that question? God help us both, Harold! Is there *no* way out of it?"

These letters were both duly received by Harold Quaritch on the following morning and threw him into a fever of anxiety and doubt. He was a just and reasonable man, and, knowing something of human nature, under the circumstances did not altogether wonder at the Squire's violence and irritation. The financial position of the de la Molle family was little, if anything, short of desperate. He could easily understand how maddening it must be to a man like Mr. de la Molle, who loved Honham, which had for centuries been the home of his race, better than he loved anything on earth, to suddenly realise that it must pass away from him and his for ever, merely because a woman happened to prefer one man to another, and that man, to his view, the less eligible of the two. So keenly did he realise this, indeed, that he greatly doubted whether or no he was justified in continuing his advances to Ida. Finally, after much thought, he wrote to the Squire as follows:

"I have received your letter, and also one from Ida, and I hope you will believe me when I say that I quite understand and sympathise with the motives which evidently led you to write it. I am unfortunately—although I never regretted it till now—a poor man, whereas my rival suitor is a rich one. I shall, of course, strictly obey your injunctions; and, moreover, I can assure you that, whatever my own feelings may be in the matter, I shall do nothing, either directly or indirectly, to influence Ida's ultimate decision. She must decide for herself."

To Ida herself he also wrote at length:

"Dearest Ida," he ended, "I can say nothing more; you must judge for yourself; and I shall accept your decision loyally whatever it may be. It is unnecessary for me to tell you how inextricably my happiness in life is interwoven with that decision, but at the same time I do not wish to influence it. It certainly to my mind does not seem right that a woman should be driven into sacrificing her whole life to secure any monetary advantage either for herself or for others, but then the world is full of things that are not right. I can give you no advice, for I do not know what advice I ought to give. I try to put myself out of the question and to consider you, and you only; but even then I fear that my judgment is not impartial. At any rate, the less we see of each other at present the better, for I do not wish to appear to be taking any undue advantage. If we are destined to pass our lives together, this temporary estrangement will not matter, and if on the other hand we are doomed to a life-long separation the sooner we begin the better. It is a hard world, and sometimes (as it does now) my heart sinks within me as from year to year I struggle on towards a happiness that ever vanishes when I stretch out my hand to clasp it; but, if I feel thus, what must you feel who have so much more to bear? My dearest love, what can I say? I can only say with you, God help us!"

This letter did not tend to raise Ida's spirits. Evidently her lover saw that there was another side to the question—the side of duty, and was too honest to hide it from her. She had said that she would have nothing to do with Edward Cossey, but she was well aware that the matter was still an open one. What should she do, what ought she to do? Abandon her love, desecrate herself and save her father and her house, or cling to her love and leave the rest to chance? It was a cruel position, nor did the lapse of time tend to make it less cruel. Her father went about the place pale and melancholy—all his jovial manner had vanished beneath the pressure of impending ruin. He treated her with studious and old-fashioned courtesy, but she could see that he was bitterly aggrieved by her conduct and that the anxiety of his position was telling on his health. If this was the case now, what, she wondered, would happen in the Spring, when steps were actually taken to sell the place?

One bright cold morning she was walking with her father through the fields down on the foot-path that led to the church, and it would have been hard to say which of the two looked the paler or the more miserable. On the previous day the Squire had seen Mr. Quest and made as much of an appeal *ad misericordiam* to him as his pride would allow, only to find the lawyer very courteous, very regretful, but hard as adamant. Also that very morning a letter had reached him from London announcing that the last hope of raising money to meet the mortgages had failed.

The path ran along towards the road past a line of oaks.

Half-way down this line they came across George, who, with his marking instrument in his hand, was contemplating some of the trees which it was proposed to take down.

"What are you doing there?" said the Squire, in a melancholy voice.

"Marking, Squire."

"Then you may as well save yourself the trouble, for the place will belong to somebody else before the sap is up in those oaks."

"Now, Squire, don't you begin to talk like that, for I don't believe it. That ain't a-going to happen."

"Ain't a-going to happen, you stupid fellow, ain't a-going to happen," answered the Squire with a dreary laugh. "Why, look there," and he pointed to a dog-cart which had drawn up on the road in such a position that they could see it without its occupants seeing them; "they are taking notes already."

George looked and so did Ida. Mr. Quest was the driver of the dog-cart, which he had pulled up in such a position as to command a view of the Castle, and his companion—in whom George recognised a well-known London auctioneer who sometimes did business in these parts—was standing up, an open notebook in his hand, alternately looking at the noble towers of the gateway and jotting down memoranda.

"Damn 'em, and so they be," said George, utterly forgetting his manners.

Ida looked up and saw her father's eyes fixed firmly upon her with an expression that seemed to say, "See, you wilful woman, see the ruin that you have brought upon us!"

She turned away; she could not bear it, and that very night she came to a determination, which in due course was communicated to Harold, and him alone. That determination was to let things be for the present, upon the chance of something happening by means of which the dilemma might be solved. But if nothing happened—and indeed it did not seem probable to her that anything would happen—then she would sacrifice herself at the last moment. She believed, indeed she knew, that she could always call Edward Cossey back to her if she liked. It was a compromise, and like all compromises had an element of weakness; but it gave time, and time to her was like breath to the dying.

"Sir," said George presently, "it's Boisingham Quarter Sessions the day after to-morrow, ain't it?" (Mr. de la Molle was chairman of Quarter Sessions.)

"Yes, of course, it is."

George thought for a minute.

"I'm a-thinking, Squire, that if I arn't wanting that day I want to go up to Lunnon about a bit of business."

"Go up to London!" said the Squire; "why what are you going to do there? You were in London the other day."

"Well, Squire," he answered, looking inexpressibly sly, "that ain't no matter of nobody's. It's a bit of private affairs."

"Oh, all right," said the Squire, his interest dying out. "You are always full of twopenny-halfpenny mysteries," and he continued his walk.

But George shook his fist in the direction of the road down which the dog-cart had driven.

"Ah! you laryer devil," he said, alluding to Mr. Quest. "If I don't make Boisingham, yes, and all England, too hot to hold you, my mother never christened me and my name ain't George. I'll give you what for, my cuckoo, that I will!"

CHAPTER XXXIV

GEORGE'S DIPLOMATIC ERRAND

George carried out his intention of going to London. On the second morning after the day when Mr. Quest had driven the auctioneer in the dog-cart to Honham, he might have been seen an hour before it was light purchasing a third class return ticket to Liverpool Street. Arriving there in safety he partook of a second breakfast, for it was ten o'clock, and then hiring a cab caused himself to be driven to the end of that street in Pimlico where he had gone with the fair "Edithia" and where Johnnie had made acquaintance with his ash stick.

Dismissing the cab he made his way to the house with the red pillars, but on arriving was considerably taken aback, for the place had every appearance of being deserted. There were no blinds to the windows, and on the steps were muddy foot-marks and bits of rag and straw which seemed to be the litter of a recent removal. Indeed, there on the road were the broad wheelmarks of the van which had carted off the furniture. He stared at this sight in dismay. The bird had apparently flown, leaving no address, and he had taken his trip for nothing.

He pressed upon the electric bell; that is, he did this ultimately. George was not accustomed to electric bells, indeed he had never seen one before, and after attempting in vain to pull it with his fingers (for he knew that it must be a bell because there was the word itself written on it), as a last resource he condescended to try his teeth. Ultimately, however, he discovered how to use it, but without result. Either the battery had been taken away, or it was out of gear. Just as he was wondering what to do next he made a discovery—the door was slightly ajar. He pushed it and it opened—revealing a dirty hall, stripped of every scrap of furniture. Entering, he shut the door and walked up the stairs to the room whence he had fled after thrashing Johnnie. Here he paused and listened, thinking that he heard somebody in the room. Nor was he mistaken, for presently a well-remembered voice shrilled out:

"Who's skulking round outside there? If it's one of those bailiffs he'd better hook it, for there's nothing left here."

George's countenance positively beamed at the sound.

"Bailiffs, marm?" he called through the door—"it ain't no varminty bailiffs, it's a friend, and just when you're a-wanting one seemingly. Can I come in?"

"Oh, yes, come in, whoever you are," said the voice. Accordingly he opened the door and entered, and this was what he saw. The room, like the rest of the house, had been stripped of everything, with the solitary exceptions of a box and a mattress, beside which were an empty bottle and a dirty glass. On the mattress sat the fair Edithia, *alias* Mrs. d'Aubigne, *alias* the Tiger, *alias* Mrs. Quest, and such a sight as she presented George had never seen before. Her fierce face bore traces of recent heavy drinking and was moreover dirty, haggard and dreadful to look upon; her hair was a frowsy mat, on some patches of which the golden dye had faded, leaving it its natural hue of doubtful grey. She wore no collar and her linen was open at the neck. On her feet were a filthy pair of white satin slippers, and on her back that same gorgeous pink satin tea-gown which Mr. Quest had observed on the occasion of his visit, now however soiled and torn. Anything more squalid or repulsive than the whole picture cannot be imagined, and though his nerves were pretty strong, and in the course of his life he had seen many a sight of utter destitution,

George literally recoiled from it.

"What's the matter?" said the hag sharply, "and who the dickens are you? Ah, I know now; you're the chap who whacked Johnnie," and she burst into a hoarse scream of laughter at the recollection. "It was mean of you though to hook it and leave me. He pulled me, and I was fined two pounds by the beak."

"Mean of *him*, marm, not me, but he was a mean varmint altogether he was; to go and pull a lady too, I niver heard of such a thing. But, marm, if I might say so, you seem to be in trouble here," and he took a seat upon the deal box.

"In trouble, I should think I was in trouble. There's been an execution in the house, that is, there's been three executions, one for rates and taxes, one for a butcher's bill, and one for rent. They all came together, and fought like wild cats for the things. That was yesterday, and you see all they have left me; cleaned out everything down to my new yellow satin, and then asked for more. They wanted to know where my jewellery was, but I did them, hee, hee!"

"Meaning, marm?"

"Meaning that I hid it, that is, what was left of it, under a board. But that ain't the worst. When I was asleep that devil Ellen, who's had her share all these years, got to the board and collared the things and bolted with them, and look what she's left me instead," and she held up a scrap of paper, "a receipt for five years' wages, and she's had them over and over again. Ah, if ever I get a chance at her," and she doubled her long hand and made a motion as of a person scratching. "She's bolted and left me here to starve. I haven't had a bit since yesterday, nor a drink either, and that's worse. What's to become of me? I'm starving. I shall have to go to the workhouse. Yes, me," she added in a scream, "me, who have spent thousands; I shall have to go to a workhouse like a common woman!"

"It's cruel, marm, cruel," said the sympathetic George, "and you a lawful wedded wife 'till death do us part.' But, marm, I saw a public over the way. Now, no offence, but you'll let me just go over and fetch a bite and a sup."

"Well," she answered hungrily, "you're a gent, you are, though you're a country one. You go, while I just make a little toilette, and as for the drink, why let it be brandy."

"Brandy it shall be," said the gallant George, and departed.

In ten minutes he returned with a supply of beef patties, and a bottle of good, strong "British Brown," which as everybody knows is a sufficient quantity to render three privates or two blue-jackets drunk and incapable.

The woman, who now presented a slightly more respectable appearance, seized the bottle, and pouring about a wine-glass and a half of its contents into a tumbler mixed it with an equal quantity of water and drank it off at a draught.

"That's better," she said, "and now for a patty. It's a real picnic, this is."

He handed her one, but she could not eat more than half of it, for alcohol destroys the healthier appetites, and she soon went back to the brandy bottle.

"Now, marm, that you are a little more comfortable, perhaps you will tell me how as you got into this way, and you with a rich husband, as I well knows, to love and cherish you."

"A husband to love and cherish me?" she said; "why, I have written to him three times to tell him that I'm starving, and never a cent has he given me—and there's no allowance due yet, and when there is they'll take it, for I owe hundreds."

"Well," said George, "I call it cruel—cruel, and he rolling in gold. Thirty thousand pounds he hev just made, that I knows on. You must be an angel, marm, to stand it, an angel without wings. If it were my husband, now I'd know the reason why."

"Ay, but I daren't. He'd murder me. He said he would."

George laughed gently. "Lord! Lord!" he said, "to see how men play it off upon poor weak women, working on their narves and that like. He kill you! Laryer Quest kill you, and he the biggest coward in Boisingham; but there it is. This is a world of wrong, as the parson says, and the poor shorn lambs must jamb their tails down and turn their backs to the wind, and so must you, marm. So it's the workhus you'll be in to-morrow. Well, you'll find it a poor place; the skilly is that rough it do fare to take the skin off your throat, and not a drop of liquor, not even of a cup of hot tea, and work too, lots of it—scrubbing, marm, scrubbing!"

This vivid picture of miseries to come drew something between a sob and a howl from the woman. There is nothing more horrible to the imagination of such people than the idea of being forced to work. If their notions of a future state of punishment could be got at, they would be found in nine cases out of ten to resolve themselves into a vague conception of hard labour in a hot climate. It was the idea of the scrubbing that particularly affected the Tiger.

"I won't do it," she said, "I'll go to chokey first—"

"Look here, marm," said George, in a persuasive voice, and pushing the brandy bottle towards her, "where's the need for you to go to the workhus or to chokey either—you with a rich husband as is bound by law to support you as becomes a lady? And, marm, mind another thing, a husband as hev wickedly deserted you—which how he could do so it ain't for me to say—and is living along of another young party."

She took some more brandy before she answered.

"That's all very well, you duffer," she said; "but how am I to get at him? I tell you I'm afraid of him, and even if I weren't, I haven't a cent to travel with, and if I got there what am I to do?"

"As for being afeard, marm," he answered, "I've told you Laryer Quest is a long sight more frightened of you than you are of him. Then as for money, why, marm, I'm a-going down to Boisingham myself by the train as leaves Liverpool Street at half-past one, and that's an hour and a bit from now, and it's proud and pleased I should be to take a lady down and be the means of bringing them as has been in holy matrimony togither again. And as to what you should do when you gets there, why, you should just walk up with your marriage lines and say, 'You are my lawful husband, and I calls on you to cease living as you didn't oughter and to take me back;' and if he don't, why then you swears an information, and it's a case of warrant for bigamy."

The woman chuckled, and then suddenly seized with suspicion looked at her visitor sharply.

"What do you want me to blow the gaff for?" she said; "you're a leery old hand, you are, for all your simple ways, and you've got some game on, I'll take my davy."

"I a game—I—!" answered George, an expression of the deepest pain spreading itself over his ugly features. "No, marm—and when one hev wanted to help a friend too. Well, if you think that—and no doubt misfortune hev made you doubtful-like—the best I can do is to bid you good-day, and to wish you well out of your troubles, workhus and all, marm, which I do according," and he rose from his box with much dignity, politely bowed to the hag on the mattress, and then turning walked towards the door.

She sprung up with an oath.

"I'll go," she said. "I'll take the change out of him; I'll teach him to let his lawful wife starve on a beggarly pittance. I don't care if he does try to kill me. I'll ruin him," and she stamped upon the floor and screamed, "I'll ruin him, I'll ruin him!" presenting such a picture of abandoned rage and wickedness that even George, whose feelings were not finely strung, inwardly shrank from her.

"Ah, marm," he said, "no wonder you're put about. When I think of what you've had to suffer, I own it makes my blood go a-biling through my veins. But if you is a-coming, mayhap it would be as well to stop cursing of and put your hat on, and we hev got to catch the train." And he pointed to a head-gear chiefly made of somewhat dilapidated peacock feathers, and an ulster which the bailiffs had either overlooked or left through pity.

She put on the hat and cloak. Then going to the hole beneath the board, out of which she said the woman Ellen had stolen her jewellery, she extracted the copy of the certificate of marriage which that lady had not apparently thought worth taking, and placed it in the pocket of her pink silk *peignoir*.

Then George having first secured the remainder of the bottle of brandy, which he slipped into his capacious pocket, they started, and drove to Liverpool Street. Such a spectacle as the Tiger upon the platform George was wont in after days to declare he never did see. But it can easily be imagined that a fierce, dissolute, hungry-looking woman, with half-dyed hair, who had drunk as much as was good for her, dressed in a hat made of shabby peacock feathers, dirty white shoes, an ulster with some buttons off, and a gorgeous but filthy pink silk tea-gown, presented a sufficiently curious appearance. Nor did it lose strength by contrast with that of her companion, the sober and melancholy-looking George, who was arrayed in his pepper-and-salt Sunday suit.

So curious indeed was their aspect that the people loitering about the platform collected round them, and George, who felt heartily ashamed of the position, was thankful enough when once the train started. From motives of economy he had taken her a third-class ticket, and at this she grumbled, saying that she was accustomed to travel, like a lady should, first; but he appeased her with the brandy bottle.

All the journey through he talked to her about her wrongs, till at last, what between the liquor and his artful incitements, she was inflamed into a condition of savage fury against Mr. Quest. When once she got to this point he would let her have no more brandy, seeing that she was now ripe for his purpose, which was of course to use her to ruin the man who would ruin the house he served.

Mr. Quest, sitting in state as Clerk to the Magistrates assembled in Quarter Sessions at the Court House, Boisingham, little guessed that the sword at whose shadow he had trembled all these years was even now falling on his head. Still less did he dream that the hand to cut the thread which held it was that of the stupid bumpkin whose warning he had despised.

CHAPTER XXXV

THE SWORD OF DAMOCLES

At last the weary journey was over, and to George's intense relief he found himself upon the platform at Boisingham. He was a pretty tough subject, but he felt that a very little more of the company of the fair Edithia would be too much for him. As it happened, the station- master was a particular friend of his, and the astonishment of that worthy when he saw the respectable George in such company could scarcely be expressed in words.

"Why boar! Well I never! Is she a furriner?" he ejaculated in astonishment.

"If you mean me," said Edithia, who was by now in fine bellicose condition, "I'm no more foreign than you are. Shut up, can't you? or—" and she took a step towards the stout station-master. He retreated precipitately, caught his heel against the threshold of the booking office and vanished backwards with a crash.

"Steady, marm, steady," said George. "Save it up now, do, and as for you, don't you irritate her none of yer, or I won't answer for the consequences, for she's an injured woman she is, and injured women is apt to be dangerous."

It chanced that a fly which had brought somebody to the station was still standing there. George bundled his fair charge into it, telling the driver to go to the Sessions House.

"Now, marm," he said, "listen to me; I'm a-going to take you to the man as hev wronged you. He's sitting as clerk to the magistrates. Do you go up and call him your husband. Thin he'll tell the policeman to take you away. Thin do you sing out for justice, because when people sings out for justice everybody's bound to hearken, and say how as you wants a warrant agin him for bigamy, and show them the marriage lines. Don't you be put down, and don't you spare him. If you don't startle him you'll niver get northing out of him."

"Spare him," she snarled; "not I. I'll have his blood. But look here, if he's put in chokey, where's the tin to come from?"

"Why, marm," answered George with splendid mendacity, "it's the best thing that can happen for you, for if they collar him you git the property, and that's law."

"Oh," she answered, "if I'd known that he'd have been collared long ago, I can tell you."

"Come," said George, seeing that they were nearing their destination. "Hev one more nip just to keep your spirits up," and he produced the brandy bottle, at which she took a long pull.

"Now," he said, "go for him like a wild cat."

"Never you fear," she said.

They got out of the cab and entered the Sessions House without attracting any particular notice. The court itself was crowded, for a case which had excited public interest was coming to a conclusion. The jury had given their verdict, and sentence was being pronounced by Mr. de la Molle, the chairman.

Mr. Quest was sitting at his table below the bench taking

some notes.

"There's your husband," George whispered, "now do you draw on."

George's part in the drama was played, and with a sigh of relief he fell back to watch its final development. He saw the fierce tall woman slip through the crowd like a snake or a panther to its prey, and some compunction touched him when he thought of the prey. He glanced at the elderly respectable-looking gentleman by the table, and reflected that he too was stalking *his* prey—the old Squire and the ancient house of de la Molle. Then his compunction vanished, and he rejoiced to think that he would be the means of destroying a man who, to fill his pockets, did not hesitate to ruin the family with which his life and the lives of his forefathers had been interwoven for many generations.

By this time the woman had fought her way through the press, bursting the remaining buttons off her ulster in so doing, and reached the bar which separated spectators from the space reserved for the officials. On the further side of the bar was a gangway, and beyond it a table at which Mr. Quest sat. He had been busy writing something all this time, now he rose, passed it to Mr. de la Molle, and then turned to sit down again.

Meanwhile his wife had craned her long lithe body forward over the bar till her head was almost level with the hither edge of the table. There she stood glaring at him, her wicked face alive with fury and malice, for the brandy she had drunk had caused her to forget her fears.

As Mr. Quest turned, his eye caught the flash of colour from the peacock feather hat. Thence it travelled to the face beneath.

He gave a gasp, and the court seemed to whirl round him. The sword had fallen indeed!

"Well, Billy!" whispered the hateful voice, "you see I've come to look you up."

With a desperate effort he recovered himself. A policeman was standing near. He beckoned to him, and told him to remove the woman, who was drunk. The policeman advanced and touched her on the arm.

"Come, you be off," he said, "you're drunk."

At that moment Mr. de la Molle ceased giving judgment.

"I ain't drunk," said the woman, loud enough to attract the attention of the whole court, which now for the first time observed her extraordinary attire, "and I've a right to be in the public court."

"Come on," said the policeman, "the clerk says you're to go."

"The clerk says so, does he?" she answered, "and do you know who the clerk is? I'll tell you all," and she raised her voice to a scream; "he's my husband, my lawful wedded husband, and here's proof of it," and she took the folded certificate from her pocket and flung it so that it struck the desk of one of the magistrates.

Mr. Quest sank into his chair, and a silence of astonishment fell upon the court.

The Squire was the first to recover himself.

"Silence," he said, addressing her. "Silence. This cannot go on here."

"But I want justice," she shrieked. "I want justice; I want a warrant against that man for *bigamy*." (Sensation.) "He's left me to starve; me, his lawful wife. Look here," and she tore open the pink satin tea-gown, "I haven't enough clothes on me; the bailiffs took all my clothes; I have suffered his cruelty for years, and borne it, and I can bear it no longer. Justice, your worships; I only ask for justice."

"Be silent, woman," said Mr. de la Molle; "if you have a criminal charge to bring against anybody there is a proper way to make it. Be silent or leave this court."

But she only screamed the more for *justice*, and loudly detailed fragments of her woes to the eagerly listening crowd.

Then policemen were ordered to remove her, and there followed a frightful scene. She shrieked and fought in such a fashion that it took four men to drag her to the door of the court, where she dropped exhausted against the wall in the corridor.

"Well," said the observant George to himself, "she hev done the trick proper, and no mistake. Couldn't have been better. That's a master one, that is." Then he turned his attention to the stricken man before him. Mr. Quest was sitting there, his face ashen, his eyes wide open, and his hands placed flat on the table before him. When silence had been restored he rose and turned to the bench apparently with the intention of addressing the court. But he said nothing, either because he could not find the words or because his courage failed him. There was a moment's intense silence, for every one in the crowded court was watching him, and the sense of it seemed to take what resolution he had left out of him. At any rate, he left the table and hurried from the court. In the passage he found the Tiger, who, surrounded by a little crowd, her hat awry and her clothes half torn from her back, was huddled gasping against the wall.

She saw him and began to speak, but he stopped and faced her. He faced her, grinding his teeth, and with such an awful fire of fury in his eyes that she shrank from him in terror, flattening herself against the wall.

"What did I tell you?" he said in a choked voice, and then

passed on. A few paces down the passage he met one of his own clerks, a sharp fellow enough.

"Here, Jones," he said, "you see that woman there. She has made a charge against me. Watch her. See where she goes to, and find out what she is going to do. Then come and tell me at the office. If you lose sight of her, you lose your place too. Do you understand?"

"Yes, sir," said the astonished clerk, and Mr. Quest was gone.

He made his way direct to the office. It was closed, for he had told his clerks he should not come back after court, and that they could go at half-past four. He had his key, however, and, entering, lit the gas. Then he went to his safe and sorted some papers, burning a good number of them. Two large documents, however, he put by his side to read. One was his will, the other was endorsed "Statement of the circumstances connected with Edith."

First he looked through his will. It had been made some years ago, and was entirely in favour of his wife, or, rather, of his reputed wife, Belle.

"It may as well stand," he said aloud; "if anything happens to me she'll take about ten thousand under it, and that was what she brought me." Taking the pen he went through the document carefully, and wherever the name of "Belle Quest" occurred he put a X, and inserted these words, "Gennett, commonly known as Belle Quest," Gennett being Belle's maiden name, and initialled the correction. Next he glanced at the Statement. It contained a full and fair account of his connection with the woman who had ruined his life. "I may as well leave it," he thought; "some day it will show Belle that I was not quite so bad as I seemed."

He replaced the statement in a brief envelope, sealed and directed it to Belle, and finally marked it, "Not to be opened till my death.—W. Quest." Then he put the envelope away in the safe and took up the will for the same purpose. Next it on the table lay the deeds executed by Edward Cossey transferring the Honham mortgages to Mr. Quest in consideration of his abstaining from the commencement of a suit for divorce in which he proposed to join Edward Cossey as co-respondent. "Ah!" he thought to himself, "that game is up. Belle is not my legal wife, therefore I cannot commence a suit against her in which Cossey would figure as co-respondent, and so the consideration fails. I am sorry, for I should have liked him to lose his thirty thousand pounds as well as his wife, but it can't be helped. It was a game of bluff, and now that the bladder has been pricked I haven't a leg to stand on."

Then, taking a pen, he wrote on a sheet of paper which he inserted in the will, "Dear B.,—You must return the Honham mortgages to Mr. Edward Cossey. As you are not my legal wife the consideration upon which he transferred them fails, and you cannot hold them in equity, nor I suppose would you wish to do so.—W. Q."

Having put all the papers away, he shut the safe at the moment that the clerk whom he had deputed to watch his wife knocked at the door and entered.

"Well?" said his master.

"Well, sir, I watched the woman. She stopped in the passage for a minute, and then George, Squire de la Molle's man, came out and spoke to her. I got quite close so as to hear, and he said, 'You'd better get out of this.'"

"'Where to?' she answered. 'I'm afraid.'"

"'Back to London,' he said, and gave her a sovereign, and she got up without a word and slunk off to the station followed by a mob of people. She is in the refreshment room now, but George sent word to say that they ought not to serve her with any drink."

"What time does the next train go—7.15, does it not?" said Mr. Quest.

"Yes, sir."

"Well, go back to the station and keep an eye upon that woman, and when the time comes get me a first-class return ticket to London. I shall go up myself and give her in charge there. Here is some money," and he gave him a five-pound note, "and look here, Jones, you need not trouble about the change."

"Thank you, sir, I'm sure," said Jones, to whom, his salary being a guinea a week, on which he supported a wife and family, a gift of four pounds was sudden wealth.

"Don't thank me, but do as I tell you. I will be down at the station at 7.10. Meet me outside and give me the ticket. That will do."

When Jones had gone Mr. Quest sat down to think.

So George had loosed this woman on him, and that was the meaning of his mysterious warnings. How did he find her? That did not matter, he had found her, and in revenge for the action taken against the de la Molle family had brought her here to denounce him. It was cleverly managed, too. Mr. Quest reflected to himself that he should never have given the man credit for the brains. Well, that was what came of underrating people.

And so this was the end of all his hopes, ambitions, shifts and struggles! The story would be in every paper in England before another twenty-four hours were over, headed, "*Remarkable occurrence at Boisingham Quarter Sessions.—Alleged bigamy of a solicitor.*" No doubt, too, the Treasury would take it up and institute a prosecution. This was the end of his strivings after respectability and the wealth that brings it. He had over-reached himself. He had plotted and schemed, and hardened his heart against the de la Molle family, and fate had made use of his success to destroy him. In another few months he had expected to be able to leave this place a wealthy and respected man—and now? He laid his hand upon the table and reviewed his past life—tracing it from year to year, and seeing how the shadow of this accursed woman had haunted him, bringing disgrace and terror and mental agony with it—making his life a misery. And now what was to be done? He was ruined. Let him fly to the utmost parts of the earth, let him burrow in the recesses of the cities of the earth, and his shame would find him out. He was an impostor, a bigamist; one who had seduced an innocent woman into a mock marriage and then taken her fortune to buy the silence of his lawful wife. More, he had threatened to bring an action for divorce against a woman to whom he knew he was not really married and made it a lever to extort large sums of money or their value.

What is there that a man in his position can do?

He can do two things—he can revenge himself upon the author of his ruin, and he be bold enough, he can put an end to his existence and his sorrows at a blow.

Mr. Quest rose and walked to the door. Halting there, he turned and looked round the office in that peculiar fashion wherewith the eyes take their adieu. Then with a sigh he went.

Reaching his own house he hesitated whether or not to enter. Had the news reached Belle? If so, how was he to face her? Her hands were not clean, indeed, but at any rate she had no mock marriage in her record, and her dislike of him had been unconcealed throughout. She had never wished to marry him, and never for one single day regarded him otherwise than with aversion.

After reflection he turned and went round by the back way into the garden. The curtains of the French windows were drawn, but it was a wet and windy night, and the draught occasionally lifted the edge of one of them. He crept like a thief up to his own window and looked in. The drawing-room was lighted, and in a low chair by the fire sat Belle. She was as usual dressed in black, and to Mr. Quest, who loved her, and who knew that he was about to bid farewell to the sight of her, she looked more beautiful now than ever she had before. A book lay open on her knee, and he noticed, not without surprise, that it was a Bible. But she was not reading it; her dimpled chin rested on her hand, her violent eyes were fixed on vacancy, and even from where he was he thought that he could see the tears in them.

She had heard nothing; he was sure of that from the expression of her face; she was thinking of her own sorrows, not of his shame.

Yes, he would go in.

CHAPTER XXXVI

HOW THE GAME ENDED

Mr. Quest entered the house by a side door, and having taken off his hat and coat went into the drawing-room. He had still half an hour to spare before starting to catch the train.

"Well," said Belle, looking up. "Why are you looking so pale?"

"I have had a trying day," he answered. "What have you been doing?"

"Nothing in particular."

"Reading the Bible, I see."

"How do you know that?" she asked, colouring a little, for she had thrown a newspaper over the book when she heard him coming in. "Yes, I have been reading the Bible. Don't you know that when everything else in life has failed them women generally take to religion?"

"Or drink," he put in, with a touch of his old bitterness. "Have you seen Mr. Cossey lately?"

"No. Why do you ask that? I thought we had agreed to drop that subject."

As a matter of fact it had not been alluded to since Edward left the house.

"You know that Miss de la Molle will not marry him after all?"

"Yes, I know. She will not marry him because you forced him to give up the mortgages."

"You ought to be much obliged to me. Are you not pleased?"

"No. I no longer care about anything. I am tired of passion, and sin and failure. I care for nothing any more."

"It seems that we have both reached the same goal, but by different roads."

"You?" she answered, looking up; "at any rate you are not tired of money, or you would not do what you have done to get it."

"I never cared for money itself," he said. "I only wanted money that I might be rich and, therefore, respected."

"And you think any means justifiable so long as you get it?"

"I thought so. I do not think so now."

"I don't understand you to-night, William. It is time for me to go to dress for dinner."

"Don't go just yet. I'm leaving in a minute."

"Leaving? Where for?"

"London; I have to go up to-night about some business."

"Indeed; when are you coming back?"

"I don't quite know—to-morrow, perhaps. I wonder, Belle," he went on, his voice shaking a little, "if you will always think as badly of me as you do now."

"I?" she said, opening her eyes widely; "who am I that I should judge you? However bad you may be, I am worse."

"Perhaps there are excuses to be made for both of us," he said; "perhaps, after all, there is no such thing as free will, and we are nothing but pawns moved by a higher power. Who knows? But I will not keep you any longer. Good-bye—Belle!"

"Yes."

"May I kiss you before I go?"

She looked at him in astonishment. Her first impulse was to refuse. He had not kissed her for years. But something in the man's face touched her. It was always a refined and melancholy face, but to-night it wore a look which to her seemed almost unearthly.

"Yes, William, if you wish," she said; "but I wonder that you care to."

"Let the dead bury their dead," he answered, and stooping he put his arm round her delicate waist and drawing her to him kissed her tenderly but without passion on her forehead. "There, good-night," he said; "I wish that I had been a better husband to you. Good-night," and he was gone.

When he reached his room he flung himself for a few moments face downwards upon the bed, and from the convulsive motion of his back an observer might almost have believed that he was sobbing. When he rose, there was no trace of tears or tenderness upon his features. On the contrary, they were stern and set, like the features of one bent upon some terrible endeavour. Going to a drawer, he unlocked it and took from it a Colt's revolver of the small pattern. It was loaded, but he extracted the cartridges and replaced them with fresh ones from a tin box. Then he went downstairs, put on a large ulster with a high collar, and a soft felt hat, the brim of which he turned down over his face, placed the pistol in the pocket of his ulster, and started.

It was a dreadful night, the wind was blowing a heavy gale, and between the gusts the rain came down in sheets of driving spray. Nobody was about the streets—the weather was far too bad; and Mr. Quest reached the station without meeting a living soul. Outside the circle of light from a lamp over the doorway he paused, and looked about for the clerk Jones. Presently, he saw him walking backwards and forwards under the shelter of a lean-to, and going up, touched him on the shoulder.

The man started back.

"Have you got the ticket, Jones?" he asked.

"Lord, sir," said Jones, "I didn't know you in that get-up. Yes, here it is."

"Is the woman there still?"

"Yes, sir; she's taken a ticket, third-class, to town. She has been going on like a wild thing because they would not give her any liquor at the refreshment bar, till at last she frightened them into letting her have six of brandy. Then she began and told the girl all sorts of tales about you, sir—said she was going back to London because she was afraid that if she stopped here you would murder her—and that you were her lawful husband, and she would have a warrant out against you, and I don't know what all. I sat by and heard her with my own ears."

"Did she—did she indeed?" said Mr. Quest, with an attempt at a laugh. "Well, she's a common thief and worse, that's what she is, and by this time to-morrow I hope to see her safe in gaol. Ah! here comes the train. Good-night, Jones. I can manage for myself now."

"What's his game?" said Jones to himself as he watched his master slip on to the platform by a gate instead of going through the booking office. "Well, I've had four quid out of it, any way, and it's no affair of mine." And Jones went home to tea.

Meanwhile Mr. Quest was standing on the wet and desolate platform quite away from the lamps, watching the white lights of the approaching train rushing on through the storm and night. Presently it drew up. No passengers got out.

"Now, mam, look sharp if you're going," cried the porter, and the woman Edith came out of the refreshment room.

"There's the third, forrard there," said the porter, running to the van to see about the packing of the mails.

On she came, passing quite close to Mr. Quest, so close that he could hear her swearing at the incivility of the porter. There was a third- class compartment just opposite, and this she entered. It was one of those carriages that are still often to be seen on provincial lines in which the partitions do not go up to the roof, and, if possible, more vilely lighted than usual. Indeed the light which should have illuminated the after-half of it had either never been lit or had gone out. There was not a soul in the whole length of the compartment.

As soon as his wife was in, Mr. Quest watched his opportunity. Slipping up to the dark carriage, he opened and shut the door as quietly as possible and took his seat in the gloom.

The engine whistled, there was a cry of "right forrard," and they were off.

Presently he saw the woman stand up in her division of the compartment and peep over into the gloom.

"Not a blessed soul," he heard her mutter, "and yet I feel as though that devil Billy was creeping about after me. Ugh! it must be the horrors. I can see the look he gave me now."

A few minutes later the train stopped at a station, but nobody got in, and presently it moved on again. "Any passengers for Effry?" shouted the porter, and there had been no response. If they did not stop at Effry there would be no halt for forty minutes. Now was his time. He waited a little till they had got up the speed. The line here ran through miles and miles of fen country, more or less drained by dykes and rivers, but still wild and desolate enough. Over this great flat the storm was sweeping furiously—even drowning in its turmoil the noise of the travelling train.

Very quietly he rose and climbed over the low partition which separated his compartment from that in which the woman was. She was seated in the corner, her head leaning back, so that the feeble light from the lamp fell on it, and her eyes were closed. She was asleep.

He slid himself along the seat till he was opposite to her, then paused to look at the fierce wicked face on which drink and paint and years of evil-thinking and living had left their marks, and looking shuddered. There was his bad genius, there was the creature who had driven him from evil to evil and finally destroyed him. Had it not been for her he might have been a good and respected man, and not what he was now, a fraudulent ruined outcast. All his life seemed to flash before his inner eye in those few seconds of contemplation, all the long weary years of struggle, crime, and deceit. And this was the end of it, and *there* was the cause of it. Well, she should not escape him; he would be revenged upon her at last. There was nothing but death before *him*, she should die too.

He set his teeth, drew the loaded pistol from his pocket, cocked it and lifted it to her breast.

What was the matter with the thing? He had never known the pull of a pistol to be so heavy before.

No, it was not *that*. He could not do it. He could not shoot a sleeping woman, devil though she was; he could not kill her in her sleep. His nature rose up against it.

He placed the pistol on his knee, and as he did so she opened her eyes. He saw the look of wonder gather in them and grow to a stare of agonised terror. Her face became rigid like a dead person's and her lips opened to scream, but no cry came. She could only point to the pistol.

"Make a sound and you are dead," he said fiercely. "Not that it matters though," he added, as he remembered that the scream must be loud which could be heard in that raging gale.

"What are you going to do?" she gasped at last. "What are you going to do with that pistol? And where do you come from?"

"I come out of the night," he answered, raising the weapon, "out of the night into which you are going."

"You are not going to kill me?" she moaned, turning up her ghastly face. "I can't die. I'm afraid to die. It will hurt, and I've been wicked. Oh, you are not going to kill me, are you?"

"Yes, I am going to kill you," he answered. "I told you months ago that I would kill you if you molested me. You have ruined me now, there is nothing but death left for *me*, and *you* shall die too, you fiend."

"Oh no! no! no! anything but that. I was drunk when I did it; that man brought me there, and they had taken all my things, and I was starving," and she glanced wildly round the empty carriage to see if help could be found, but there was none. She was alone with her fate.

She slipped down upon the floor of the carriage and clasped his knees. Writhing in her terror upon the ground, in hoarse accents she prayed for mercy.

"You used to kiss me," she said; "you cannot kill a woman you used to kiss years ago. Oh, spare me, spare me!"

He set his lips and placed the muzzle of the pistol against her head. She shivered at the contact, and her teeth began to chatter.

He could not do it. He must let her go, and leave her to fate. After all, she could hurt him no more, for before another sun had set he would be beyond her reach.

His pistol hand fell against his side, and he looked down with loathing not unmixed with pity at the abject human snake who was writing at his feet.

She caught his eye, and her faculties, sharpened by the imminent peril, read relentment there. For the moment, at any rate, he was softened. If she could master him now while he was off his guard—he was not a very strong man! But the pistol—

Slowly, still groaning out supplications, she rose to her feet.

"Yes," he said, "be quiet while I think if I can spare you," and he half turned his head away from her. For a moment nothing was heard but the rush of the gale and the roll of the wheels running over and under bridges.

This was her opportunity. All her natural ferocity arose within her, intensified a hundred times by the instinct of self-protection. With a sudden blow she struck the pistol from his hand; it fell upon the floor of the carriage. And then with a scream she sprang like a wild cat straight at his throat. So sudden was the attack that the long lean hands were gripping his windpipe before he knew it had been made. Back she bore him, though he seized her round the waist. She was the heavier of the two, and back they went, *crash* against the carriage door.

It gave! Oh, God, the worn catch gave! Out together, out with a yell of despair into the night and the raging gale; down together through sixty feet of space into the black river beneath. Down together, deep into the watery depths—into the abyss of Death.

The train rushed on, the wild winds blew, and the night was as the night had been. But there in the black water, though there was never a star to see them, there, locked together in death as they had been locked together in life, the fierce glare of hate and terror yet staring from their glazed eyes, two bodies rolled over and over as they sped silently towards the sea.

CHAPTER XXXVII

SISTER AGNES

Ten days had passed. The tragedy had echoed through all the land. Numberless articles and paragraphs had been written in numberless papers, and numberless theories had been built upon them. But the echoes were already beginning to die away. Both actors in the dim event were dead, and there was no pending trial to keep the public interest alive.

The two corpses, still linked in that fierce dying grip, had been picked up on a mudbank. An inquest had been held, at which an open verdict was returned, and they were buried. Other events had occurred, the papers were filled with the reports of new tragedies, and the affair of the country lawyer who committed bigamy and together with his lawful wife came to a tragic and mysterious end began to be forgotten.

In Boisingham and its neighbourhood much sympathy was shown with Belle, whom people still called Mrs. Quest, though she had no title to that name. But she received it coldly and kept herself secluded.

As soon as her supposed husband's death was beyond a doubt Belle had opened his safe (for he had left the keys on his dressing-table), and found therein his will and other papers, including the mortgage deeds, to which, as Mr. Quest's memorandum advised her, she had no claim. Nor, indeed, had her right to them been good in law, would she have retained them, seeing that they were a price wrung from her late lover under threat of an action that could not be brought.

So she made them into a parcel and sent them to Edward Cossey, together with a formal note of explanation, greatly wondering in her heart what course he would take with reference to them. She was not left long in doubt. The receipt of the deeds was acknowledged, and three days afterwards she heard that a notice calling in the borrowed money had been served upon Mr. de la Molle on behalf of Edward Cossey.

So he had evidently made up his mind not to forego this new advantage which chance threw in his way. Pressure and pressure alone could enable him to attain his end, and he was applying it unmercifully. Well, she had done with him now, it did not matter to her; but she could not help faintly wondering at the extraordinary tenacity and hardness of purpose which his action showed. Then she turned her mind to the consideration of another matter, in connection with which her plans were approaching maturity.

It was some days after this, exactly a fortnight from the date of Mr. Quest's death, that Edward Cossey was sitting one afternoon brooding over the fire in his rooms. He had much business awaiting his attention in London, but he would not go to London. He could not tear himself away from Boisingham, and such of the matters as could be attended to there were left without attention. He was still as determined as ever to marry Ida, more determined if possible, for from constant brooding on the matter he had arrived at a condition approaching monomania. He had been quick to see the advantage resulting to him from Mr. Quest's tragic death and the return of the deeds, and though he knew that Ida would hate him the more for doing it, he instructed his lawyers to call in the money and make use of every possible legal means to harass and put pressure upon Mr. de la Molle. At the same time he had written privately to the Squire, calling his attention to the fact that matters were now once more as they had been at the beginning, but that he was as before willing to carry out the arrangements which he had already specified, provided that Ida could be persuaded to consent to marry him. To this Mr. de la Molle had answered courteously enough, notwithstanding his grief and irritation at the course his would-be son-in-law had taken about the mortgages on the death of Mr. Quest, and the suspicion (it was nothing more) that he now had as to the original cause of their transfer to the lawyer. He said what he had said before, that he could not force his daughter into a marriage with him, but that if she chose to agree to it he should offer no objection. And there the matter stood. Once or twice Edward had met Ida walking or driving. She bowed to him coldly and that was all. Indeed he had only one crumb of comfort in his daily bread of disappointment, and the hope deferred which, where a lady is concerned, makes the heart more than normally sick, and it was that he knew his hated rival, Colonel Quaritch, had been forbidden the Castle, and that intercourse between him and Ida was practically at an end.

But he was a dogged and persevering man; he knew the power of money and the shifts to which people can be driven who are made desperate by the want of it. He knew, too, that it is no rare thing for women who are attached to one man to sell themselves to another of their own free will, realising that love may pass, but wealth (if the settlements are properly drawn) does not. Therefore he still hoped that with so many circumstances bringing an ever-increasing pressure upon her, Ida's spirit would in time be broken, her resistance would collapse, and he would have his will. Nor, as the sequel will show, was that hope a baseless one.

As for his infatuation there was literally no limit to it. It broke out in all sorts of ways, and for miles round was a matter of public notoriety and gossip. Over the mantelpiece in his sitting-room was a fresh example of it. By one means and another he had obtained several photographs of Ida, notably one of her in a court dress which she had worn two or three years before, when her brother James had insisted upon her being presented. These photographs he caused to be enlarged and then, at the cost of 500 pounds, commissioned a well-known artist to paint from them a full-length life-size portrait of Ida in her court dress. This order had been executed, and the portrait, which although the colouring was not entirely satisfactory was still an effective likeness and a fine piece of work, now hung in a splendid frame over his mantelpiece.

There, on the afternoon in question, he sat before the fire, his eyes fixed upon the portrait, of which the outline was beginning to grow dim in the waning December light, when the servant girl came in and announced that a lady wished to speak to him. He asked what her name was, and the girl said that she did not know, because she had her veil down and was wrapped up in a big cloak.

In due course the lady was shown up. He had relapsed into his reverie, for nothing seemed to interest him much now unless it had to do with Ida—and he knew that the lady could not be Ida, because the girl said that she was short. As it happened, he sat with his right ear, in which he was deaf, towards the door, so that between his infirmity and his dreams he never heard Belle—for it was she—enter the room.

For a minute or more she stood looking at him as he sat with his eyes fixed upon the picture, and while she looked an expression of pity stole across her sweet pale face.

"I wonder what curse there is laid upon us that we should be always doomed to seek what we cannot find?" she said aloud.

He heard her now, and looking up saw her standing in the glow and flicker of the firelight, which played upon her white face and black- draped form. He started violently; as he did so she loosed the heavy cloak and hood that she wore and it fell behind her. But where was the lovely rounded form, and where the clustering golden curls? Gone, and in their place a coarse robe of blue serge, on which hung a crucifix, and the white hood of the nun.

He sprang from his chair with an exclamation, not knowing if he dreamed or if he really saw the woman who stood there like a ghost in the firelight.

"Forgive me, Edward," she said presently, in her sweet low voice. "I daresay that this all looks theatrical enough—but I have put on this dress for two reasons: firstly, because I must leave this town in an hour's time and wish to do so unknown; and secondly, to show that you need not fear that I have come to be troublesome. Will you light the candles?"

He did so mechanically, and then pulled down the blinds. Meanwhile Belle had seated herself near the table, her face buried in her hands.

"What is the meaning of all this, Belle?" he said.

"'Sister Agnes,' you must call me now," she said, taking her hands from her face. "The meaning of it is that I have left the world and entered a sisterhood which works among the poor in London, and I have come to bid you farewell, a last farewell."

He stared at her in amazement. He did not find it easy to connect the idea of this beautiful, human, loving creature with the cold sanctuary of a sisterhood. He did not know that natures like this, whose very intensity is often the cause of their destruction, are most capable of these strange developments. The man or woman who can really love and endure—and they are rare—can also, when their passion has utterly broken them, turn to climb the stony paths that lead to love's antipodes.

"Edward," she went on, speaking very slowly, "you know in what relation we have stood to each other, and what that relationship means to woman. You know this—I have loved you with all my heart, and all my strength, and all my soul—" Here she trembled and broke down.

"You know, too," she continued presently, "what has been the end of all this, the shameful end. I am not come to blame you. I do not blame you, for the fault was mine, and if I have anything to forgive I forgive it freely. Whatever memories may still live in my heart I swear I put away all bitterness, and that my most earnest wish is that you may be happy, as happiness is to you. The sin was mine; that is it would have been mine were we free agents, which perhaps we are not. I should have loved my husband, or rather the man whom I thought my husband, for with all his faults he was of a different clay to you, Edward."

He looked up, but said nothing.

"I know," she went on, pointing to the picture over the mantelpiece, "that your mind is still set upon her, and I am nothing, and less than nothing, to you. When I am gone you will scarcely give me a thought. I cannot tell you if you will succeed in your end, and I think the methods you are adopting wicked and shameful. But whether you succeed or not, your fate also will be what my fate is—to love a person who is not only indifferent to you but who positively dislikes you, and reserves all her secret heart for another man, and I know no greater penalty than is to be found in that daily misery."

"You are very consoling," he said sulkily.

"I only tell you the truth," she answered. "What sort of life do you suppose mine has been when I am so utterly broken, so entirely robbed of hope, that I have determined to leave the world and hide myself and my shame in a sisterhood? And now, Edward," she went on, after a pause, "I have something to tell you, for I will not go away, if indeed you allow me to go away at all after you have heard it, until I have confessed." And she leant forward and looked him full in the face, whispering —"*I shot you on purpose, Edward!*"

"What!" he said, springing from his chair; "you tried to murder me?"

"Yes, yes; but don't think too hardly of me. I am only flesh and blood, and you drove me wild with jealousy—you taunted me with having been your mistress and said that I was not fit to associate with the lady whom you were going to marry. It made me mad, and the opportunity offered—the gun was there, and I shot you. God forgive me, I think that I have suffered more than you did. Oh! when day after day I saw you lying there and did not know if you would live or die, I thought that I should have gone mad with remorse and agony!"

He listened so far, and then suddenly walked across the room towards the bell. She placed herself between him and it.

"What are you going to do?" she said.

"Going to do? I am going to send for a policeman and give you into custody for attempted murder, that is all."

She caught his arm and looked him in the face. In another second she had loosed it.

"Of course," she said, "you have a right to do that. Ring and send for the policeman, only remember that nothing is known now, but the whole truth will come out at the trial."

This checked him, and he stood thinking.

"Well," she said, "why don't you ring?"

"I do not ring," he answered, "because on the whole I think I had better let you go. I do not wish to be mixed up with you any more. You have done me mischief enough; you have finished by attempting to murder me. Go; I think that a convent is the best place for you; you are too bad and too dangerous to be left at large."

"*Oh!*" she said, like one in pain. "*Oh!* and you are the man for whom I have come to this! Oh, God! it is a cruel world." And she pressed her hands to her heart and stumbled rather than walked to the door.

Reaching it she turned, and her hands still pressing the coarse blue gown against her heart, she leaned against the door.

"Edward," she said, in a strained whisper, for her breath came thick, "Edward—I am going for ever—have you *no* kind word —to say to me?"

He looked at her, a scowl upon his handsome face. Then by way of answer he turned upon his heel.

And so, still holding her hands against her poor broken heart, she went out of the house, out of Boisingham and of touch and knowledge of the world. In after years these two were fated to meet once again, and under circumstances sufficiently tragic; but the story of that meeting does not lie within the scope of this history. To the world Belle is dead, but there is another world of sickness, and sordid unchanging misery and shame, where the lovely face of Sister Agnes moves to and fro like a ray of heaven's own light. There those who would know her must go to seek her.

Poor Belle! Poor shamed, deserted woman! She was an evil-doer, and the fatality of love and the unbalanced vigour of her mind, which might, had she been more happily placed, have led her to all things that are pure, and true, and of good report, combined to drag her into shame and wretchedness. But the evil that she did was paid back to her in full measure, pressed down and running over. Few of us need to wait for a place of punishment to get the due of our follies and our sins. *Here* we expiate them. They are with us day and night, about our path and about our bed, scourging us with the whips of memory, mocking us with empty longing and the hopelessness of despair. Who can escape the consequence of sin, or even of the misfortune which led to sin? Certainly Belle did not, nor Mr. Quest, nor even that fierce-hearted harpy who hunted him to his grave.

And so good-bye to Belle. May she find peace in its season!

CHAPTER XXXVIII

COLONEL QUARITCH EXPRESSES HIS VIEWS

Meanwhile things had been going very ill at the Castle. Edward Cossey's lawyers were carrying out their client's instructions to the letter with a perseverance and ingenuity worthy of a County Court solicitor. Day by day they found a new point upon which to harass the wretched Squire. Some share of the first expenses connected with the mortgages had, they said, been improperly thrown upon their client, and they again and again demanded, in language which was almost insolent, the immediate payment of the amount. Then there was three months' interest overdue, and this also they pressed and clamoured for, till the old gentleman was nearly driven out of his senses, and as a consequence drove everybody about the place out of theirs.

At last this state of affairs began to tell upon his constitution, which, strong as he was, could not at his age withstand such constant worry. He grew to look years older, his shoulders acquired a stoop, and his memory began to fail him, especially on matters connected with the mortgages and farm accounts. Ida, too, became pale and ill; she caught a heavy cold, which she could not throw off, and her face acquired a permanently pained and yet listless look.

One day, it was on the 15th of December, things reached a climax. When Ida came down to breakfast she found her father busy poring over some more letters from the lawyers.

"What is it now, father?" she said.

"What is it now?" he answered irritably. "What, it's another claim for two hundred, that's what it is. I keep telling them to write to my lawyers, but they won't, at least they write to me too. There, I can't make head or tail of it. Look here," and he showed her two sides of a big sheet of paper covered with statements of accounts. "Anyhow, I have not got two hundred, that's clear. I don't even know where we are going to find the money to pay the three months' interest. I'm worn out, Ida, I'm worn out! There is only one thing left for me to do, and that is to die, and that's the long and short of it. I get so confused with these figures. I'm an old man now, and all these troubles are too much for me."

"You must not talk like that, father," she answered, not knowing what to say, for affairs were indeed desperate.

"Yes, yes, it's all very well to talk so, but facts are stubborn. Our family is ruined, and we must accept it."

"Cannot the money be got anyhow? Is there *nothing* to be done?" she said in despair.

"What is the good of asking me that? There is only one thing that can save us, and you know what it is as well as I do. But you are your own mistress. I have no right to put pressure on you. I don't wish to put pressure on you. You must please yourself. Meanwhile I think we had better leave this place at once, and go and live in a cottage somewhere, if we can get enough to support us; if not we must starve, I suppose. I cannot keep up appearances any longer."

Ida rose, and with a strange sad light of resolution shining in her eyes, came to where her father was sitting, and putting her hands upon his shoulders, looked him in the face.

"Father," she said, "do you wish me to marry that man?"

"Wish you to marry him? What do you mean?" he said, not without irritation, and avoiding her gaze. "It is no affair of mine. I don't like the man, if that's what you mean. He is acting like—well, like the cur that he is, in putting on the screw as he is doing; but, of course, that is the way out of it, and the only way, and there you are."

"Father," she said again, "will you give me ten days, that is, until Christmas Day? If nothing happens between this and then I will marry Mr. Edward Cossey."

A sudden light of hope shone in his eyes. She saw it, though he tried to hide it by turning his head away.

"Oh, yes," he answered, "as you wish; settle it one way or the other on Christmas Day, and then we can go out with the new year. You see your brother James is dead, I have no one left to advise me now, and I suppose that I am getting old. At any rate, things seem to be too much for me. Settle it as you like; settle it as you like," and he got up, leaving his breakfast half swallowed, and went off to moon aimlessly about the park.

So she made up her mind at last. This was the end of her struggling. She could not let her old father be turned out of house and home to starve, for practically they would starve. She knew her hateful lover well enough to be aware that he would show no mercy. It was a question of the woman or the money, and she was the woman. Either she must let him take her or they must be destroyed; there was no middle course. And in these circumstances there was no room for hesitation. Once more her duty became clear to her. She must give up her life, she must give up her love, she must give up herself. Well, so be it. She was weary of the long endeavour against fortune, now she would yield and let the tide of utter misery sweep over her like a sea—to bear her away till at last it brought her to that oblivion in which perchance all things come right or are as though they had never been.

She had scarcely spoken to her lover, Harold Quaritch, for

some weeks. She had as she understood it entered into a kind of unspoken agreement with her father not to do so, and that agreement Harold had realised and respected. Since their last letters to each other they had met once or twice casually or at church, interchanged a few indifferent words, though their eyes spoke another story, touched each other's hands and parted. That was absolutely all. But now that Ida had come to this momentous decision she felt he had a right to learn it, and so once more she wrote to him. She might have gone to see him or told him to meet her, but she would not. For one thing she did not dare to trust herself on such an errand in his dear company, for another she was too proud, thinking if her father came to hear of it he might consider that it had a clandestine and underhand appearance.

And so she wrote. With all she said we need not concern ourselves. The letter was loving, even passionate, more passionate perhaps than one would have expected from a woman of Ida's calm and stately sort. But a mountain may have a heart of fire although it is clad in snows, and so it sometimes is with women who seem cold and unemotional as marble. Besides, it was her last chance—she could write him no more letters and she had much to say.

"And so I have decided, Harold," she said after telling him of all her doubts and troubles. "I must do it, there is no help for it, as I think you will see. I have asked for ten days' respite. I really hardly know why, except that it is a respite. And now what is there left to say to you except good-bye? I love you, Harold, I make no secret of it, and I shall never love any other. Remember all your life that I love you and have not forgotten you, and never can forget. For people placed as we are there is but one hope—the grave. In the grave earthly considerations fail and earthly contracts end, and there I trust and believe we shall find each other—or at the least forgetfulness. My heart is so sore I know not what to say to you, for it is difficult to put all I feel in words. I am overwhelmed, my spirit is broken, and I wish to heaven that I were dead. Sometimes I almost cease to believe in a God who can allow His creatures to be so tormented and give us love only that it may be daily dishonoured in our sight; but who am I that I should complain, and after all what are our troubles compared to some we know of? Well, it will come to an end at last, and meanwhile pity me and think of me.

"Pity me and think of me; yes, but never see me more. As soon as this engagement is publicly announced, go away, the further the better. Yes, go to New Zealand, as you suggested once, and in pity of our human weakness never let me see your face again. Perhaps you may write to me sometimes—if Mr. Cossey will allow it. Go there and occupy yourself, it will divert your mind—you are still too young a man to lay yourself upon the shelf—mix yourself up with the politics of the place, take to writing; anything, so long as you can absorb yourself. I sent you a photograph of myself (I have nothing better) and a ring which I have worn night and day since I was a child. I think that it will fit your little finger and I hope you will always wear it in memory of me. It was my mother's. And now it is late and I am tired, and what is there more that a woman can say to the man she loves—and whom she must leave for ever? Only one word—Good-bye. Ida."

When Harold got this letter it fairly broke him down. His hopes had been revived when he thought that all was lost, and now again they were utterly dashed and broken. He could see no way out of it, none at all. He could not quarrel with Ida's decision, shocking as it was, for the simple reason that he knew in his heart she was acting rightly and even nobly. But, oh, the thought of it made him mad. It is probable that to a man of imagination and deep feeling hell itself can invent no more hideous torture than he must undergo in the position in which Harold Quaritch found himself. To truly love some good woman or some woman whom he thinks good—for it comes to the same thing—to love her more than life, to hold her dearer even than his honour, to be, like Harold, beloved in turn; and then to know that this woman, this one thing for which he would count the world well lost, this light that makes his days beautiful, has been taken from him by the bitterness of Fate (not by Death, for that he could bear), taken from him, and given—for money or money's worth—to some other man! It is, perhaps, better that a man should die than that he should pass through such an experience as that which threatened Harold Quaritch now: for though the man die not, yet will it kill all that is best in him; and whatever triumphs may await him, whatever women may be ready in the future to pin their favours to his breast, life will never be for him what it might have been, because his lost love took its glory with her.

No wonder, then, that he despaired. No wonder, too, that there rose up in his breast a great anger and indignation against the man who had brought this last extremity of misery upon them. He was just, and could make allowances for his rival's infatuation—which, indeed, Ida being concerned, it was not difficult for him to understand. But he was also, and above all things, a gentleman; and the spectacle of a woman being inexorably driven into a distasteful marriage by money pressure, put on by the man who wished to gain her, revolted him beyond measure, and, though he was slow to wrath, moved him to fiery indignation. So much did it move him that he took a resolution; Mr. Cossey should know his mind about the matter, and that at once. Ringing the bell, he ordered his dog-cart, and drove to Edward Cossey's rooms with the full intention of giving that gentleman a very unpleasant quarter-of-an-hour.

Mr. Cossey was in. Fearing lest he should refuse to see him, the Colonel followed the servant up the stairs, and entered almost as she announced his name. There was a grim and even a formidable look upon his plain but manly face, and something of menace, too, in his formal and soldierly bearing; nor did his aspect soften when his eyes fell upon the full-length picture of Ida over the mantelpiece.

Edward Cossey rose with astonishment and irritation, not unmixed with nervousness, depicted on his face. The last person whom he wished to see and expected a visit from was Colonel Quaritch, whom in his heart he held in considerable awe. Besides, he had of late received such a series of unpleasant calls that it is not wonderful that he began to dread these interviews.

"Good-day," he said coldly. "Will you be seated?"

The Colonel bowed his head slightly, but he did not sit down.

"To what am I indebted for the pleasure?" began Edward Cossey with much politeness.

"Last time I was here, Mr. Cossey," said the Colonel in his deep voice, speaking very deliberately, "I came to give an explanation; now I come to ask one."

"Indeed!"

"Yes. To come to the point, Miss de la Molle and I are attached to each other, and there has been between us an understanding that this attachment might end in marriage."

"Oh! has there?" said the younger man with a sneer.

"Yes," answered the Colonel, keeping down his rising temper as well as he could. "But now I am told, upon what appears to be good authority, that you have actually condescended to bring, directly and indirectly, pressure of a monetary sort to bear upon Miss de la Molle and her father in order to force her into a distasteful marriage with yourself."

"And what the devil business of yours is it, sir," asked Cossey, "what I have or have not done? Making every allowance for the disappointment of an unsuccessful suitor, for I presume that you appear in that character," and again he sneered, "I ask, what business is it of yours?"

"It is every business of mine, Mr. Cossey, because if Miss de la Molle is forced into this marriage, I shall lose my wife."

"Then you will certainly lose her. Do you suppose that I am going to consider you? Indeed," he went on, being now in a towering passion, "I should have thought that considering the difference of age and fortune between us, you might find other reasons than you suggest to account for my being preferred, if I should be so preferred. Ladies are apt to choose the better man, you know."

"I don't quite know what you mean by the 'better man,' Mr. Cossey," said the Colonel quietly. "Comparisons are odious, and I will make none, though I admit that you have the advantage of me in money and in years. However, that is not the point; the point is that I have had the fortune to be preferred to *you* by the lady in question, and *not* you to me. I happen to know that the idea of her marriage with you is as distasteful to Miss de la Molle as it is to me. This I know from her own lips. She will only marry you, if she does so at all, under the pressure of direst necessity, and to save her father from the ruin you are deliberately bringing upon him."

"Well, Colonel Quaritch," he answered, "have you quite done lecturing me? If you have, let me tell you, as you seem anxious to know my mind, that if by any legal means I can marry Ida de la Molle I certainly intend to marry her. And let me tell you another thing, that when once I am married it will be the last that you shall see of her, if I can prevent it."

"Thank you for your admissions," said Harold, still more quietly. "So it seems that it is all true; it seems that you are using your wealth to harass this unfortunate gentleman and his daughter until you drive them into consenting to this marriage. That being so, I wish to tell you privately what I shall probably take some opportunity of telling you in public, namely, that a man who does these things is a cur, and worse than a cur, he is a *blackguard*, and *you* are such a man, Mr. Cossey."

Edward Cossey's face turned perfectly livid with fury, and he drew himself up as though to spring at his adversary's throat.

The Colonel held up his hand. "Don't try that on with me," he said. "In the first place it is vulgar, and in the second you have only just recovered from an accident and are no match for me, though I am over forty years old. Listen, our fathers had a way of settling their troubles; I don't approve of that sort of thing as a rule, but in some cases it is salutary. If you think yourself aggrieved it does not take long to cross the water, Mr. Cossey."

Edward Cossey looked puzzled. "Do you mean to suggest that I should fight a duel with you?" he said.

"To challenge a man to fight a duel," answered the Colonel with deliberation, "is an indictable offence, therefore I make no such challenge. I have made a suggestion, and if that suggestion falls in with your views as," and he bowed, "I hope it may, we might perhaps meet accidentally abroad in a few days' time, when we could talk this matter over further."

"I'll see you hanged first," answered Cossey. "What have I to gain by fighting you except a very good chance of being shot? I have had enough of being shot as it is, and we will play this game out upon the old lines, until I win it."

"As you like," said Harold. "I have made a suggestion to you which you do not see fit to accept. As to the end of the game, it is not finished yet, and therefore it is impossible to say who will win it. Perhaps you will be checkmated after all. In the meanwhile allow me again to assure you that I consider you both a cur and a blackguard, and to wish you good-morning." And he bowed himself out, leaving Edward Cossey in a curious condition of concentrated rage.

CHAPTER XXXIX

THE COLONEL GOES TO SLEEP

The state of mind is difficult to picture which could induce a peaceable christian-natured individual, who had moreover in the course of his career been mixed up with enough bloodshed to have acquired a thorough horror of it, to offer to fight a duel. Yet this state had been reached by Harold Quaritch.

Edward Cossey wisely enough declined to entertain the idea, but the Colonel had been perfectly in earnest about it. Odd as it may appear in the latter end of this nineteenth century, nothing would have given him greater pleasure than to put his life against that of his unworthy rival. Of course, it was foolish and wrong, but human nature is the same in all ages, and in the last extremity we fall back by instinct on those methods which men have from the beginning adopted to save themselves from intolerable wrong and dishonour, or, be it admitted, to bring the same upon others.

But Cossey utterly declined to fight. As he said, he had had enough of being shot, and so there was an end of it. Indeed, in after days the Colonel frequently looked back upon this episode in his career with shame not unmingled with amusement, reflecting when he did so on the strange potency of that passion which can bring men to seriously entertain the idea of such extravagances.

Well, there was nothing more to be done. He might, it is true, have seen Ida, and working upon her love and natural inclinations have tried to persuade her to cut the knot by marrying him off-hand. Perhaps he would have succeeded, for in these affairs women are apt to find the arguments advanced by their lovers weighty and well worthy of consideration. But he was not the man to adopt such a course. He did the only thing he could do—answered her letter by saying that what must be must be. He had learnt that on the day subsequent to his interview with his rival the Squire had written to Edward Cossey informing him that a decided answer would be given to him on Christmas Day, and that thereon all vexatious proceedings on the part of that gentleman's lawyers had been stayed for the time. He could now no longer doubt what the answer would be. There was only one way out of the trouble, the way which Ida had made up her mind to adopt.

So he set to work to make his preparations for leaving Honham and this country for good and all. He wrote to land agents and put Molehill upon their books to be sold or let on lease, and also to various influential friends to obtain introductions to the leading men in New Zealand. But these matters did not take up all his time, and the rest of it hung heavily on his hands. He mooned about the place until he was tired. He tried to occupy himself in his garden, but it was weary work sowing crops for strange hands to reap, and so he gave it up.

Somehow the time wore on until at last it was Christmas Eve; the eve, too, of the fatal day of Ida's decision. He dined alone that night as usual, and shortly after dinner some waits came to the house and began to sing their cheerful carols outside. The carols did not chime in at all well with his condition of mind, and he sent five shillings out to the singers with a request that they would go away as he had a headache.

Accordingly they went; and shortly after their departure the great gale for which that night is still famous began to rise. Then he fell to pacing up and down the quaint old oak-panelled parlour, thinking until his brain ached. The hour was at hand, the evil was upon him and her whom he loved. Was there no way out of it, no possible way? Alas! there was but one way and that a golden one; but where was the money to come from? He had it not, and as land stood it was impossible to raise it. Ah, if only that great treasure which old Sir James de la Molle had hid away and died rather than reveal, could be brought to light, now in the hour of his house's sorest need! But the treasure was very mythical, and if it had ever really existed it was not now to be found. He went to his dispatch box and took from it the copy he had made of the entry in the Bible which had been in Sir James's pocket when he was murdered in the courtyard. The whole story was a very strange one. Why did the brave old man wish that his Bible should be sent to his son, and why did he write that somewhat peculiar message in it?

Suppose Ida was right and that it contained a cypher or cryptograph which would give a clue to the whereabouts of the treasure? If so it was obvious that it would be one of the simplest nature. A man confined by himself in a dungeon and under sentence of immediate death would not have been likely to pause to invent anything complicated. It would, indeed, be curious that he should have invented anything at all under such circumstances, and when he could have so little hope that the riddle would be solved. But, on the other hand, his position was desperate; he was quite surrounded by foes; there was no chance of his being able to convey the secret in any other way, and he *might* have done so.

Harold placed the piece of paper upon the mantelpiece, and sitting down in an arm-chair opposite began to contemplate it earnestly, as indeed he had often done before. In case its exact wording should not be remembered, it is repeated here. It ran: "*Do not grieve for me, Edward, my son, that I am thus suddenly and wickedly done to death by rebel murderers, for nought happeneth but according to God's will. And now farewell, Edward, till we shall meet in heaven. My moneys have I hid, and on account thereof I die unto this world, knowing that not one piece shall Cromwell touch. To whom God shall appoint shall all my treasure be, for nought can I communicate.*"

Harold stared and stared at this inscription. He read it forwards, backwards, crossways, and in every other way, but absolutely without result. At last, wearied out with misery of mind and the pursuit of a futile occupation, he dropped off sound asleep in his chair. This happened about a quarter to eleven o'clock. The next thing he knew was that he suddenly woke up; woke up completely, passing as quickly from a condition of deep sleep to one of wakefulness as though he had never shut his eyes. He used to say afterwards that he felt as though somebody had come and aroused him; it was not like a natural waking. Indeed, so unaccustomed was the sensation, that for a moment the idea flashed through his brain that he had died in his sleep, and was now awakening to a new state of existence.

This soon passed, however. Evidently he must have slept some time, for the lamp was out and the fire dying. He got up and hunted about in the dark for some matches, which at last he found. He struck a light, standing exactly opposite to the bit of paper with the copy of Sir James de la Molle's dying message on it. This message was neatly copied long-ways upon a half-sheet of large writing paper, such as the Squire generally used. It's first line ran as it was copied:

"*Do not grieve for me, Edward, my son, that I am thus suddenly and wickedly done.*"

Now, as the match burnt up, by some curious chance, connected probably with the darkness and the sudden striking of light upon his eyeballs, it came to pass that Harold, happening to glance thereon, was only able to read four letters of this first line of writing. All the rest seemed to him but as a blue connecting those four letters. They were:

D..............E..............a..............d

being respectively the initials of the first, the sixth, the eleventh, and the sixteenth words of the line given above.

The match burnt out, and he began to hunt about for another.

"D-E-A-D," he said aloud, repeating the letters almost automatically. "Why it spells '*Dead.*' That is rather curious."

Something about this accidental spelling awakened his interest very sharply—it was an odd coincidence. He lit some candles, and hurriedly examined the line. The first thing which struck him was that the four letters which went to make up the word "dead" were about equi-distant in the line of writing. Could it be? He hurriedly counted the words in the line. There were sixteen of them. That is after the first, one of the letters occurred at the commencement of every fifth word.

This was certainly curious. Trembling with nervousness he took a pencil and wrote down the initial letter of every fifth word in the message, thus:

> Do not grieve for me, Edward my son, that I am thus suddenly and D E a
>
> wickedly done to death by rebel murderers, for naught happeneth d m
>
> but according to God's will. And now farewell, Edward, till we a n
>
> shall meet in heaven. My moneys have I hid, and on account thereof s m o
>
> I die unto this world, knowing that not one piece shall Cromwell u n
>
> touch. To whom God shall appoint shall all my treasure be, for t a b
>
> nought can I communicate. c

When he had done he wrote these initials in a line:

DEadmansmountabc

He stared at them for a little—then he saw.

Great heaven! he had hit upon the reading of the riddle.

The answer was:

"Dead Man's Mount,"

followed by the mysterious letters A.B.C.

Breathless with excitement, he checked the letters again to see if by any chance he had made an error. No, it was perfectly corrcct.

"Dead Man's Mount." That was and had been for centuries the name of the curious tumulus or mound in his own back garden. It was this mount that learned antiquarians had discussed the origin of so fiercely, and which his aunt, the late Mrs. Massey, had roofed at the cost of two hundred and fifty pounds, in order to prove that the hollow in the top had once been the agreeable country seat of an ancient British family.

Could it then be but a coincidence that after the first word the initial of every fifth word in the message should spell out the name of this remarkable place, or was it so arranged? He sat down to think it over, trembling like a frightened child. Obviously, it was *not* accident; obviously, the prisoner of more than two centuries ago had, in his helplessness, invented this simple cryptograph in the hope that his son or, if not his son, some one of his descendants would discover it, and thereby become master of the hidden wealth. What place would be more likely for the old knight to have chosen to secrete the gold than one that even in those days had the uncanny reputation of being haunted? Who would ever think of looking for modern treasure in the burying place of the ancient dead?

In those days, too, Molehill, or Dead Man's Mount, belonged to the de la Molle family, who had re-acquired it on the break up of the Abbey. It was only at the Restoration, when the Dofferleigh branch came into possession under the will of the second and last baronet, Edward de la Molle, who died in exile, that they failed to recover this portion of the property. And if this was so, and Sir James, the murdered man, had buried his treasure in the mount, what did the mysterious letters A.B.C. mean? Were they, perhaps, directions as to the line to be taken to discover it? Harold could not imagine, nor, as a matter of fact, did he or anybody else ever find out either then or thereafter.

Ida, indeed, used afterwards to laughingly declare that old Sir James meant to indicate that he considered the whole thing as plain as A.B.C., but this was an explanation which did not commend itself to Harold's practical mind.

CHAPTER XL

BUT NOT TO BED

Harold glanced at the clock; it was nearly one in the morning, time to go to bed if he was going. But he did not feel inclined to go to bed. If he did, with this great discovery on his mind he should not sleep. There was another thing; it was Christmas Eve, or rather Christmas Day, the day of Ida's answer. If any succour was to be given at all, it must be given at once, before the fortress had capitulated. Once let the engagement be renewed, and even if the money should subsequently be forthcoming, the difficulties would be doubled. But he was building his hopes upon sand, and he knew it. Even supposing that he held in his hand the key to the hiding place of the long-lost treasure, who knew whether it would still be there, or whether rumour had not enormously added to its proportions? He was allowing his imagination to carry him away.

Still he could not sleep, and he had a mind to see if anything could be made of it. Going to the gun-room he put on a pair of shooting- boots, an old coat, and an ulster. Next he provided himself with a dark lantern and the key of the summer-house at the top of Dead Man's Mount, and silently unlocking the back door started out into the garden. The night was very rough, for the great gale was now rising fast, and bitterly cold, so cold that he hesitated for a moment before making up his mind to go on. However, he did go on, and in another two minutes was climbing the steep sides of the tumulus. There was a wan moon in the cold sky—the wind whistled most drearily through the naked boughs of the great oaks, which groaned in answer like things in pain. Harold was not a nervous or impressionable man, but the place had a spectral look about it, and he could not help thinking of the evil reputation it had borne for all those ages. There was scarcely a man in Honham, or in Boisingham either, who could have been persuaded to stay half an hour by himself on Dead Man's Mount after the sun was well down. Harold had at different times asked one or two of them what they saw to be afraid of, and they had answered that it was not what they saw so much as what they felt. He had laughed at the time, but now he admitted to himself that he was anything but comfortable, though if he had been obliged to put his feelings into words he could probably not have described them better than by saying that he had a general impression of somebody being behind him.

However, he was not going to be frightened by this nonsense, so consigning all superstitions to their father the Devil, he marched on boldly and unlocked the summer-house door. Now, though this curious edifice had been designed for a summer-house, and for that purpose lined throughout with encaustic tiles, nobody as a matter of fact had ever dreamed of using it to sit in. To begin with, it roofed over a great depression some thirty feet or more in diameter, for the top of the mount was hollowed out like one of those wooden cups in which jugglers catch balls. But notwithstanding all the encaustic tiles in the world, damp will gather in a hollow like this, and the damp alone was an objection. The real fact was, however, that the spot had an evil reputation, and even those who were sufficiently well educated to know the folly of this sort of thing would not willingly have gone there for purposes of enjoyment. So it had suffered the general fate of disused places, having fallen more or less out of repair and become a receptacle for garden tools, broken cucumber frames and lumber of various sorts.

Harold pushed the door open and entered, shutting it behind him. It was, if anything, more disagreeable in the empty silence of the wide place than it had been outside, for the space roofed over was considerable, and the question at once arose in his mind, what was he to do now that he had got there? If the treasure was there at all, probably it was deep down in the bowels of the great mound. Well, as he was on the spot, he thought that he might as well try to dig, though probably nothing would come of it. In the corner were a pickaxe and some spades and shovels. Harold got them, advanced to the centre of the space and, half laughing at his own folly, set to work. First, having lit another lantern which was kept there, he removed with the sharp end of the pickaxe a large patch of the encaustic tiles exactly in the centre of the depression. Then having loosened the soil beneath with the pick he took off his ulster and fell to digging with a will. The soil proved to be very sandy and easy to work. Indeed, from its appearance, he soon came to the conclusion that it was not virgin earth, but worked soil which had been thrown there.

Presently his spade struck against something hard; he picked it up and held it to the lantern. It proved to be an ancient spear-head, and near it were some bones, though whether or no they were human he could not at the time determine. This was very interesting, but it was scarcely what he wanted, so he dug on manfully until he found himself chest deep in a kind of grave. He had been digging for an hour now, and was getting very tired. Cold as it was the perspiration poured from him. As he paused for breath he heard the church clock strike two, and very solemnly it sounded down the wild ways of the wind-torn winter night. He dug on a little more, and then seriously thought of giving up what he was somewhat ashamed of having undertaken. How was he to account for this great hole to his gardener on the following morning? Then and there he made up his mind that he would not account for it. The gardener, in common with the rest of the village, believed that the place was haunted. Let him set down the hole to the "spooks" and their spiritual activity.

Still he dug on at the grave for a little longer. It was by now becoming a matter of exceeding labour to throw the shovelfuls of soil clear of the hole. Then he determined to stop, and with this view scrambled, not without difficulty, out of the amateur tomb. Once out, his eyes fell on a stout iron crowbar which was standing among the other tools, such an implement as is used to make holes in the earth wherein to set hurdles and stakes. It occurred to him that it would not be a bad idea to drive this crowbar into the bottom of the grave which he had dug, in order to ascertain if there was anything within its reach. So he once more descended into the hole and began to work with the iron crow, driving it down with all his strength. When he had got it almost as deep as it would go, that is about two feet, it struck something—something hard—there was no doubt of it. He worked away in great excitement, widening the hole as much as he could.

Yes, it was masonry, or if it was not masonry it was something uncommonly like it. He drew the crow out of the hole, and, seizing the shovel, commenced to dig again with renewed vigour. As he could no longer conveniently throw the earth from the hole he took a "skep" or leaf basket, which lay handy, and, placing it beside him, put as much of the sandy soil as he could carry into it, and then lifting shot it on the edge of the pit. For three-quarters of an hour he laboured thus most manfully, till at last he came down on the stonework. He cleared a patch of it and examined it attentively, by the light of the dark lantern. It appeared to be rubble work built in the form of an arch. He struck it with the iron crow and it gave back a hollow sound. There was a cavity of some sort underneath.

His excitement and curiosity redoubled. By great efforts he widened the spot of stonework already laid bare. Luckily the soil, or rather sand, was so friable that there was very little exertion required to loosen it. This done he took the iron crow, and inserting it beneath a loose flat stone levered it up. Here was a beginning, and having got rid of the large flat stone he struck down again and again with all his strength, driving the sharp point of the heavy crow into the rubble work beneath. It began to give, he could hear bits of it falling into the cavity below. There! it went with a crash, more than a square foot of it.

He leant over the hole at his feet, devoutly hoping that the ground on which he was standing would not give way also, and tried to look down. Next second he threw his head back coughing and gasping. The foul air rushing up from the cavity or chamber, or whatever it was, had half poisoned him. Then not without difficulty he climbed out of the grave and sat down on the pile of sand he had thrown up. Clearly he must allow the air in the place to sweeten a little. Clearly also he must have assistance if he was to descend into the great hole. He could not undertake this by himself.

He sat upon the edge of the pit wondering who there was that he might trust. Not his own gardener. To begin with he would never come near the place at night, and besides such people talk. The Squire? No, he could not rouse him at this hour, and also, for obvious reasons, they had not met lately. Ah, he had it. George was the man! To begin with he could be relied upon to hold his tongue. The episode of the production of the real Mrs. Quest had taught him that George was a person of no common powers. He could think and he could act also.

Harold threw on his coat, extinguished the large stable lantern, and passing out, locked the door of the summer-house and started down the mount at a trot. The wind had risen steadily during his hours of work, and was now blowing a furious gale. It was about a quarter to four in the morning and the stars shone brightly in the hard clean-blown sky. By their light and that of the waning moon he struggled on in the teeth of the raging tempest. As he passed under one of the oaks he heard a mighty crack overhead, and guessing what it was ran like a hare. He was none too soon. A circular gust of more than usual fierceness had twisted the top right out of the great tree, and down it came upon the turf with a rending crashing sound that made his blood turn cold. After this escape he avoided the neighbourhood of the groaning trees.

George lived in a neat little farmhouse about a quarter of a mile away. There was a shot cut to it across the fields, and this he took, breathlessly fighting his way against the gale, which roared and howled in its splendid might as it swept across the ocean from its birthplace in the distances of air. Even the stiff hawthorn fences bowed before its breath, and the tall poplars on the skyline bent like a rod beneath the first rush of a salmon.

Excited as he was, the immensity and grandeur of the sight and sounds struck upon him with a strange force. Never before had he felt so far apart from man and so near to that dread Spirit round Whose feet thousands of rolling worlds rush on, at Whose word they are, endure, and are not.

He struggled forward until at last he reached the house. It was quite silent, but in one of the windows a light was burning. No doubt its occupants found it impossible to sleep in that wild gale. The next thing to consider was how to make himself heard. To knock at the door would be useless in that turmoil. There was only one thing to be done—throw stones at the window. He found a good-sized pebble, and standing underneath, threw it with such goodwill that it went right through the glass. It lit, as he afterwards heard, full upon the sleeping Mrs. George's nose, and nearly frightened that good woman, whose nerves were already shaken by the gale, into a fit. Next minute a red nightcap appeared at the window.

"George!" roared the Colonel, in a lull of the gale.

"Who's there?" came the faint answer.

"I—Colonel Quaritch. Come down. I want to speak to you."

The head was withdrawn and a couple of minutes afterwards Harold saw the front door begin to open slowly. He waited till there was space enough, and then slipped in, and together they forced it to.

"Stop a bit, sir," said George; "I'll light the lamp;" and he did.

Next minute he stepped back in amazement.

"Why, what on arth hev you bin after, Colonel?" he said, contemplating Harold's filth-begrimed face, and hands, and clothes. "Is anything wrong up at the Castle, or is the cottage blown down?"

"No, no," said Harold; "listen. You've heard tell of the treasure that old Sir James de la Molle buried in the time of the Roundheads?"

"Yes, yes. I've heard tell of that. Hev the gale blown it up?"

"No, but by heaven I believe that I am in a fair way to find it."

George took another step back, remembering the tales that Mrs. Jobson had told, and not being by any means sure but that the Colonel was in a dangerous condition of lunacy.

"Give me a glass of something to drink, water or milk, and I'll tell you. I've been digging all night, and my throat's like a limeskin."

"Digging, why where?"

"Where? In Dead Man's Mount!"

"In Dead Man's Mount?" said George. "Well, blow me, if that ain't a funny place to dig at on a night like this," and, too amazed to say anything more, he went off to get the milk.

Harold drank three glasses of milk, and then sat down to tell as much of his moving tale as he thought desirable.

CHAPTER XLI

HOW THE NIGHT WENT

George sat opposite to him, his hands on his knees, the red nightcap on his head, and a comical expression of astonishment upon his melancholy countenance.

"Well," he said, when Harold had done, "blow me if that ain't a master one. And yet there's folks who say that there ain't no such thing as Providence—not that there's anything prowided yet—p'raps there ain't nawthing there after all."

"I don't know if there is or not, but I'm going back to see, and I want you to come with me."

"Now?" said George rather uneasily. "Why, Colonel, that bain't a very nice spot to go digging about in on a night like this. I niver heard no good of that there place—not as I holds by sich talk myself," he added apologetically.

"Well," said the Colonel, "you can do as you like, but I'm going back at once, and going down the hole, too; the gas must be out of it by now. There are reasons," he added, "why, if this money is to be found at all, it should be found this morning. To-day is Christmas Day, you know."

"Yes, yes, Colonel; I knows what you mean. Bless you, I know all about it; the old Squire must talk to somebody; if he don't he'd bust, so he talks to me. That Cossey's coming for his answer from Miss Ida this morning. Poor young lady, I saw her yesterday, and she looks like a ghost, she du. Ah, he's a mean one, that Cossey. Laryer Quest warn't in it with him after all. Well, I cooked his goose for him, and I'd give summut to have a hand in cooking that banker chap's too. You wait a minute, Colonel, and I'll come along, gale and ghostesses and all. I only hope it mayn't be after a fool's arrand, that's all," and he retired to put on his boots. Presently he appeared again, his red nightcap still on his head, for he was afraid that the wind would blow a hat off, and carrying an unlighted lantern in his hand.

"Now, Colonel, I'm ready, sir, if you be;" and they started.

The gale was, if anything, fiercer than ever. Indeed, there had been no such wind in those parts for years, or rather centuries, as the condition of the timber by ten o'clock that morning amply testified.

"This here timpest must be like that as the Squire tells us on in the time of King Charles, as blew the top of the church tower off on a Christmas night," shouted George. But Harold made no answer, and they fought their way onward without speaking any more, for their voices were almost inaudible. Once the Colonel stopped and pointed to the sky-line. Of all the row of tall poplars which he had seen bending like whips before the wind as he came along but one remained standing now, and as he pointed that vanished also.

Reaching the summer house in safety, they entered, and the Colonel shut and locked the door behind them. The frail building was literally rocking in the fury of the storm.

"I hope the roof will hold," shouted George, but Harold took no heed. He was thinking of other things. They lit the lanterns, of which they now had three, and the Colonel slid down into the great grave he had so industriously dug, motioning to George to follow. This that worthy did, not without trepidation. Then they both knelt and stared down through the hole in the masonry, but the light of the lanterns was not strong enough to enable them to make out anything with clearness.

"Well," said George, falling back upon his favourite expression in his amazement, as he drew his nightcapped head from the hole, "if that ain't a master one, I niver saw a masterer, that's all.

"What be you a-going to du now, Colonel? Hev you a ladder here?"

"No," answered Harold, "I never thought of that, but I've a good rope: I'll get it."

Scrambling out of the hole, he presently returned with a long coil of stout rope. It belonged to some men who had been recently employed in cutting boughs off such of the oaks that needed attention.

They undid the rope and let the end down to see how deep the pit was. When they felt that the end lay upon the floor they pulled it up. The depth from the hole to the bottom of the pit appeared to be about sixteen feet or a trifle more.

Harold took the iron crow, and having made the rope fast to it fixed the bar across the mouth of the aperture. Then he doubled the rope, tied some knots in it, and let it fall into the pit, preparatory to climbing down it.

But George was too quick for him. Forgetting his doubts as to the wisdom of groping about Dead Man's Mount at night, in the ardour of his burning curiosity he took the dark lantern, and holding it with his teeth passed his body through the hole in the masonry, and cautiously slid down the rope.

"Are you all right?" asked Harold in a voice tremulous with excitement, for was not his life's fortune trembling on the turn?

"Yes," answered George doubtfully. Harold looking down could see that he was holding the lantern above his head and staring at something very hard.

Next moment a howl of terror echoed up from the pit, the lantern was dropped upon the ground and the rope began to be agitated with the utmost violence.

In another two seconds George's red nightcap appeared followed by a face that was literally livid with terror.

"Let me up for Goad's sake," he gasped, "or he'll hev me by the leg!"

"He! who?" asked the Colonel, not without a thrill of superstitious fear, as he dragged the panting man through the hole.

But George would give no answer until he was out of the grave. Indeed had it not been for the Colonel's eager entreaties, backed to some extent by actual force, he would by this time have been out of the summer-house also, and half-way down the mount.

"What is it?" roared the Colonel in the pit to George, who shivering with terror was standing on its edge.

"It's a blessed ghost, that's what it is, Colonel," answered George, keeping his eyes fixed upon the hole as though he momentarily expected to see the object of his fears emerge.

"Nonsense," said Harold doubtfully. "What rubbish you talk. What sort of a ghost?"

"A white un," said George, "all bones like."

"All bones?" answered the Colonel, "why it must be a skeleton."

"I don't say that he ain't," was the answer, "but if he be, he's nigh on seven foot high, and sitting airing of hissel in a stone bath."

"Oh, rubbish," said the Colonel. "How can a skeleton sit and air himself? He would tumble to bits."

"I don't know, but there he be, and they don't call this here place 'Dead Man's Mount' for nawthing."

"Well," said the Colonel argumentatively, "a skeleton is a perfectly harmless thing."

"Yes, if he's dead maybe, sir, but this one's alive, I saw him nod his head at me."

"Look here, George," answered Harold, feeling that if this went on much longer he should lose his nerve altogether. "I'm not going to be scared. Great heavens, what a gust! I'm going down to see for myself."

"Very good, Colonel," answered George, "and I'll wait here till you come up again—that is if you iver du."

Thrice did Harold look at the hole in the masonry and thrice did he shrink back.

"Come," he shouted angrily, "don't be a fool; get down here and hand me the lantern."

George obeyed with evident trepidation. Then Harold scrambled through the opening and with many an inward tremor, for there is scarcely a man on the earth who is really free from supernatural fears, descended hand over hand. But in so doing he managed to let the lantern fall and it went out. Now as any one will admit this was exceedingly trying. It is not pleasant to be left alone in the dark and underground in the company of an unknown "spook." He had some matches, but what between fear and cold it was some time before he could get a light. Down in this deep place the rush of the great gale reached his ears like a faint and melancholy sighing, and he heard other tapping noises, too, or he thought he did, noises of a creepy and unpleasant nature. Would the matches never light? The chill and death-like damp of the place struck to his marrow and the cold sweat poured from his brow. Ah! at last! He kept his eyes steadily fixed upon the lantern till he had lit it and the flame was burning brightly. Then with an effort he turned and looked round him.

And this is what he saw.

There, three or four paces from him, in the centre of the chamber of Death sat or rather lay a figure of Death. It reclined in a stone chest or coffin, like a man in a hip bath which is too small for him. The bony arms hung down on either side, the bony limbs projected towards him, the great white skull hung forward over the massive breast bone. It moved, too, of itself, and as it moved, the jaw-bone tapped against the breast and the teeth clacked gently together.

Terror seized him while he looked, and, as George had done, he turned to fly. How could that thing move its head? The head ought to fall off.

Seizing the rope, he jerked it violently in the first effort of mounting.

"Hev he got yew, Colonel?" sung out George above; and the sound of a human voice brought him back to his sense.

"No," he answered as boldly as he could, and then setting his teeth, turned and tottered straight at the Horror in the chest.

He was there now, and holding the lantern against the thing, examined it. It was a skeleton of enormous size, and the skull was fixed with rusty wire to one of the vertebrae.

At this evidence of the handiwork of man his fears almost vanished. Even in that company he could not help remembering that it is scarcely to be supposed that spiritual skeletons carry about wire with which to tie on their skulls.

With a sigh of relief he held up the lantern and looked round. He was standing in a good-sized vault or chamber, built of rubble stone. Some of this rubble had fallen in to his left; but otherwise, though the workmanship showed that it must be of extreme antiquity, the stone lining was still strong and good. He looked upon the floor, and then for the first time saw that the nodding skeleton before him was not the only one. All round lay remnants of the dead. There they were, stretched out in the form of a circle, of which the stone kist was the centre.[*] One place in the circle was vacant; evidently it had once been occupied by the giant frame which now sat within the kist. Next he looked at the kist itself. It had all the appearance of one of those rude stone chests in which the very ancient inhabitants of this island buried the ashes of their cremated dead. But, if this was so, whence came the uncremated skeletons?

> [*] At Bungay, in Suffolk, there stood a mound or tumulus, on which was a windmill. Some years ago the windmill was pulled down, and the owner of the ground wishing to build a house upon its site, set to work to cart away the mound. His astonishment may be conceived when he found in the earth a great number of skeletons arranged in circles. These skeletons were of large size, and a gentleman who saw them informed me that he measured one. It was that of a man who must have been nearly seven feet high. The bones were, unhappily, carted away and thrown into a dyke. But no house has been built upon the resting-place of those unknown warriors.—Author.

Perhaps a subsequent race or tribe had found the chamber ready prepared, and used it to bury some among them who had fallen in battle. It was impossible to say more, especially as with one exception there was nothing buried with the skeletons which would assist to identify their race or age. That exception was a dog. A dog had been placed by one of the bodies. Evidently from the position of the bones of its master's arms he had been left to his last sleep with his hand resting on the hound's head.

Bending down, Harold examined the seated skeleton more closely. It was, he discovered, accurately jointed together with strong wire. Clearly this was the work of hands which were born into the world long after the flesh on those mighty bones had crumbled into dust.

But where was the treasure? He saw none. His heart sank as the idea struck him that he had made an interesting archaeological discovery, and that was all. Before undertaking a closer search he went under the hole and halloaed to George to come down as there was nothing but some bones to frighten him.

This the worthy George was at length with much difficulty persuaded to do.

When at last he stood beside him in the vault, Harold explained to him what the place was and how ridiculous were his fears, without however succeeding in allaying them to any considerable extent.

And really when one considers the position it is not wonderful that George was scared. For they were shut up in the bowels of a place which had for centuries owned the reputation of being haunted, faced by a nodding skeleton of almost superhuman size, and surrounded by various other skeletons all "very fine and large," while the most violent tempest that had visited the country for years sighed away outside.

"Well," he said, his teeth chattering, "if this ain't the masterest one that iver I did see." But here he stopped, language was not equal to the expression of his feelings.

Meanwhile Harold, with a heart full of anxiety, was turning the lantern this way and that in the hope of discovering some traces of Sir James's treasure, but naught could he see. There to the left the masonry had fallen in. He went to it and pulled aside some of the stones. There was a cavity behind, apparently a passage, leading no doubt to the secret entrance to the vault, but he could see nothing in it. Once more he searched. There was nothing. Unless the treasure was buried somewhere, or hidden away in the passage, it was non-existent.

And yet what was the meaning of that jointed skeleton sitting in the stone bath? It must have been put there for some purpose, probably to frighten would-be plunderers away. Could he be sitting on the money? He rushed to the chest and looked through the bony legs. No, his pelvis rested on the stone bottom of the kist.

"Well, George, it seems we're done," said Harold, with a ghastly attempt at a laugh. "There's no treasure here."

"Maybe it's underneath that there stone corn bin," suggested George, whose teeth were still chattering. "It should be here or hereabouts, surely."

This was an idea. Helping himself to the shoulder-blade of some deceased hero, Harold, using it as a trowel, began to scoop away the soft sand upon which the stone chest stood. He scooped and scooped manfully, but he could not come to the bottom of the kist.

He stepped back and looked at it. It must be one of two things—either the hollow at the top was but a shallow cutting in a great block of stone, or the kist had a false bottom.

He sprang at it. Seizing the giant skeleton by the spine, he jerked it out of the kist and dropped it on one side in a bristling bony heap. Just as he did so there came so furious a gust of wind that, buried as they were in the earth, they literally felt the mound rock beneath it. Instantly it was followed by a frightful crash overhead.

George collapsed in terror, and for a moment Harold could not for the life of him think what had happened. He ran to the hole and looked up. Straight above him he could see the sky, in which the first cold lights of dawn were quivering. Mrs. Massey's summer-house had been blown bodily away, and the "ancient British Dwelling Place" was once more open to the sky, as it had been for centuries.

"The summer-house has gone, George," he said. "Thank goodness that we were not in it, or we should have gone too."

"Oh, Lord, sir," groaned the unhappy George, "this is an awful business. It's like a judgment."

"It might have been if we had been up above instead of safe down here," he answered. "Come, bring that other lantern."

George roused himself, and together they bent over the now empty kist, examining it closely.

The stone bottom was not of quite the same colour as the walls of the chest, and there was a crack across it. Harold felt in his pocket and drew out his knife, which had at the back of it one of those strong iron hooks that are used to extract stones from the hoofs of horses. This hook he worked into the crack and managed before it broke to pull up a fragment of stone. Then, looking round, he found a long sharp flint among the rubbish where the wall had fallen in. This he inserted in the hole and they both levered away at it.

Half of the cracked stone came up a few inches, far enough to allow them to get their fingers underneath it. So it *was* a false bottom.

"Catch hold," gasped the Colonel, "and pull for your life."

George did as he was bid, and setting their knees against the hollowed stone, they tugged till their muscles cracked.

"It's a-moving," said George. "Now thin, Colonel."

Next second they both found themselves on the flat of their backs. The stone had given with a run.

Up sprang Harold like a kitten. The broken stone was standing edgeways in the kist. There was something soft beneath it.

"The light, George," he said hoarsely.

Beneath the stone were some layers of rotten linen.

Was it a shroud, or what?

They pulled the linen out by handfuls. One! two! three!

Oh, great heaven!

There, under the linen, were row on row of shining gold coins set edgeways.

For a moment everything swam before Harold's eyes, and his heart stopped beating. As for George, he muttered something inaudible about its being a "master one," and collapsed.

With trembling fingers Harold managed to pick out two pieces of gold which had been disturbed by the upheaval of the stone, and held them to the light. He was a skilled numismatist, and had no difficulty in recognising them. One was a beautiful three-pound piece of Charles I., and the other a Spur Rial of James I.

That proved it. There was no doubt that this was the treasure hidden by Sir James de la Molle. He it must have been also who had conceived the idea of putting a false bottom to the kist and setting up the skeleton to frighten marauders from the treasure, if by any chance they should enter.

For a minute or two the men stood staring at each other over the great treasure which they had unearthed in that dread place, shaking with the reaction of their first excitement, and scarcely able to speak.

"How deep du it go?" said George at length.

Harold took his knife and loosed some of the top coins, which were very tightly packed, till he could move his hand in them freely. Then he pulled out handful after handful of every sort of gold coin. There were Rose Nobles of Edward IV.; Sovereigns and Angels of Henry VII. and VIII.; Sovereigns, Half-Sovereigns and gold Crowns of Edward VI.; Sovereigns, Rials, and Angels of Mary; Sovereigns, Double Crowns and Crowns of Elizabeth; Thirty-shilling pieces, Spur Rials, Angels, Unites and Laurels of James I.; Three-pound pieces, Broads, and Half Broads of Charles I.; some in greater quantity and some in less; all were represented. Handful after handful did he pull out, and yet the bottom was not reached. At last he came to it. The layer of gold pieces was about twenty inches broad by three feet six long.

"We must get this into the house, George, before any one is about," gasped the Colonel.

"Yes, sir, yes, for sure we must; but how be we a-going to carry it?"

Harold thought for a minute, and then acted thus. Bidding George stay in the vault with the treasure, which he was with difficulty persuaded to do, he climbed the improvised rope ladder, and got in safety through the hole. In his excitement he had forgotten about the summer- house having been carried away by the gale, which was still blowing, though not with so much fury as before. The wind-swept desolation that met his view as he emerged into the dawning light broke upon him with a shock. The summer-house was clean gone, nothing but a few uprights remained of it; and fifty yards away he thought he could make out the crumpled shape of the roof. Nor was that all. Quite a quarter of the great oaks which were the glory of the place were down, or splintered and ruined.

But what did he care for the summer-house or the oaks now? Forgetting his exhaustion, he ran down the slope and reached the house, which he entered as softly as he could by the side door. Nobody was about yet, or would be for another hour. It was Christmas Day, and not a pleasant morning to get up on, so the servants would be sure to lie a-bed. On his way to his bed-room he peeped into the dining-room, where he had fallen asleep on the previous evening. When he had woke up, it may be remembered, he lit a candle. This candle was now flaring itself to death, for he had forgotten to extinguish it, and by its side lay the paper from which he had made the great discovery. There was nothing in it, of course, but somehow the sight impressed him very much. It seemed months since he awoke to find the lamp gone out. How much may happen between the lighting of a candle and its burning away! Smiling at this trite reflection, he blew that light out, and, taking another, went to his room. Here he found a stout hand-bag, with which he made haste to return to the Mount.

"Are you all right, George?" he shouted down the hole.

"Well, Colonel, yes, but not sorry to see you back. It's lonesome like down here with these deaders."

"Very well. Look out! There's a bag. Put as much gold in it as you can lift comfortably, and then make it fast to the rope."

Some three minutes passed, and then George announced that the bagful of gold was ready. Harold hauled away, and with a considerable effort brought it to the surface. Then, lifting the bag on his shoulder he staggered with it to the house. In his room stood a massive sea-going chest, the companion of his many wanderings. It was about half full of uniforms and old clothes, which he bundled unceremoniously on to the floor. This done, he shot the bagful of shining gold, as bright and uncorrupted now as when it was packed away two and a half centuries ago, into the chest, and returned for another load.

About twenty times did he make this journey. At the tenth something happened.

"Here's a writing, sir, with this lot," shouted George. "It was packed away in the money."

He took the "writing," or rather parchment, out of the mouth of the bag, and put it in his pocket unread.

At length the store, enormous as it was, was exhausted.

"That's the lot, sir," shouted George, as he sent up the last bagful. "If you'll kindly let down that there rope, I'll come up too."

"All right," said the Colonel, "put the skeleton back first."

"Well, sir," answered George, "he looks wonderful comfortable where he lay, he du, so if you're agreeable I think I'll let him be."

Harold chuckled, and presently George arrived, covered with filth and perspiration.

"Well, sir," he said, "I never did think that I should get dead tired of handling gold coin, but it's a rum world, and that's a fact. Well, I niver, and the summer-house gone, and jist look at thim there oaks. Well, if that beant a master one."

"You never saw a masterer, that's what you were going to say, wasn't it? Well, and take one thing with another, nor did I, George, if that's any comfort to you. Now look here, just cover over this hole with some boards and earth, and then come in and get some breakfast. It's past eight o'clock and the gale is blowing itself out. A merry Christmas to you, George!" and he held out his hand, covered with cuts, grime and blood.

George shook it. "Same to you, Colonel, I'm sure. And a merry Christmas it is. God bless you, sir, for what you've done to-night. You've saved the old place from that banker chap, that's what you've done; and you'll hev Miss Ida, and I'm durned glad on it, that I am. Lord! won't this make the Squire open his eyes," and the honest fellow brushed away a tear and fairly capered with joy, his red nightcap waving on the wind.

It was a strange and beautiful sight to see the solemn George capering thus in the midst of that storm-swept desolation.

Harold was too moved to answer, so he shouldered his last load of treasure and limped off with it to the house. Mrs. Jobson and her talkative niece were up now, but they did not happen to see him, and he reached his room unnoticed. He poured the last bagful of gold into the chest, smoothed it down, shut the lid and locked it. Then as he was, covered with filth and grime, bruised and bleeding, his hair flying wildly about his face, he sat down upon it, and from his heart thanked heaven for the wonderful thing that had happened to him.

So exhausted was he that he nearly fell asleep as he sat, but remembering himself rose, and taking the parchment from his pocket cut the faded silk with which it was tied and opened it.

On it was a short inscription in the same crabbed writing which he had seen in the old Bible that Ida had found.

It ran as follows:

> "Seeing that the times be so troublous that no man can be sure of his own, I, Sir James de la Molle, have brought together all my substance in money from wheresoever it lay at interest, and have hid the same in this sepulchre, to which I found the entry by a chance, till such time as peace come back to this unhappy England. This have I done on the early morn of Christmas Day, in the year of our Lord 1642, having ended the hiding of the gold while the great gale was blowing.

"James de la Molle."

Thus on a long gone Christmas Day, in the hour of a great wind, was the gold hid, and now on this Christmas Day, when another great wind raged overhead, it was found again, in time to save a daughter of the house of de la Molle from a fate sore as death.

CHAPTER XLII

IDA GOES TO MEET HER FATE

Most people of a certain age and a certain degree of sensitiveness, in looking back down the vista of their lives, whereon memory's melancholy light plays in fitful flashes like the alternate glow of a censer swung in the twilight of a tomb, can recall some one night of peculiar mental agony. It may have come when first we found ourselves face to face with the chill and hopeless horror of departed life; when, in our soul's despair, we stretched out vain hands and wept, called and no answer came; when we kissed those beloved lips and shrunk aghast at contact with their clay, those lips more eloquent now in the rich pomp of their unutterable silence than in the brightest hour of their unsealing. It may have come when our honour and the hope of all our days lay at our feet shattered like a sherd on the world's hard road. It may have come when she, the star of our youth, the type of completed beauty and woman's most perfect measure, she who held the chalice of our hope, ruthlessly emptied and crushed it, and, as became a star, passed down our horizon's ways to rise upon some other sky. It may have come when Brutus stabbed us, or when a child whom we had cherished struck us with a serpent-fang of treachery and left the poison to creep upon our heart. One way or another it has been with most of us, that long night of utter woe, and all will own that it is a ghastly thing to face.

And so Ida de la Molle had found it. The shriek of the great gale rushing on that Christmas Eve round the stout Norman towers was not more strong than the breath of the despair which shook her life. She could not sleep—who could sleep on such a night, the herald of such a morrow? The wail and roar of the wind, the crash of falling trees, and the rattle of flying stones seemed to form a fit accompaniment to the turmoil of her mind.

She rose, went to the window, and in the dim light watched the trees gigantically tossing in struggle for their life. An oak and a birch were within her view. The oak stood the storm out—for a while. Presently there came an awful gust and beat upon it. It would not bend, and the tough roots would not give, so beneath the weight of the gale the big tree broke in two like a straw, and its spreading top was whirled into the moat. But the birch gave and bent; it bent till its delicate filaments lay upon the wind like a woman's streaming hair, and the fierceness of the blast wore itself away and spared it.

"See what happens to those who stand up and defy their fate," said Ida to herself with a bitter laugh. "The birch has the best of it."

Ida turned and closed the shutters; the sight of the tempest affected her strained nerves almost beyond bearing. She began to walk up and down the big room, flitting like a ghost from end to end and back again, and again back. What could she do? What should she do? Her fate was upon her: she could no longer resist the inevitable—she must marry him. And yet her whole soul revolted from the act with an overwhelming fierceness which astonished even herself. She had known two girls who had married people whom they did not like, being at the time, or pretending to be, attached to somebody else, and she had observed that they accommodated themselves to their fate with considerable ease. But it was not so with her; she was fashioned of another clay, and it made her faint to think of what was before her. And yet the prospect was one on which she could expect little sympathy. Her own father, although personally he disliked the man whom she must marry, was clearly filled with amazement that she should prefer Colonel

Quaritch, middle-aged, poor, and plain, to Edward Cossey—handsome, young, and rich as Croesus. He could not comprehend or measure the extraordinary gulf which her love dug between the two. If, therefore, this was so with her own father, how would it be with the rest of the world?

She paced her bedroom till she was tired; then, in an access of despair, which was sufficiently distressing in a person of her reserved and stately manner, flung herself, weeping and sobbing, upon her knees, and resting her aching head upon the bed, prayed as she had never prayed before that this cup might pass from her.

She did not know—how should she?—that at this very moment her prayer was being answered, and that her lover was then, even as she prayed, lifting the broken stone and revealing the hoard of ruddy gold. But so it was; she prayed in despair and agony of mind, and the prayer carried on the wild wings of the night brought a fulfilment with it. Not in vain were her tears and supplications, for even now the deliverer delved among

"The dust and awful treasures of the dead,"

and even now the light of her happiness was breaking on her tortured night as the cold gleams of the Christmas morning were breaking over the fury of the storm without.

And then, chilled and numb in body and mind, she crept into her bed again and at last lost herself in sleep.

By half-past nine o'clock, when Ida came down to breakfast, the gale had utterly gone, though its footprints were visible enough in shattered trees, unthatched stacks, and ivy torn in knotty sheets from the old walls it clothed. It would have been difficult to recognise in the cold and stately lady who stood at the dining-room window, noting the havoc and waiting for her father to come in, the lovely, passionate, dishevelled woman who some few hours before had thrown herself upon her knees praying to God for the succour she could not win from man. Women, like nature, have many moods and many aspects to express them. The hot fit had passed, and the cold fit was on her now. Her face, except for the dark hollows round the eyes, was white as winter, and her heart was cold as winter's ice.

Presently her father came in.

"What a gale," he said, "what a gale! Upon my word I began to think that the old place was coming down about our ears, and the wreck among the trees is dreadful. I don't think there can have been such a wind since the time of King Charles I., when the top of the tower was blown right off the church. You remember I was showing you the entry about it in the registers the other day, the one signed by the parson and old Sir James de la Molle. The boy who has just come up with the letters tells me he hears that poor old Mrs. Massey's summer-house on the top of Dead Man's Mount has been blown away, which is a good riddance for Colonel Quaritch. Why, what's the matter with you, dear? How pale you look!"

"The gale kept me awake. I got very little sleep," answered Ida.

"And no wonder. Well, my love, you haven't wished me a merry Christmas yet. Goodness knows we want one badly enough. There has not been much merriment at Honham of late years."

"A merry Christmas to you, father," she said.

"Thank you, Ida, the same to you; you have got most of your Christmases before you, which is more than I have. God bless me, it only seems like yesterday since the big bunch of holly tied to the hook in the ceiling there fell down on the breakfast table and smashed all the cups, and yet it is more than sixty years ago. Dear me! how angry my poor mother was. She never could bear the crockery to be broken—it was a little failing of your grandmother's," and he laughed more heartily than Ida had heard him do for some weeks.

She made no answer but busied herself about the tea. Presently, glancing up she saw her father's face change. The worn expression came back upon it and he lost his buoyant bearing. Evidently a new thought had struck him, and she was in no great doubt as to what it was.

"We had better get on with breakfast," he said. "You know that Cossey is coming up at ten o'clock."

"Ten o'clock?" she said faintly.

"Yes. I told him ten so that we could go to church afterwards if we wished to. Of course, Ida, I am still in the dark as to what you have made up your mind to do, but whatever it is I thought that he had better once and for all hear your final decision from your own lips. If, however, you feel yourself at liberty to tell it to me as your father, I shall be glad to hear it."

She lifted her head and looked him full in the face, and then paused. He had a cup of tea in his hand, and held it in the air half way to his mouth, while his whole face showed the over-mastering anxiety with which he was awaiting her reply.

"Make your mind easy, father," she said, "I am going to marry Mr. Cossey."

He put the cup down in such a fashion that he spilt half the tea, most of it over his own clothes, without even noticing it, and then turned away his face.

"Well," he said, "of course it is not my affair, or at least only indirectly so, but I must say, my love, I congratulate you on the decision which you have come to. I quite understand that you have been in some difficulty about the matter; young women often have been before you, and will be again. But to be frank, Ida, that Quaritch business was not at all suitable, either in age, fortune, or in anything else. Yes, although Cossey is not everything that one might wish, on the whole I congratulate you."

"Oh, pray don't," broke in Ida, almost with a cry. "Whatever you do, pray do not congratulate me!"

Her father turned round again and looked at her. But Ida's face had already recovered its calm, and he could make nothing of it.

"I don't quite understand you," he said; "these things are generally considered matters for congratulation."

But for all he might say and all that he might urge in his mind to the contrary, he did more or less understand what her outburst meant. He could not but know that it was the last outcry of a broken spirit. In his heart he realised then, if he had never clearly realised it before, that this proposed marriage was a thing hateful to his daughter, and his conscience pricked him sorely. And yet—and yet—it was but a woman's fancy—a passing fancy. She would become reconciled to the inevitable as women do, and when her children came she would grow accustomed to her sorrow, and her trouble would be forgotten in their laughter. And if not, well it was but one woman's life which would be affected, and the very existence of his race and the very cradle that had nursed them from century to century were now at stake. Was all this to be at the mercy of a girl's whim? No! let the individual suffer.

So he argued. And so at his age and in his circumstances most of us would argue also, and, perhaps, considering all things, we should be right. For in this world personal desires must continually give way to the welfare of others. Did they not do so our system of society could not endure.

No more was said upon the subject. Ida made pretence of eating a piece of toast; the Squire mopped up the tea upon his clothes, and then drank some more.

Meanwhile the remorseless seconds crept on. It wanted but five minutes to the hour, and the hour would, she well knew, bring the man with it.

The five minutes passed slowly and in silence. Both her father and herself realised the nature of the impending situation, but neither of them spoke of it. Ah! there was the sound of wheels upon the gravel. So it had come.

Ida felt like death itself. Her pulse sunk and fluttered; her vital forces seemed to cease their work.

Another two minutes went by, then the door opened and the parlour-maid came in.

"Mr. Cossey, if you please, sir."

"Oh," said the Squire. "Where is he?"

"In the vestibule, sir."

"Very good. Tell him I will be there in a minute."

The maid went.

"Now, Ida," said her father, "I suppose that we had better get this business over."

"Yes," she answered, rising; "I am ready."

And gathering up her energies, she passed out to meet her fate.

CHAPTER XLIII

GEORGE IS SEEN TO LAUGH

Ida and her father reached the vestibule to find Edward Cossey standing with his face to the mantelpiece and nervously toying with some curiosities upon it. He was, as usual, dressed with great care, and his face, though white and worn from the effects of agitation of mind, looked if anything handsomer than ever. As soon as he heard them coming, which owing to his partial deafness he did not do till they were quite close to him, he turned round with a start, and a sudden flush of colour came upon his pale face.

The Squire shook hands with him in a solemn sort of way, as people do when they meet at a funeral, but Ida barely touched his outstretched fingers with her own.

A few random remarks followed about the weather, which really for once in a way was equal to the conversational strain put upon it. At length these died away and there came an awful pause. It was broken by the Squire, who, standing with his back to the fire, his eyes fixed upon the wall opposite, after much humming and hawing, delivered himself thus:

"I understand, Mr. Cossey, that you have come to hear my daughter's final decision on the matter of the proposal of marriage which you have made and renewed to her. Now, of course, this is a very important question, very important indeed, and it is one with which I cannot presume even to seem to interfere. Therefore, I shall without comment leave my daughter to speak for herself."

"One moment before she does so," Mr. Cossey interrupted, drawing indeed but a poor augury of success from Ida's icy looks. "I have come to renew my offer and to take my final answer, and I beg Miss de la Molle to consider how deep and sincere must be that affection which has endured through so many rebuffs. I know, or at least I fear, that I do not occupy the place in her feelings that I should wish to, but I look to time to change this; at any rate I am willing to take my chance. As regards money, I repeat the offer which I have already made."

"There, I should not say too much about that," broke in the Squire impatiently.

"Oh, why not?" said Ida, in bitter sarcasm. "Mr. Cossey knows it is a good argument. I presume, Mr. Cossey, that as a preliminary to the renewal of our engagement, the persecution of my father which is being carried on by your lawyers will cease?"

"Absolutely."

"And if the engagement is not renewed the money will of course be called in?"

"My lawyers advise that it should be," he answered sullenly; "but see here, Ida, you may make your own terms about money. Marriage, after all, is very much a matter of bargaining, and I am not going to stand out about the price."

"You are really most generous," went on Ida in the same bitter tone, the irony of which made her father wince, for he understood her mood better than did her lover. "I only regret that I cannot appreciate such generosity more than I do. But it is at least in my power to give you the return which you deserve. So I can no longer hesitate, but once and for all—"

She stopped dead, and stared at the glass door as though she saw a ghost. Both her father and Edward Cossey followed the motion of her eyes, and this was what they saw. Up the steps came Colonel Quaritch and George. Both were pale and weary-looking, but the former was at least clean. As for George, this could not be said. His head was still adorned with the red nightcap, his hands were cut and dirty, and on his clothes was an unlimited quantity of encrusted filth.

"What the dickens—" began the Squire, and at that moment George, who was leading, knocked at the door.

"You can't come in now," roared the Squire; "don't you see that we are engaged?"

"But we must come in, Squire, begging your pardon," answered George, with determination, as he opened the door; "we've got that to say as won't keep."

"I tell you that it must keep, sir," said the old gentleman, working himself into a rage. "Am I not to be allowed a moment's privacy in my own house? I wonder at your conduct, Colonel Quaritch, in forcing your presence upon me when I tell you that it is not wanted."

"I am sure that I apologise, Mr. de la Molle," began the Colonel, utterly taken aback, "but what I have to say is—"

"The best way that you can apologise is by withdrawing," answered the Squire with majesty. "I shall be most happy to hear what you have to say on another occasion."

"Oh, Squire, Squire, don't be such a fule, begging your pardon for the word," said George, in exasperation. "Don't you go a-knocking of your head agin a brick wall."

"Will you be off, sir?" roared his master in a voice that made the walls shake.

By this time Ida had recovered herself. She seemed to feel that her lover had something to say which concerned her deeply—probably she read it in his eyes.

"Father," she said, raising her voice, "I won't have Colonel Quaritch turned away from the door like this. If you will not admit him I will go outside and hear what it is that he has to say."

In his heart the Squire held Ida in some awe. He looked at her, and saw that her eyes were flashing and her breast heaving. Then he gave way.

"Oh, very well, since my daughter insists on it, pray come in," and he bowed. "If such an intrusion falls in with your ideas of decency it is not for me to complain."

"I accept your invitation," answered Harold, looking very angry, "because I have something to say which you must hear, and hear at once. No, thank you, I will stand. Now, Mr. de la Molle, it is this, wonderful as it may seem. It has been my fortune to discover the treasure hidden by Sir James de la Molle in the year 1643!"

There was a general gasp of astonishment.

"*What!*" exclaimed the Squire. "Why, I thought that the whole thing was a myth."

"No, that it ain't, sir," said George with a melancholy smile, "cos I've seen it."

Ida had sunk into a chair.

"What is the amount?" she asked in a low eager voice.

"I have been unable to calculate exactly, but, speaking roughly, it cannot be under fifty thousand pounds, estimated on the value of the gold alone. Here is a specimen of it," and Harold pulled out a handful of rials and other coins, and poured them on to the table.

Ida hid her face in her hand, and Edward Cossey realising what this most unexpected development of events might mean for him, began to tremble.

"I should not allow myself to be too much elated, Mr. de la Molle," he said with a sneer, "for even if this tale be true, it is treasure trove, and belongs to the Crown."

"Ah," said the Squire, "I never thought of that."

"But I have," answered the Colonel quietly. "If I remember right, the last of the original de la Molles left a will in which he especially devised this treasure, hidden by his father, to your ancestor. That it is the identical treasure I am fortunately in a position to prove by this parchment," and he laid upon the table the writing he had found with the gold.

"Quite right—quite right," said the Squire, "that will take it out of the custom."

"Perhaps the Solicitor to the Treasury may hold a different opinion," said Cossey, with another sneer.

Just then Ida took her hand from her face. There was a dewy look about her eyes, and the last ripples of a happy smile lingered round the corners of her mouth.

"Now that we have heard what Colonel Quaritch had to say," she said in her softest voice, and addressing her father, "there is no reason why we should not finish our business with Mr. Cossey."

Here Harold and George turned to go. She waved them back imperiously, and began speaking before any one could interfere, taking up her speech where she had broken it off when she caught sight of the Colonel and George coming up the steps.

"I can no longer hesitate," she said, "but once and for all I decline to marry you, Mr. Cossey, and I hope that I shall never see your face again."

At this announcement the bewildered Squire put his hand to his head. Edward Cossey staggered visibly and rested himself against the table, while George murmured audibly, "That's a good job."

"Listen," said Ida, rising from her chair, her dark eyes flashing as the shadow of all the shame and agony that she had undergone rose up within her mind. "Listen, Mr. Cossey," and she pointed her finger at him; "this is the history of our connection. Some months ago I was so foolish as to ask your help in the matter of the mortgages which your bank was calling in. You then practically made terms that if it should at any time be your wish I should become engaged to you; and I, seeing no option, accepted. Then, in the interval, while it was inconvenient to you to enforce those terms, I gave my affection elsewhere. But when you, having deserted the lady who stood in your way—no, do not interrupt me, I know it, I know it all, I know it from her own lips—came forward and claimed my promise, I was forced to consent. But a loophole of escape presented itself and I availed myself of it. What followed? You again became possessed of power over my father and this place, you insulted the man I loved, you resorted to every expedient that the law would allow to torture my father and myself. You set your lawyers upon us like dogs upon a hare, you held ruin over us and again and again you offered me money, as much money as I wished, if only I would sell myself to you. And then you bided your time, leaving despair to do its work.

"I saw the toils closing round us. I knew that if I did not yield my father would be driven from his home in his old age, and that the place he loved would pass to strangers—would pass to you. No, father, do not stop me, I *will* speak my mind!

"And at last I determined that cost what it might I would yield. Whether I could have carried out my determination God only knows. I almost think that I should have killed myself upon my marriage day. I made up my mind. Not five minutes ago the very words were upon my lips that would have sealed my fate, when deliverance came. And now *go*. I have done with you. Your money shall be paid to you, capital and interest, down to the last farthing. I tender back my price, and knowing you for what you are, I—I despise you. That is all I have to say."

"Well, if that beant a master one," ejaculated George aloud.

Ida, who had never looked more beautiful than she did in this moment of passion, turned to seat herself, but the tension of her feelings and the torrent of her wrath and eloquence had been too much for her. She would have fallen had not Harold, who had been listening amazed to this overpowering outburst of nature, run up and caught her in his arms.

As for Edward Cossey, he had shrunk back involuntarily beneath the volume of her scorn, till he stood with his back against the panelled wall. His face was white as a sheet; despair and fury shone in his dark eyes. Never had he desired this woman more fiercely than he did now, in the moment when he knew that she had escaped him for ever. In a sense he was to be pitied, for passion tore his heart in twain. For a moment he stood thus. Then with a spring rather than a step, he advanced across the room till he was face to face with Harold, who, with Ida still half fainting in his arms, and her head upon his shoulder, was standing on the further side of the fire-place.

"Damn you," he said, "I owe this to you—you half-pay adventurer," and he lifted his arm as though to strike him.

"Come, none of that," said the Squire, speaking for the first time. "I will have no brawling here."

"No," put in George, edging his long form between the two,

"and begging your pardon, sir, don't you go a-calling of better men than yourself adwenturers. At any rate, if the Colonel is an adwenturer, he hev adwentured to some purpose, as is easy for to see," and he pointed to Ida.

"Hold your tongue, sir," roared the Squire, as usual relieving his feelings on his retainer. "You are always shoving your oar in where it isn't wanted."

"All right, Squire, all right," said George the imperturbable; "thin his manners shouldn't be sich."

"Do you mean to allow this?" said Cossey, turning fiercely to the old gentleman. "Do you mean to allow this man to marry your daughter for her money?"

"Mr. Cossey," answered the Squire, with his politest and most old-fashioned bow, "whatever sympathy I may have felt for you is being rapidly alienated by your manner. I told you that my daughter must speak for herself. She has spoken very clearly indeed, and, in short, I have absolutely nothing to add to her words."

"I tell you what it is," Cossey said, shaking with fury, "I have been tricked and fooled and played with, and so surely as there is a heaven above us I will have my revenge on you all. The money which this man says that he has found belongs to the Queen, not to you, and I will take care that the proper people are informed of it before you can make away with it. When that is taken from you, if, indeed, the whole thing is not a trick, we shall see what will happen to you. I tell you that I will take this property and I will pull this old place you are so fond of down stone by stone and throw it into the moat, and send the plough over the site. I will sell the estate piecemeal and blot it out. I tell you I have been tricked—you encouraged the marriage yourself, you know you did, and forbade that man the house," and he paused for breath and to collect his words.

Again the Squire bowed, and his bow was a study in itself. You do not see such bows now-a-days.

"One minute, Mr. Cossey," he said very quietly, for it was one of his peculiarities to become abnormally quiet in circumstances of real emergency, "and then I think that we may close this painful interview. When first I knew you I did not like you. Afterwards, through various circumstances, I modified my opinion and set my dislike down to prejudice. You are quite right in saying that I encouraged the idea of a marriage between you and my daughter, also that I forbade the house to Colonel Quaritch. I did so because, to be honest, I saw no other way of avoiding the utter ruin of my family; but perhaps I was wrong in so doing. I hope that you may never be placed in a position which will force you to such a decision. Also at the time, indeed never till this moment, have I quite realised how the matter really stood. I did not understand how strongly my daughter was attached in another direction, perhaps I was unwilling to understand it. Nor did I altogether understand the course of action by which it seems you obtained a promise of marriage from my daughter in the first instance. I was anxious for the marriage because I believed you to be a better man than you are, also because I thought that it would place my daughter and her descendants in a much improved position, and that she would in time become attached to you. I forbade Colonel Quaritch the house because I considered that an alliance with him would be undesirable for everybody concerned. I find that in all this I was acting wrongly, and I frankly admit it. Perhaps as we grow old we grow worldly also, and you and your agents pressed me very hard, Mr. Cossey. Still I have always told you that my daughter was a free agent and must decide for herself, and therefore I owe you no apology on this score. So much then for the question of your engagement to Miss de la Molle. It is done with.

"Now as regards the threats you make. I shall try to meet them as occasion arises, and if I cannot do so it will be my misfortune. But one thing they show me, though I am sorry to have to say it to any man in a house which I can still call my own—they show me that my first impressions of you were the correct ones. *You are not a gentleman*, Mr. Cossey, and I must beg to decline the honour of your further acquaintance," and with another bow he opened the vestibule door and stood holding the handle in his hand.

Edward Cossey looked round with a stare of rage. Then muttering one most comprehensive curse he stalked from the room, and in another minute was driving fast through the ancient gateway.

Let us pity him, for he also certainly received his due.

George followed him to the outer door and then did a thing that nobody had seen him do before; he burst out into a loud laugh.

"What are you making that noise about?" asked his master sternly. "This is no laughing matter."

"*Him!*" replied George, pointing to the retreating dog-cart—"*he's* a-going to pull down the Castle and throw it into the moat and to send the plough over it, is he? *Him*—that varmint! Why, them old towers will be a-standing there when his beggarly bones is dust, and when his name ain't no more a name; and there'll be one of the old blood sitting in them too. I knaw it, and I hev allus knawed it. Come, Squire, though you allus du say how as I'm a fule, what did I tell yer? Didn't I tell yer that Prowidence weren't a-going to let this place go to any laryers or bankers or thim sort? Why, in course I did. And now you see. Not but what it is all owing to the Colonel. He was the man as found it, but then God Almighty taught him where to dig. But he's a good un, he is; and a gintleman, not like *him*," and once more he pointed with unutterable scorn to the road down which Edward Cossey had vanished.

"Now, look here," said the Squire, "don't you stand talking all day about things you don't understand. That's the way you waste time. You be off and look after this gold; it should not be left alone, you know. We will come down presently to

Molehill, for I suppose that is where it is. No, I can't stop to hear the story now, and besides I want Colonel Quaritch to tell it to me."

"All right, Squire," said George, touching his red nightcap, "I'll be off," and he started.

"George," halloaed his master after him, but George did not stop. He had a trick of deafness when the Squire was calling, that is if he wanted to go somewhere else.

"Confound you," roared the old gentleman, "why don't you stop when I call you?"

This time George brought his long lank frame to a standstill.

"Beg pardon, Squire."

"Beg pardon, yes—you're always begging pardon. Look here, you had better bring your wife and have dinner in the servants' hall to-day, and drink a glass of port."

"Thank you, Squire," said George again, touching his red nightcap.

"And look here, George. Give me your hand, man. Here's a merry Christmas to you. We've gone through some queerish times about this place together, but now it almost looks as though we were going to end our days in peace and plenty."

"Same to you, Squire, I'm sure, same to you," said George, pulling off his cap. "Yes, yes, we've had some bad years, what with poor Mr. James and that Quest and Cossey (he's the master varmint of the lot he is), and the bad times, and Janter, and the Moat Farm and all. But, bless you, Squire, now that there'll be some ready money and no debts, why, if I don't make out somehow so that you all get a good living out of the place I'm a Dutchman. Why, yes, it's been a bad time and we're a-getting old, but there, that's how it is, the sky almost allus clears toward night-fall. God Almighty hev a mind to let one down easy, I suppose."

"If you would talk a little less about your Maker, and come to church a little more, it would be a good thing, as I've told you before," said the Squire; "but there, go along with you."

And the honest fellow went.

CHAPTER XLIV

CHRISTMAS CHIMES

The Squire turned and entered the house. He generally was fairly noisy in his movements, but on this occasion he was exceptionally so. Possibly he had a reason for it.

On reaching the vestibule he found Harold and Ida standing side by side as though they were being drilled. It was impossible to resist the conclusion that they had suddenly assumed that attitude because it happened to be the first position into which they could conveniently fall.

There was a moment's silence, then Harold took Ida's hand and led her up to where her father was standing.

"Mr. de la Molle," he said simply, "once more I ask you for your daughter in marriage. I am quite aware of my many disqualifications, especially those of my age and the smallness of my means; but Ida and myself hope and believe that under all the circumstances you will no longer withhold your consent," and he paused.

"Quaritch," answered the Squire, "I have already in your presence told Mr. Cossey under what circumstances I was favourably inclined to his proposal, so I need not repeat all that. As regards your means, although they would have been quite insufficient to avert the ruin which threatened us, still you have, I believe, a competence, and owing to your wonderful and most providential discovery the fear of ruin seems to have passed away. It is owing to you that this discovery, which by the way I want to hear all about, has been made; had it not been for you it never would have been made at all, and therefore I certainly have no right to say anything more about your means. As to your age, well, after all forty-four is not the limit of life, and if Ida does not object to marrying a man of those years, I cannot object to her doing so. With reference to your want of occupation, I think that if you marry Ida this place will, as times are, keep your hands pretty full, especially when you have an obstinate donkey like that fellow George to deal with. I am getting too old and stupid to look after it myself, and besides things are so topsy-turvy that I can't understand them. There is one thing more that I want to say: I forbade you the house. Well, you are a generous- minded man, and it is human to err, so I think that perhaps you will understand my action and not bear me a grudge on that account. Also, I dare say that at the time, and possibly at other times, I said things I should be sorry for if I could remember what they were, which I can't, and if so, I apologise to you as a gentleman ought when he finds himself in the wrong. And so I say God bless you both, and I hope you will be happy in life together; and now come here, Ida, my love, and give me a kiss. You have been a good daughter all your life, and so Quaritch may be sure that you will be a good wife too."

Ida did as she was bid. Then she went over to her lover and took him by his hand, and he kissed her on the forehead. And thus after all their troubles they finally ratified the contract.

* * * * *

And we, who have followed them thus far, and have perhaps been a little moved by their struggles, hopes, and fears, will surely not grudge to re-echo the Squire's old-fashioned prayer, "God bless them both."

God bless them both. Long may they live, and happily.

Long may they live, and for very long may their children's children of the race, if not of the name of de la Molle, pass in and out through the old Norman gateway and by the sturdy Norman towers. The Boisseys, who built them, here had their habitation for six generations. The de la Molles who wedded the heiress of the Boisseys lived here for thirteen generations. May the Quaritchs whose ancestor married Ida, heiress of the de la Molles, endure as long!

Surely it is permitted to us to lift a corner of the curtain of futurity and in spirit see Ida Quaritch, stately and beautiful as we knew her, but of a happier countenance. We see her seated on some Christmas Eve to come in the drawing-room of the Castle, telling to the children at her knees the wonderful tale of how their father and old George on this very night, when the gale blew long years ago, discovered the ruddy pile of gold, hoarded in that awful storehouse amid the bones of Saxon or Danish heroes, and thus saved her to be their mother. We can see their wide wondering eyes and fixed faces, as for the tenth time they listen to a story before which the joys of Crusoe will grow pale. We can hear the eager appeal for details made to the military-looking gentleman, very grizzled now, but grown better-looking with the advancing years, who is standing before the fire, the best, most beloved husband and father in all that country side.

Perhaps there may be a vacant chair, and another tomb among the ranks of the departed de la Molles; perhaps the ancient walls will no longer echo to the sound of the Squire's stentorian voice. And what of that? It is our common lot.

But when he goes the country side will lose a man of whom they will not see the like again, for the breed is dead or dying; a man whose very prejudices, inconsistencies, and occasional wrong-headed violence will be held, when he is no longer here, to have been endearing qualities. And for manliness, for downright English God-fearing virtues, for love of Queen, country, family and home, they may search in vain to find his equal among the cosmopolitan Englishmen of the dawning twentieth century. His faults were many, and at one time he went near to sacrificing his daughter to save his house, but he would not have been the man he was without them.

And so to him, too, farewell. Perchance he will find himself better placed in the Valhalla of his forefathers, surrounded by those stout old de la Molles whose memory he regarded with so much affection, than here in this thin-blooded Victorian era. For as has been said elsewhere the old Squire would undoubtedly have looked better in a chain shirt and bearing a battle axe than ever he did in a frock coat, especially with his retainer George armed to the teeth behind him.

* * * * *

They kissed, and it was done.

Out from the church tower in the meadows broke with clash and clangour a glad sound of Christmas bells. Out it swept over layer, pitle and fallow, over river, plantain, grove and wood. It floated down the valley of the Ell, it beat against Dead Man's Mount (henceforth to the vulgar mind more haunted than ever), it echoed up the Castle's Norman towers and down the oak-clad vestibule. Away over the common went the glad message of Earth's Saviour, away high into the air, startling the rooks upon their airy courses, as though the iron notes of the World's rejoicing would fain float to the throned feet of the World's Everlasting King.

Peace and goodwill! Ay and happiness to the children of men while their span is, and hope for the Beyond, and heaven's blessing on holy love and all good things that are. This is what those liquid notes seemed to say to the most happy pair who stood hand in hand in the vestibule and thought on all they had escaped and all that they had won.

* * * * *

"Well, Quaritch, if you and Ida have quite done staring at each other, which isn't very interesting to a third party, perhaps you will not mind telling us how you happened on old Sir James de la Molle's hoard."

Thus adjured, Harold began his thrilling story, telling the whole history of the night in detail, and if his hearers had expected to be astonished certainly their expectations were considerably more than fulfilled.

"Upon my word," said the Squire when he had done, "I think I am beginning to grow superstitious in my old age. Hang me if I don't believe it was the finger of Providence itself that pointed out those letters to you. Anyway, I'm off to see the spoil. Run and get your hat, Ida, my dear, and we will all go together."

And they went and looked at the chest full of red gold, yes, and passed down, all three of them, into those chill presences in the bowels of the Mount. Then coming thence awed and silent they sealed up the place for ever.

CONCLUSION

GOOD-BYE

On the following morning such of the inhabitants of Boisingham as chanced to be about were much interested to see an ordinary farm tumbrel coming down the main street. It was being driven, or rather led, by no less a person than George himself, while behind it walked the well-known form of the old Squire, arm-in-arm with Colonel Quaritch.

They were still more interested, however, when the tumbrel drew up at the door of the bank—not Cossey's, but the opposition bank—where, although it was Boxing Day, the manager and the clerk were apparently waiting for its arrival.

But their interest culminated when they perceived that the cart only contained a few bags, and yet that each of these bags seemed to require three or four men to lift it with any comfort.

Thus was the gold safely housed. Upon being weighed its value was found to be about fifty-three thousand pounds of modern money. But as some of the coins were exceedingly rare, and of great worth to museums and collectors, this value was considerably increased, and the treasure was ultimately sold for fifty-six thousand two hundred and fifty-four pounds. Only Ida kept back enough of the choicest coins to make a gold waistband or girdle and a necklace for herself, destined no doubt in future days to form the most cherished heirloom of the Quaritch family.

On that same evening the Squire and Harold went to London and opened up communications with the Solicitor to the Treasury. Fortunately they were able to refer to the will of Sir Edward de la Molle, the second baronet, in which he specially devised to his cousin, Geoffrey Dofferleigh, and his heirs for ever, not only his estates, but his lands, "together with the treasure hid thereon or elsewhere by my late murdered father, Sir James de la Molle." Also they produced the writing which Ida had found in the old Bible, and the parchment discovered by George among the coin. These three documents formed a chain of evidence which even officials interested for the Treasury could not refuse to admit, and in the upshot the Crown renounced its claims, and the property in the gold passed to the Squire, subject to the payment of the same succession duty which he would have been called upon to meet had he inherited a like sum from a cousin at the present time.

And so it came to pass that when the mortgage money was due it was paid to the last farthing, capital and interest, and Edward Cossey lost his hold upon Honham for ever.

As for Edward Cossey himself, we may say one more word about him. In the course of time he sufficiently recovered from his violent passion for Ida to allow him to make a brilliant marriage with the only daughter of an impecunious peer. She keeps her name and title and he plays the part of the necessary husband. Anyhow, my reader, if it is your fortune to frequent the gilded saloons of the great, you may meet Lady Honoria Tallton and Mr. Cossey. If you do meet him, however, it may be as well to avoid him, for the events of his life have not been of a nature to improve his temper. This much then of Edward Cossey.

If after leaving the gilded saloons aforesaid you should happen to wander through the London streets, you may meet another character in this history. You may see a sweet pale face, still stamped with a child-like roundness and simplicity, but half hidden in the coarse hood of the nun. You may see her, and if you care to follow you may find what is the work wherein she seeks her peace. It would shock you; but it is her work of mercy and loving kindness and she does it unflinchingly. Among her sister nuns there is no one more beloved than Sister Agnes. So good-bye to her also.

Harold Quaritch and Ida were married in the spring and the village children strewed the churchyard path with primroses and violets—the same path where in anguish of soul they had met and parted on that dreary winter's night.

And there at the old church door, when the wreath is on her brow and the veil about her face, let us bid farewell to Ida and her husband, Harold Quaritch.

THE END

ABOUT THE AUTHOR

Sir Henry Rider Haggard (June 22, 1856 – May 14, 1925), born in Norfolk, England, was a Victorian writer of adventure novels set in locations considered exotic by readers in his native England.

Haggard had some firsthand experience of these locations, thanks to his extensive travels. He first travelled to Natal Colony in 1875, as secretary to the colonial Governor Bulwer. It was in this role that Haggard was present in Pretoria for the official announcement of the British annexation of the Boer Republic of the Transvaal. In fact, Haggard was forced to read out much of the proclamation following the loss of voice of the official originally entrusted with the duty.

In 1878 he became Registrar of the High Court in the Transvaal, in the region that was to become part of South Africa. He was eventually to return to England to find a wife, bringing Mariana Louisa Margitson back to Africa with him as a bride. Later they had a son named Jock (who died of measles at the age of 10) and three daughters.

Returning again to England in 1882, the couple settled in Ditchingham, Norfolk. Later he lived in Kessingland and had connections with the church in Bungay, Suffolk.

Choose from Thousands of 1stWorldLibrary Classics By

Friedrich Kerst
Friedrich Nietzsche
Fyodor Dostoyevsky
G.A. Henty
G.K. Chesterton
Gabrielle E. Jackson
Garrett P. Serviss
Gaston Leroux
George A. Warren
George Ade
Geroge Bernard Shaw
George Cary Eggleston
George Durston
George Ebers
George Eliot
George Gissing
George MacDonald
George Meredith
George Orwell
George Sylvester Viereck
George Tucker
George W. Cable
George Wharton James
Gertrude Atherton
Gordon Casserly
Grace E. King
Grace Gallatin
Grace Greenwood
Grant Allen
Guillermo A. Sherwell
Gulielma Zollinger
Gustav Flaubert
H. A. Cody
H. B. Irving
H.C. Bailey
H. G. Wells
H. H. Munro
H. Irving Hancock
H. R. Naylor
H. Rider Haggard
H. W. C. Davis
Haldeman Julius
Hall Caine
Hamilton Wright Mabie
Hans Christian Andersen
Harold Avery
Harold McGrath
Harriet Beecher Stowe
Harry Castlemon
Harry Coghill
Harry Houidini
Hayden Carruth
Helent Hunt Jackson
Helen Nicolay
Hendrik Conscience
Hendy David Thoreau
Henri Barbusse
Henrik Ibsen
Henry Adams
Henry Ford
Henry Frost
Henry James
Henry Jones Ford
Henry Seton Merriman
Henry W Longfellow
Herbert A. Giles
Herbert Carter
Herbert N. Casson
Herman Hesse
Hildegard G. Frey
Homer
Honore De Balzac
Horace B. Day
Horace Walpole
Horatio Alger Jr.
Howard Pyle
Howard R. Garis
Hugh Lofting
Hugh Walpole
Humphry Ward
Ian Maclaren
Inez Haynes Gillmore
Irving Bacheller
Isabel Cecilia Williams
Isabel Hornibrook
Israel Abrahams
Ivan Turgenev
J.G.Austin
J. Henri Fabre
J. M. Barrie
J. M. Walsh
J. Macdonald Oxley
J. R. Miller
J. S. Fletcher
J. S. Knowles
J. Storer Clouston
J. W. Duffield
Jack London
Jacob Abbott
James Allen
James Andrews
James Baldwin
James Branch Cabell
James DeMille
James Joyce
James Lane Allen
James Lane Allen
James Oliver Curwood
James Oppenheim
James Otis
James R. Driscoll
Jane Abbott
Jane Austen
Jane L. Stewart
Janet Aldridge
Jens Peter Jacobsen
Jerome K. Jerome
Jessie Graham Flower
John Buchan
John Burroughs
John Cournos
John F. Kennedy
John Gay
John Glasworthy
John Habberton
John Joy Bell
John Kendrick Bangs
John Milton
John Philip Sousa
John Taintor Foote
Jonas Lauritz Idemil Lie
Jonathan Swift
Joseph A. Altsheler
Joseph Carey
Joseph Conrad
Joseph E. Badger Jr
Joseph Hergesheimer
Joseph Jacobs
Jules Vernes
Julian Hawthrone
Julie A Lippmann
Justin Huntly McCarthy
Kakuzo Okakura
Karle Wilson Baker
Kate Chopin
Kenneth Grahame
Kenneth McGaffey
Kate Langley Bosher
Kate Langley Bosher
Katherine Cecil Thurston
Katherine Stokes
L. A. Abbot
L. T. Meade

L. Frank Baum
Latta Griswold
Laura Dent Crane
Laura Lee Hope
Laurence Housman
Lawrence Beasley
Leo Tolstoy
Leonid Andreyev
Lewis Carroll
Lewis Sperry Chafer
Lilian Bell
Lloyd Osbourne
Louis Hughes
Louis Joseph Vance
Louis Tracy
Louisa May Alcott
Lucy Fitch Perkins
Lucy Maud Montgomery
Luther Benson
Lydia Miller Middleton
Lyndon Orr
M. Corvus
M. H. Adams
Margaret E. Sangster
Margret Howth
Margaret Vandercook
Margaret W. Hungerford
Margret Penrose
Maria Edgeworth
Maria Thompson Daviess
Mariano Azuela
Marion Polk Angellotti
Mark Overton
Mark Twain
Mary Austin
Mary Catherine Crowley
Mary Cole
Mary Hastings Bradley
Mary Roberts Rinehart
Mary Rowlandson
M. Wollstonecraft Shelley
Maud Lindsay
Max Beerbohm
Myra Kelly
Nathaniel Hawthrone
Nicolo Machiavelli
O. F. Walton
Oscar Wilde

Owen Johnson
P.G. Wodehouse
Paul and Mabel Thorne
Paul G. Tomlinson
Paul Severing
Percy Brebner
Percy Keese Fitzhugh
Peter B. Kyne
Plato
Quincy Allen
R. Derby Holmes
R. L. Stevenson
R. S. Ball
Rabindranath Tagore
Rahul Alvares
Ralph Bonehill
Ralph Henry Barbour
Ralph Victor
Ralph Waldo Emmerson
Rene Descartes
Ray Cummings
Rex Beach
Rex E. Beach
Richard Harding Davis
Richard Jefferies
Richard Le Gallienne
Robert Barr
Robert Frost
Robert Gordon Anderson
Robert L. Drake
Robert Lansing
Robert Lynd
Robert Michael Ballantyne
Robert W. Chambers
Rosa Nouchette Carey
Rudyard Kipling
Saint Augustine
Samuel B. Allison
Samuel Hopkins Adams
Sarah Bernhardt
Sarah C. Hallowell
Selma Lagerlof
Sherwood Anderson
Sigmund Freud
Standish O'Grady
Stanley Weyman
Stella Benson
Stella M. Francis

Stephen Crane
Stewart Edward White
Stijn Streuvels
Swami Abhedananda
Swami Parmananda
T. S. Ackland
T. S. Arthur
The Princess Der Ling
Thomas A. Janvier
Thomas A Kempis
Thomas Anderton
Thomas Bailey Aldrich
Thomas Bulfinch
Thomas De Quincey
Thomas Dixon
Thomas H. Huxley
Thomas Hardy
Thomas More
Thornton W. Burgess
U. S. Grant
Upton Sinclair
Valentine Williams
Various Authors
Vaughan Kester
Victor Appleton
Victor G. Durham
Victoria Cross
Virginia Woolf
Wadsworth Camp
Walter Camp
Walter Scott
Washington Irving
Wilbur Lawton
Wilkie Collins
Willa Cather
Willard F. Baker
William Dean Howells
William le Queux
W. Makepeace Thackeray
William W. Walter
William Shakespeare
Winston Churchill
Yei Theodora Ozaki
Yogi Ramacharaka
Young E. Allison
Zane Grey

www.ingramcontent.com/pod-product-compliance
Lightning Source LLC
LaVergne TN
LVHW090548110826
845146LV00001B/56